EXPLORING ENGLISH I

S.S.

Duty desk.

Agent (415) 373-8519

(415) 214) - 3550

David GRUEN

(415) 576 - 1210

EXPLORING ENGLISH I

An Anthology of Short Stories
for Intermediate Certificate

Edited by
AUGUSTINE MARTIN

Gill & Macmillan

Gill & Macmillan
Hume Avenue, Park West, Dublin 12
www.gillmacmillanbooks.ie

© Introduction and Notes, Augustine Martin, 1967
© Foreword, Dermot Bolger, 2011

978 07171 5041 0

Typeset in the Republic of Ireland
Printed in the UK by TJ International Ltd, Padstow, Cornwall

A CIP catalogue record for this book is available
from the British Library.

5 7 9 8 6

CONTENTS

CONTENTS

SHORT STORIES BY OTHER AUTHORS

ACKNOWLEDGEMENTS

THE publishers wish to thank the following for permission to include copyright material in the present edition of this book:

The Estate of the late Daniel Corkery for 'The Breath of Life' and 'Vanity' from *A Munster Twilight* by Daniel Corkery. 'His First Flight', 'The Reaping Race', 'The Wren's Nest', 'Three Lambs' and 'The Rockfish' from *The Short Stories of Liam O'Flaherty* by Liam O'Flaherty, reprinted by permission of the Random House Group Ltd. 'The Wild Duck's Nest', 'The Road to the Shore' and 'The Poteen Maker' from Michael McLaverty's *Collected Short Stories* (Blackstaff Press 2002) are reproduced by permission of Blackstaff Press on behalf of the Estate of Michael McLaverty. 'The Secret Life of Walter Mitty' from *My World and Welcome to It* by James Thurber, © 1942 by Rosemary A. Thurber, reprinted by arrangement with Rosemary A. Thurber and The Barbara Hogenson Agency; all rights reserved. 'First Confession' from *Traveller's Samples* by Frank O'Connor (Copyright © The Estate of Frank O'Connor 1951); 'The Majesty of the Law' from *The Bones of Contention* by Frank O'Connor (Copyright © the Estate of Frank O'Connor 1938) and 'Guests of the Nation' by Frank O'Connor (Copyright © the Estate of Frank O'Connor 1931) are all reproduced by permission of PFD (www.pfd. co.uk) on behalf of the Estate of Frank O'Connor. 'The Fly in the Ointment ' from *The Saint and Other Stories* by V.S. Pritchett (© V.S. Pritchett 1966), and 'The Web' and 'Janey Mary' from *The Trusted and the Maimed* by James Plunkett (© James Plunkett 1969) are all reproduced by permission of PFD on behalf of the Estates of V.S. Pritchett and James Plunkett. 'Brother Boniface' from *Tales from Bective Bridge* by Mary Lavin is published with the permission of Elizabeth Walsh Peavoy and Faber & Faber Ltd. 'The Story of the Widow's Son' from *The Stories of Mary Lavin* by Mary Lavin is published with the permission of Elizabeth Walsh Peavoy. 'Louise' by William Somerset Maugham is reproduced by permission of A.P. Watt on behalf of The Royal Literary Fund. 'The Diamond Maker' by H.G. Wells is published with the permission of A.P.Watt on behalf of the Literary Executors of the Estate of H.G. Wells. 'Among the Ruins' (from *Selected Stories* 1962, 1979), 'A Man's World' (from *A Man's World*, 1962, 2010) and 'The Potato Gatherers' (from *Selected Stories*, 1962, 1979) by Brian Friel are all reproduced by kind permission of the author and The Gallery Press, Loughcrew, Oldcastle, Co. Meath. 'The Confirmation Suit' by Brendan Behan from *Brendan Behan's Island* is reprinted by kind permission of the Estate of Brendan Behan and The Sayle Literary Agency, © Estate of Brendan Behan 1962. 'The Dogs in the Great Glen' from *The Journey to the Seven Streams* by Benedict Kiely is reprinted with kind permission from the Estate of Benedict Kiely through the Jonathan Williams Literary Agency. 'Billy the Kid' from *The Hot Gates* by William Golding published with the permission of Faber & Faber Ltd. 'The Trout' and 'Up the Bare Stairs' by Sean O'Faolain are published by kind permission of Julia O'Faolain. 'The Holy Kiss' from *The Lion-Tamer* and 'The Windows of Wonder' from *The Red Petticoat* by Bryan MacMahon are published by kind permission of Maurice MacMahon.

FOREWORD

ON the Saturday of the FA Cup Final in 1972, I sat my entrance exam into secondary school. Following a letter of acceptance, I bowed out of primary school a month ahead of schedule and commenced an extra-long summer that remains extraordinarily vivid in my mind, because three things of personal import happened.

First, I commenced my first paid employment as an under-age helper on a Palm Grove Ice Cream delivery van, which dispensed largesse of choices to shops along the chain of small seaside towns that necklace the north Dublin coastline. Second, I began to scribble down my (often conflicted) thoughts in words that became lines and, I gradually realised, poems. Third, I inherited my big brother's Intermediate Certificate English textbooks and, most especially, *Exploring English Book 1*, edited by Augustine Martin.

I can see sunlight streaming into the back bedroom in Finglas Park – the room where I was born – as I lay on the bed at the age of thirteen, tentatively opening my brother's copy of this book and suddenly feeling older and on the cusp of a new world. It felt like a passport, heralding a different life. That copy of the book presented me with new names to wonder about – and only half of them were writers. It is true that the official contents page listed authors with whom I was previously unacquainted: Mary Lavin, Liam O'Flaherty, James Plunkett and Katherine Mansfield. But because this was a volume inherited from an older sibling, the back cover contained a second inventory of names – this time handwritten – which charted the rock bands he and his long-haired friends were listening to: bands like Led Zeppelin, Yes, Thin Lizzy, Procol Harum and Jethro Tull. This duality of names was exciting and important to me, because both lists represented future worlds which, during the summer, I found myself eager to explore.

Like many younger brothers, I was regularly dispatched on errands that involved the lending of precious vinyl albums by these bands. I was starting to understand the alchemy of lyrics by Phil Lynott or Neil Young. While listening to the (sometimes scratched) albums by the bands listed on the back of that inherited textbook in the summer evenings of 1972 – before I ever set foot in secondary school – I began to discover a different alchemy and magic by repeatedly devouring every short story in *Exploring English 1*.

I still possess my original and now very battered copy of that book. I associate it with the start of adolescence, standing on the verge of a different phase of life that felt exciting and daunting, with the advent of new friendships and emotions and summer nights spent sitting up talking with the intensity that only young people possess.

In later years, I often met people who had similarly started to dip into *Exploring English 1* in the summer before they entered secondary school: youngsters who spent summers in the 1970s wandering suburban streets or country lanes amid clusters of fellow teenagers, discussing teachers, dissecting the opposite sex or planning to attend weekend discos. I met them when I worked in mobile libraries or drank in pubs or caught my breath at half time in a football match or, even much later, when I had become a young parent chatting with other young parents while we watched our children clamber around playgrounds.

There was one thing that we found we shared in common, and we shared it in common with almost everybody educated in the Irish Republic for almost quarter of a century. On our walks to and from school, during the first three years of our secondary education, we had each carried in our bags a copy of *Exploring English 1*.

The book was lovingly edited by Professor Gus Martin. He included short biographical notes and informed explorations and exercises that whetted the appetite and the imagination.

All these years later, it is hard to realise just how revolutionary *Exploring English 1* was in 1967 for introducing the short story to the school curriculum for the first time. The choice of stories was made by a syllabus committee of the Department of Education, who were in turn influenced by an energetic Association of Teachers of English, among whom Augustine Martin, Veronica O'Brien, Tom O'Dea and Fr Joe Veale were prominent. But while a committee may have helped to select the stories, Martin's approach of 'exploring' the texts was equally revolutionary in terms of conventional teaching and of opening up the imaginative possibilities of language to the relatively young minds who were being exposed to adult themes and ideas.

There are ongoing debates now about what should or should not be compulsory in secondary education, but it seems to me that every school child in Ireland should be exposed, as a right, to Frank O'Connor's 'Guests of the Nation' as a seminal national text. Few children who read it will ever shed the impact of that ending where 'the birds and the bloody stars were all far away, and I was somehow very small and very lost and lonely like a child astray in the snow. And anything that happened to me afterwards, I never felt the same about again'.

It would be an exaggeration to say that 'anything that happened to me afterwards, I never felt the same about again' after reading the stories assembled in *Exploring English 1*, but it would be true to say that every book I had read before, I never felt the same about again. Because the lives that I encountered in these short stories were more real and vivid than the lives I had previously encountered in the children's books I borrowed from the public library. There was far less adventure here, very few pyrotechnics or trick endings – though it was hard for a young mind to shed the shocking impact of the final two paragraphs of 'An Occurrence at Owl Creek Bridge' – but it was the very ordinariness of the worlds conjured up here that made them so believable.

There was humour in O'Connor's 'First Confession' and Behan's 'The Confirmation Suit', and my young mind loved Gus Martin's footnote about having carried out 'extensive research in Dublin Northside pubs' to try, in vain, to establish a meaning for the word 'capernosity'. There was almost unbearable pathos in reading James Plunkett's 'Janey Mary' and a shock at reading James Thurber's 'The Secret Life of Walter Mitty', because I discovered that I was not the only person who seemed to occasionally fantasise about an alternative version of my life, where I was the star and matinee hero.

But of far greater impact – indeed, almost every person I have discussed this anthology with brings up this same story – was the wonderfully true notion, propounded in Mary Lavin's 'The Story of the Widow's Son', that any story (and, by extension, any event in our lives) could have two contradictory but equally valid endings; that the outcome of our entire lives could hinge upon how we, and others, react to tiny decisions.

Exploring English 1 was actually the first of a trio of textbooks; the second book being a selection of prose extracts, edited by James Carey, and the third a poetry anthology, edited jointly by Martin and Carey. All three were published in 1967 to coincide with the introduction of a new syllabus for English in the Intermediate Certificate and continued in use until another syllabus for English was introduced in the early 1990s. But it is book one, the anthology of short stories, that remains so vivid and affectionately treasured in people's minds.

Not all of the roughly half a million students who studied this book were enamored by the stories it contained. Indeed, many probably gleefully destroyed it – and every other Inter Cert textbook – as soon as their exams were finished. But if they look back, a remarkably large number can probably still talk about some character in some story who resonated and lodged, almost unnoticed, in their subconscious.

Exploring English 1 lay on bedroom floors while girls chatted on impossibly heavy house phones, too excited about their lives to get around to studying. It was opened on buses as terrified students tried to cram in the last days before exams. Initials and love hearts and random notes were scrawled in its margins, a shorthand code of teenage life jotted down in blank spaces. But the book remains infused with Gus Martin's love for literature and his desire to inspire that same love in several generations of teenagers.

This was a book that helped to shape our imaginations. Recalling the book in *The Princeton University Library Chronicle* in 2011, the Booker Prize winning novelist, Anne Enright, noted how 'our sensibilities were shaped by the fine choices of ... [such stories] as Michael McLaverty's "The Road to the Shore", a story that revealed as much to me about aesthetic possibilities and satisfactions as it did about nuns'.

Most of us threw away our copies of *Exploring English 1*. We were probably wise, because, with the advent of married life, those hand-drawn hearts and entwined initials on the back covers might have taken some explaining. It is wonderful, however, to see it republished with its original cover, complete with added graffiti and stains to make it look authentic. It might be the perfect book to share with someone special, whom you didn't know back when you both read these stories for the first time with Led Zeppelin playing in the background. It also still serves its initial purpose – for readers of any age – as a great introduction to the art of the short story.

Dermot Bolger, 2011

INTRODUCTION

Most young people seem to have a natural taste for reading. Children don't have to be urged to read comics. They delight in these simple, fast-moving tales of romance or adventure with their well-worn phrases, predictable endings and improbable heroes. Some people pass on naturally from the comics to more valuable forms of literature—novels, short stories, plays or poems that treat life in greater depth and with far greater skill. Others when they 'grow out' of comics give up reading altogether, except for news items in the evening papers. Others remain in the world of comics all their lives—they read, endlessly and tirelessly, 'romantic' love stories and detective or western novels, all with incredible heroes and heroines, well-worn phrases and happy endings. They remain, that is, in the world of literary childhood.

The purpose of the English class is to help the ordinary boy or girl to move from the world of literary childhood into the world of genuine literature, to help the young reader develop a taste for good novels, stories, plays and poems. This requires a willingness on the part of the student. One might compare his state to that of the prospective swimmer. Some people, either through laziness or timidity, are content to paddle in the shallows all their lives and they get a certain shallow pleasure from it. Others are determined to swim however great the effort of learning and they earn the right to a far greater pleasure and excitement. Most of us have to make similar efforts in becoming good readers but, as in the case of the swimmer, the rewards make it well worth while. The present collection of stories provides this sort of challenge and promises, I believe, this sort of reward.

The first mark of a good reader is his sensitivity to words, their sound, meaning and associations. Every work of literature is, basically, an arrangement of words on a page. These words may be used simply, as in a ballad like *Sir Patrick Spens*, or subtly, as in a Shakespearean sonnet. A good reader has learned to

1

respond sensitively to the words as they guide him towards the author's mood, theme and purpose. When the anonymous poet writes

> They hadna sailed a league, a league,
>   A league but barely three,
> When the lift grew dark, and the wind blew loud,
>   And gurly grew the sea

the skilful reader will not waste time searching for hidden meanings. He will respond rather to the rugged energy of the words and enter imaginatively into the rude seafaring world of the mariners. In doing this he will, of course, relish the sound effects, the repetitions, the alliterations, the growling quaintness of ' gurly,' all of which combine to create that world and atmosphere. On the other hand, when he reads Shakespeare's

> When to the sessions of sweet silent thought
> I summon up remembrance of things past

he will realise that the poet is using a legal image which creates a mood of solemnity suitable to the grave meditation that follows. The good reader will also be alert to the cadence of the words and notice how the whispering ' s ' sounds in both lines contribute towards the central effect. He may not, in either case, stop and reflect every time a phrase pleases him ; he will read on, pleasantly conscious that the poet knows what he is about.

Similarly with prose. At the end of Frank O'Connor's story, " Guests of the Nation," when the two hostages have been executed, the young revolutionary looks up and sees the ' bloody stars ' ; clearly the word has been chosen with great care to help us see how the world to him will never be the same again. When Janey Mary goes out into ' the ancient crookedness of streets ' the attentive reader is made aware of how cruel, old and meaningless the city must seem to the little girl. When in " Occurrence at Owl Creek Bridge " the soldiers faced the bridge, ' staring stonily, motionless ' the words give us a powerful impression of men dehumanised by war. Furthermore, the student who thinks that sound is not important in mere prose might study how the middle word shares its initial consonant with the word that goes before it and its dominant vowel with the word that comes after ;

he might also note how the accent, falling heavily on the first syllable of each word, contributes to the same sense of unthinking brutality. Similar effects are to be found in the lighter stories. For instance, the reader who knows the meaning of ' punitive expedition ' as a military term will be especially amused to see it in "The Lumber Room," used to describe the cruel aunt's hastily organised trip to the seaside.

But the careless reader misses all this : he lacks the eye for the stars and the ear for the soldiers ; he skims over the ' ancient crookedness of streets,' and ' the punitive expedition ' is so much verbiage to him. He merely wants to know what happened next. He reads the work of literature as if it were a badly written and rather long-winded tale out of the comics.

The most characteristic mark of the untrained or non-literary reader is this overmastering interest in ' what happens next.' C. S. Lewis, in his valuable book, *An Experiment in Criticism*, puts it like this :

> As the unmusical listener wants only the Tune, so the unliterary reader wants only the Event. The one ignores nearly all the sounds the orchestra is actually making ; he wants to hum the tune. The other ignores nearly all that the words before him are doing ; he wants to know what happened next.
>
> He reads only narrative because only there will he find an Event. He is deaf to the aural side of what he reads because rhythm and melody do not help him to discover who married . . . whom. He likes ' strip ' narratives and almost wordless films because in them nothing stands between him and the Event. And he likes speed because a very swift story is all events.

Once such a reader has found out how the story ends it no longer has any attraction for him. He ejects it from his mind like a used cartridge. He will hardly ever read it again except by accident. In fact he has not ' read ' the story at all ; he has merely used it.

This sort of careless, headlong reading will be quite useless for the modern short story. The reader who is looking merely for swift action will be brutally disappointed by many of the stories in this book. Here he will find, for instance, a story like " The Fly " where nothing at all seems to happen, or " The Majesty of the Law " which begins at a point where all the exciting events are over, or " Brother Boniface," which moves back and forth in time without warning and without any obvious outward pattern. In a certain sense the unprepared student might well be forgiven for claiming that these are not stories at all. And this leads us to consider the nature of the modern short story as an art form.

THE MODERN SHORT STORY

The false expectations with which some readers approach the modern short story may have their origin in the development of the short story itself. In his book on the subject O'Connor begins with the words :

> " By the hokies, there was a man in this place one time by the name of Ned Sullivan, and a queer thing happened him late one night and he coming up the Valley Road from Durlas." That is how, even in my own lifetime, stories began. In its earlier phases storytelling, like poetry and drama, was a public art, though unimportant beside them because of its lack of a rigorous technique. But the short story, like the novel, is a modern art form ; that is to say, it represents, better than poetry or drama, our attitude to life.

There is still, perhaps, the tendency to look in the short story for ' queer things ' happening, for action, excitement and surprises. It need not necessarily start with ' By the hokies ' but it might begin

> Wild Bill looked down the twin barrels of the sawed-off shotgun, and then into the steely eyes of the man who held it.
> " Go ahead and shoot," he said evenly.

The reader who is looking for ' kicks ' like this in the modern short story will be disappointed by a simple description of a ewe giving birth to three lambs or an old man longing for an obituary in a provincial newspaper. This is not to say that action and violence are necessarily ruled out. Writers such as Kipling, Hemingway and Liam O'Flaherty have dealt superbly with such material in their work. It is the treatment that counts. James Plunkett in " The Web " shows how a gifted writer can take the framework of a war thriller and turn it into art by informing it with a genuine sense of character, motive and atmosphere.

Just as the fire-side folktale and the conventional thriller do not qualify as short stories in the strict sense—one lacking verisimilitude and the other depth—neither does the ' anecdote.' An anecdote is the simple telling of a single—often interesting— incident. The anecdote does not concern itself with such things as character, motivation or atmosphere. Many excellent short stories are, of course, built round an anecdote. There is an interesting anecdote in the bare events of stories like " The Reaping Race," or " Up the Bare Stairs." But when we think back on these stories it is not the bare events, the anecdotal element in them, that we remember. They live in our memory for the human personalities that inhabit them, the atmosphere which the author has created around them, the glimpses into our human condition that they have granted us. In other words the anecdote has been fused into a vivid pattern of human thought and action and turned by the writer's craft and inspiration into a short story. Other stories in the book tend to hover on the borderline between anecdote and art. O. Henry's delightful little piece, " The Green Door," has all the qualities of an anecdote brilliantly told. The events are deftly organised to give the reader a series of pleasant shocks and surprises but the characters are very thinly sketched and there is little attempt to engage our emotions. Once we have read it and discovered its secret we have little desire to read it again.

The short story was not invented ; it evolved, like every other art, from earlier forms. Since the rise of the novel in the eighteenth century there had always been a steady readership for collections of ' tales ' and ' sketches ' by distinguished writers. These were especially popular in the nineteenth century with the spread of magazines. These pieces had no set form or convention and included moral tales, narrative essays, curious anecdotes, accounts of folk-tales, ' Gothick ' horror stories and even short novels. The emergence of the short story proper as a special art-form is usually associated with the great Russian writers, Gogol, Turgenev, and Chekhov. Turgenev—whose *Sportsman's Sketchbook* had a great influence on the Irish short story—was in the habit of saying that the modern short story ' came out from under Gogol's overcoat.' A useful comment that requires a little explanation.

Gogol's story is about a poor Russian clerk who is robbed of his new overcoat. It is a simple but moving story about an ordinary man in a rather commonplace situation. There are no clever twists to the plot, no surprises, no marvels or curiosities. Like most good short stories it deals with one significant event of everyday life and deals with it in some depth. Frank O'Connor suggests that this was ' the first appearance in fiction of the little man,' and in his book, *The Lonely Voice*, he suggests that the short story, as an art-form, is essentially the literature of lonely men. While the statement may not hold universally, it has a good deal of truth in it. The reason is fairly obvious. Within the limits of a short story there simply isn't space to encompass the rise and fall of princes, the bankruptcy of great firms, the deliberations of governments. It must isolate the significant moments in the lives of ordinary men and try to render them with economy and psychological insight : it must strive for ' great riches in a little room.'

Edgar Allan Poe, who is also named as a pioneer in the form, defined it as a narrative that can be read at one sitting, in the space of a half-hour to two hours ; a narrative that aims at a ' certain unique and single effect ' to which everything in the story is subordinate. It differs from the novel, therefore, not only in length but in its singleness of purpose and unity of action. It cannot allow sub-plots to develop, it cannot accommodate a large cast of characters and it must be rigorously selective about the events it chooses to describe. Frank O'Connor develops this point when he writes—

> Every great short story represents a struggle with time—the novelist's time—a refusal to allow it to establish its majestic rhythms (Chapter 1, A Walk on the Heath). It attempts to reach some point of vantage, some glowing centre of action from which past and future will be equally visible.

This valuable insight might be usefully applied to every story in the present book. It helps us to understand the special problems facing each writer as he grapples with his material and tries to shape it into unity. It helps us to see why one author chooses a point in time that will enable him to look back on the entire action, while another chooses to plunge us immediately into the midst of the situation from the first word ; it enables us to appreciate why one author chooses to tell the story in the third person while another makes use of a fictional narrator.

Some Critical Terms

In settling on his ' unique single effect ' and in looking for his ' glowing centre of action,' the writer is making up his mind about the *theme* of his story. This is the first and perhaps the most important critical term to be explained. There is in every good short story a central idea that lies behind the outward events and actions. This is called the theme of the story. Though it may not be stated, one is always conscious of its presence as it determines the emphasis of the action and imposes a unity on it. Sometimes the theme is announced in the title. The theme of " Vanity " is that foolish vanity that sometimes dominates lonely old people ; the theme of Bryan MacMahon's " The Windows of Wonder " is also indicated in the title : behind its events and dialogue lies the author's conviction that children must be stimulated to a sense of the marvellous. In other stories the theme is not always so obvious, and readers may disagree as to what precisely it is. Is " Occurrence at Owl Creek Bridge " about the brutality of war or the deceptiveness of earthly time ? Is "Among the Ruins " about man's tendency to dream or the constant failure of children and parents to understand each other ? In deciding questions such as these a great deal depends on the author's skill in placing his emphasis and the reader's skill in receiving his message. Where there is sharp disagreement within a class about the central theme of a story it is, I think, wiser for the teacher to avoid being dogmatic. But he must insist that any proffered interpretation is solidly grounded in the text. With that very important proviso, each reader is entitled to his own opinion.

If theme lies at the very inner core of the story, *plot* stands at the outside. By plot is meant the organisation of the story's outer events. When we say that a story has almost no plot we mean that the events are few or that they have not been organised into any obvious pattern. For instance " The Fly in the Ointment " is almost plotless : a man gets out of a taxi, enters a deserted factory and has a conversation with his father in the course of which the old man tries vainly to swat a fly. " The Lumber Room " has a very carefully worked plot beginning at the breakfast table and ending in a note of triumph at the tea table.

"The Queer Feet," being a detective story, could not have existed without its ingenious and carefully ordered plot.

Occasionally there is reference to *action*. By this is meant the inner as well as the outer movement of a story. The action of "A Fly in the Ointment" involves not only the physical movements of the characters but the subtle interplay of their thoughts and words, their private reflections and emotions, their decisions and resolutions.

By the *structure* of a story we mean the over-all design or organisation of the work : the way in which the elements of plot, action, character and language are woven together to bring out the theme. The *climax* or *crisis* of a story is its point of greatest tension where the action reaches its highest point and then turns : the climax of "The Majesty of the Law" comes where the Sergeant asks ' I suppose you're not thinking of paying that little fine, Dan ? ' and waits for a reply. The climax of "The Holy Kiss" comes when the grandmother decides to yield the kiss to the mother. Some stories have no discernible climax ; in some the question is open to dispute. In such cases it is perhaps best left alone. Reading must never become a game of ' hunt the climax.'

When we speak of *imagery* or *figurative language* we mean that the author is making use of images, metaphors, similes, symbols, word-pictures—to illustrate his meaning. The nature of the story will usually dictate whether the language will be figurative or conceptual. When Mary Lavin tells her simple parable about the fate of the widow's son she confines herself largely to bare, conceptual language : her theme does not really need the support of imagery. But when she writes about the vague undefined longings of a young man for the contemplative life, in "Brother Boniface," she makes skilful use of imagery to express what might be otherwise inexpressible. Imagery can be taken to mean any word, phrase or series of phrases that presents a meaningful picture to the eye. In "Brother Boniface," for instance, the man sowing in the field represents for the hero the active life, while the monk standing looking up to heaven symbolises for him, at that moment, the life of contemplation.

The only really difficult term under this heading is *symbol*. While a simile is a formal comparison between two things of different natures, and metaphor is an implied comparison, the symbol does not involve a direct comparison of two things. A symbol is some object or event in a story that exists in its own right yet carries further significance. For instance when, in "The Web," Freddie watches the spider 'spreading its dexterous web between two barrels' the spider is real. But it also suggests to the reader, as well as to the character, the web of treachery that is closing in on the fugitives. It is being used as a symbol not only for the undisclosed informer who has given them away but also for betrayal, cunning and cruel patience. We find symbols used in stories such as "The Fly," "The Fly in the Ointment," "Janey Mary" and others.

There is frequent reference to *irony* in the notes and questions. This is a difficult element to define though easy to recognise. At its simplest it is the author or character saying the opposite to what he means. At its subtlest it involves a conspiracy of understanding between the author and the reader at the expense of the character. For instance in Somerset Maugham's story, "Louise," the heroine strikes a number of attitudes and makes a number of statements that everyone in the story believes in, except the author. But the author and the reader share the knowledge that she is, in fact, a fraud. One gets an added pleasure in sharing this secret knowledge and a further dimension is added to everything she says and does. The final irony comes when, at the end, she seems to confirm her own estimate of herself by actually dying. Mary Lavin's story of the widow's son is based on a deliberate irony : no matter what had happened, the widow and her son were doomed to misunderstanding and unhappiness. "The Green Door" is based entirely on what we sometimes call 'an ironic twist of fate.' The aunt in "The Lumber Room" trapped in the garden pond is ironically placed : she finds her own words about the temptations of the Evil One used against her and can do nothing about it.

The question of irony raises the question of *tone*. Every story has its own peculiar tone. The tone of a story is similar to a tone of voice. A boy may, for instance, say 'I'm off to school to-morrow' in many different tones of voice and the precise meaning of the statement will depend to a great extent on the tone in which he says it. If he is looking forward to seeing his friends and bored with holidays it may be a shout of joy. If he hates school it can be a cry of disgust. It may, on the other hand, be a simple statement of fact—the tone may be neutral.

With the written word it is harder to judge the tone, as there is no accompanying gesture or facial expression. The skilled reader, however, can quickly distinguish whether the tone is mocking or enthusiastic, simple or ironical, grave or gay, angry or complacent. He will notice from the first word that O. Henry takes a genial, optimistic tone, that H. G. Wells is calm and factual, that James Plunkett—in "Janey Mary "—is at once angry and compassionate. It is the tone that reveals the author's attitude towards his characters and towards the reader. If the reader is alert to the signs he is rarely at a loss to know what attitude a good writer wishes him to adopt towards the actors in a story.

It is hardly necessary to say that when reference is made to the *hero* or *heroine* of a story the term means the central character, however unheroic he may be. By the *narrator* is meant the person who tells the story. If the narrator is the central character he is called simply the *hero/narrator*.

By *style* is meant the writer's characteristic manner of expressing himself, his use of language, his management of sentences, his use of imagery. It is important to realise that style is not something that is put on from without like paint on wood. Cardinal Newman described it as ' a thinking out into language.' It is dictated by the temper of the writer's mind and the sort of material that he is dealing with. Liam O'Flaherty tends to write in short, simple sentences using simple, concrete words and seldom resorting to figurative language. Frank O'Connor usually stays very close to the idiom of the spoken word and his stories often have the style of fireside narrative. Mary Lavin demonstrates in the present book that the same writer may use two different styles in response to two different kinds of experience. Style is, in the last analysis, the most distinctive aspect of a writer's craft. Many writers are immediately recognisable by their style : Dr. Johnson could never be mistaken for Ernest Hemingway, nor Liam O'Flaherty for G. K. Chesterton. It is this individual quality of style that Sean O'Faolain refers to when he speaks of ' communicated personality.'

How to Use this Book

This anthology has been arranged according to a few simple, definite principles. The stories are there to be enjoyed, consequently nothing has been allowed to stand between the reader and the story. The biographical notes are relegated to the back of the book and the glosses, confined to a minimum, are supplied at the end of each story. In these notes no words are explained that can be found in a pocket dictionary—a piece of equipment that no student of English should lack—and the informative glossing is deliberately sparse. It did not seem necessary for instance, to investigate the scientist Daubrée, referred to in Wells's " The Diamond Maker," but it seemed useful to give a little information about the American Civil War in the case of Ambrose Bierce's story. In other words where the understanding of an allusion is important to the understanding of a story the information is briefly given. Where such information might prove merely distracting it is omitted.

The questions that come immediately after the story, under the title " Explorations " are meant primarily for class discussion though the individual pupil may also find them useful in private study. Their purpose is to guide the reader into the heart of the story, its central theme, and from there to considerations of treatment and technique. But there is no rigid pattern ; each story required a different approach, a different point of entry. For instance, the fly episode is central to " The Fly in the Ointment," but it would, I think, be ill-judged to start a class discussion on the point. It seemed better to explore the relationship between son and father that the author so carefully builds up before entering the difficult area of symbol. By the time this initial exploration is over and the questions more or less satisfactorily answered the student is perhaps in a position to see for himself what the fly stands for.

Some stories, of course, demand far more strenuous probing than others. The impact of an O'Flaherty story, for instance, is powerful, simple and immediate. He rarely uses symbols or concerns himself with more than one level of meaning. In his case the questions are fewer and in the case of " Three Lambs " questions seemed not only unnecessary but impertinent. On the other hand stories like "A Man's World " and " The Poteen Maker " may be greeted by the students with a sense of cheated indignation. What is the point of the story, they may ask ? Nothing much seems to happen ; nothing begins, develops and ends—there seems to be no plot, no meaningful action, no moral.

This is an understandable and healthy reaction and could make a useful point of departure for a deeper examination of the story. Before the student turns away from it in disgust or frustration and retreats into his comic, western or detective novel—the world of reliable, predictable, undemanding narrative—the teacher must gently bring him back to the story he is about to dismiss. This, I believe, can best be done by asking questions. Why did the character behave in such a way at such a time ? What light does this piece of dialogue or that phrase throw on it ? Why does the author dwell at such length on this object or that incident ? In this way the hidden design of the story will slowly reveal itself and the student will have the added pleasure of discovering most of it for himself.

Though a good deal of thought has gone into devising these questions the individual teacher may find more effective questions himself or use the questions provided in quite a different order. They are supplied both as practical teaching tools and examples of a general method. The teacher, in many cases, will find it necessary to expand and augment them. And it is important to bear in mind that the bright student may discover levels of meaning in a story that may have escaped both teacher and editor.

The "Exercises" are meant, in most cases, for written rather than oral work. Some of them, however, invite the student to read a similar story from the anthology as a preparation for discussion and comparison in a subsequent class. It is strongly urged that the written exercises be short because it would be a pity if the stories were to become an occasion for labour and boredom. For this reason the exercises are ' creative ' rather than critical. Instead of asking the pupil to write an ' appreciation ' of the story he is asked to describe an incident, fill out a piece of dialogue, or relate an allied experience from his own life. It might be desirable, for this reason, to let the pupil choose his own exercise from those given ; his imagination will probably respond best to the material that attracts him most. In tackling these written exercises the student will learn a great deal about life as well as the craft of writing. First of all he will learn humility : he will have a greater respect for the skill involved in writing a good story when he has attempted to write one himself. Consequently he must not be disappointed if his performance falls sharply below the story that inspired it. A single good phrase should, in many cases, prove sufficient reward and justification for the effort. Apart from that the exercise will liberate his imagination ; it will teach him to analyse and evaluate his own experience ; it will help him to appreciate the richness of human life around him ; it will give him a respect for words, their power to evoke, suggest, define. Another effect of these exercises—especially the oral ones—should be to encourage the student to range at large throughout the anthology and from there to other collections of short stories. The more stories he reads the better reader he will become.

A final advantage of the interrogative method is that it protects student, teacher and editor against dogmatism. Instead of forcing a single, rigid interpretation or evaluation on the young reader, the questions invite him to lay creative hold on the material and form his own judgments. Literature is a field where every reader must reach his own individual insights and opinions. In guiding him towards these the teacher must merely insist that these judgments are supported by intelligent reference to the text. The well-directed question is, perhaps, the best way of doing this. Because the question, unlike the assertion, opens the windows of wonder and inquiry instead of closing them.

AUGUSTINE MARTIN.

SHORT STORIES

BY

IRISH AUTHORS

THE BREATH OF LIFE

The opera company which I had accompanied as first violinist on so many tours suddenly collapsing, I found myself rather unexpectedly out of an engagement. I communicated with my Society, and after a day's delay I was ordered to go at once to Clonmoyle.

I was in the worst of humours. Clonmoyle, I found, was one of those places which instead of increasing in size and importance as places ought, seem to have become accustomed to doing the very opposite. Once a city, it was now but a straggling town. What had brought an opera company to try its fortunes there I could make no guess at, yet there it was, and with difficulties accumulating about it. Here was I myself, for instance, in Clonmoyle because the manager had found it impossible to supplement his scanty travelling orchestra with local players ; and several others as well as I had to travel day and night to be in time for the opening performance. Only one local musician had been dug up ; and of him this story.

In everything he stood apart from us. He was old, well over sixty, however young in appearance. He was large and heavy in build, easy-going, ruminative. We, the others in the band, were rather meagre, high-strung, irritable, worried—as is the way of our tribe ; on this trip particularly so (consider my own case : a first-class violinist in such surroundings !) He, on the other hand, smiled the whole day long, and his voice whispered rather than spoke. It did not seem to trouble him that the old ramshackle theatre was mouldy, damp, foul-smelling. He did not seem to notice the cruel draughts that swept us while we played, and benumbed our fingers. It made no difference to him if the manager was in a vile temper over the receipts, and our conductor still worse, his rheumatism playing old Harry with him.

At our very first rehearsal I discovered he could not play in tune. " I'm in for it ! " I said, for a week of such fellowship I knew only too well would leave me a wreck. And even as I said this I saw the conductor staring hard at where the two of us were sitting side by side ; was it possible he thought it was I who was playing like that ! He might well have thought so, for my companion's face was not a guilty face ; how anyone could play so consistently flat and still smile was a problem beyond me. Yes, Ignatius O'Byrne, such was his name, still smiled and still flattened. The fact is, he was the happiest man alive ; it was as if he had come into an inheritance. Here he was fiddling away in his beloved operas, and it was thirty years since he had last done so. These long thirty years, he explained to me in an interval, he had been rehearsing them in his untidy lodgings in a back street, and more than that, he had been thinking them out, phrase by phrase, " walking in the mists upon these rainsoaked hills "—I give his very words. As he spoke he swept his hand in a half-circle as if even there in the theatre he could still behold them, the dreary hills that surround Clonmoyle on every side and overlay it, as it were, with a sort of perpetual gloom. And then he added : " Behind music is the breath of life." A curious man, surely ; I watched his face. It was glowing, glowing, as long as the music held. And once when in some happy passage the whole band was singing like one, " Bravo, Bravo ! " I heard him whisper, and later on " Bravissimo ! " and he ceased playing, ceased, until I thought of nudging him with my elbow. And so, little by little, I came to forgive him his flat playing and his awkward bowing.

Our conductor, a brute of a man, his body twisted into a knot by rheumatism, was now constantly looking in our direction; but whenever I saw him doing so I would make my violin sing for all it was worth : were we not brothers in the same craft, this old man and I ? At rehearsal the second day my efforts to cover his wretched playing failed ; the conductor left his place, tied up and all as he was in that knot of pain, shuffled over to where we sat, and stood between us ! That settled for him which of us two was playing flat. He scowled at the old resurrected musician, hissed out a fierce, wicked word under his breath, and hobbled back to his place. That night, just to make matters worse, I suppose, old Byrne played altogether vilely ! He had scarce a phrase in tune. When the curtain fell he had to face a little tragic opera of his own—the tragedy of old age and failing powers. He took it all without a word. " The breath of life is behind music," he whispered to me as he came from the interview ;

then he bent down, carefully wrapped his fiddle in a piece of baize cloth, put it in his case and made off.

The final explosion came at the rehearsal next day. He and I were the first to arrive. The score of last night's opera, it was *The Marriage of Figaro*, still lay on the conductor's stand. He turned the pages. They were pencilled all over with directions as to the tempos of the various movements. Along these pencillings old Byrne ran his finger. I could see he was having his revenge. I could see him lift his brows—just a little—as if he were partly amused, partly astonished. But no word escaped him. Soon the conductor came in and we began. We had not got far when we heard " Get out ! " roared in a terrible voice, the voice of one who had not slept for several nights. The old man rose up, wrapped his baize cloth around his instrument, and moved between the chairs. As he went how still the empty house was, only a chair moving, and his own almost silent feet ! And how we watched him ! But when he got as far as the conductor's chair he paused, glanced once more at the open score, and laughed a tiny little laugh !

I felt his going more than I should care to tell. Will you believe me ? I had told that old musician, that stranger, the whole story of the sorrows of my life. Yes, I told him things I had hardly ever made clear even to myself ! And he replied : " Is it not behind music, the breath of life ? " as if sorrow was there for the one purpose of being transmuted into sweet sound ! I recalled his words as I went to my task that night.

And that night the extraordinary thing happened ; our conductor failed to make an appearance ; his rheumatism had conquered. There was then a call for our leader. He was found. Alas! he was not in a condition to conduct anything. He could scarcely stand. And he became quite cross about it ; we had to leave him there in his corner, resining his bow like anything and scowling like mad. What between principals, chorus, and band, all thinking they stood a chance of losing a night's pay, and the manager flustering about like a whirlwind, our little den beneath the stage was deafening ; I slipped quietly out into the house. There outside the rail was old Byrne ! " What's the matter ? " he whispered. As I told him, up came the manager.

" Mr. Melton," he said to me, " will you please take the baton to-night ? "

A very flattering compliment indeed, and I should have taken that baton if our band did not happen to be the scraggiest ever scraped together from the ends of the earth ; our leader was in the condition I have mentioned. I had to lead ! As we spoke I saw the players getting into their places, a tempting sight, yet still I hesitated, foreseeing collapse and ignominy.

" It is not possible," I began, but over the rail old Byrne was climbing like a boy. He had clutched the baton from the manager's hand. He had leaped into the conductor's chair. He gave but one glance to the right, to the left. " Now, boys," he said, and at the words we swam, sank, buried ourselves in the rich, broad, gentle strains of the overture to *Faust*. Some wide gesture he had used, some thrill in his tone had bidden us to do so—to lose ourselves in the soul of the music. At the first chord we had got within the skin of it, as the saying is. And never was the mood broken ; every progression told, and not a colour tone was faulty or blurred. That memorable waltz, which use has almost spoiled, he made a new thing of it—we were all spirits in thin air, so lightly it went. But our triumph was the tremendous trio at the close. The old man stood up to it, hiding the stage from a large sector of the house. What did he care ! We felt his huge shabby figure above us as a darkness, a vastness of great potency. It commanded stage, orchestra, house, with a strong yet benign power. The voices—tenor, soprano, bass—all the instruments, strings, brass, wood, drums, the very shell of the old house itself, became as one instrument and sang the great strain with such strength and spirit that some of us trembled lest we should fall down with excitement and spoil everything.

" Oh ! " we all sighed when it was over. For such moments does the artist live. I was so glad I had told him the story of my sorrows !

Now, sir, around Clonmoyle, as I have said, is a rampart of dark hills, bleak and rain-sodden, treeless and desolate. Why do I again mention them ? " Wherever did you learn to conduct ? " I asked him, as we made for our lodgings.

" There ! " he answered, and his outstretched hand gestured around the deserted hills, " behind music we must get at the breath of life." Bare, wind-swept hills !—curious place to find out the secrets of life ! Or what did he mean by " Life ! " It cannot be that the breath of life that is behind all great music is the sigh of loneliness ?

" And you took him with the company ? "

" No, sir ; an opera company, like any other company, must pay its way."

— *A Munster Twilight*

Explorations

1. Ignatius O'Byrne is distinguished from everyone else in the story by his physical appearance. Is he distinguished in any other way ?

2. Why do you think Ignatius O'Byrne was such a wretched violinist and at the same time such an inspired conductor ?

3. Why, in your opinion, does the narrator tell the old man ' the sorrows of his life ' ?

4. In the last sentence the narrator suggests that, much as they might have liked to, the company could not afford to take the old man with them. Can you suggest why, particularly as O'Byrne would hardly have demanded a large salary ?

5. The old man keeps saying that ' music is the breath of life.' Is this statement true of the old man himself ? Is it true of the other characters in the story—the narrator, the original conductor, the drunken leader ?

6. Is it an apt title for the story ? Why ?

7. Do you find the character of the old man convincing ? If you do, try to explain how Corkery managed to make him so, taking account of his actions, his words, the comments of the narrator about him. If you think the author failed to make him convincing, try, in the same way to explain where he may have failed.

8. The author tries to suggest that there is a deep bond between Ignatius O'Byrne and his music and also between him and the surrounding hills. What is the purpose of these associations ?

9. Is there any difference between the ways in which the narrator and O'Byrne see Clonmoyle and the surrounding country ? If so, is it important ?

Exercises

1. Tell the story from the point of view of the leader who gets drunk at the last moment.

2. Write down honestly what you thought about the first orchestra conductor you ever saw perform.

VANITY

I

From that great mountain-wall which divides Cork from Kerry great spurs of broken and terraced rock run out on the Cork side like vast buttresses ; and in the flanks of these great buttresses are round-ended glens, or cooms, as they are called in Irish. Those on the northern flanks of such spurs are gloomy beyond belief.

The dwellers in these cold valleys are of such an austere, puritanic type that the exception among them who is given to the vanities of the world shows out with indescribable, if unholy lustre. In Lyrenascaul old Diarmuid Mac Coitir was such a man ; it may be more correct to say had been such a man, for he was now of great age and mostly confined to his bed. In the little dark back-room—it was dark because a sheer slab of rock, grey, lichened and damp, rose up behind the house — he passed the long hours of day and night. Between the darkness of the room itself and the darkness that was coming over his eyes, there was not much difference for him now between day and night, except that in the day he could still hear the little stir of life—very little indeed it was—that went on around the miserable bit of a farm that he had made over to his son. In the few other houses that clung against the sides of Lyrenascaul there were here and there other bed-ridden ancients ; these you beheld with their beads in their hands, night as well as day, and a certain pallor, a quiet peacefulness that lay always on their features, told you they had long since put this world aside and were now calmly awaiting the call to the next world. Diarmuid had never been of the same mind as these ; and instead of that great calmness of theirs, it would be a thick sort of smile that would come slowly crawling over his features, sometimes disguising them for quite long spells.

He lived there with his wife, who was almost as old as himself and as unworldly as he was worldly ; and the only other person in the house was their only remaining son, the still unmarried Michael, now an old man himself, one too who had inherited much of the worldliness and hardness of the ancient who day after day lay bed-ridden in the little dark back-room.

Into that out-of-the-world coom—it was miles from any main road—it was seldom a stray newspaper from Cork or Dublin made its way. You might even to-day live there a long six months and not see one ; and I am told that many people easily remember the time when no papers at all entered with their strange tales of the outside world. Old Diarmuid could not read (indeed his son could hardly do as much) but even if he could what interest would he have found in the news of a world he had never been in, more especially when that news would consist of a series of unrelated facts, with, for him, no yesterday, no to-morrow ? News of fairs and markets he might have fathomed, if there were any such. There usually was not. In every paper, however, that chanced to find its way into that forgotten world, there would be a series of paragraphs that always came home to him and gripped his thoughts—these were the death notices. For many years these notices were such a novelty that he learned each of them by heart from some other person's reading, and would recite the latest to his gossips, and compare it with ones he had earlier learned, and go on to speak of the difference between one which mentioned that a Requiem Mass had been sung and one which was content with the modest : R.I.P.

At that stage he was when without warning he was one day struck with paralysis. One evening he sat up, thinking of what had befallen him. He called to his son :

" Hi ! " he said, " Michael, Michael ! "

Michael had been chopping furze to give as food to their poor sorry nag ; he came in, chopper in hand :

" Well ? "

" Tell me this, Michael, if 'twas dead you found me this day, or any other day, would you put a little biteen of a notice in the paper—just a little biteen of a wan with R.I.P. at the end of it ? "

Michael looked at him and noticed how strong and sturdy he was. He smiled, not sweetly or lovingly. He threw an eye around the dark, almost empty little house; he took a step to the

open door and glanced with scorn at the scraggy patch of land
that was their farm ; he came back and said :

" Isn't it well you deserve it from me ? "

" Don't be hard, Michael, boy, there's a good time coming ;
you won't have to face what I had to face, the struggling with
landlords, and the law—the law that would leave a rich man
poor and a poor man broken. Give me your word, Michael, boy,
when it pleases God to call me you'll put a little biteen of a notice
in the paper so that—— "

" I won't then give you me word. An old man like you, 'tis
something else should be troubling you besides having your name
stuck in the paper and you cold on the bed—." And then, just
as he was about to begin his furze-chopping again, he called out :

" Was there ever anyone from Lyrenascaul in the paper and
he dead ? "

" That's why ! " said the old man, sitting up suddenly, while
quite a glow came back into his heavy face.

Not long after there did really happen to be a death-notice
from Lyrenascaui in the paper. It was American gold put it
there. Old John Kevane had died. The news had been leisurely
enough sent to his son in America. A few days after its arrival
there the notice appeared in the Cork and Dublin papers—
cabled from America ! Whereupon old Diarmuid Mac Coitir
renewed his importunity, not however with more success.
" There's a great fear of you dying, a great fear indeed ! " his
son would answer, and pass the thing off as a joke.

II

It was long after midnight when the old man heard his son's
horse-and-cart jolting up the rock-strewn bohereen. In that dead
hour he could hear it even when a great way off. He had not
expected Michael earlier, he had been at Inchigeela fair. Some
little brightness came into the dull face to hear the sound of the
wheels. That fair day used to be a bright feature in his own life
in the years now gone for ever ; he thought it meant the same
for his son, as in some measure it did ; and with each recurrence
of the event some little trace of his old alertness would struggle
up in the old man's face, and that unlovely smile was sure to

follow. After long waiting he heard the son putting up his horse. He entered and his face was a great broad smile.

" 'Tis a queer thing I'm after hearing this day," he said to his father.

" What was it ? " and the old man scanned his son's face, rather pleased, perhaps, as well as a little jealous, to find in it the excitement and jollity of strong drink.

" What was it ? " he said.

" Well, then, 'tis this : I'm after learning, and from good authority, that if yourself and herself died together on the wan day on me I'd get a notice in the paper for the same money as if it was only one of ye was in it ! " And he sat on a stool, with one gaiter dangling in his hand, and he laughed stupidly, and with such loudness as seemed sacrilegious in that solemn mountain glen, in that great darkness and silence.

" Wouldn't ye do it, and I promise ye, ye'd get it—the notice ! "

" Do what ? "

" Die, the pair of ye, on the wan day ! "

The old man growled at him and turned away. The son went off in a great fit of laughter. Likely enough his horse had often heard him laugh that night as he came the long twenty-seven miles of bogland and mountain. And the great joke held him for several weeks !

Although he had answered not a word, this new idea took possession of the old man's mind. But whereas formerly in those odd moments when in imagination he would behold his neighbours passing the paper that contained his own death-notice from hand to hand, he always felt nothing but joy and pride, now there was in the dream some shadowy fear he could not fathom, could not put aside. There was certainly no feeling of pride left in him. In fact he soon came to trying to avoid the vision ; it had now, however, become part of himself, so keenly had he desired it, so frequently had he indulged it. He could not avoid it. At any moment of great stillness, it would suddenly stand before him—a group of his neighbours—old Padraig Lynch, old Tadhg Cremin, old Steve Casey, with his one eye, old Morty Shea, with his high, white forehead and glasses—there they were, all gathered together around the Master while he read out to them, "At their son's residence in Lyrenascaul, at an advanced age, Jeremiah and Mary Cotter . . . " Ah ! that was it : there were now always the two names coupled together in the death-notice he beheld his neighbours reading. Yet in spite of his new-sprung hatred he couldn't banish the vision, couldn't prevent its reappearance at the most unexpected hours.

If he woke up in the still night what else was there for him to think about ? In fact it seemed as if he had been waked up for the one purpose of seeing the vision, as if indeed the vision had been waiting for him to awaken. In great and terrifying clearness there was Morty Shea, that calm, saintly-looking man with the white forehead and the glasses, there was Steve Casey, with the one eye, a black slit where the other should be, listening, intently listening ; there, too, was —. All joy had passed away out of old Diarmuid's mind.

When his wife, who was now almost ninety—he himself was ninety-three—brought in a ponny of milk to him he would strain whatever sight he had left to look slyly up in her face ; he would also pass his hand over hers—he was glad if it felt distinctly hotter or distinctly colder ; he was depressed if it seemed the same as his own ! He would make sly inquiries of his son as to how she was in health.

It was another fair day, a mellow harvest-golden day in September ; the son was again from home. He would not be home till late. Towards evening the old woman brought in some milk and home-made bread to the bed-ridden man. They had nothing to say to one another. They were too old. She waited till he had finished, she then carried out the vessels again. He settled himself for a comfortable sleep ; he would then wake up refreshed and be ready to receive the news of the fair ; it had become a point of honour with him to be awake on such occasions. He had not been long asleep when he awoke with a curious tingling sensation, and there was that terrible vision once again, the same faces, the same attitudes. And he was disturbed. He should not have awakened so soon.

" Maire ! " he called out in his wheezy voice.

He got no answer.

" Maire ! Maire ! I'm queer."

There was no sound, except the water running down that-slab of rock behind the house.

" Maire ! Maire ! "

Even while he called, it was of his own fear he was thinking. And then, horribly real—the people in the vision began to move, a hand was lifted, an eye turned—

" Don't forget the R.I.P., Master," said their son. " If that wasn't in it he wouldn't be satisfied, even how long we made it."

" I have R.I.P. in it."

" Read it now."

" At their son's residence, Lyrenascaul, Jeremiah and Mary—— "

— A Munster Twilight

Explorations

1. Why is the story entitled ' Vanity ' ?

2. In ordinary circumstances would the desire to have a death notice printed in the paper be considered a great vanity ?

3. In the circumstances which Corkery describes do you consider it vanity ? Why ?

4. Corkery devotes a good deal of space to the scenery. Is this done for its own sake ? Or is he trying to suggest that there is some connection between the landscape and the mentality of its people ? If so, what sort of relationship do you think he is trying to suggest ? Examine the story closely in arriving at your answer.

5. What sort of relationship exists between Diarmuid and his son ? Is there any evidence that there is love between them ? Or hatred ? Or indifference ? Is Michael's treatment of the old man cruel ? Does Diarmuid regard it as cruel ? Is it a normal father/son relationship ?

6. Are any of the characters religious people ? Does the author introduce the notion of religion, however tactfully, at any stage in the story ? Where ? Why ?

7. This is a story about rather primitive people and conditions. Do you think the author's style is suitable to the material ? Give reasons for your answer. Try briefly to describe the chief qualities of the style, taking in the narrative, descriptive and dialogue passages.

8. The death of the old couple is suggested rather than described. Do you think that this was the best way to handle the ending ? Give your reasons.

9. The character of the mother is barely mentioned at all. What, in fact, is said about her ? Answer this without going back to the story and then check your answer against the text. Do you think that the author was wise in telling us so little about her ? Why ?

10. The old man is described as smiling an 'unlovely smile.' Does the phrase suggest a spiritual or a merely physical lack of beauty ? Comment on any other words or phrases that strike you.

11. The old man is accused of ' worldliness ' several times in the course of the story. Does he, on the evidence of the story, deserve the charge ?

12. The old couple die on the same day. What do you think Corkery means to convey by this ? In answering, bear in mind the title and look again at the story from the words ' although he had answered not a word ' to the end.

13. The character of Michael, the son, is not developed in depth. Is he developed sufficiently for the purposes of the story ? Or would you like to know more about him ?

Exercises

1. Try to imagine the conversation that took place between the priest when he was called, and Michael, on the death of the old people.

2. Compose a description of your own landscape—be it town or city or country—similar to the opening passage of the present story and try to suggest the influence which their surroundings might have on the people who live there.

3. The author uses a number of words and terms not in common use—' coom ' for glen, ' ponny '—meaning a tin cup or porringer. Examine the story for words such as these and say whether they add anything special to the story.

4. Frank O'Connor has stated that ' there is in the short story at its most characteristic something we do not often find in the novel—an intense awareness of human loneliness.' Discuss this statement in relation to one or both of these Corkery stories.

3

HIS FIRST FLIGHT

The young seagull was alone on his ledge. His two brothers and his sister had already flown away the day before. He had been afraid to fly with them. Somehow when he had taken a little run forward to the brink of the ledge and attempted to flap his wings he became afraid. The great expanse of sea stretched down beneath, and it was such a long way down—miles down. He felt certain that his wings would never support him, so he bent his head and ran away back to the little hole under the ledge where he slept at night. Even when each of his brothers and his little sister, whose wings were far shorter than his own, ran to the brink, flapped their wings, and flew away, he failed to muster up courage to take that plunge which appeared to him so desperate. His father and mother had come around calling to him shrilly, upbraiding him, threatening to let him starve on his ledge unless he flew away. But for the life of him he could not move.

That was twenty-four hours ago. Since then nobody had come near him. The day before, all day long, he had watched his parents flying about with his brothers and sister, perfecting them in the art of flight, teaching them how to skim the waves and how to dive for fish. He had, in fact, seen his older brother catch his first herring and devour it, standing on a rock, while his parents circled around raising a proud cackle. And all the morning the whole family had walked about on the big plateau midway down the opposite cliff, taunting him with his cowardice.

The sun was now ascending the sky, blazing warmly on his ledge that faced the south. He felt the heat because he had not eaten since the previous nightfall. Then he had found a dried piece of mackerel's tail at the far end of his ledge. Now there was not a single scrap of food left. He had searched every inch, rooting among the rough, dirt-caked straw nest where he and his brothers and sister had been hatched. He even gnawed at the dried pieces of spotted eggshell. It was like eating part of himself. He had then trotted back and forth from one end of the ledge to the other, his grey body the colour of the cliff, his long grey legs stepping daintily, trying to find some means of reaching his parents without having to fly. But on each side of him the ledge ended in a sheer fall of precipice, with the sea beneath. And between him and his parents there was a deep, wide chasm. Surely he could reach them without flying if he could only move northwards along the cliff face ? But then on what could he walk ? There was no ledge, and he was not a fly. And above him he could see nothing. The precipice was sheer, and the top of it was perhaps farther away than the sea beneath him.

He stepped slowly out to the brink of the ledge, and, standing on one leg with the other hidden under his wing, he closed one eye, then the other, and pretended to be falling asleep. Still they took no notice of him. He saw his two brothers and his sister lying on the plateau dozing, with their heads sunk into their necks. His father was preening the feathers on his white back. Only his mother was looking at him. She was standing on a little high hump on the plateau, her white breast thrust forward. Now and again she tore at a piece of fish that lay at her feet, and then scraped each side of her beak on the rock. The sight of the food maddened him. How he loved to tear food that way, scraping his beak now and again to whet it ! He uttered a low cackle. His mother cackled too, and looked over at him.

" Ga, ga, ga," he cried, begging her to bring him over some food. " Gaw-ool-ah," she screamed back derisively. But he kept calling plaintively, and after a minute or so he uttered a joyful scream. His mother had picked up a piece of the fish and was flying across to him with it. He leaned out eagerly, tapping the rock with his feet, trying to get nearer to her as she flew across. But when she was just opposite to him, abreast of the ledge, she halted, her legs hanging limp, her wings motionless, the piece of fish in her beak almost within reach of his beak. He waited a moment in surprise, wondering why she did not come nearer, and then, maddened by hunger, he dived at the fish. With a loud scream he fell outwards and downwards into space. His mother had swooped upwards. As he passed beneath her he heard the swish of her wings. Then a monstrous terror seized him and his heart stood still. He could hear nothing. But it only lasted a moment. The next moment he felt his wings spread outwards. The wind rushed against his breast feathers, then under his stomach and against his wings. He could feel the tips of his wings cutting through the air. He was not falling headlong now. He was soaring gradually downwards and outwards. He was no longer afraid. He just felt a bit dizzy. Then he flapped his wings once and he soared upwards. He uttered a joyous scream and flapped them again. He soared higher. He raised his breast and banked against the wind. " Ga, ga, ga. Ga, ga, ga. Gaw-ool-ah." His mother swooped past him, her wings making a loud noise. He answered her with another scream. Then his father flew over him screaming. Then he saw his two brothers and sister flying around him curveting and banking and soaring and diving.

Then he completely forgot that he had not always been able to fly, and commenced himself to dive and soar and curvet, shrieking shrilly.

He was near the sea now, flying straight over it, facing straight out over the ocean. He saw a vast green sea beneath him, with little ridges moving over it, and he turned his beak sideways and crowed amusedly. His parents and his brothers and sister had landed on this green floor in front of him. They were beckoning to him, calling shrilly. He dropped his legs to stand on the green sea. His legs sank into it. He screamed with fright and attempted to rise again, flapping his wings. But he was tired and weak with hunger and he could not rise, exhausted by the strange exercise. His feet sank into the green sea, and then his belly touched it and he sank no farther. He was floating on it. And around him his family was screaming, praising him, and their beaks were offering him scraps of dog-fish.

He had made his first flight.

— Short Stories of Liam O'Flaherty

Explorations

1.   In the story do you find yourself involved in the predicament of
the young seagull ? Do you find yourself wishing he would take the
plunge ? Do you pity him in his agony of indecision ? If so, try to
discover how the author manages to involve you in the fate of the bird.
If not, try to discover the flaw in yourself or in the story that may be
responsible.

2.   How would you describe the language of the story : simple or
elaborate ? clear or obscure? natural or artificial? economical or
long-winded ? Is this style suited to the subject matter ? Why ?

3.   Where would you locate the climax of the story ? Give your
reasons.

4.   Do you think this is a proper subject for a story at all ? Why ?

Exercises

1.   Describe the mother's feelings as she tries to get the young
bird to take the plunge.

2.   Describe some moment of drama in the animal world that
you personally witnessed and try to write, with some precision, and
in the right words, what the animal in question may have been feeling.

THE REAPING RACE

At dawn the reapers were already in the rye field. It was the big rectangular field owned by James McDara, the retired engineer. The field started on the slope of a hill and ran down gently to the sea-road that was covered with sand. It was bound by a low stone fence, and the yellow heads of the rye-stalks leaned out over the fence all round in a thick mass, jostling and crushing one another as the morning breeze swept over them with a swishing sound.

McDara himself, a white-haired old man in grey tweeds, was standing outside the fence on the sea-road, waving his stick and talking to a few people who had gathered even at that early hour. His brick-red face was all excitement, and he waved his black-thorn stick as he talked in a loud voice to the men about him.

" I measured it out yesterday," he was saying, " as even as it could be done. Upon my honour there isn't an inch in the difference between one strip and another of the three strips. D'ye see ? I have laid lines along the length of the field so they can't go wrong. Come here and I'll show ye."

He led the men along from end to end of the field and showed how he had measured it off into three even parts and marked the strips with white lines laid along the ground.

" Now it couldn't be fairer," cried the old man, as excited as a schoolboy. " When I fire my revolver they'll all start together, and the first couple to finish their strip gets a five-pound note."

The peasants nodded their heads and looked at old McDara seriously, although each one of them thought he was crazy to spend five pounds on the cutting of a field that could be cut for two pounds. They were, however, almost as excited as McDara himself, for the three best reapers in the whole island of Inverara had entered for the competition. They were now at the top of the field on the slope of the hill ready to commence. Each had his wife with him to tie the sheaves as they were cut and bring food and drink.

They had cast lots for the strips by drawing three pieces of seaweed from McDara's hat. Now they had taken up position on their strips awaiting the signal. Although the sun had not yet warmed the earth and the sea breeze was cold, each man had stripped to his shirt. The shirts were open at the chest and the sleeves were rolled above the elbow. They wore grey woollen shirts. Around his waist each had a multi-coloured " crios," a long knitted belt made of pure wool. Below that they wore white frieze drawers with the ends tucked into woollen stockings that were embroidered at the tops. Their feet were protected by raw-hide shoes. None of them wore a cap. The women all wore red petticoats, with a little shawl tied around their heads.

On the left were Michael Gill and his wife, Susan. Michael was a long wiry man, with fair hair that came down over his forehead and was cropped to the bone all around the skull. He had a hook nose, and his lean jaws were continually moving backwards and forwards. His little blue eyes were fixed on the ground, and his long white eyelashes almost touched his cheek-bones, as if he slept. He stood motionless, with his reaping-hook in his right hand and his left hand in his belt. Now and again he raised his eyelashes, listening for the signal to commence. His wife was almost as tall as himself, but she was plump and rosy-cheeked. A silent woman, she stood there thinking of her eight-months-old son whom she had left at home in the charge of her mother.

In the middle Johnny Bodkin stood with his arms folded and his legs spread wide apart, talking to his wife in a low serious voice. He was a huge man, with fleshy limbs and neck, and black hair that had gone bald over his forehead. His forehead was very white and his cheeks were very red. He always frowned, twitching his black eyebrows. His wife, Mary, was short, thin, sallow-faced, and her upper teeth protruded slightly over her lower lip.

On the right were Pat Considine and his wife, Kate. Kate was very big and brawny, with a freckled face and a very marked moustache on her upper lip. She had a great mop of sandy-coloured curly hair that kept coming undone. She talked to her husband in a loud, gruff, masculine voice, full of good humour. Her husband, on the other hand, was a small man, small and slim, and beginning to get wrinkles in his face, although he was not yet forty. His face had once been a brick-red colour, but now it was becoming sallow. He had lost most of his front teeth. He stood loosely, grinning towards McDara, his little, loose, slim body hiding its strength.

Then McDara waved his stick. He lifted his arm. A shot rang out. The reaping race began. In one movement the three men sank to their right knees like soldiers on parade at musketry practice. Their left hands in the same movement closed about a bunch of rye-stalks. The curved reaping-hooks whirled in the air, and then there was a crunching sound, the sound that hungry cows make eating long fresh grass in spring. Then three little slender bunches of rye-stalks lay flat on the dewy grass beneath the fence, one bunch behind each reaper's bent left leg. The three women waited in nervous silence for the first sheaf. It would be an omen of victory or defeat. One, two, three, four bunches . . . Johnny Bodkin, snorting like a furious horse, was dropping his bunches almost without stopping. With a loud cheer he raised his reaping-hook in the air and spat on it, crying " First sheaf ! " His wife dived at it with both hands. Separating a little bunch of stalks, she encircled the head of the sheaf and then bound it with amazing rapidity, her long thin fingers moving like knitting needles. The other reapers and their wives had not paused to look. All three reapers had cut their first sheaves and their wives were on their knees tying.

Working in the same furious manner in which he had begun, Bodkin was soon far ahead of his competitors. He was cutting his sheaves in an untidy manner, and he was leaving hummocks behind him on the ground owing to the irregularities of his strokes, but his speed and strength were amazing. His great hands whirled the hook and closed on the stalks in a ponderous manner, and his body hurtled along like the carcass of an elephant trotting through a forest, but there was a rhythm in the never-ending movement of his limbs that was not without beauty. And behind came his wife, tying, tying speedily, with her hard face gathered together in a serious frown like a person meditating on a grave decision.

Considine and his wife were second. Considine, now that he was in action, showed surprising strength and an agility that was goat-like. When his lean, long, bony arms moved to slash the rye, muscles sprang up all over his bent back like an intricate series of springs being pressed. Every time he hopped on his right knee to move along his line of reaping he emitted a sound like a groan cut short. His wife, already perspiring heavily, worked almost on his heels, continually urging him on, laughing and joking in her habitual loud hearty voice.

Michael Gill and his wife came last. Gill had begun to reap with the slow methodic movements of a machine driven at low pressure. He continued at exactly the same pace, never changing, never looking up to see where his opponents were. His long lean hands moved noiselessly, and only the sharp crunching rush of the teeth of his reaping-hook through the yellow stalks of the rye could be heard. His long drooping eyelashes were always directed towards the point where his hook was cutting. He never looked behind to see had he enough for a sheaf before beginning another. All his movements were calculated beforehand, calm, monotonous, deadly accurate. Even his breathing was light, and came through his nose like one who sleeps healthily. His wife moved behind him in the same manner, tying each sheaf daintily, without exertion.

As the day advanced people gathered from all quarters watching the reapers. The sun rose into the heaven. There was a fierce heat. Not a breath of wind. The rye-stalks no longer moved. They stood in perfect silence, their heads a whitish colour, their stalks golden. Already there was a large irregular gash in the rye, ever increasing. The bare patch, green with little clover plants that had been sown with the rye, was dotted with sheaves, already whitening in the hot sun. Through the hum of conversation the regular crunching of the reaping-hooks could be heard.

A little before noon Bodkin had cut half his strip. A stone had been placed on the marking line at half-way, and when Bodkin reached that stone he stood up with the stone in his hand and yelled : " This is a proof," he cried, " that there was never a man born in the island of Inverara as good as Johnny Bodkin." There was an answering cheer from the crowd on the fence, but big Kate Considine humorously waved a sheaf above her head and yelled in her rough man's voice : " The day is young yet, Bodkin of the soft flesh ! " The crowd roared with laughter, and Bodkin fumed, but he did not reply. His wits were not very sharp. Gill and his wife took no notice. They did not raise their eyes from the reaping.

Bodkin's wife was the first to go for the midday meal. She brought a can full of cold tea and a whole oven cake of white flour, cut in large pieces, each piece coated heavily with butter. She had four eggs, too, boiled hard. The Bodkin couple had no children, and on that account they could afford to live well, at least far better than the other peasants. Bodkin just dropped his reaping-hook and ravenously devoured three of the eggs, while his wife, no less hungry, ate the fourth. Then Bodkin began to eat the bread-and-butter and drink the cold tea with as much speed as he had reaped the rye. It took him and his wife exactly two minutes and three-quarters to finish that great quantity of food and drink. Out of curiosity, Gallagher, the doctor, counted the time down on the shore-road. As soon as they had finished eating they set to work again as fiercely as ever.

Considine had come level with Bodkin, just as Bodkin resumed work, and instead of taking a rest for their meal, Considine and his wife ate in the ancient fashion current among Inverara peasants during contests of the kind. Kate fed her husband as he worked with buttered oaten cake. Now and again she handed him the tea-can and he paused to take a drink. In that way he was still almost level with Bodkin when he had finished eating. The spectators were greatly excited at this eagerness on the part of Considine, and some began to say that he would win the race.

Nobody took any notice of Gill and his wife, but they had never stopped to eat, and they had steadily drawn nearer to their opponents. They were still some distance in the rear, but they seemed quite fresh, whereas Bodkin appeared to be getting exhausted, handicapped by his heavy meal, and Considine was obviously using up the reserves of his strength. Then, when they reached the stone at half-way, Gill quietly laid down his hook and told his wife to bring the meal. She brought it from the fence, buttered oaten bread and a bottle of new milk, with oatmeal in the bottom of the bottle. They ate slowly, and then rested for a while. People began to jeer at them when they saw them resting, but they took no notice. After about twenty minutes they got up to go to work again. A derisive cheer arose, and an

old man cried out : " Yer a disgrace to me name, Michael."
" Never mind, father," called Michael, " the race isn't finished
yet." Then he spat on his hands and seized his hook once more.

Then, indeed, excitement rose to a high pitch, because the Gill
couple resumed work at a great speed. Their movements were as
mechanical and regular as before, but they worked at almost
twice the speed. People began to shout at them. Then betting
began among the gentry. Until now the excitement had not been
intense because it seemed a foregone conclusion that Bodkin
would win since he was so far ahead. Now, however, Bodkin's
supremacy was challenged. He still was a long way ahead of
Gill, but he was visibly tired, and his hook made mistakes now
and again, gripping the earth with its point. Bodkin was lathered
with sweat. He now began to look behind him at Gill, irritated by
the shouts of the people.

Just before four o'clock Considine suddenly collapsed, utterly
exhausted. He had to be carried over to the fence. A crowd
gathered around, and the rector, Mr. Robertson, gave him a swig
from his brandy-flask that revived him. He made an effort to
go back to work, but he was unable to rise. " Stay there," said
his wife angrily, " you're finished. I'll carry on myself." Rolling
up her sleeves farther on her fat arms, she went back to the reaping
hook, and with a loud yell began to reap furiously. " Bravo,"
cried McDara, " I'll give the woman a special prize. Gallagher,"
he cried, hitting the doctor on the shoulder, " after all . . . the
Irish race . . . ye know what I mean . . . man, alive."

But all centred their attention on the struggle between Bodkin
and Gill. Spurred by rage, Bodkin had made a supreme effort,
and he began to gain ground once more. His immense body,
moving from left to right and back again across his line of reaping,
seemed to swallow the long yellow rye-stalks, so quickly did they
fall before it. And as the sheaf was completed his lean wife grabbed
it up and tied it. But still, when Bodkin paused at five o'clock to
cast a look behind him, there was Gill coming with terrible
regularity. Bodkin suddenly felt all the weariness of the day overcome him.

It struck him first in the shape of an intense thirst. He sent his
wife up to the fence for their extra can of tea. When she came
back with it he began to drink. But the more he drank the

thirstier he became. His friends in the crowd of spectators shouted at him in warning, but his thirst maddened him. He kept drinking. The shore-wall and victory were very near now. He kept looking towards it in a dazed way as he whirled his hook. And he kept drinking. Then his senses began to dull. He became sleepy. His movements became almost unconscious. He only saw the wall, and he fought on. He began to talk to himself. He reached the wall at one end of his strip. He had only to cut down to the other end and finish. Three sheaves more, and then . . . Best man in Inverara . . . Five-Pound Note . . .

But just then a ringing cheer came to his ears, and the cry rose on the air : " Gill has won." Bodkin collapsed with a groan.

— Short Stories of Liam O'Flaherty

Explorations

1. As it is the story of a contest the writer must acquaint us with the background and the rules of the game. How does he do this ? Does he do it well ?

2. One of the elements in such a story must be suspense. What methods does the writer use to build up suspense before the contest begins ? Where are they, in your opinion, particularly effective ?

3. As the contestants line up, the author describes them briefly. Some of these details are directly relevant to their skill as reapers. Some are calculated to make us interested in them as individuals. What details do you find particularly effective in achieving each of these purposes ?

4. Each contestant has his own peculiar style of reaping. How well, in your opinion, does the author describe each technique ? Mention some of the descriptive phrases that strike you as particularly vivid. Is the reaping style, in your opinion, typical of the contestant as the author has described him ? Give reasons for your answer.

5. Are you surprised at the outcome of the race ? Go back and examine the early descriptions of the contestants. Has the author given any hint as to who might win ? If so, name the phrases in

question. On looking back, has the author in any way cheated in order to build up the suspense ? Does the victory of the Gill team seem to have been inevitable ? Why ?

6.   Which of the teams do you like best as people ? Why ?

Exercises

1.   As old Mr. Gill watches the race he probably makes frequent comments to his neighbours. Try to imagine these comments at the various stages of the race described by the author.

2.   Try to describe the thoughts of MacDara as the race reaches it later stages—from the moment when he notices that Considine may collapse. If you wish, punctuate his thought with remarks that he may have made to the people standing near him.

3.   Write a paragraph about the daily lives of these island people without going beyond the story for evidence.

4.   Liam O'Flaherty has written another story of a sporting event entitled *The Wing Three-Quarter*. Read it and compare the stories as tales of excitement and suspense.

5

THE WREN'S NEST

It was a summer's evening just before sunset. Little Michael and Little Jimmy, both twelve-year-old boys, set out to look for birds' nests. They were both dressed alike, except that Little Michael's blue sweater and grey flannel trousers were of better quality than Little Jimmy's, since the latter was the son of a farm labourer and Little Michael's father was the magistrate and a retired army officer. They were both barefooted, with cuts on their toes, and each had a bandage on the big toe of the right foot. They skirmished along south of the village, crossing the crags, picking berries and talking about the nests they had. No use looking for a nest until one came to the hollow there beyond Red Dick's potato garden. There was a cliff there overlooking a grassy glen. The cliff was awfully hard to climb and so was unexplored, and there was where they were going to search. It would be a great feat to climb the cliff anyway, since the only person who had climbed it was Black Peter, the bird catcher, and of course he was sold to the devil and could do anything. No boy had ever been able to climb it beyond the little ledge about a quarter of the way up, a ledge that was always covered with bird dirt and discoloured with cliff water that dripped on to it from a spring in the cliff face.

The two boys came to the cliff face and looked up. Then they looked at one another, their mouths open. " You go first," said Little Michael. " No, you go," said Little Jimmy. " No, you go." They argued a long time about it, but neither moved. "Aw," said Little Michael, " I think it's too late to climb it anyway today. Let us wait until tomorrow, and put on stockings. Black Peter always wears stockings. Stockings stick to the cliff face." " You're afraid," said Little Jimmy, wiping his nose with the sleeve of his coat. " Who is afraid ? My father fought in ten battles." " Climb it then." "All right, let's climb it together." " Then who'll watch ? We might be caught. Your father would summon me. That's certain." They kept silent for a minute and then lay on

E.E. 1—3

their stomachs on the grass looking up at the cliff. Sparrows were chirping hidden in the ivy. Right at the top, about sixty feet above the level of the glen, there was a deep slit in the cliff and several broods of starlings were croaking there.

"There must be twenty nests there," said Little Michael. "There are forty. I counted them the other day," said Little Jimmy. "Let's throw stones at them." They threw a few stones up into the ivy and a number of birds flew out screaming. Then they lay down again on the grass and watched. Suddenly Little Jimmy said "Hist!" His dirty face was lit up with sudden excitement. "What's that?" whispered Little Michael. "Hist!" said Little Jimmy, "I see a wren. Look." He pointed to a point far down in the cliff about five feet from the ground, where just a shred of ivy was growing, an offshoot from the main growth farther up. Little Michael nearly shut his eyes looking closely and saw a little brown ball moving slightly. The two boys held their breaths for a long time, lying quite still. Presently a tiny head peered out of the ivy. Then it disappeared again. Then it appeared again, looked around, and presently a wren flew out, circled around a little and landed on the fence to the left. Then it chirped lowly and sped away. Another little wren came out of the cliff in answer to the chirp and followed it.

"It's a nest," gasped both the boys together. They jumped to their feet and raced to the cliff, each trying to get there first.

They arrived at the cliff together and each thrust a hand into the little clump of ivy to get at the nest. There was a rustle of green leaves, a panting of breaths, and then their hands met in the ivy and they paused. They looked at one another and there was poisoned hatred in their eyes. "I got it first," said Little Michael. "I touched it first." "Ye're a liar," said Little Jimmy, "I saw the wren first." "You call me a liar and your father was in jail twice." "I can beat you. I beat Johnny Derrane, and he beat you."

"Oh, you just try." They stood back from the cliff and looked one another up and down, each afraid of the other. The situation was intensely embarrassing, but just then one of the wrens flew back over the fence carrying a little wisp of moss in its mouth and saved the situation. They both looked at the wren, and said "Hist!" glad of some excuse to prevent them from fighting. The wren alighted on a fence to the left and became very busy pretending to have a nest in the fence. " Come away," said Little Michael, " if he sees us looking at the nest he will forsake it, and a forsaken nest doesn't count. That's well known."

" Oh, let's see how many eggs in it," said Little Jimmy. " Nobody will believe us if we can't say how many eggs in it." " You leave it alone," said Little Michael ; " that's my nest. If you look at it, I'll tell my father." " Ha, spy," said Little Jimmy. Little Michael became very conscious of having made a fool of himself and didn't know what to say or do. He had an impulse to hit Little Jimmy, but he was afraid to hit him. No use fighting anyway when nobody was looking. Nobody ever heard of anybody fighting when there was nobody looking, unless two brothers, maybe, or a boy and his sister. " Maybe you think I'm afraid," he said at last. " Take care now, Little Jimmy, that you'd think I'm afraid."

"Aw, I don't care," said Little Jimmy, dabbing his toe into the grass with a swagger. " I'm going to look at this nest any- way." He moved forward and Little Michael caught him by the two hands and they struggled. " Let me go," cried Little Michael. " You let me go," cried Little Jimmy. The two wrens were now hovering about screaming in an agonised state, but the boys took no heed of them. Each was trying to grab at the nest and the other trying to prevent him. The ivy was soon torn from the cliff and a little round hole became visible, a beautiful little round hole, suggestive of beauty within, and around the little round hole was a house built of moss. Then Little Jimmy grabbed at the nest, caught it in the tips of his fingers, and as Little Michael pulled him suddenly, the nest came out of the niche and tumbled to the ground. It fell on the ground on its side and a little egg, a tiny egg, tumbled out. It was so light that it landed between two blades of grass and stayed there poised. The wrens on the fence set up a terrible chatter and then flew away high above the ground. They would never come back.

The two boys looked at the nest in silence. " Now see what you've done," said Little Michael ; " the nest is no use to us." " It's all your fault," said Little Jimmy ; " you were afraid to look at it." " Who was afraid ? " said Little Michael heatedly ; " what do I care about a wren's nest," and he kicked the nest with his foot. The structure of dried moss burst in two pieces and several eggs scattered around. Both boys laughed, and began to kick the pieces of the nest and then tore them to shreds. The inside was coated wonderfully with feathers and down, interlaced with an art that could not be rivalled by human beings. The boys tore it into shreds and scattered the shreds. Then they pelted one another with the eggs, laughing excitedly. Then they paused, uncertain what to do, and they both sighed, from satisfaction. They were friendly again, the cause of their quarrel had vanished, destroyed by their hands.

" I got a rabbit's nest with three young ones in it," said Little Jimmy.

" Show it to me," said Little Michael, " and I'll show you a blackbird's nest with three eggs in it." "All right," said Little Jimmy, and they scampered off, over the fence where the wrens flew away. Two fields farther on they passed the wrens, already looking for another niche, but they did not recognise them. If they had they would probably have thrown a few stones at them.

— *Short Stories of Liam O'Flaherty*

Explorations

1. Do you find this story believable ? Give reasons for your answer.

2. Do the boys set out with the intention of robbing birds' nests ? Why do they destroy the nest ? In each case confine your answer to the evidence of the story.

3. Is their action the result of cruelty or thoughtlessness ? Don't forget that they throw stones at the nests on the cliff-side at the beginning.

4. At one point the author mentions the beauty of the nest. Are the boys at any stage interested in its beauty ? Or is their interest totally selfish ? Examine the evidence in the text and cite it in support of your opinion.

5. Is the last sentence justified in view of what we have learned about the two boys ? Does it add anything to the story ? Does it damage the story in any way ? Why ?

6. Which of the boys is more responsible for the destruction ? Or are they equally to blame ?

7. When the work of destruction is over the boys ' sighed, from satisfaction.' Do you find it strange that they show no signs of remorse ? Explain your point of view.

8.   Can you believe that this is the same Little Michael as in ' Three Lambs ' ?

9.   Is there irony in the constant use of *Little* to describe Michael and Jimmy ? Explain.

Exercises

1.   Did you ever rob a bird's nest, or do anything to an animal or bird that you are now ashamed of ? If so, try to describe your feelings at the time and contrast them with your feelings about it now. Don't confine yourself to one incident.

2.   In *Snaring* and *Birdnesting* Wordsworth deals with a young boy's life in the countryside. In different ways Wordsworth and O'Flaherty seem to suggest that the human being is at his best when he is acting in harmony with nature ; that he is at fault when he breaks this harmony. Discuss the points of difference between their treatments of the theme.

3.   Tell the story of the wren's nest as seen through the eyes of Little Michael or Little Jimmy.

4.   Read McLaverty's 'The Wild Duck's Nest' and be able to compare the two stories in next day's discussion.

6

THREE LAMBS

Little Michael rose before dawn. He tried to make as little noise as possible. He ate two slices of bread and butter and drank a cup of milk, although he hated cold milk with bread and butter in the morning. But on an occasion like this, what did it matter what a boy ate? He was going out to watch the black sheep having a lamb. His father had mentioned the night before that the black sheep was sure to lamb that morning, and of course there was a prize, three pancakes, for the first one who saw the lamb.

He lifted the latch gently and stole out. It was best not to let his brother John know he was going. He would be sure to want to come too. As he ran down the lane, his sleeves, brushing against the evergreen bushes, were wetted by the dew, and the tip of his cap was just visible above the hedge, bobbing up and down as he ran. He was in too great a hurry to open the gate and tore a little hole in the breast of his blue jersey climbing over it. But he didn't mind that. He would get another one on his thirteenth birthday.

He turned to the left from the main road, up a lane that led to the field where his father, the magistrate, kept his prize sheep. It was only a quarter of a mile, that lane, but he thought that it would never end and he kept tripping among the stones that strewed the road. It was so awkward to run on the stones wearing shoes, and it was too early in the year yet to be allowed to go barefooted. He envied Little Jimmy, the son of the farm labourer, who was allowed to go barefooted all the year round, even in the depths of winter, and who always had such wonderful cuts on his big toes, the envy of all the little boys in the village school.

He climbed over the fence leading into the fields, and, clapping his hands together, said " Oh, you devil," a swear word he had

46

learned from Little Jimmy and of which he was very proud. He took off his shoes and stockings and hid them in a hole in the fence. Then he ran jumping, his bare heels looking like round brown spots as he tossed them up behind him. The grass was wet and the ground was hard, but he persuaded himself that it was great fun.

Going through a gap into the next field, he saw a rabbit nibbling grass. He halted suddenly, his heart beating loudly. Pity he hadn't a dog. The rabbit stopped eating. He cocked up his ears. He stood on his tail, with his neck craned up and his forefeet hanging limp. Then he came down again. He thrust his ears forward. Then he lay flat with his ears buried in his back and lay still. With a great yell Little Michael darted forward imitating a dog barking and the rabbit scurried away in short sharp leaps. Only his white tail was visible in the grey light.

Little Michael went into the next field, but the sheep were nowhere to be seen. He stood on a hillock and called out " Chowin, chowin," three times. Then he heard " Mah-m-m-m " in the next field and ran on. The sheep were in the last two fields, two oblong little fields, running in a hollow between two crags, surrounded by high thick fences, the walls of an old fort. In the nearest of the two fields he found ten of the sheep, standing side by side, looking at him, with their fifteen lambs in front of them also looking at him curiously. He counted them out loud and then he saw that the black sheep was not there. He panted with excitement. Perhaps she already had a lamb in the next field. He hurried to the gap leading into the next field, walking stealthily, avoiding the spots where the grass was high, so as to make less noise. It was bad to disturb a sheep that was lambing. He peered through a hole in the fence and could see nothing. Then he crawled to the gap and peered around the corner. The black sheep was just inside standing with her forefeet on a little mound.

Her belly was swollen out until it ended on each side in a sharp point and her legs appeared to be incapable of supporting her body. She turned her head sharply and listened. Little Michael held his breath, afraid to make a noise. It was of vital importance not to disturb the sheep. Straining back to lie down he burst a button on his trousers and he knew his braces were undone. He said, " Oh, you devil," again and decided to ask his mother to let him wear a belt instead of a braces, same as Little Jimmy wore. Then he crawled farther back from the gap and taking off his braces altogether made it into a belt. It hurt his hips, but he felt far better and manly.

Then he came back again to the gap and looked. The black sheep was still in the same place. She was scratching the earth with her forefeet and going around in a circle, as if she wanted to lie down but was afraid to lie down. Sometimes she ground her teeth and made an awful noise, baring her jaws and turning her head around sideways. Little Michael felt a pain in his heart in pity for her, and he wondered why the other sheep didn't come to keep her company. Then he wondered whether his mother had felt the same pain when she had Ethna the autumn before. She must have, because the doctor was there.

Suddenly the black sheep went on her knees. She stayed a few seconds on her knees and then she moaned and sank to the ground and stretched herself out with her neck on the little hillock and her hindquarters falling down the little slope. Little Michael forgot about the pain now. His heart thumped with excitement. He forgot to breathe, looking intently. "Ah," he said. The sheep stretched again and struggled to her feet and circled around once, stamping and grinding her teeth. Little Michael moved up to her slowly. She looked at him anxiously, but she was too sick to move away. He broke the bladder and he saw two little feet sticking out. He seized them carefully and pulled. The sheep moaned again and pressed with all her might. The lamb dropped on the grass.

Little Michael sighed with delight and began to rub its body with his finger nails furiously. The sheep turned around and smelt it, making a funny happy noise in its throat. The lamb, its white body covered with yellow slime, began to move, and presently it tried to stand up, but it fell again and Little Michael kept rubbing it, sticking his fingers into its ears and nostrils to clear them. He was so intent on this work that he did not notice the sheep had moved away again, and it was only when the lamb was able to stand up and he wanted to give it suck, that he noticed the sheep was lying again giving birth to another lamb.

" Oh, you devil," gasped Little Michael, " six pancakes."

The second lamb was white like the first but with a black spot on its right ear. Little Michael rubbed it vigorously, pausing now and again to help the first lamb to its feet as it tried to stagger about. The sheep circled around making low noises in her throat, putting her nostrils to each lamb in turn, stopping nowhere, as giddy as a young schoolgirl, while the hard pellets of earth that stuck to her belly jingled like beads when she moved. Little Michael then took the first lamb and tried to put it to suck, but it refused to take the teat, stupidly sticking its mouth into the wool. Then he put his finger in its mouth and gradually got the teat in with his other hand. Then he pressed the teat and the hot milk squirted into the lamb's mouth. The lamb shook its tail, shrugged its body, made a little drive with its head, and began to suck.

Little Michael was just going to give the second lamb suck, when the sheep moaned and moved away again. He said, " chowin, chowin, poor chowin," and put the lamb to her head, but she turned away moaning and grinding her teeth and stamping. " Oh, you devil," said Little Michael, " she is going to have another lamb."

The sheep lay down again, with her foreleg stretched out in front of her and, straining her neck backwards, gave birth to a third lamb, a black lamb.

Then she rose smartly to her feet, her two sides hollow now. She shrugged herself violently and, without noticing the lambs, started to eat grass fiercely, just pausing now and again to say " mah-m-m-m."

Little Michael, in an ecstasy of delight, rubbed the black lamb until it was able to stand. Then he put all the lambs to suck, the sheep eating around her in a circle, without changing her feet, smelling a lamb now and again. " Oh, you devil," Little Michael kept saying, thinking he would be quite famous now, and talked about for a whole week. It was not every day that a sheep had three lambs.

He brought them to a sheltered spot under the fence. He wiped the birth slime from his hands with some grass. He opened his penknife and cut the dirty wool from the sheep's udder, lest the lambs might swallow some and die. Then he gave a final look at them, said, " Chowin, chowin," tenderly, and turned to go.

He was already at the gap when he stopped with a start. He raced back to the lambs and examined each of them. " Three she lambs," he gasped. " Oh, you devil, that never happened before. Maybe father will give me half-a-crown."

And as he raced homeward, he barked like a dog in his delight.

— Short Stories of Liam O'Flaherty

Explorations

1. Do you find this an utterly beautiful story ? If not, please read it again.

Exercises

1. If you like this story, write down your thoughts about it now without discussion.

7

THE ROCKFISH

Flop. The cone-shaped bar of lead tied to the end of the fishing-line dropped into the sea without causing a ripple. It sank rapidly through the long seaweed that grew on the face of the rock. It sank twenty-five feet and then struck the bottom. It tumbled around and then lay on its side in a niche at the top of a round pool. The man on top of the rock hauled in his line until it was taut. The bar of lead bobbed up and down twice. Then it rested straight on its end in the niche. Three short plaits of stiff horsehair extended crookedly like tentacles from the line above the leaden weight at regular intervals. At the end of each plait was a hook baited all over with shelled periwinkle. A small crab, transfixed through the belly, wriggled on the lowest hook. The two upper hooks had a covering of crushed crab tied by thin strings around the periwinkles. The three baited hooks swung round and round, glistening white through the red strands of broad seaweed that hung lazily from their stems in the rock face. Dark caverns at the base of the rock cast long shadows out over the bottom of the sea about the hooks. Little bulbous things growing in groups on the bottom spluttered methodically as they stirred.

The man sitting above on the top of the rock spat into the sea. Resting his fishing-rod in the crutch of his right arm, he began to fill his pipe, yawning.

A little rockfish came rushing out from a cavern under the rock. He whisked his tail and stopped dead behind a huge blade of seaweed when he saw the glistening baits. His red scaly body was the colour of the weed. It tapered from the middle to the narrow tail and to the triangular-shaped head. He stared at the baits for a long time without moving his body. His gills rose and fell steadily. Then he flapped his tail and glided to the upper hook. He touched it with his snout. He nibbled at it timorously three times. Then he snatched at the top of it and darted away back into the cavern with a piece of periwinkle in his mouth. The man on the rock sat up excitedly, threw his pipe on the rock, and seized the rod with both hands, breathing through his nose.

Several rockfish gathered around the little fellow in the cavern. They tried to snatch the piece of periwinkle from his mouth. But he dived under a ledge of rock and bolted it hurriedly. Then, all the rockfish darted out to the hooks. The little ones scurried around hither and thither. Three middle-sized ones stood by the two upper hooks, sniffing at them. Then they began to nibble carefully. One little rockfish stood on his head over the bottom hook and sniffed at it. But the crab wriggled one leg and the rockfish darted away at a terrific speed. All the rockfish darted away after it into the cavern. Then one of the middle-sized ones came back again alone. He went up to the highest hook and grabbed at it immediately. He took the whole bait from it. The hook grazed his lower lip as it slipped from his mouth. The rockfish dropped the bait, turned a somersault, and dived into the cavern.

The man on the rock swung his rod back over his head, and dropped it forward again with an oath when he found the line coming slack. " Missed," he said. Then the leaden weight slipped back again into the niche. A crowd of rockfish quarrelled over the pieces of periwinkle fallen from the middle-sized fellow's mouth. The pieces, too light to sink, kept floating about. Then they disappeared one by one into the fishes' mouths.

A huge rockfish prowled in from the deep. He stood by the corner of a rock watching the little ones quarrel over the pieces of fallen bait. He was as big as all the others together. He must have been three feet long and his middle was as thick as a bulldog's chest. The scales on his back were all the colours of the rainbow. His belly was a dun colour. He stood still for a time, watching like an old bull, his gills showing large red cavities in his throat as they opened. Then he swooped in among the little ones. They dived away from him into the cavern. He gobbled the remaining pieces of bait. Then he turned around slowly twice and swam close to the bottom towards the hooks. He saw the crab wriggling on the lowest hook. With a rush he swallowed the crab and the hook, turned about and rushed away with it, out towards his lair in the deep. The leaden weight rushed along the bottom with him. The line went taut with a snap over his back. The fishing-rod was almost wrenched from the hands of the man on the rock. Its tip touched the water. Then the man heaved the rod over his head and grasped the line. The hook was wrenched back out of the rockfish's gullet and its points tore through the side of his mouth.

The rockfish was whirled about by the wrench and dragged backwards headlong. With a swishing sound he heaved straight through the water towards the cavern. Then the line went taut again as the man hauled in. The rockfish was tugged up along the face of the rock. He jumped twice and heaved. He tore a strip of the soft thick skin, in which the hook was embedded, from his jaw at one end. Hanging to the hook by this strip, he came up gasping through the hanging weeds. The man groaned as he heaved.

Then the bared top hook got caught in a broad blade of seaweed. It combed its way through to the hard stem and then got stuck. The man heaved and could draw it no farther. The rockfish hung exhausted from the bottom hook. The man stuck his right foot against a ledge and leaning back with the line held in his two hands across his stomach he pulled with all his might. The top hook broke. The line jerked up. The rockfish reached the surface. He tried to breathe with wide open mouth. Then he hurled himself into the air and dived headlong downwards. The hanging strip of skin parted from his jaw. He was free.

— Short Stories of Liam O'Flaherty

Explorations

1. The author takes great care to describe objects and their movements in close detail. Are these descriptions well done? What is their purpose within the story? Give examples.

2. The American writer Ernest Hemingway constantly stated that it was very important for a writer to see the thing as it is, and to describe it as it is. Does O'Flaherty do this? Where and how? Is there any writer in the anthology who strikes you as careless or inaccurate in his description of things? State your criticisms of him.

3. As between fish and fisherman, does the author show any more sympathy for one than for the other? Make sure that your answer is based on the text.

4. Unlike the smaller fish, the rockfish is a formidable opponent for the fisherman. How does O'Flaherty suggest this to us?

5. Does O'Flaherty make much use of metaphor or simile in his work? Examine his stories in the present anthology and see when he chooses to use figurative language. Then try to decide why.

Exercises

1. As each tug comes on the line you can imagine the mental or indeed vocal muttering of the fisherman. Try to put into words and phrases, not necessarily grammatical, the thoughts of the fisherman during these moments of suspense and frustration.

2. No doubt he related the incident at his home or in his public house that evening. Tell the story as he might have told it.

3. Try to describe your first, or your most memorable, struggle to land a fish. Try to get the details as accurately as O'Flaherty does. Even if you can only manage a paragraph make sure you find the right words to convey your meaning.

4. Read Hemingway's story *The Old Man and the Sea* and try to find similarities and points of difference between the two stories.

8

THE MAJESTY OF THE LAW

Old Dan Bride was breaking brosna for the fire when he heard a step on the path. He paused, a bundle of saplings on his knee.

Dan had looked after his mother while the life was in her, and after her death no other woman had crossed his threshold. Signs on it, his house had that look. Almost everything in it he had made with his own hands in his own way. The seats of the chairs were only slices of log, rough and round and thick as the saw had left them, and with the rings still plainly visible through the grime and polish that coarse trouser-bottoms had in the course of long years imparted. Into these Dan had rammed stout knotted ash-boughs that served alike for legs and back. The deal table, bought in a shop, was an inheritance from his mother and a great pride and joy to him though it rocked whenever he touched it. On the wall, unglazed and fly-spotted, hung in mysterious isolation a Marcus Stone print, and beside the door was a calendar with a picture of a racehorse. Over the door hung a gun, old but good, and in excellent condition, and before the fire was stretched an old setter who raised his head expectantly whenever Dan rose or even stirred.

He raised it now as the steps came nearer and when Dan, laying down the bundle of saplings, cleaned his hands thoughtfully in the seat of his trousers, he gave a loud bark, but this expressed no more than a desire to show off his own watchfulness. He was half human and knew people thought he was old and past his prime.

A man's shadow fell across the oblong of dusty light thrown over the half-door before Dan looked round.

"Are you alone, Dan ? " asked an apologetic voice.

" Oh, come in, come in, sergeant, come in and welcome," exclaimed the old man, hurrying on rather uncertain feet to the door which the tall policeman opened and pushed in. He stood there, half in sunlight, half in shadow, and seeing him so, you would have realised how dark the interior of the house really was. One side of his red face was turned so as to catch the light, and behind it an ash-tree raised its boughs of airy green against the sky. Green fields, broken here and there by clumps of red-brown rock, flowed downhill, and beyond them, stretched all across the horizon, was the sea, flooded and almost transparent with light. The sergeant's face was fat and fresh, the old man's face, emerging from the twilight of the kitchen, had the colour of wind and sun, while the features had been so shaped by the struggle with time and the elements that they might as easily have been found impressed upon the surface of a rock.

" Begor, Dan," said the sergeant, " 'tis younger you're getting."

" Middling I am, sergeant, middling," agreed the old man in a voice which seemed to accept the remark as a compliment of which politeness would not allow him to take too much advantage. " No complaints."

" Begor, 'tis as well because no one would believe them. And the old dog doesn't look a day older."

The dog gave a low growl as though to show the sergeant that he would remember this unmannerly reference to his age, but indeed he growled every time he was mentioned, under the impression that people had nothing but ill to say of him.

"And how's yourself, sergeant ? "

" Well, now, like the most of us, Dan, neither too good nor too bad. We have our own little worries, but, thanks be to God, we have our compensations."

"And the wife and family ? "

" Good, praise be to God, good. They were away from me for a month, the lot of them, at the mother-in-law's place in Clare."

" In Clare, do you tell me ? "

" In Clare. I had a fine quiet time."

The old man looked about him and then retired to the bed-room, from which he returned a moment later with an old shirt. With this he solemnly wiped the seat and back of the log-chair nearest the fire.

" Sit down now, sergeant. You must be tired after the journey. 'Tis a long old road. How did you come ? "

" Teigue Leary gave me the lift. Wisha now, Dan, don't be putting yourself out. I won't be stopping. I promised them I'd be back inside an hour."

" What hurry is on you ? " asked Dan. " Look, your foot was only on the path when I made up the fire."

"Arrah, Dan, you're not making tea for me ? "

" I am not making it for you, indeed ; I'm making it for myself, and I'll take it very bad of you if you won't have a cup."

" Dan, Dan, that I mightn't stir, but 'tisn't an hour since I had it at the barracks ! "

"Ah, whisht, now, whisht ! Whisht, will you ! I have something here to give you an appetite."

The old man swung the heavy kettle on to the chain over the open fire, and the dog sat up, shaking his ears with an expression of the deepest interest. The policeman unbuttoned his tunic, opened his belt, took a pipe and a plug of tobacco from his breast pocket, and crossing his legs in an easy posture, began to cut the tobacco slowly and carefully with his pocket knife. The old man went to the dresser and took down two handsomely decorated cups, the only cups he had, which, though chipped and handleless, were used at all only on very rare occasions ; for himself he preferred his tea from a basin. Happening to glance into them, he noticed that they bore signs of disuse and had collected a lot of the fine white turf-dust that always circulated in the little smoky cottage. Again he thought of the shirt, and, rolling up his sleeves with a stately gesture, he wiped them inside and out till they shone. Then he bent and opened the cupboard. Inside was a quart bottle of pale liquid, obviously untouched. He removed the cork and smelt the contents, pausing for a moment in the act as though to recollect where exactly he had noticed that particular smoky smell before. Then, reassured, he stood up and poured out with a liberal hand.

" Try that now, sergeant," he said with quiet pride.

The sergeant, concealing whatever qualms he might have felt at the idea of drinking illegal whiskey, looked carefully into the cup, sniffed, and glanced up at old Dan.

" It looks good," he commented.

" It should be good," replied Dan with no mock modesty.

" It tastes good too," said the sergeant.

"Ah, sha," said Dan, not wishing to praise his own hospitality in his own house, " 'tis of no great excellence."

" You'd be a good judge, I'd say," said the sergeant without irony.

" Ever since things became what they are," said Dan, carefully guarding himself against a too-direct reference to the peculiarities of the law administered by his guest, " liquor isn't what it used to be."

" I've heard that remark made before now, Dan," said the sergeant thoughtfully. " I've heard it said by men of wide experience that it used to be better in the old days."

" Liquor," said the old man, " is a thing that takes time. There was never a good job done in a hurry."

" 'Tis an art in itself."

" Just so."

"And an art takes time."

"And knowledge," added Dan with emphasis. " Every art has its secrets, and the secrets of distilling are being lost the way the old songs were lost. When I was a boy there wasn't a man in the barony but had a hundred songs in his head, but with people running here, there and everywhere, the songs were lost . . . Ever since things became what they are," he repeated on the same guarded note, " there's so much running about the secrets are lost."

" There must have been a power of them."

" There was. Ask any man today that makes whiskey do he know how to make it out of heather."

"And was it made of heather ? " asked the policeman.

" It was."

" You never drank it yourself ? "

" I didn't, but I knew old men that did, and they told me that no whiskey that's made nowadays could compare with it."

" Musha, Dan, I think sometimes 'twas a great mistake of the law to set its hand against it."

Dan shook his head. His eyes answered for him, but it was not in nature for a man to criticise the occupation of a guest in his own home.

" Maybe so, maybe not," he said non-committally.

" But sure, what else have the poor people ? "

" Them that makes the laws have their own good reasons."

"All the same, Dan, all the same, 'tis a hard law."

The sergeant would not be outdone in generosity. Politeness required him not to yield to the old man's defence of his superiors and their mysterious ways.

" It is the secrets I'd be sorry for," said Dan, summing up.
" Men die and men are born, and where one man drained another
will plough, but a secret lost is lost forever."

" True," said the sergeant mournfully. " Lost forever."

Dan took his cup, rinsed it in a bucket of clear water by the
door and cleaned it again with the shirt. Then he placed it carefully at the sergeant's elbow. From the dresser he took a jug of
milk and a blue bag containing sugar ; this he followed up with a
slab of country butter and—a sure sign that he had been expecting
a visitor—a round cake of homemade bread, fresh and uncut. The
kettle sang and spat and the dog, shaking his ears, barked at it
angrily.

" Go away, you brute ! " growled Dan, kicking him out of his
way.

He made the tea and filled the two cups. The sergeant cut himself a large slice of bread and buttered it thickly.

" It is just like medicines," said the old man, resuming his
theme with the imperturbability of age. " Every secret there was
is lost. And leave no one tell me that a doctor is as good a man as
one that had the secrets of old times."

" How could he be ? " asked the sergeant with his mouth full.

" The proof of that was seen when there were doctors and wise
people there together."

" It wasn't to the doctors the people went, I'll engage."

" It was not. And why ? " With a sweeping gesture the old man
took in the whole world outside his cabin. " Out there on the
hillsides is the sure cure for every disease. Because it is written "
—he tapped the table with his thumb—" it is written by the poets
' wherever you find the disease you will find the cure.' But people
walk up the hills and down the hills and all they see is flowers.
Flowers ! As if God Almighty—honour and praise to Him !—had
nothing better to do with His time than be making old flowers ! "

" Things no doctor could cure the wise people cured," agreed
the sergeant.

"Ah, musha, 'tis I know it," said Dan bitterly. " I know it, not
in my mind but in my own four bones."

" Have you the rheumatics at you still ? " the sergeant asked in
a shocked tone.

" I have. Ah, if you were alive, Kitty O'Hara, or you, Nora
Malley of the Glen, 'tisn't I'd be dreading the mountain wind or

the sea wind ; 'tisn't I'd be creeping down with my misfortunate' red ticket for the blue and pink and yellow dribble-drabble of their ignorant dispensary."

" Why then indeed," said the sergeant, " I'll get you a bottle for that."

"Ah, there's no bottle ever made will cure it."

" That's where you're wrong, Dan. Don't talk now till you try it. It cured my own uncle when he was that bad he was shouting for the carpenter to cut the two legs off him with a handsaw."

"I'd give fifty pounds to get rid of it," said Dan magniloquently. " I would and five hundred."

The sergeant finished his tea in a gulp, blessed himself and struck a match which he then allowed to go out as he answered some question of the old man. He did the same with a second and third, as though titillating his appetite with delay. Finally he succeeded in getting his pipe alight and the two men pulled round their chairs, placed their toes side by side in the ashes, and in deep puffs, lively bursts of conversation, and long, long silences, enjoyed their smoke.

" I hope I'm not keeping you ? " said the sergeant, as though struck by the length of his visit.

"Ah, what would you keep me from ? "

" Tell me if I am. The last thing I'd like to do is waste another man's time."

" Begor, you wouldn't waste my time if you stopped all night."

" I like a little chat myself," confessed the policeman.

And again they became lost in conversation. The light grew thick and coloured and, wheeling about the kitchen before it disappeared, became tinged with gold ; the kitchen itself sank into cool greyness with cold light on the cups and basins and plates of the dresser. From the ash tree a thrush began to sing. The open hearth gathered brightness till its light was a warm, even splash of crimson in the twilight.

Twilight was also descending outside when the sergeant rose to go. He fastened his belt and tunic and carefully brushed his clothes. Then he put on his cap, tilted a little to side and back.

" Well, that was a great talk," he said.

" 'Tis a pleasure," said Dan, " a real pleasure."

" And I won't forget the bottle for you."

" Heavy handling from God to you ! "

" Good-bye now, Dan."

" Good-bye, sergeant, and good luck."

Dan didn't offer to accompany the sergeant beyond the door. He sat in his old place by the fire, took out his pipe once more, blew through it thoughtfully, and just as he leaned forward for a twig to kindle it, heard the steps returning. It was the sergeant. He put his head a little way over the half-door.

" Oh, Dan ! " he called, softly.

"Ay, sergeant ? " replied Dan, looking round, but with one hand still reaching for the twig. He couldn't see the sergeant's face, only hear his voice.

" I suppose you're not thinking of paying that little fine, Dan ? "

There was a brief silence. Dan pulled out the lighted twig, rose slowly and shambled towards the door, stuffing it down in the almost empty bowl of the pipe. He leaned over the half-door while the sergeant with hands in the pockets of his trousers gazed rather in the direction of the laneway, yet taking in a considerable portion of the sea line.

" The way it is with me, sergeant," replied Dan unemotionally, " I am not."

" I was thinking that, Dan ; I was thinking you wouldn't."

There was a long silence during which the voice of the thrush grew shriller and merrier. The sunken sun lit up rafts of purple cloud moored high above the wind.

" In a way," said the sergeant, " that was what brought me."

" I was just thinking so, sergeant, it only struck me and you going out the door."

" If 'twas only the money, Dan, I'm sure there's many would be glad to oblige you."

" I know that, sergeant. No, 'tisn't the money so much as giving that fellow the satisfaction of paying. Because he angered me, sergeant."

The sergeant made no comment on this and another long silence ensued.

" They gave me the warrant," the sergeant said at last, in a tone which dissociated him from all connection with such an unneighbourly document.

" Did they so ? " exclaimed Dan, as if he was shocked by the thoughtlessness of the authorities.

" So whenever 'twould be convenient for you—— "

" Well, now you mention it," said Dan, by way of throwing out a suggestion for debate, " I could go with you now."

"Ah, sha, what do you want going at this hour for ? " protested the sergeant with a wave of his hand, dismissing the notion as the tone required.

" Or I could go tomorrow," added Dan, warming to the issue.

" Would it be suitable for you now ? " asked the sergeant, scaling up his voice accordingly.

" But, as a matter of fact," said the old man emphatically, " the day that would be most convenient to me would be Friday after dinner, because I have some messages to do in town, and I wouldn't have the journey for nothing."

" Friday will do grand," said the sergeant with relief that this delicate matter was now practically disposed of. " If it doesn't they can damn well wait. You could walk in there yourself when it suits you and tell them I sent you."

" I'd rather have yourself there, sergeant, if it would be no inconvenience. As it is, I'd feel a bit shy."

" Why then, you needn't feel shy at all. There's a man from my own parish there, a warder ; one Whelan. Ask for him ; I'll tell him you're coming, and I'll guarantee when he knows you're a friend of mine he'll make you as comfortable as if you were at home."

" I'd like that fine," Dan said with profound satisfaction. " I'd like to be with friends, sergeant."

" You will be, never fear. Good-bye again now, Dan. I'll have to hurry."

" Wait now, wait till I see you to the road."

Together the two men strolled down the laneway while Dan explained how it was that he, a respectable old man, had had the grave misfortune to open the head of another old man in such a way as to require his removal to hospital, and why it was that he couldn't give the old man in question the satisfaction of paying in cash for an injury brought about through the victim's own unmannerly method of argument.

" You see, sergeant," Dan said, looking at another little cottage up the hill, " the way it is, he's there now, and he's looking at us as sure as there's a glimmer of sight in his weak, wandering, watery eyes, and nothing would give him more gratification than for me to pay. But I'll punish him. I'll lie on bare boards for him. I'll suffer for him, sergeant, so that neither he nor any of his children after him will be able to raise their heads for the shame of it."

On the following Friday he made ready his donkey and butt and set out. On his way he collected a number of neighbours who wished to bid him farewell. At the top of the hill he stopped to send them back. An old man, sitting in the sunlight, hastily made his way indoors, and a moment later the door of his cottage was quietly closed.

Having shaken all his friends by the hand, Dan lashed the old donkey, shouted : " Hup there ! " and set out alone along the road to prison.

— The Stories of Frank O'Connor

Explorations

1. This is, in fact, the story of an arrest. Is it an ordinary arrest ? Explain.

2. Why does the Sergeant greet Dan in an ' apologetic voice ' ?

3. Why does the Sergeant not come to the point of his visit immediately ?

4. Dan Bride lives among crude and primitive furnishings. Is he, in fact, a crude or primitive man ? Give reasons for your answer.

5. Dan Bride strikes another old man over the head. Is he, in your opinion, a violent or a brutal man ? Why ?

6. He struck the other man for his ' unmannerly method of argument.' Does this strike you as a sufficient provocation for the attack ? Is there any evidence in the story that Dan Bride, in particular, might find the lack of manners offensive ?

7. Is the Sergeant a good law officer ? Is he a good human being ?

8. Does the story suggest in any way that there is a code of behaviour that is finer, deeper or higher than the legal code ? How does it suggest it ? Can you attempt to formulate that code ?

9. Read the quotation from O'Connor on page 6 of the Introduction and then try to decide why the author takes up the story at a point when it is almost over. Why is the actual purpose of the Sergeant's visit not disclosed till so near the end ? Why is the actual fight given so little space ? Are you satisfied with the ending ? Would it have been better to have described Dan Bride going into the police station ? Or into the jail ?

10. There are fairly long discussions in the story about the making of illicit liquor, about traditional cures, about ' secrets.' Have these discussions any other significance ? Are they in any way symbolic ? In what way ? What use does the author make of them to reveal the attitudes of the characters towards the central issue of the story ?

11. There are descriptions of furniture, scenery, household vessels. Are these descriptions interesting in themselves ? Are they convincing ? What do they contribute to the total meaning of the story ?

Exercises

1. Tell the entire story in your own words, describing the events that the author merely mentions and referring to the events which the author details.

2. Reconstruct in your own way the scene and the argument that led up to Dan Bride hitting his companion over the head.

3. For other stories dealing with the Irish countryman's attitude to Law, read O'Connor's *Peasants* and *On the Train*.

9

FIRST CONFESSION

All the trouble began when my grandfather died and my grandmother—my father's mother—came to live with us. Relations in the one house are a strain at the best of times, but, to make matters worse, my grandmother was a real old countrywoman and quite unsuited to the life in town. She had a fat, wrinkled old face, and, to Mother's great indignation, went round the house in bare feet—the boots had her crippled, she said. For dinner she had a jug of porter and a pot of potatoes with—sometimes—a bit of salt fish, and she poured out the potatoes on the table and ate them slowly, with great relish, using her fingers by way of a fork.

Now, girls are supposed to be fastidious, but I was the one who suffered most from this. Nora, my sister, just sucked up to the old woman for the penny she got every Friday out of the old-age pension, a thing I could not do. I was too honest, that was my trouble ; and when I was playing with Bill Connell, the sergeant-major's son, and saw my grandmother steering up the path with the jug of porter sticking out from beneath her shawl, I was mortified. I made excuses not to let him come into the house, because I could never be sure what she would be up to when we went in.

When Mother was at work and my grandmother made the dinner I wouldn't touch it. Nora once tried to make me, but I hid under the table from her and took the bread-knife with me for protection. Nora let on to be very indignant (she wasn't, of course, but she knew Mother saw through her, so she sided with Gran) and came after me. I lashed out at her with the bread-knife, and after that she left me alone. I stayed there till Mother came in from work and made my dinner, but when Father came in later, Nora said in a shocked voice : " Oh, Dadda, do you know what Jackie did at dinnertime ? " Then, of course, it all came out ; Father gave me a flaking ; Mother interfered, and for days after that he didn't speak to me and Mother barely spoke to Nora.

And all because of that old woman ! God knows, I was heart-scalded.

Then, to crown my misfortunes, I had to make my first confession and communion. It was an old woman called Ryan who prepared us for these. She was about the one age with Gran ; she was well-to-do, lived in a big house on Montenotte, wore a black cloak and bonnet, and came every day to school at three o'clock when we should have been going home, and talked to us of hell. She may have mentioned the other place as well, but that could only have been by accident, for hell had the first place in her heart.

She lit a candle, took out a new half-crown, and offered it to the first boy who would hold one finger—only one finger !—in the flame for five minutes by the school clock. Being always very ambitious I was tempted to volunteer, but I thought it might look greedy. Then she asked were we afraid of holding one finger— only one finger !—in a little candle flame for five minutes and not afraid of burning all over in roasting hot furnaces for all eternity. "All eternity ! Just think of that! A whole lifetime goes by and it's nothing, not even a drop in the ocean of your sufferings." The woman was really interesting about hell, but my attention was all fixed on the half-crown. At the end of the lesson she put it back in her purse. It was a great disappointment ; a religious woman like that, you wouldn't think she'd bother about a thing like a half-crown.

Another day she said she knew a priest who woke one night to find a fellow he didn't recognise leaning over the end of his bed. The priest was a bit frightened—naturally enough—but he asked the fellow what he wanted, and the fellow said in a deep, husky voice that he wanted to go to confession. The priest said it was an awkward time and wouldn't it do in the morning, but the fellow said that last time he went to confession, there was one sin he kept back, being ashamed to mention it, and now it was always on his mind. Then the priest knew it was a bad case, because the fellow was after making a bad confession and committing a mortal sin. He got up to dress, and just then the cock crew in the yard outside, and—lo and behold !—when the priest looked round there was no sign of the fellow, only a smell of burning timber, and when the priest looked at his bed didn't he see the print of two hands burned in it? That was because the fellow had made a bad confession. This story made a shocking impression on me.

But the worst of all was when she showed us how to examine our conscience. Did we take the name of the Lord, our God, in vain? Did we honour our father and our mother? (I asked her did this include grandmothers and she said it did.) Did we love our neighbours as ourselves? Did we covet our neighbour's goods? (I thought of the way I felt about the penny that Nora got every Friday.) I decided that, between one thing and another, I must have broken the whole ten commandments, all on account of that old woman, and so far as I could see, so long as she remained in the house, I had no hope of ever doing anything else.

I was scared to death of confession. The day the whole class went, I let on to have a toothache, hoping my absence wouldn't be noticed; but at three o'clock, just as I was feeling safe, along comes a chap with a message from Mrs. Ryan that I was to go to confession myself on Saturday and be at the chapel for communion with the rest. To make it worse, Mother couldn't come with me and sent Nora instead.

Now, that girl had ways of tormenting me that Mother never knew of. She held my hand as we went down the hill, smiling sadly and saying how sorry she was for me, as if she were bringing me to the hospital for an operation.

" Oh, God help us! " she moaned. " Isn't it a terrible pity you weren't a good boy? Oh, Jackie, my heart bleeds for you! How will you ever think of all your sins? Don't forget you have to tell him about the time you kicked Gran on the shin."

" Lemme go! " I said, trying to drag myself free of her. " I don't want to go to confession at all."

" But sure, you'll have to go to confession, Jackie," she replied in the same regretful tone. " Sure, if you didn't, the parish priest would be up to the house, looking for you. 'Tisn't, God knows, that I'm not sorry for you. Do you remember the time you tried to kill me with the bread-knife under the table? And the language you used to me? I don't know what he'll do with you at all, Jackie. He might have to send you up to the bishop."

I remember thinking bitterly that she didn't know the half of what I had to tell—if I told it. I knew I couldn't tell it, and understood perfectly why the fellow in Mrs. Ryan's story made a bad confession ; it seemed to me a great shame that people wouldn't stop criticising him.   I remember that steep hill down to the church, and the sunlit hillsides beyond the valley of the river, which I saw in the gaps between the houses like Adam's last glimpse of Paradise.

Then, when she had manoeuvred me down the long flight of steps to the chapel yard, Nora suddenly changed her tone.   She became the raging malicious devil she really was.

"There you are !" she said with a yelp of triumph, hurling me through the church door. "And I hope he'll give you the penitential psalms, you dirty little caffler."

I knew then I was lost, given up to eternal justice.   The door with the coloured-glass panels swung shut behind me, the sunlight went out and gave place to deep shadow, and the wind whistled outside so that the silence within seemed to crackle like ice under my feet.   Nora sat in front of me by the confession box. There were a couple of old women ahead of her, and then a miserable-looking poor devil came and wedged me in at the other side, so that I couldn't escape even if I had the courage. He joined his hands and rolled his eyes in the direction of the roof, muttering aspirations in an anguished tone, and I wondered had he a grandmother too.   Only a grandmother could account for a fellow behaving in that heartbroken way, but he was better off than I, for he at least could go and confess his sins ; while I would make a bad confession and then die in the night and be continually coming back and burning people's furniture.

Nora's turn came, and I heard the sound of something slamming, and then her voice as if butter wouldn't melt in her mouth, and then another slam, and out she came.   God, the hypocrisy of women !   Her eyes were lowered, her head was bowed, and her hands were joined very low down on her stomach, and she walked up the aisle to the side altar looking like a saint.   You never saw such an exhibition of devotion ; and I remembered the devilish malice with which she had tormented me all the way from our door, and wondered were all religious people like that, really.   It was my turn now.   With the fear of damnation in my soul I went in, and the confessional door closed of itself behind me.

It was pitch-dark and I couldn't see priest or anything else. Then I really began to be frightened.   In the darkness it was a matter between God and me, and He had all the odds.   He knew what my intentions were before I even started ; I had no chance. All I had ever been told about confession got mixed up in my mind, and I knelt to one wall and said : " Bless me, father, for I have sinned ; this is my first confession." I waited for a few minutes, but nothing happened, so I tried it on the other wall. Nothing happened there either. He had me spotted all right.

It must have been then that I noticed the shelf at about one height with my head. It was really a place for grown-up people to rest their elbows, but in my distracted state I thought it was probably the place you were supposed to kneel. Of course, it was on the high side and not very deep, but I was always good at climbing and managed to get up all right. Staying up was the trouble. There was room only for my knees, and nothing you could get a grip on but a sort of wooden moulding a bit above it. I held on to the moulding and repeated the words a little louder, and this time something happened all right. A slide was slammed back ; a little light entered the box, and a man's voice said : " Who's there ? "

" 'Tis me, father," I said for fear he mightn't see me and go away again. I couldn't see him at all. The place the voice came from was under the moulding, about level with my knees, so I took a good grip of the moulding and swung myself down till I saw the astonished face of a young priest looking up at me. He had to put his head on one side to see me, and I had to put mine on one side to see him, so we were more or less talking to one another upside-down. It struck me as a queer way of hearing confessions, but I didn't feel it my place to criticise.

" Bless me, father, for I have sinned ; this is my first confession," I rattled off all in one breath, and swung myself down the least shade more to make it easier for him.

" What are you doing up there ? " he shouted in an angry voice, and the strain the politeness was putting on my hold of the moulding, and the shock of being addressed in such an uncivil tone, were too much for me. I lost my grip, tumbled, and hit the door an unmerciful wallop before I found myself flat on my back in the middle of the aisle. The people who had been waiting stood up with their mouths open. The priest opened the door of the middle box and came out, pushing his biretta back from his forehead ; he looked something terrible. Then Nora came scampering down the aisle.

" Oh, you dirty little caffler ! " she said. " I might have known
you'd do it.   I might have known you'd disgrace me.   I can't
leave you out of my sight for one minute."

Before I could even get to my feet to defend myself she bent
down and gave me a clip across the ear.   This reminded me that
I was so stunned I had even forgotten to cry, so that people might
think I wasn't hurt at all, when in fact I was probably maimed
for life.   I gave a roar out of me.

" What's all this about ? " the priest hissed, getting angrier than
ever and pushing Nora off me.   " How dare you hit the child like
that, you little vixen ? "

" But I can't do my penance with him, father," Nora cried,
cocking an outraged eye up at him.

" Well, go and do it, or I'll give you some more to do," he said,
giving me a hand up.   " Was it coming to confession you were,
my poor man ? " he asked me.

" 'Twas, father," said I with a sob.

" Oh," he said respectfully, " a big hefty fellow like you must
have terrible sins.   Is this your first ? "

" 'Tis, father," said I.

" Worse and worse," he said gloomily.   " The crimes of a lifetime.   I don't know will I get rid of you at all today.   You'd better
wait now till I'm finished with these old ones.   You can see by
the looks of them they haven't much to tell."

" I will, father," I said with something approaching joy.

The relief of it was really enormous.   Nora stuck out her tongue
at me from behind his back, but I couldn't even be bothered
retorting.   I knew from the very moment that man opened his
mouth that he was intelligent above the ordinary.   When I had
time to think, I saw how right I was.   It only stood to reason that a
fellow confessing after seven years would have more to tell than
people that went every week.   The crimes of a lifetime, exactly as
he said.   It was only what he expected, and the rest was the
cackle of old women and girls with their talk of hell, the bishop,
and the penitential psalms.   That was all they knew.   I started to
make my examination of conscience, and barring the one bad
business of my grandmother, it didn't seem so bad.

The next time, the priest steered me into the confession box
himself and left the shutter back, the way I could see him get in
and sit down at the further side of the grille from me.

" Well, now," 'he said, " what do they call you ? "

" Jackie, father," said I.

"And what's a-trouble to you, Jackie ? "

" Father," I said, feeling I might as well get it over while I had him in good humour, " I had it all arranged to kill my grandmother."

He seemed a bit shaken by that, all right, because he said nothing for quite a while.

" My goodness," he said at last, " that'd be a shocking thing to do. What put that into your head ? "

" Father," I said, feeling very sorry for myself, " she's an awful woman."

" Is she ? " he asked. " What way is she awful ? "

" She takes porter, father," I said, knowing well from the way Mother talked of it that this was a mortal sin, and hoping it would make the priest take a more favourable view of my case.

" Oh, my ! " he said, and I could see he was impressed.

"And snuff, father," said I.

" That's a bad case, sure enough, Jackie," he said.

"And she goes round in her bare feet, father," I went on in a rush of self-pity, " and she knows I don't like her, and she gives pennies to Nora and none to me, and my da sides with her and flakes me, and one night I was so heart-scalded I made up my mind I'd have to kill her."

"And what would you do with the body ? " he asked with great interest.

" I was thinking I could chop that up and carry it away in a barrow I have," I said.

" Begor, Jackie," he said, " do you know you're a terrible child ? "

" I know, father," I said, for I was just thinking the same thing myself. " I tried to kill Nora too with a bread-knife under the table, only I missed her."

" Is that the little girl that was beating you just now ? " he asked.

" 'Tis, father."

" Someone will go for her with a bread-knife one day, and he won't miss her," he said rather cryptically. " You must have great courage. Between ourselves, there's a lot of people I'd like to, do the same to, but I'd never have the nerve. Hanging is an awful death."

" Is it, father ? " I asked with the deepest interest—I was always very keen on hanging. " Did you ever see a fellow hanged ? "

" Dozens of them," he said solemnly. "And they all died roaring."

" Jay ! " I said.

" Oh, a horrible death ! " he said with great satisfaction. " Lots of the fellows I saw killed their grandmothers too, but they all said 'twas never worth it."

He had me there for a full ten minutes talking, and then walked out the chapel yard with me. I was genuinely sorry to part with him, because he was the most entertaining character I'd ever met in the religious line. Outside, after the shadow of the church, the sunlight was like the roaring of waves on a beach ; it dazzled me ; and when the frozen silence melted and I heard the screech of trams on the road, my heart soared. I knew now I wouldn't die in the night and come back, leaving marks on my mother's furniture. It would be a great worry to her, and the poor soul had enough.

Nora was sitting on the railing, waiting for me, and she put on a very sour puss when she saw the priest with me. She was mad jealous because a priest had never come out of the church with her.

" Well," she asked coldly, after he left me, " what did he give you ? "

" Three Hail Marys," I said.

" Three Hail Marys," she repeated incredulously. " You mustn't have told him anything."

" I told him everything," I said confidently.

"About Gran and all ? "

"About Gran and all."

(All she wanted was to be able to go home and say I'd made a bad confession.)

" Did you tell him you went for me with the bread-knife ? " she asked with a frown.

" I did to be sure."

"And he only gave you three Hail Marys ? "

" That's all."

She slowly got down from the railing with a baffled air. Clearly, this was beyond her. As we mounted the steps back to the main road, she looked at me suspiciously.

" What are you sucking ? " she asked.

" Bullseyes."

" Was it the priest gave them to you ? "

" 'Twas."

" Lord God," she wailed bitterly, " some people have all the luck ! 'Tis no advantage to anybody trying to be good. I might just as well be a sinner like you."

— *The Stories of Frank O'Connor*

Explorations

1. This is, in one sense, a story of persecution. The child is surrounded by people who are consciously or unconsciously tormenting him. Name the chief of these. Briefly describe the nature of each kind of persecution.

2. In your opinion is the child ever really terrified ? In answering consider the tone of the story.

3. In your opinion is the child ever really angry ? Why do you think so ?

4. Are the events funny to the young boy as he experiences them ? Or are they merely humorous to the mature man looking back on them ?

5. Arising out of your answer to question 4, is it a true description of childhood, or are the terror and anger softened by the distance from which they are viewed ?

6. Read the quotation from O'Connor on p. 4 of the Introduction ; then consider the opening sentence of the story and try to decide how much, in fact, Frank O'Connor may owe to the old fireside storytelling manner. In how far is it the tone of a man speaking ? Examine the story, the words, phrases and rhythms with this in mind.

7. In his characterisation O'Connor has been praised for his use of ' significant detail '—that is his skill in selecting the detail that will convey a great deal in terms of character and atmosphere. Find examples of this in the character of the grandmother, the sister, Mrs. Ryan, the priest. Try to indicate what impressions these details convey.

8. Are you convinced by the priest's change from annoyance at the young boy to sympathy ? If so, how does O'Connor make this change convincing ?

9. Was the priest an understanding confessor ? In answering this, study carefully his remarks on, and reactions to, the little boy's sins. How does his theology compare with Mrs. Ryan's ?

10. Do you find this a comic story ? Try to define where its comedy lies—the characters, the situations, the language, the style ?

11. Might it have been a tragic or serious story ? What changes would be necessary to make it such ?

Exercises

1. Tell the entire story from the viewpoint of the little girl.

2. Tell the story as the priest might have told it to a fellow curate over dinner.

3. Make up another story involving the two children and the grandmother.

4. For comparison read O'Connor's other child/parent stories— *My Oedipus Complex*, *The Drunkard*, *Old Fellows* and *My Da*.

10

GUESTS OF THE NATION

I

At dusk the big Englishman, Belcher, would shift his long legs out of the ashes and say " Well, chums, what about it ? " and Noble and myself would say "All right, chum " (for we had picked up some of their curious expressions), and the little Englishman, Hawkins, would light the lamp and bring out the cards. Sometimes Jeremiah Donovan would come up and supervise the game, and get excited over Hawkins' cards, which he always played badly, and shout at him as if he was one of our own, "Ah, you divil, why didn't you play the tray ? "

But ordinarily Jeremiah was a sober and contented poor devil like the big Englishman, Belcher, and was looked up to only because he was a fair hand at documents, though he was slow even with them. He wore a small cloth hat and big gaiters over his long pants, and you seldom saw him with his hands out of his pockets. He reddened when you talked to him, tilting from toe to heel and back, and looking down all the time at his big farmer's feet. Noble and myself used to make fun of his broad accent, because we were both from the town.

I could not at the time see the point of myself and Noble guarding Belcher and Hawkins at all, for it was my belief that you could have planted that pair down anywhere from this to Claregalway and they'd have taken root there like a native weed. I never in my short experience saw two men take to the country as they did.

They were passed on to us by the Second Battalion when the search for them became too hot, and Noble and myself, being young, took them over with a natural feeling of responsibility, but Hawkins made us look like fools when he showed that he knew the country better than we did.

" You're the bloke they call Bonaparte," he says to me. " Mary Brigid O'Connell told me to ask what you'd done with the pair of her brother's socks you borrowed."

For it seemed, as they explained it, that the Second had little evenings, and some of the girls of the neighbourhood turned up, and, seeing they were such decent chaps, our fellows could not leave the two Englishmen out. Hawkins learned to dance " The Walls of Limerick," " The Siege of Ennis " and " The Waves of Tory " as well as any of them, though he could not return the compliment, because our lads at that time did not dance foreign dances on principle.

So whatever privileges Belcher and Hawkins had with the Second they just took naturally with us, and after the first couple of days we gave up all pretence of keeping an eye on them. Not that they could have got far, because they had accents you could cut with a knife, and wore khaki tunics and overcoats with civilian pants and boots, but I believe myself they never had any idea of escaping and were quite content to be where they were.

It was a treat to see how Belcher got off with the old woman in the house where we were staying. She was a great warrant to scold, and cranky even with us, but before ever she had a chance of giving our guests, as I may call them, a lick of her tongue, Belcher had made her his friend for life. She was breaking sticks, and Belcher, who had not been more than ten minutes in the house, jumped up and went over to her.

"Allow me, madam," he said, smiling his queer little smile. " Please allow me," and he took the hatchet from her. She was too surprised to speak, and after that, Belcher would be at her heels, carrying a bucket, a basket or a load of turf. As Noble said, he got into looking before she leapt, and hot water, or any little thing she wanted, Belcher would have ready for her. For such a huge man (and though I am five foot ten myself I had to look up at him) he had an uncommon lack of speech. It took us a little while to get used to him, walking in and out like a ghost, without speaking. Especially because Hawkins talked enough for a platoon, it was strange to hear Belcher with his toes in the ashes come out with a solitary " Excuse me, chum," or " That's right, chum." His one and only passion was cards, and he was a remarkably good card player. He could have skinned myself and Noble, but whatever we lost to him, Hawkins lost to us, and Hawkins only played with the money Belcher gave him.

Hawkins lost to us because he had too much old gab, and we probably lost to Belcher for the same reason. Hawkins and Noble argued about religion into the early hours of the morning, and Hawkins worried the life out of Noble, who had a brother a priest, with a string of questions that would puzzle a cardinal. Even in treating of holy subjects, Hawkins had a deplorable tongue. I never met a man who could mix such a variety of cursing and bad language into any argument. He was a terrible man, and a fright to argue. He never did a stroke of work, and when he had no one else to argue with, he got stuck in the old woman.

He met his match in her, for when he tried to get her to complain profanely of the drought she gave him a great comedown by blaming it entirely on Jupiter Pluvius (a deity neither Hawkins nor I had ever heard of, though Noble said that among the pagans it was believed that he had something to do with the rain). Another day he was swearing at the capitalists for starting the German war when the old lady laid down her iron, puckered up her little crab's mouth and said : " Mr. Hawkins, you can say what you like about the war, and think you'll deceive me because I'm only a simple poor countrywoman, but I know what started the war. It was the Italian Count that stole the heathen divinity out of the temple of Japan. Believe me, Mr. Hawkins, nothing but sorrow and want can follow people who disturb the hidden powers."

A queer old girl, all right.

II

One evening we had our tea and Hawkins lit the lamp and we all sat into cards. Jeremiah Donovan came in too, and sat and watched us for a while, and it suddenly struck me that he had no great love for the two Englishmen. It came as a surprise to me because I had noticed nothing of it before.

Late in the evening a really terrible argument blew up between Hawkins and Noble about capitalists and priests and love of country.

" The capitalists pay the priests to tell you about the next world so that you won't notice what the bastards are up to in this," said Hawkins.

" Nonsense, man ! " said Noble, losing his temper. " Before ever a capitalist was thought of people believed in the next world."

Hawkins stood up as though he was preaching.

" Oh, they did, did they ? " he said with a sneer. " They believed all the things you believe—isn't that what you mean ? And you believe God created Adam, and Adam created Shem, and Shem created Jehoshophat. You believe all that silly old fairytale about Eve and Eden and the apple. Well listen to me, chum ! If you're entitled to a silly belief like that, I'm entitled to my own silly belief—which is that the first thing your God created was a bleeding capitalist, with morality and Rolls-Royce complete. Am I right, chum ? " he says to Belcher.

" You're right, chum," says Belcher with a smile, and he got up from the table to stretch his long legs into the fire and stroke his moustache. So, seeing that Jeremiah Donovan was going, and that there was no knowing when the argument about religion would be over, I went out with him. We strolled down to the village together, and then he stopped, blushing and mumbling, and said I should be behind, keeping guard. I didn't like the tone he took with me, and anyway I was bored with life in the cottage, so I replied by asking what the hell we wanted to guard them for at all.

He looked at me in surprise and said : " I thought you knew we were keeping them as hostages."

" Hostages ? " I said.

" The enemy have prisoners belonging to us, and now they're talking of shooting them," he said. " If they shoot our prisoners, we'll shoot theirs."

" Shoot Belcher and Hawkins ? " I said.

" What else did you think we were keeping them for ? " he said.

" Wasn't it very unforeseen of you not to warn Noble and myself of that in the beginning ? " I said.

" How was it ? " he said. " You might have known that much."

" We could not know it, Jeremiah Donovan," I said. " How could we when they were on our hands so long ? "

" The enemy have our prisoners as long and longer," he said.

" That's not the same thing at all," said I.

" What difference is there ? " said he.

I couldn't tell him, because I knew he wouldn't understand. If it was only an old dog that you had to take to the vet's, you'd try and not get too fond of him, but Jeremiah Donovan was not a man who would ever be in danger of that.

"And when is this to be decided ? " I said.

" We might hear tonight," he said. " Or tomorrow or the next day at latest. So if it's only hanging round that's a trouble to you, you'll be free soon enough."

It was not the hanging round that was a trouble to me at all by this time. I had worse things to worry about. When I got back to the cottage the argument was still on. Hawkins was holding forth in his best style, maintaining that there was no next world, and Noble saying that there was ; but I could see that Hawkins had had the best of it.

" Do you know what, chum ? " he was saying with a saucy smile. " I think you're just as big a bleeding unbeliever as I am. You say you believe in the next world, and you know just as much about the next world as I do, which is sweet damn-all. What's heaven ? You don't know. Where's heaven ? You don't know. You know sweet damn-all ! I ask you again, do they wear wings ? "

" Very well, then," said Noble. " They do. Is that enough for you ? They do wear wings."

" Where do they get them then ? Who makes them ? Have they a factory for wings ? Have they a sort of store where you hand in your chit and take your bleeding wings ? "

" You're an impossible man to argue with," said Noble. " Now, listen to me—— " And they were off again.

It was long after midnight when we locked up and went to bed. As I blew out the candle I told Noble. He took it very quietly. When we'd been in bed about an hour he asked if I thought we should tell the Englishmen. I didn't, because I doubted if the English would shoot our men. Even if they did, the Brigade officers, who were always up and down to the Second Battalion and knew the Englishmen well, would hardly want to see them plugged. " I think so too," said Noble. " It would be great cruelty to put the wind up them now."

" It was very unforeseen of Jeremiah Donovan, anyhow," said I.

It was next morning that we found it so hard to face Belcher and Hawkins. We went about the house all day, scarcely saying a word. Belcher didn't seem to notice ; he was stretched into the ashes as usual, with his usual look of waiting in quietness for something unforeseen to happen, but Hawkins noticed it and put it down to Noble's being beaten in the argument of the night before.

" Why can't you take the discussion in the proper spirit ? " he said severely. " You and your Adam and Eve ! I'm a Communist, that's what I am. Communist or Anarchist, it all comes to much the same thing." And he went round the house, muttering when the fit took him : "Adam and Eve ! Adam and Eve ! Nothing better to do with their time than pick bleeding apples ! "

III

I don't know how we got through that day, but I was very glad when it was over, the tea things were cleared away, and Belcher said in his peaceable way : " Well, chums, what about it ? " We sat round the table and Hawkins took out the cards, and just then I heard Jeremiah Donovan's footsteps on the path and a dark presentiment crossed my mind. I rose from the table and caught him before he reached the door.

" What do you want ? " I asked.

" I want those two soldier friends of yours," he said, getting red.

" Is that the way, Jeremiah Donovan ? " I asked.

" That's the way. There were four of our lads shot this morning, one of them a boy of sixteen."

" That's bad," I said.

At that moment Noble followed me out, and the three of us walked down the path together, talking in whispers. Feeney, the local intelligence officer, was standing by the gate.

" What are you going to do about it ? " I asked Jeremiah Donovan.

" I want you and Noble to get them out ; tell them they're being shifted again ; that'll be the quietest way."

" Leave me out of that," said Noble, under his breath.

Jeremiah Donovan looked at him hard.

"All right," he says. " You and Feeney get a few tools from the shed and dig a hole by the far end of the bog. Bonaparte and myself will be after you. Don't let anyone see you with the tools. I wouldn't like it to go beyond ourselves."

We saw Feeney and Noble go round to the shed and went in ourselves. I left Jeremiah Donovan to do the explanations. He told them that he had orders to send them back to the Second Battalion. Hawkins let out a mouthful of curses, and you could see that though Belcher didn't say anything, he was a bit upset too. The old woman was for having them stay in spite of us, and she didn't stop advising them until Jeremiah Donovan lost his temper and turned on her. He had a nasty temper, I noticed. It was pitch-dark in the cottage by this time, but no one thought of lighting the lamp, and in the darkness the two Englishmen fetched their topcoats and said good-bye to the old woman.

"Just as a man makes a home of a bleeding place, some bastard at headquarters thinks you're too cushy and shunts you off," said Hawkins, shaking her hand.

"A thousand thanks, madam," said Belcher. "A thousand thanks for everything "—as though he'd made it up.

We went round to the back of the house and down towards the bog. It was only then that Jeremiah Donovan told them. He was shaking with excitement.

" There were four of our fellows shot in Cork this morning and now you're to be shot as a reprisal."

" What are you talking about ? " snaps Hawkins. " It's bad enough being mucked about as we are without having to put up with your funny jokes."

" It isn't a joke," says Donovan. " I'm sorry, Hawkins, but it's true," and begins on the usual rigmarole about duty and how unpleasant it is. I never noticed that people who talk a lot about duty find it much of a trouble to them.

" Oh, cut it out ! " said Hawkins.

"Ask Bonaparte," said Donovan, seeing that Hawkins wasn't taking him seriously. " Isn't it true, Bonaparte ? "

" It is," I said, and Hawkins stopped.

"Ah, for Christ's sake, chum ! "

" I mean it, chum," I said.

" You don't sound as if you meant it."

" If he doesn't mean it, I do," said Donovan, working himself up.

" What have you against me, Jeremiah Donovan ? "

" I never said I had anything against you. But why did your people take out four of your prisoners and shoot them in cold blood ? "

He took Hawkins by the arm and dragged him on, but it was impossible to make him understand that we were in earnest. I had the Smith and Wesson in my pocket and I kept fingering it and wondering what I'd do if they put up a fight for it or ran, and wishing to God they'd do one or the other. I knew if they did run for it, that I'd never fire on them. Hawkins wanted to know was Noble in it, and when we said yes, he asked us why Noble wanted to plug him. Why did any of us want to plug him ? What had he done to us ? Weren't we all chums ? Didn't we understand him and didn't he understand us ? Did we imagine for an instant that he'd shoot us for all the so-and-so officers in the so-and-so British Army ?

By this time we'd reached the bog, and I was so sick I couldn't even answer him. We walked along the edge of it in the darkness, and every now and then Hawkins would call a halt and begin all over again, as if he was wound up, about our being chums, and I knew that nothing but the sight of the grave would convince him that we had to do it. And all the time I was hoping that something would happen ; that they'd run for it or that Noble would take over the responsibility from me. I had the feeling that it was worse on Noble than on me.

IV

At last we saw the lantern in the distance and made towards it. Noble was carrying it, and Feeney was standing somewhere in the darkness behind him, and the picture of them so still and silent in the bogland brought it home to me that we were in earnest, and banished the last bit of hope I had.

Belcher, on recognising Noble, said : " Hallo, chum," in his quiet way, but Hawkins flew at him at once, and the argument began all over again, only this time Noble had nothing to say for himself and stood with his head down, holding the lantern between his legs.

It was Jeremiah Donovan who did the answering. For the twentieth time, as though it was haunting his mind, Hawkins asked if anybody thought he'd shoot Noble.

" Yes, you would," said Jeremiah Donovan.

" No, I wouldn't, damn you ! "

" You would, because you'd know you'd be shot for not doing it."

" I wouldn't, not if I was to be shot twenty times over. I wouldn't shoot a pal. And Belcher wouldn't—isn't that right, Belcher ? "

" That's right, chum," Belcher said, but more by way of answering the question than of joining in the argument. Belcher sounded as though whatever unforeseen thing he'd always been waiting for had come at last.

"Anyway, who says Noble would be shot if I wasn't ? What do you think I'd do if I was in his place, out in the middle of a blasted bog ? "

" What would you do ? " asked Donovan.

" I'd go with him wherever he was going, of course. Share my last bob with him and stick by him through thick and thin. No one can ever say of me that I let down a pal."

" We had enough of this," said Jeremiah Donovan, cocking his revolver. " Is there any message you want to send ? "

" No, there isn't."

" Do you want to say your prayers ? "

Hawkins came out with a cold-blooded remark that even shocked me and turned on Noble again.

" Listen to me, Noble," he said. " You and me are chums. You can't come over to my side, so I'll come over to your side. That show you I mean what I say ? Give me a rifle and I'll go along with you and the other lads."

Nobody answered him. We knew that was no way out.

" Hear what I'm saying ? " he said. " I'm through with it. I'm a deserter or anything else you like. I don't believe in your stuff, but it's no worse than mine. That satisfy you ? "

Noble raised his head, but Donovan began to speak and he lowered it again without replying.

" For the last time, have you any messages to send ? " said Donovan in a cold, excited sort of voice.

" Shut up, Donovan ! You don't understand me, but these lads do. They're not the sort to make a pal and kill a pal. They're not the tools of any capitalist."

I alone of the crowd saw Donovan raise his Webley to the back of Hawkins's neck, and as he did so I shut my eyes and tried to pray. Hawkins had begun to say something else when Donovan fired, and as I opened my eyes at the bang, I saw Hawkins stagger at the knees and lie out flat at Noble's feet, slowly and as quiet as a kid falling asleep, with the lantern-light on his lean legs and bright farmer's boots. We all stood very still, watching him settle out in the last agony.

Then Belcher took out a handkerchief and began to tie it about his own eyes (in our excitement we'd forgotten to do the same for Hawkins), and, seeing it wasn't big enough, turned and asked for the loan of mine. I gave it to him and he knotted the two together and pointed with his foot at Hawkins.

" He's not quite dead," he said. " Better give him another."

Sure enough, Hawkins's left knee was beginning to rise. I bent down and put my gun to his head ; then, recollecting myself, I got up again. Belcher understood what was in my mind.

" Give him his first," he said. " I don't mind. Poor bastard, we don't know what's happening to him now."

I knelt and fired. By this time I didn't seem to know what I was doing. Belcher, who was fumbling a bit awkwardly with the handkerchiefs, came out with a laugh as he heard the shot. It was the first time I had heard him laugh and it sent a shudder down my back ; it sounded so unnatural.

" Poor bugger ! " he said quietly. "And last night he was so curious about it all. It's very queer, chums, I always think. Now he knows as much about it as they'll ever let him know, and last night he was all in the dark."

Donovan helped him to tie the handkerchiefs about his eyes. " Thanks, chum," he said. Donovan asked if there were any messages he wanted sent.

" No, chum," he said. " Not for me. If any of you would like to write to Hawkins's mother, you'll find a letter from her in his pocket. He and his mother were great chums. But my missus left me eight years ago. Went away with another fellow and took the kid with her. I like the feeling of a home, as you may have noticed, but I couldn't start another again after that."

It was an extraordinary thing, but in those few minutes Belcher said more than in all the weeks before. It was just as if the sound of the shot had started a flood of talk in him and he could go on the whole night like that, quite happily, talking about himself. We stood around like fools now that he couldn't see us any longer. Donovan looked at Noble, and Noble shook his head. Then Donovan raised his Webley, and at that moment Belcher gave his queer laugh again. He may have thought we were talking about him, or perhaps he noticed the same thing I'd noticed and couldn't understand it.

" Excuse me, chums," he said. " I feel I'm talking the hell of a lot, and so silly, about my being so handy about a house and things like that. But this thing came on me suddenly. You'll forgive me, I'm sure."

" You don't want to say a prayer ? " asked Donovan.

" No, chum," he said. " I don't think it would help. I'm ready, and you boys want to get it over."

" You understand that we're only doing our duty ? " said Donovan.

Belcher's head was raised like a blind man's, so that you could only see his chin and the top of his nose in the lantern-light.

" I never could make out what duty was myself," he said. " I think you're all good lads, if that's what you mean. I'm not complaining."

Noble, just as if he couldn't bear any more of it, raised his fist at Donovan, and in a flash Donovan raised his gun and fired. The big man went over like a sack of meal, and this time there was no need of a second shot.

I don't remember much about the burying, but that it was worse than all the rest because we had to carry them to the grave. It was all mad lonely with nothing but a patch of lantern-light between ourselves and the dark, and birds hooting and screeching all round, disturbed by the guns. Noble went through Hawkins's belongings to find the letter from his mother, and then joined his hands together. He did the same with Belcher. Then, when we'd filled in the grave, we separated from Jeremiah Donovan and Feeney and took our tools back to the shed. All the way we didn't speak a word. The kitchen was dark and cold as we'd left it, and the old woman was sitting over the hearth, saying her beads. We walked past her into the room, and Noble struck a match to light the lamp. She rose quietly and came to the doorway with all her cantankerousness gone.

" What did ye do with them ? " she asked in a whisper, and Noble started so that the match went out in his hand.

" What's that ? " he asked without turning round.

" I heard ye," she said.

" What did you hear ? " asked Noble.

" I heard ye. Do ye think I didn't hear ye, putting the spade back in the houseen ? "

Noble struck another match and this time the lamp lit for him.

" Was that what ye did to them ? " she asked.

Then, by God, in the very doorway, she fell on her knees and began praying, and after looking at her for a minute or two Noble did the same by the fireplace. I pushed my way out past her and left them at it. I stood at the door, watching the stars and listening to the shrieking of the birds dying out over the bogs. It is so strange what you feel at times like that that you can't describe it. Noble says he saw everything ten times the size, as though there were nothing in the whole world but that little patch of bog with the two Englishmen stiffening into it, but with me it was as if the patch of bog where the Englishmen were was a million miles away, and even Noble and the old woman, mumbling behind me, and the birds and the bloody stars were all far away, and I was somehow very small and very lost and lonely like a child astray in the snow. And anything that happened to me afterwards, I never felt the same about again.

— *Collection Two*

Explorations

1.   What is the attitude of Jeremiah Donovan to the execution ? From the evidence of the story what sort of man would you say he is ?

2.   Why, in your opinion, does Noble refuse to take part in the killing ? Give your impressions of Noble as a character.

3.   Hawkins asserts at the end that he would not have done the same had the positions been reversed. Do you believe him ? Why ? Comment on the character of Hawkins.

4. The word 'duty' occurs many times in the story. Different people seem to have different attitudes towards it. Define briefly the attitudes of Bonaparte, Donovan, Hawkins and Belcher towards it. Which of these attitudes strike you as the most worthy?

5. Noble is a Christian. Does his faith help him at the moment of crisis? If so how? If not why?

6. Bonaparte and Noble are profoundly shaken by the execution. How does the author make us aware of this?

7. How does the author manage so well to show us that Belcher and Hawkins fitted into the Irish scene? Examine the text carefully with this in view.

8. There are many discussions about religion and the afterlife. Are these there merely to indicate the passing of time or have they a larger significance?

9. By what means does the author convey the sense of intimacy and friendship in the household?

10. In this context who is the real outsider? Who is the real enemy? Ponder this a little.

11. The language of the story is a mixture of the colloquial and the literary. Or is it? What are its chief merits? Quote instances.

12. In this story the characters are mostly likable human beings. Does this add or detract from the sense of horror one feels at their fate?

13. There is a sense of darkness and bleakness at the end. How is this conveyed in the language? Examine the last movement of the story carefully to see how the author builds up this atmosphere.

14. The constant references to the stars, the bog, the night, the cold make a contrast with the earlier household scenes. What is the purpose of that contrast? Is it effective?

Exercises

1. Tell the story from the viewpoint of Donovan, Noble, Hawkins, or Belcher and try to find words appropriate to their character.

2. At the crisis of the story Noble seems to be about to strike Donovan. Assume that he did and write what you think would have happened.

3. Read O'Connor's other war stories, *Laughter* and *Freedom*, so that you can compare them with 'Guests of the Nation.'

11

THE TROUT

One of the first places Julia always ran to when they arrived in G—— was The Dark Walk. It is a laurel walk, very old ; almost gone wild ; a lofty midnight tunnel of smooth, sinewy branches. Underfoot the tough brown leaves are never dry enough to crackle : there is always a suggestion of damp and cool trickle.

She raced right into it. For the first few yards she always had the memory of the sun behind her, then she felt the dusk closing swiftly down on her so that she screamed with pleasure and raced on to reach the light at the far end ; and it was always just a little too long in coming so that she emerged gasping, clasping her hands, laughing, drinking in the sun. When she was filled with the heat and glare, she would turn and consider the ordeal again.

This year she had the extra joy of showing it to her small brother, and of terrifying him as well as herself. And for him the fear lasted longer because his legs were so short and she had gone out at the far end while he was still screaming and racing.

When they had done this many times, they came back to the house to tell everybody that they had done it. He boasted. She mocked. They squabbled.

" Cry babby ! "

" You were afraid yourself, so there ! "

" I won't take you any more."

" You're a big pig."

" I hate you."

Tears were threatening, so somebody said, " Did you see the well ? " She opened her eyes at that and held up her long lovely neck suspiciously and decided to be incredulous. She was twelve and at that age little girls are beginning to suspect most stories : they have already found out too many, from Santa Claus to the stork. How could there be a well ? In The Dark Walk ? That she had visited year after year ? Haughtily she said, " Nonsense."

But she went back, pretending to be going somewhere else, and she found a hole scooped in the rock at the side of the walk, choked with damp leaves, so shrouded by ferns that she uncovered it only after much searching. At the back of this little cavern there was about a quart of water. In the water she suddenly perceived a panting trout. She rushed for Stephen and dragged him to see, and they were both so excited that they were no longer afraid of the darkness as they hunched down and peered in at the fish panting in his tiny prison, his silver stomach going up and down like an engine.

Nobody knew how the trout got there. Even old Martin in the kitchen garden laughed and refused to believe that it was there, or pretended not to believe, until she forced him to come down and see. Kneeling and pushing back his tattered old cap he peered in.

" Be cripes, you're right. How the divil in hell did that fella get there ? "

She stared at him suspiciously.

" You knew ? " she accused ; but he said, " The divil a' know," and reached down to lift it out. Convinced, she hauled him back. If she had found it, then it was her trout.

Her mother suggested that a bird had carried the spawn. Her father thought that in the winter a small streamlet might have carried it down there as a baby, and it had been safe until the summer came and the water began to dry up. She said, " I see," and went back to look again and consider the matter in private. Her brother remained behind, wanting to hear the whole story of the trout, not really interested in the actual trout but much interested in the story which his mummy began to make up for him on the lines of, " So one day Daddy Trout and Mammy Trout . . ." When he retailed it to her she said, " Pooh !"

It troubled her that the trout was always in the same position ; he had no room to turn ; all the time the silver belly went up and down ; otherwise he was motionless. She wondered what he ate, and in between visits to Joey Pony and the boat, and a bathe to get cool, she thought of his hunger. She brought him down bits of dough ; once she brought him a worm. He ignored the food. He just went on panting. Hunched over him, she thought how all the winter, while she was at school, he had been in there. All the winter, in The Dark Walk, all day, all night, floating around alone. She drew the leaf of her hat down around her ears and chin and stared. She was still thinking of it as she lay in bed.

It was late June, the longest days of the year. The sun had sat still for a week, burning up the world. Although it was after ten o'clock, it was still bright and still hot. She lay on her back under a single sheet, with her long legs spread, trying to keep cool. She could see the D of the moon through the fir tree— they slept on the ground floor. Before they went to bed, her mummy had told Stephen the story of the trout again, and she, in her bed, had resolutely presented her back to them and read her book. But she had kept one ear cocked.

"And so, in the end, this naughty fish who would not stay at home got bigger and bigger and bigger, and the water got smaller and smaller. . . ."

Passionately she had whirled and cried, " Mummy, don't make it a horrible old moral story ! " Her mummy had brought in a fairy godmother then, who sent lots of rain, and filled the well, and a stream poured out and the trout floated away down to the river below. Staring at the moon she knew that there are no such things as fairy godmothers and that the trout, down in The Dark Walk, was panting like an engine. She heard somebody unwind a fishing reel. Would the *beasts* fish him out ?

She sat up. Stephen was a hot lump of sleep, lazy thing. The Dark Walk would be full of little scraps of moon. She leaped up and looked out the window, and somehow it was not so lightsome now that she saw the dim mountains far away and the black firs against the breathing land and heard a dog say *bark-bark*. Quietly she lifted the ewer of water and climbed out the window and scuttled along the cool but cruel gravel down to the maw of the tunnel. Her pyjamas were very short, so that when she splashed water, it wet her ankles. She peered into the tunnel. Something alive rustled inside there. She raced in, and up and down she raced, and flurried, and cried aloud, " Oh, gosh, I can't find it," and then at last she did. Kneeling down in the damp she put her hand into the slimy hole. When the body lashed, they were both mad with fright. But she gripped him and shoved him into the ewer and raced, with her teeth ground, out to the other end of the tunnel and down the steep paths to the river's edge.

All the time she could feel him lashing his tail against the side of the ewer. She was afraid he would jump right out. The gravel cut into her soles until she came to the cool ooze of the river's bank where the moon mice on the water crept into her feet. She poured out, watching until he plopped. For a second he was visible in the water. She hoped he was not dizzy. Then all she saw was the glimmer of the moon in the silent-flowing river, the dark firs, the dim mountains, and the radiant pointed face laughing down at her out of the empty sky.

She scuttled up the hill, in the window, plonked down the ewer, and flew through the air like a bird into bed. The dog said *bark-bark*. She heard the fishing reel whirring. She hugged herself and giggled. Like a river of joy, her holiday spread before her.

In the morning, Stephen rushed to her, shouting that " he " was gone, and asking " where " and " how." Lifting her nose in the air, she said superciliously, " Fairy godmother, I suppose ? " and strolled away, patting the palms of her hands.

— *The Finest Stories of Sean O'Faolain*

Explorations

1. Early in the story the author tells us that Julia was beginning to suspect most stories 'from Santa Claus to the stork'. Can you find any other hints of Julia's changing attitude to the world of children ?

2. Why does she hate her mother's making a ' horrible old moral story ' out of it ? Work out your answer to this carefully.

3. 'She heard the fishing reel whirring. She hugged herself and giggled. Like a river of joy her holiday spread before her'. What in your opinion, is the cause of the joy ? Why is this holiday going to be so special ?

4. What do you think the author meant to convey by showing that Julia and her brother reacted differently to the trout's predicament ?

5. Why does the girl go out into the night to rescue the trout ? Take your time answering this.

6. On the evidence of the story what sort of girl is Julia ?

7. Outline in a couple of sentences the plot of this story.

8. Where is the story's climax ?

Exercises

1. The author takes great care to describe physical details—the tunnel, the trout itself and so on. Point out some descriptions that strike you as particularly real or vivid, and say what appeals to you in them. In a final paragraph try to say why he took such care to get them right.

2. Did you ever hold a live fish in your hand ? If so, try to describe your feelings at the time. If you have held a frog or a bird describe those also.

3. We get snatches of the mother's 'moral tale' to young Stephen. Try to reconstruct this tale in full.

4. Can you recall any incident in your own life around the age of twelve when you felt that you had taken a definite step in growing up ? If so, describe it and any incident since then that has advanced the process.

12

UP THE BARE STAIRS

A pity beyond all telling is hid in the heart of love.

All the way from Dublin my travelling companion had not spoken
a dozen words. After a casual interest in the countryside as we
left Kingsbridge, he had wrapped a rug about his legs, settled into
his corner, and dozed.

He was a bull-shouldered man, about sixty, with coarse, sallow
skin stippled with pores, furrowed by deep lines on either side of
his mouth : I could imagine him dragging these little dikes open
when shaving. He was dressed so conventionally, that he might
be a judge, a diplomat, a shopwalker, a shipowner, or an old-time
Shakespearian actor : black coat, striped trousers, grey spats,
white slip inside his waistcoat, butterfly collar folded deeply, and
a black cravat held by a gold clasp with a tiny diamond.

The backs of his fingers were hairy : he wore an amethyst ring
almost as big as a bishop's. His temples were greying and brushed
up in two sweeping wings—wherefore the suggestion of the actor.
On the rack over his head was a leather hat-case with the initials
F.J.N. in Gothic lettering. He was obviously an Englishman who
had crossed the night before. Even when the steam of the train
lifted to show the black January clouds sweeping across the Galtees,
and a splash of sleet hit the window by his ear, he did not waken.
Just then the ticket checker came in from the corridor and tipped
his shoulder. As he received back his ticket he asked, " What
time do we arrive in Cork ? " He said the word *Cork* as only a
Corkman can say it, giving the *r* its distinctively delicate palatal
trill, not saying " Corrrk," or " Cohk." He was unmistakably a
Corkonian.

At Mallow I came back from tea to find him stretching his
legs on the platform and taking notice. He had bought the
evening paper and was tapping his thigh with it as he watched,
with a quizzical smile, two tipsy old countrymen in amiable
dispute, nose to nose, outside the bar. A fine man on his feet ;
at least six foot two. I bought a paper, also, at the bookstall and
as we went on our way, we both read.

My eye floated from a heading about a licensing case—the usual long verbatim report, two men found hiding under the stairs, six men with bottles in the stable, much laughter in court, and so on—to a headline beside it : CORKMAN IN BIRTHDAY HONOURS LIST. The paragraph referred to " Francis James Nugent, Baronet : for War Services." I looked across at him.

" Did you say something ? " he asked.

" No, no ! Or, rather, I don't think so."

" Pretty cold," he said, in a friendly way. " Though I will say one thing for the G.S.R., they do heat their trains."

" Yes, it's nice and warm today. They're not, of course, the G.S.R. now, you know. They're called Coras Iompair Eireann."

" What's that ? Irish for G.S.R. ? "

" More or less."

We talked a bit about the revival of the language. Not that he was interested ; but he was tolerant, or perhaps the right word is indifferent. After a bit I said :

" I see there's a Corkman in the new honours list."

" Oh ? "

I glanced up at the rack and said, with a grin :

" I see the initials on your hatbox."

He chuckled, pleased.

" I suppose I'd better plead guilty."

" Congratulations."

" Thank you."

" What does it feel like ? "

He glanced out at the wheeling fields, with their lochs of water and cowering cattle, and then looked back at me with a cynical smile.

" It doesn't feel any different. By the time you get it you've pretty well enjoyed everything it stands for. Still, it helps."

" I see from the paper that you went to the same school as myself."

"Are you the old Red and Green, too ? "

" Up the Abbey ! "

He laughed, pleased again.

" Does all that go on just the same as before ? "

" It goes on. Perhaps not just the same as before."

We talked of West Abbey. I knew none of the men he knew, but he thawed out remembering them.

"Are all the old photographs still in the main hall ? Chaps in the Indian Civil, the Canadian Mounted, the Navy, the Indian Police ? God, I used to stare at them when I was a kid."

" They're gone. They've been replaced by Confirmation groups all wearing holy medals."

He made a bored face.

" I suppose in those days you little thought you'd be coming back to Cork one day as Sir Francis Nugent."

He peered at me through his cigarette smoke and nodded sagely.

" I knew."

" You did ! "

" I shouldn't have said that. I couldn't know. But I had a pretty good idea."

Then he leaned forward and let down all his reserves. As he began, my heart sank. He was at the favourite theme of every successful man : " How I Began." But as he went on, I felt mean and rebuked. I doubt if he had ever told anyone, and before he finished I could only guess why he chose to tell me now.

" You know, it's extraordinary the things that set a fellow going. I always knew I'd get somewhere. Not merely that, but I can tell you the very day, the very hour, I made up my mind I was going to get there. I don't think I was more than fourteen or fifteen at the time. Certainly not more than fifteen. It was as simple as that "—clicking his fingers. " It was all on account of a little man named Angelo—one of the monks who was teaching us. He's gone to God by now. There was a time when I thought he was the nicest little man in the whole school. Very handsome. Cheeks as red as a girl's, black bristly hair, blue eyes, and the most perfect teeth I've ever seen between a man's lips. He was absolutely full of life, bursting with it. He was really just a big boy and that's probably why we got on so well with him. I've seen him get as much fun out of solving a quadratic equation or a problem in Euclid as a kid with a new toy. He had a marvellous trick of flinging his *cappa* over one shoulder, shoving his two wrists out of his sleeves like a conjurer, snapping up a bit of chalk and saying, ' Watch what I'm going to do now,' that used to make us sit bolt upright in our desks as if . . . well, as if he was going to do a conjuring trick. And if you could only have seen the way he'd kick ball with us in the yard—you know, the old yard at the back of West Abbey—all we had was a lump of paper tied with twine—shouting and racing like any of us. He really was a good chap. We were very fond of him.

" Too fond of him, I've often thought. He knew it, you see, and it made him put too much of himself into everything we did. And the result was that we were next door to helpless without him. He made us depend on him too much. Perhaps he wasn't the best kind of teacher ; perhaps he was too good a teacher— I don't know—have it whichever way you like. If he was tired, or had a headache, or sagged, we sagged. If he was away sick and somebody else had to take charge of us, we were a set of duffers. They could be just as cross as he was—he was very severe, he'd take no excuses from anybody—or they could be as merry as he was : it just wasn't the same thing. They had a job to do, and they did the best they could, but with him, it wasn't a job, it was his life, it was his joy and his pleasure. You could tell how much the fellows liked him by the way they'd crowd around him at play hour, or at the end of the holidays to say good-bye.

" One particularly nice thing about him was that he had no favourites, no pets, as we used to call them. Did you call them that in your time ? But he was—what shall I say ?—more than a little partial to me. And for a very, if you like to call it, silly reason. In those days, you see, politics were very hot in Cork city ; very hot, very passionate. Of course, they were the old Irish Party days, long before your time, when politics were taken much more seriously than I've ever seen them taken anywhere else. John Redmond had one party called the Molly Maguires, and William O'Brien had another party called the All for Irelanders. Mind you, if you asked me now what it was all about, I'd find it very hard to tell you, because they were all the one party at Westminster, and they were all agreed about home rule, but once it came to election time, they tore one another to pieces. Fights in the street every night, baton charges, clashes between rival bands, instruments smashed on the pave-ments. One night, with my own eyes, I saw a big six-foot countryman take a running jump down the Grand Parade and land right on top of a big drum.

" Well, Angelo was a Molly, and I needn't tell you he was just as excited about politics as he was about everything else, and I was also a Molly and a very hot one. Not that I understood anything at all about it, but just that my father was one of the hottest Redmondites in the city of Cork. And, of course, nothing would do Angelo but to bring politics into class. He'd divide the class into Mollies and All Fors and when we'd be doing Euclid or reciting poetry, he'd set one team against the other, and he'd work up the excitement until the fellows would be clambering across the desks, and if any fellow let down his side, we'd glare at him until he'd want to creep away out of sight, and if he scored a point, we'd cheer him as if he'd kicked a goal in an All Ireland Final.

" It was on one of these days that it happened. We were at the Eighth Problem. The Mollies wanted one point to pull even. I was the last man in—and I muffed it. And no wonder, with Angelo shouting at me like a bull, ' Come on, now, Frankie. If A.B. be placed on C.D. . . . Up the Mollies ! Go on, Frankie. Go on. If A.B. . . . '

" The All Fors won. Angelo laughed it off with, ' Very good, very good, back to yeer places now. Work is work. This isn't the Old Market Place. Now for tomorrow,' and so on.

" But he kept me in after school. There I sat, alone in the empty classroom upstairs—you know the one, near the ball alley—with the crows outside in the yard picking up the crusts, and the dusk falling over the city, and Angelo, never speaking a word, walking up and down the end of the room reading his office. As a rule we were let out at three. He kept me there until five o'clock rang. Then he told me to go home and went off himself up to the monastery.

" I walked out of the yard behind him, and at that moment if I had had a revolver in my hand I'd have shot him. I wouldn't have cared if he'd beaten me black and blue. I wouldn't have cared if he'd given me extra work to do at home. He deliberately got me into trouble with my father and mother, and what that meant, he understood exactly. Perhaps you don't. You don't know my background as he knew it. When I tell you that my father was a tailor and my mother was a seamstress, I needn't tell you any more. When a kid's mother has to work as hard as his father to push him through school, you can guess the whole picture. I don't seem to remember an hour, except for Sundays, when one or other, or both, of these machines wasn't whirring in that little room where we lived, down by the distillery, sometimes until twelve or one o'clock at night. I remember that day as I walked home, I kept saying to myself over and over again, 'If only my mummy wasn't sick.' All the way. Past the distillery. Around by the tannery. You possibly know the little terrace of houses. They've been there since the eighteenth century. Dark. We had only two rooms. In the hall. I can still get that stuffy smell that had been locked up there for a hundred and fifty years—up the bare stairs. On the landing there was a tap dripping into an old leaden trough that had been there since the year dot. I could hear the machine whirring. I remember I stopped at the window and picked a dead leaf from the geraniums. I went up the last few steps and I lifted the latch. My father was bent over the machine ; specs on his forehead, black skeins of thread around his neck, bare arms. My mother was wrapped in shawls in the old basket chair before the fire. I could draw that room ; the two machines, my bed in one corner, my dinner waiting on the table, the tailor's goose heating on the grate. The machine stopped.

" ' In the name of God what happened to you, boy ? ' says my father. ' Is there anything wrong ? What kept you ? Your poor mother there is out of her head worrying about you.'

" 'Ah, I was just kept in, sir,' says I, passing it off as airily as I could. ' How are you, Mummy ? '

" The old man caught me by the arm.

" 'Kept in ? ' says he, and the way he said it, you'd think I was after coming out of the lockup. ' Why were you kept in ? '

" 'Ah, 'twas just a bit of Euclid I didn't know, that's all.'

" It was only then I noticed that the mother was asleep. I put my hands to my lips begging him not to waken her. He let a roar out of him.

" 'A nice disgrace ! Kept in because you didn't know your Euclid ! '

" ' What is it, what is it, Frankie ? ' she says, waking up in a fright. ' What did they do to you, boy ? '

" ' 'Twas nothing at all, Mummy, just that I didn't know a bit of Euclid. I had to stay back to learn it.'

" 'A nice how d'ye do ! And why didn't you know your Euclid ? '—and he had me up against the wall and his fist raised.

" ' It wasn't really Euclid at all, Father. It was all Angelo's fault. It was all politics. He divided the class into All Fors and Mollies and because the All Fors won, he kept me in out of spite. Honestly, that's all it was, Mummy, there was nothing else to it.'

" ' Holy God,' whispers the old man. ' So it wasn't only the Euclid, but lettin' down John Redmond in front of the whole class. That's what you did, is it ? '

" ' Oh, for God's sake, Billy,' says the mother, ' don't mind John Redmond. 'Tis little John Redmond or any other John Redmond cares about us, but 'tis the work, the work. What are we slaving for, boy, day and night, and all the rest of it ? There's your poor father working himself to the bone to send you through school. And so on. Nothing matters, boy, but the work ! The work ! '

" ' 'Tisn't only the work,' says the old man. ' 'Tisn't only the work,' and he was sobbing over it. ' But to think of poor John Redmond fighting night after night for Ireland, standing up there in the House of Commons, and you—you brat—couldn't even do a sum in Euclid to stand by him ! In your own school ! Before everybody ! Look at him,' he wails, with his arm up to the picture of John Redmond on the wall, with his hooked nose and his jowls like an old countrywoman. ' Look at the dacent gentleman. A man that never let down his side. A gentleman to the tips of his toes if there ever was one. And you couldn't do a simple sum in Euclid to help him ! Th'other fellows could do it. The All Fors could do it. But my son couldn't do it ! '

"And with that he gave me a crack that nearly sent me into the fire.

" The end of it was that I was on my knees with my head on the mother's lap, blubbering, and the old man with his two hands up to John Redmond, and the tears flowing down his face like rain, and the mother wailing, ' Won't you promise, Frankie, won't you promise to work, boy ? ' and I promising and promising anything if she'd only stop crying.

" That was the moment that I swore to myself to get on. But wait ! You won't understand why, until I've finished.

" The next day Angelo took the same problem, at the same

hour, and he asked me to do it again. Now, kids are no fools. I
knew by the look on his face why he asked me to do it. He
wanted to make friends with me, to have everything the same
as if yesterday had never happened. But he didn't know what
had happened inside in me the night before. I went through the
problem, step by step—I knew it perfectly—down to the Q.E.D.

" ' Now, isn't it a pity, Frankie,' he says, smiling at me, ' that
you wouldn't do that yesterday ? '

" ' Oh,' I said, in a very lordly, tired voice, ' I just didn't feel
like it.'

" I knew what was coming to me, and I wanted it, and to make
sure that I got it, I gave him that sort of insolent smile that
drives grownups mad with children. I've seen that smile on my
own children's faces now and again, and when I see it, I have
to go outside the door for fear I'd knock them the length of the
room. That is what Angelo did to me. I got up off the floor
and I sat back in my place and I had the same insolent smile on
my face.

" ' Now, if you please,' says Angelo, reaching for his cane and
he was as white as his teeth, ' will you kindly do the next problem?'

" I did it, step by step, calm as a breeze, down to the Q.E.D.
I'd prepared it the night before.

" ' Right,' says Angelo, and his voice was trembling with rage.
' Do the next problem.'

" I had him where I wanted him. He was acting unfairly, and
he knew it, and the class knew it. I had that problem prepared
too. Just to tease him I made a couple of slips, but just as he'd
be reaching for the cane, I'd correct them. I was a beast, but
he'd made me a beast. I did it, down to the Q.E.D., and I
smiled at him, and he looked at me. We both knew that from
that moment it was war to the knife.

" I worked that night until twelve o'clock : and I worked
every night until I left school until twelve o'clock. I never gave
him a chance. I had to, because until the day I left that place,
he followed me. He followed me into Middle Grade. And into
Senior Grade. He made several efforts to make it up with me,
but I wouldn't let him. He was too useful to me the other way.
I sat for the Civil Service and I got first place in the British Isles
in three subjects out of five, geometry, chemistry and history,
third in mathematics, fifth in German. I did worst in German

because I didn't have Angelo for German. I think I can say without arrogance that I was the most brilliant student that ever passed out of West Abbey School."

Sir Francis leaned back.

" You must have worked like a black."

" I did."

" Well, it was worth it ! "

He looked out over the fields which were now becoming colourless in the falling dusk and his voice sank to a murmur, as if he were thinking aloud.

" I don't know. For me ? Yes, perhaps. I had no youth. For them ? I don't know. I didn't work to get on; I worked to get out. I didn't work to please my mother or my father. I hated my mother and I hated my father from the day they made me cry. They did the one thing to me that I couldn't stand up against. They did what that little cur Angelo planned they'd do. They broke my spirit with pity. They made me cry with pity. Oh, I needn't say I didn't go on hating them. A boy doesn't nourish hatred. He has his life before him. I was too sorry for them. But that's where they lost everything. A boy can be sorry for people who are weak and pitiable, but he can't respect them. And you can't love people if you don't respect them. I pitied them and I despised them. That's the truth."

He leaned back again.

" You don't look like a man whose spirit was ever broken," I laughed, a little embarrassed.

" The spirit is always broken by pity. Oh, I patched it up pretty well. I made a man of myself. Or, rather," he said with passion, " with what was left of myself after they'd robbed me of my youth that I spent slaving to get away from them."

" You'd have slaved anyway. You were full of ambition."

" If I did, I'd have done it for ambition alone. I tell you I did it for pity and hate and pride and contempt and God knows what other reason. No. They broke my spirit all right. I know it. The thing I've put in its place is a very different thing. I know it. I've met plenty of men who've got along on ambition and they're whole men. I know it. I'm full of what they put into me—pity and hate and rage and pride and contempt for the weak and anger against all bullying, but, above all, pity, chock-a-block with it. I know it. Pity is the most disintegrating of all human emotions. It's the most disgusting of all human emotions. I know it."

" What happened to Angelo ? "

" I don't know. Nor care. Died, I suppose."

"And . . . your father ? "

" Fifteen years after I left Cork he died. I never saw him. I brought my mother to live with me in London."

" That was good. You were fond of her."

" I was sorry for her. That's what she asked me for when I was a boy. I've been sorry for her all my life. Ah ! "

His eyes lit up. I looked sideways to see what had arrested him. It was the first lights of Cork, and, mingling with the smoke over the roofs, the January night. Behind the violet hills the last cinder of the sun made a saffron horizon. As the train roared into the tunnel we could see children playing in the streets below the steep embankment, and he was staring at them thirstily, and I must have imagined that I heard their happy shouts. Then the tunnel opened and swallowed us.

There were no lights in the carriage. All I could see was the occasional glow of his cigarette. Presently the glow moved and my knee was touched. His voice said :

" She's with me on this train. My mother. I'm bringing her back to Cork."

" Will she like that ? "

" She's dead."

The train roared on through the tunnel. As we passed under the first tunnel vent a drip of water fell on the roof. The tiny glow swelled and ebbed softly.

" I'm very sorry."

His voice said, in the darkness :

" I meant to bury her in London. But I couldn't do it. Silly, wasn't it ? "

After a while another drip of water splashed on the roof. The windows were grey.

" You did the kind thing."

His voice was so low that I barely heard it.

" Kind ! "

In a few more minutes we were drawing up in steam alongside the lighted platform. He was standing up, leaning over his hatbox. From it he lifted a silk topper and a dark scarf. He put on his black frock coat. "Good-bye," he said politely, and beckoned for a porter.

From the platform I watched him walk down towards the luggage van where a tiny group already stood waiting. They were all poor people. There was a bent old woman there in a black shawl, and three or four humble-looking men in bowler hats and caps. As I watched him bow to them and doff his hat to the old woman and introduce himself, the yellow pine-and-brass of the coffin was already emerging from the van and the undertaker's men in their brass-buttoned coats were taking it from the porters. Among his poor relations he walked reverently, bareheaded, out into the dark station-yard.

They slid the coffin into the motor hearse ; he showed his relatives into the carriages, and, stooping, he went in after them. Then the little procession moved slowly out into the streets on its way to whatever chapel would take her for the night into its mortuary.

— *The Finest Stories of Sean O'Faolain*

Explorations

It need hardly be pointed out that the story deals harshly, even brutally, with the subject of the child and his relationship with both parents and teacher. Consequently it calls for an unusual maturity of response, and ought to be read several times in order that its full significance be appreciated.

1. When the hero says 'I had no youth' what precisely does he mean ? Think out your answer carefully.

2. The hero says that he refused to let Brother Angelo make it up with him because 'He was too useful to me the other way'. What does he mean by this ?

3. The teacher and his parents are obviously out for his good yet the hero resents what they do for him. Why ? Is his resentment justified ? Give your reasons.

4. The hero looking back feels no compunction for the way in which he treated Angelo. Do you think he ought ? Why ?

5. Does Nugent still actually hate Angelo ? Explain.

6. The narrator persists in believing that there is love and kindness in the actions of the hero towards his mother, but the hero ascribes much lower motives to himself. What are these motives ? Examine the story carefully to discover them. Examine for instance his last word, 'Kind! ' Then decide whether the hero or the author is right.

7. The hero is not sure whether it was all 'worth it'. What do you think ?

8. Why does the author choose the train journey to tell this story. In answering bear in mind Frank O'Connor's belief that the short story writer must choose 'some glowing centre of action from which the past and future will be equally visible.' (See Introduction p. 6.)

9. The author must get us interested in the man he meets on the train. The story is to be a revelation of this man's mind and history. Examine the first sentence and consider how much it tells us, or promises to tell. Consider the two following descriptive paragraphs and see how he builds up our curiosity. Why, for example, does he list five possible professions ? Why does he leave 'actor' for last ? Notice how gradually the author reveals feature after feature. In view of the entire story why is it all done so gradually ?

10. We begin and end with an external view of the man. Why ?

11. The man's memory is increasingly awakened and stimulated. How does the author indicate this ?

12. The author makes use of dialogue. Point out where you think the conversation is especially real and interesting, saying why you think so.

13. A good storyteller must have a sense of timing. Does Sean O'Faolain have this ? In answering consider when he chooses to reveal that the mother's remains are on the train. Had this fact been revealed at any other time would it have helped or hindered the story ?

Exercises

1. Assume that, contrary to Nugent's statement, Brother Angelo is still alive at the time of telling. Assume that the author goes to him in order to find out his side of the story. Write the dialogue that takes place between them : begin like this : 'I see that F. J. Nugent has made the Honours List. Isn't he one of your past pupils, Brother Angelo ?'

2. Have you ever been seriously hurt in your feelings by an adult— teacher, relative or parent ? If so, describe the occasion as accurately and vividly as you can.

3. Has the reverse ever happened ? Describe your feelings with equal accuracy.

4. 'You'd have slaved anyway. You were full of ambition.' Discuss Nugent's character as man and boy in the light of these remarks. In doing so answer both these questions, giving reasons : Would you have liked him as a boy ? Was he a happy man ?

5. For background reading on this story look up Chapter Seven of the author's autobiography, *Vive Moi*.

13

BROTHER BONIFACE

Brother Boniface sat in the sun. The sun shone full on the monastery wall, and brightened the gold coins of its ancient lichen. It fell full on the rough stone seat where Brother Boniface sat smiling. It fell through the leaves of the elm trees and littered the grass with its yellow petals. It splattered the green and white palings that shut off the kitchen garden from the blazing flower beds on the lawn.

There was no one to be seen out under the hot midday sun but Brother Boniface and the monastery cats. There were five cats. There was a great yellow fellow, stretching his long paws up the bark of an elm. He had green eyes. There was an old white cat sitting in the grass. He kept his eyes shut tight against the piercing sun rays. There were two fat cats abask on the stone seat, one each side of Brother Boniface. And there would have been a great peace over the sunny place had it not been for the fifth cat. The fifth cat was very young. She was pretty and slender and she ran among the grasses. Her fur was grey with markings of gold. Her eyes were amber-yellow. She ran at the waving grasses. She ran at the falling leaves. She caught at the flies in the air. She ran at the splatters of sunlight and pinned them against the palings with her paw. Brother Boniface watched her for a little while, but when he saw the other cats with their great eyes closing every few minutes, blinking and narrowing and closing, his own eyelids began to grow heavy and he fell into a little sleep.

Brother Boniface was sleeping lightly, with his chin in his cowl, when a cinnamon-coloured butterfly, with black and brown spots on its wings, flew unsteadily into the sunlight and went towards the blazing flowers. At once the young grey cat sprang after it, leaping lightly through the grass and springing after the butterfly into the very centre of the laden flower bed. Under her weight the flower stems snapped and broke. The fat cats opened their eyes. The white cat sat up. Brother Boniface jerked his head upwards and looked from right to left. When

he saw the bent stems of the lovely blossoms he rose up unsteadily
to his feet and clapped his hands together, and shuffled the gravel
with his sandalled feet and called out to the cat :

" Pussy ! Pussy ! Pussy ! Come out of that at once ! "

He waved his arms in distress.

" Pussy ! Pussy ! Pussy ! Come out of that at once ! "

The young cat started up with a pretty fright. She laid her
ears back against her sleek grey head and she arched her back
fantastically. She looked at Brother Boniface and forgot the
cinnamon butterfly, who fluttered away through the grass. She
looked at him while he waved his arms and soon she slackened
the arch of her body and pricked up her ears once more, and
then she leaped out of the flower plot and ran after a splatter of
sun petals ; capricious, giddy, but full of grace.

Brother Boniface stood in the sun for a while and watched
her as she went away, scrambling from shadow to shadow as
the trees moved lightly in the breeze. His warm brown habit
fell in heavy folds about him and seemed to tug at him with
their weight. When he was a young monk he used to think
that the folds of his sleeves and the folds of his cowl gave him
an added speed as he strode the corridors, in the way that the
sails of a ship speed it on before the wind, but at eighty he felt
a weariness in the weight of the brown wool, although, in places,
it was worn thin enough to be little more than a network of
woollen threads. When the young cat disappeared around the
bole of a tree, Brother Boniface went over and bent down to
examine the broken flowers. He picked up three that were
severed from their stems and he laid them gently on the grass
border. There would be three flowers less before the great marble
altar on the feast of Corpus Christi, and Brother Boniface was
saddened at the thought. He was looking forward to the great
feast day, when there would be a thousand candles blazing before
the Host and a thousand flowers as well. Even three blossoms
were a loss. He went back to his stone seat, moving slowly over the
smooth pebbles that made the pathway from the rectory to the
chapel.

The pebbles on this path were all very smooth and round.
They were smoothed over by the soles of a thousand sandalled
feet and every day they were carefully raked by Brother
Gardener. Brother Gardener had come to join the order exactly

ten years after Brother Boniface, and so Brother Boniface always looked upon him as a very young man, although Brother Gardener had been now fifty years in the garb of the order.

The day that Brother Gardener came up the driveway with a red carpet-bag in his hand, Brother Boniface was clipping the ivy on the chapel wall and the air was scented with the bitter green sap from its stems. The young man asked to see the Father Abbot, and Brother Boniface got down from the ladder and went around with him to the door of the Abbot's reception room. While they stood waiting for the Father Abbot to come out, they began to talk.

" You shouldn't cut ivy at this time of the year," said the young man, who had been a gardener in the world before he got the idea of entering a monastery.

Just as Brother Boniface was going to answer him the old Abbot, Brother Anselm—God be good to his soul—opened the door, and hearing the last sentence, joined in the conversation as if he had known the young man all his life.

" Will it grow again ? " he asked.

" Nothing will stop ivy from growing, once it has started," said the young man, " but it looks better if it's clipped before the new growth has started for the year."

" I'm glad to know that," said the Abbot. " Still, we can't leave it the way it is now." He looked at the wall where there was a great grey patch of clipped twigs, and another great patch of hanging leaves that fluttered in the wind. He turned back to the young man and glanced at his red carpet-bag, and looked him straight in the eye for a minute, and then he spoke again.

" Leave your bag in the hall, young man," he said, " and finish clipping that ivy. See that you cut it at the right time next year," he paused, " and the year after, and every year," he said, and he took the shears out of Brother Boniface's hand and gave them to the new man.

" You can help Brother Sacristan to clean the brasses," he said to Boniface. That was the kind of man he was, Brother Anselm, God be good to his soul. And Brother Boniface was very fond of him.

The new young man was given the name of Jennifer, but it wasn't very long till he was known as Brother Gardener, in the same way that Brother Boas was called Brother Sacristan, and

Brother Lambert was called Brother Vintner. But Brother Boniface always kept his own name because he never did anything well enough to be left at it for long. He was changed from one task to another. He cleaned the brasses and snuffed the candles. He sharpened the knives and he fed the chickens. He waxed the oak pews and he chopped pine logs for the fire. He peeled apples and turned the churn and in October every year he went out with a basket and picked the purple elderberries. Later he took the scum off the vats. He had a thousand tasks to do, and he loved doing them all. He helped with everything, and one day Father Abbot said that he should have been called Brother Jack, because he was Jack-of-all-trades.

But Father Abbot sent for Brother Boniface when he felt that his end had come, and although all the monks clustered round him, he wouldn't let anyone minister to him but Brother Boniface. It was Brother Boniface who wet his lips. It was Brother Boniface who held the crucifix up for him to kiss, and it was he who held the candle firm in the old man's hand when he finally freed his soul to God. And when the soul of the Abbot had fled its clay, the hands of the corpse and the hands of Brother Boniface were bound together by a twisted rope of wax that had knotted its way downward, drop by drop, from the candlewick to their clasped hands.

Every year when the ivy was cut, and its bitter scent freed upon the air, Brother Boniface thought of the past and he prayed for the old Abbot. There was very little time for thinking about the past, but it was still very vivid in Brother Boniface's mind. Memories stay greener where memories are few.

And as the old monk sat in the sun, basking in its warmth with the lovely indolent cats, he had the first hours of leisure that he ever had in his life, and he thought about the years that had fled. They had gone by swiftly one after another till it seemed now as if they had been but a flight of swallows coming out one after another from under the eaves of the barn.

The earliest thing that Brother Boniface could remember was standing between his father's knees in a big wagonette with yellow leather cushions as it rolled along a road in the middle of the night. He had been on a picnic with his father and his mother, but he could only remember the ride home in the dark.

The brake was rolling along the roads, under the rustling poplar trees. The songs of the picnic party volleyed through the valley. The horse-hooves rang on the road. He, Barney, had never been out so late before. His mother hadn't wanted to bring him. She thought it would be bad for him to stay up so late. But his father had insisted on taking him. He said that he could sleep in the brake coming home.

But the brake, going home, had been the real enchantment for Barney and was the only part of the picnic that he remembered clearly. The rest of the day was only a broken memory of sun and trestle tables and people laughing and swaying from side to side on benches. He remembered a tall man pouring out lemonade from foaming bottles, and he remembered a lady with a green feather in her hat who kept telling him to run away and play like a normal child. But he could remember every moment of the drive home, along the darkening roads through the valleys. He remembered looking down over the sides of the brake at the travelling road, and he remembered his mother pulling him by the sleeve.

" Look up, Barney Boy," she said. " It will make you sick to lean down over the sides like that." So he looked up, and when he did the wonder of the world came upon him for the first time. As his head jerked up he saw a shower of brilliant sparks riding down through the skies, riding straight towards them it seemed, and he screamed with fear and excitement, and everyone in the party glanced their way.

" Oh, look ! Look, Father," he shouted, as the gilt stars rode downwards towards him.

" Where ? " said his father, looking up in fright. " What do you see ? "

" Look," shouted Barney, and he pointed at the stars.

" Is it the stars you mean ? " said his father, laughing, and looking around at the rest of the party.

" Is that what you call them ? " said Barney. " Why are they up in the sky ? "

" They're always in the sky," said his father. " You often saw them before." He looked around uneasily, hoping that no one was listening.

" Were they there last night ? "

" I suppose they were."

" Why didn't I see them ? "

" You were in bed."

" Were they there Sunday night ? "

" They were. Now that's enough about them," said his father.

" When will I see them again ? " said Barney, and his father slapped his hand on his knee.

" It will be many a long day before you see them again, if I have my way," he said, turning around and laughing with the lady who wore the green feather in her hat ; and after that everyone began to laugh and they laughed for a long time, while the brake rolled along the road under the rustling poplar trees, and Barney stared upwards until his head began to reel.

After that every night he asked to be let stay up until the stars came out. But long before they rode out into the sky Barney was in bed, and although he tried hard to remain awake he was always asleep before the first of them rode forth. And so, in time, he forgot them. And when he went to school he learned, among other things, that it was silly to get excited about common things like stars and rainbows and whirls of wind, flowers and rain and drifts of snow. They were natural phenomena, the teacher said. And she spent two days teaching Barney how to spell the word phenomena, because Barney was backward at his books.

All the way along his school career, Barney was slow and it took him all his time to avoid being made the butt of the master's jokes. And only for one poor lad that was simple, he would have been always at the foot of his class. Of course, if he had had more time to look over his lessons he might have made more progress, but his father was a man who could not believe that any real work could be done sitting on a chair, and so Barney was more often helping in the shop than he was reading his books. His father kept him always on the move.

At nine o'clock he opened the shop, although no one ever came into it till long after ten. But between the time of taking down the lice-eaten shutters, and the entry of the first customer, there were a hundred things to be done. He had to sprinkle the floor with tea leaves to keep down the dust while he swept the floor. And often before he swept the floor he had to undo the twig of bound faggots and fasten them up tighter with a thong of leather.

One morning when he was sweeping out the dust into the gutter his father came out and saw that he had sprinkled tea leaves on the pavement as well. His father gave him a clout on the ear.

"Waste not, want not," his father said, and after that Barney had to be more attentive than ever.

Then sometimes there were large packing cases to be splintered open with a gimlet, and cups and saucers and statues and lamp globes to be taken out and counted, one by one, and the sticky tissue paper that wrapped them to be peeled off with a penknife. Then they had to be arranged on the shelves, and after that the sawdust had to be swept up, and the shavings picked out by hand from the cracks in the boards, and carried into the kitchen fire without letting any fall. There was something to be done every minute, and on a Fair Day there was so much to be done that he had to stay at home from school.

On the morning of a Fair Day Barney had to be up at four o'clock, and out in front of the shop with a big ash plant in his hand to beat off the cattle that came too near the windows. The night before a Fair Day there were beer barrels rolled out to the front of the shop windows and boards were nailed across them to make a barrier, and to protect the plate glass ; but all the same, Barney had to be there, because sometimes a beast was strong enough to break through the barrier and puck at the glass with his horns.

One terrible morning, when Barney stood with his stick in the dawn, a great red heifer gave a puck to the barrels and before Barney could raise his stick she had butted against the barrels with such force that the nails of the boards were lifted out and the boards rose up and crashed through the glass. That was the worst day in Barney's life. He stood in the grey street while his father roared at him and the drovers all came up and gaped at the hole in the window. The cattle themselves were excited and they butted one another, backward and forward, some of them slipping on the dirty street and falling, while the men yelled at them and kicked their rumps and caused such confusion that Barney couldn't even hear the curses that were hurled at him.

But later in the morning when his mother stroked his head, and begged him to stop crying, and promised to ask his father

to forgive him, Barney began to remember some of the things
that had been shouted at him, and it seemed to him that, more
than anything else his father had said, the thing that was the
most terrible was the question he kept shouting : " Where are
your eyes ? Where are your eyes ? Why weren't you looking at
what you were doing ? Where were your eyes ? Why didn't
you see the beast ? "

And Barney was frightened because he couldn't remember
looking at anything but the big red-chalked barrels, and the
dry dusty boards, and the great steaming nostrils of the cattle.
He had been looking at them all the time, and if he looked
away it could only have been for a minute when a wisp of scarlet
cloud floated out between the chimney of the barrack and the
spire of the church. The cloud had only floated there for a
moment, before it was blown out of sight, but it was such a strange
and beautiful colour that Barney had stared at it. And when he
cried with his head in his mother's lap it was not because he was
beaten, but because he began to feel faintly that there was something odd about himself, and that ordinary successful people,
people who were respected in the town, like his own father, would
never be foolish enough to stand with their hands down by them,
doing nothing, as he longed to do, for hours and hours, just staring
at the trees or the grasses or the stars or the rains.

But if Barney himself was beginning to notice his difference
from other young men of his age, his father was beginning to
notice it too, and if it bewildered Barney, it had a more positive
effect on his father. One night the merchant was coming back
from the station late at night, where he had been lading crates
of china, and he came upon Barney, who was leaning against the
yard gate staring up into the sky. There was nothing in the sky
but the usual display of gaudy stars and the tinsel moon, and
Barney's father was filled with rage against the stupidity of his
only son.

"Are you getting soft in the head, I wonder ? " he said as he
pushed past him and went into the yard, and Barney could
hear his voice through the kitchen window, as he told Barney's
mother : " That son of ours is abroad at the gate," he said,
" leaning up against the piers with his hands in his pockets and
staring up into the sky like a half-wit. Can he never find anything to do for himself without being driven ? "

" Leave him alone," said his mother. " You drive him too much as it is. You're always yelling at him, and sending him here and sending him there. He never gets a moment to rest his poor feet."

" He's not resting his feet out there, gaping up at the sky," said his father, and then Barney heard his heavy steps on the stairs, and he knew that his mother was alone. He looked around him once more at the strange splendour of the heavens, and he looked around at the dark town, where every window was shuttered and curtained and he shivered suddenly, partly because of the cold night air and partly because of the great loneliness that he felt in his heart when he thought of his difference from other men. Even from his own warm-hearted mother he felt a difference that made him dread going in to the lighted kitchen where she would be waiting for him. But he opened the door and went inside.

"Are you cold? Sit over here by the fire," his mother said, looking at him sharply, and pulling a hard chair across the tiles with a clattering sound that jarred his nerves.

" What were you doing out there in the dark by yourself? " she said.

" Nothing," said Barney, and he felt her glance upon him although he was staring into the flames.

" People will think you're daft if you stand about like that gaping at the stars," she said, and he felt that there was a questioning tone in her voice, and that she was asking for an explanation rather than giving advice. He knew that the slightest explanation would have won her over to be his champion, but the feelings that drove him out into the starlight were too vague to be expressed even in thought, much less in speech. They remained mere feelings, drawing him out of doors, drawing him into silent places, drawing him away from his fellows.

His mother put her hands on her hips. She felt rebuffed.

" It's true for your father," she said. " You must be getting soft in the head. I don't know what kind of a person you are at all. But I know one thing ! The devil makes work for idle hands to do ! That's an old saying and it's a true one." She picked up a candle and went out into the hall with her head held high and her lips pursed together with annoyance, but as she went upstairs she leaned down over the banisters and watched him for a few minutes where he sat by the fire. He knew she was watching him, and his perplexity deepened and darkened his soul. He wanted to please his parents, but every hour that passed was bringing him a surer knowledge that their way of life was small and mean and that there must be a way of life that would leave time for glorying in the loveliness of field and flower and in the blazonry of stars.

After the night that his father found him gazing into vacancy, Barney was given more to do than ever he had been given before, and even at evening time, when the shop-boys were gone off to the ball-alley to play handball, or off with their girls to walk on the old town ramparts, Barney was often sent out into the country on his bicycle to deliver some parcel that might easily have been delivered the next day. They were determined to keep him from idling. They were determined to keep him moving.

But although for a long time there seems to be something vague and indecisive about our destiny, after a certain point has been reached it is often clear not only that there was a con-tinuous progress, but that events which seemed at first to impede are later seen to have facilitated it. So, riding along the country roads on messages that were intended to keep him from strange dreaming, at every new delight of nature along the way he was forced to wonder more and more how it was that all the men he knew spent their leisure hours as drearily as their working hours, and only exchanged the stuffiness of the storehouse for the stuffiness of the billiard room.

At first when he went into the country lanes Barney was little better than a city man, exclaiming at the blatant beauties that paraded more brazenly in the hedgerows, the powdery haw-thorn and the rambling honeysuckle. But after a time he grew in knowledge of the secrets and subtleties of nature, and he passed by the blossoming trees almost heedlessly and went into the deeps of the fields to seek out the secret scents that are released from the grass when the heavy cattle tread it down. And it was in the very depths of a pasture at evening, with the heavy cattle standing idle beside him in the clover, that he vowed to evade the way of life that had been destined for him by his father and his mother.

At first his pale rebellious dreams merely freed him from the dread of spending his life behind the dusty counters of the shop ; but he soon realised that he must choose an alternative way of earning his bread, and he set out to choose the one that would allow him to appreciate the qualities of the earth. From then on he began to wander around the town and take an interest, for the first time, in the rest of the townspeople. He spent many stolen hours walking around the town, in such apparent search for something that people came out into the road, after he had turned the corner, and furtively shuffled a foot in the gutter in the hope of some anonymous gain. But Barney was only looking for an idea. He stood at the great dark doorway of the smithy and watched the sparks threading up the flue. He stood at the door of the livery stable in the east side of the town and watched the horses with their trembling withers, while they were groomed and soothed by the stable-boys. There were strange dappled roans, strawberry and grey, and there were bays and chestnuts that were dappled with their own sweat. He watched the farmers bringing home the goodlihead of golden grain. He watched at the doors of shops that were bigger than his father's, and the only real difference that he could see between them was that the big shops were noisier than his father's and had more spits on the floor.

One evening, just before the last of the light went out of the sky, Barney saw a man sowing seeds in the last few furrows of his field. The picture that he made against the darkening skies of evening was one that startled Barney and made him think for a moment that he had found the beautiful life at last. But as he came nearer he saw that although the tall man made a picture of great grandeur as he stood out against the skies with his raised arm flinging the unseen seed, he himself was unaware of the grandeur of the scene, because he never lifted his eyes higher than the hand he swung in the air, tossing the grain, before he groped in his bag for another fistful. And realising this, Barney stepped back from the top of the ditch where he had been standing in a trance, and went away in sadness.

His sadness deepened as he walked along the road ; for it seemed to him that whether you cobbled or whether you hammered, whether you measured up rice in a scales or whether you led a young colt round and round in a training ring, or whether you opened or closed your hand to let fall a shower of seeds, you had to keep your eyes upon what you were doing, and soon you forgot that there was a sky over you and grass under your feet, and that flowers blew for your delight and birds sang in the bushes all day long.

At last Barney settled down to follow the life his father had planned for him, and he let his mother buy him a yellow canvas coat to keep his trousers clean when he would be weighing out whiting or weed-killer that might put dust on his clothes. And everyone said that he was shaping out much better than they would have expected. The canvas coat kept the dust from getting on Barney's trousers ; but there was dust getting into his mind, and soon he would have been using half a sheet of paper instead of a whole sheet, and weighing the whiting in the bag to make weight, and it is probable that in no time at all he would have been taking down the shutters from the windows five minutes before eight in the hope of catching another penny. Just before he had relinquished the last shreds of his dream, however, a message came down from the Abbot of the monastery that was situated outside the town, to know if the monks could be supplied with a gallon of colza oil three times a week.

"There's no need for you to go with it, Barney," said his father, " I'll send one of the boys "—because he was anxious not to impose too much on Barney at the moment when he was beginning to show some taste for money-making.

" I think I should go myself," said Barney. " I might arrange to supply them with candles as well."

His father took the yellow coat out of his hand.

" I'll hang that up for you, my boy," he said, and he saved Barney two or three steps across the shop, calling back as he hung up the coat on a nail behind the door, " Take your tea before you go. It's a long push on a bicycle out to that monastery, and as well as I remember there's a rise on the road most of the way."

There was a rise on the road, and Barney was so tired by the time he reached the monastery gate that he left the bicycle at the gate lodge and began to walk up the avenue. The night was coming down gently between the dark yews and cypress trees, and a scent of flowers rose from some hidden place behind the walls. But Barney's mind was filled with thoughts of the interview with the monks, and he was planning what he would say to the monk who would open the door.

It was an old monk who came to the door, and he seemed to be deaf. He took the can from Barney and he looked out past him through the open door, and then he pointed to a hard oak seat in the hall, and told him to wait for the can. He went away down a corridor and left Barney sitting all alone in the bare hallway with the yellow waxed floor, and he felt very young all of a sudden. He began to look around him. There were high-pointed windows, and through them he saw the high pointed stars, and they reminded him of something far away and indistinct in his childhood but he could not know what it was exactly. It was something sad and beautiful, and it was something that he had lost a long time ago. And he began to wonder why it was that the memory came back to him now ; and then he noticed that the windows were without any curtains, and his thoughts raced away on another speculation ; and it seemed to him suddenly that of all the silly things in the world the silliest was hanging heavy curtains across the windows to blot out the glory of the night with its sky and its moon and its welter of stars.

The old man came back with the empty oil-can. Barney took it silently and went out into the dark. There was no sound but the closing of the door, and he thought of all the foolish words that another man would have wasted upon the simple transaction. He is a wise old man, Barney thought, and he wondered about him as he went down the driveway.

Half-way down the avenue there was a great sycamore tree, and when Barney had nearly passed by it he saw that under its great shade of leaves there was a young monk standing ; and there was such a strange stillness in his standing figure that Barney turned around when he had gone a few paces farther and looked back at him. His face was turned upwards to the stars, and his hands were lifted in adoration of their Creator. Barney tilted up his head too, and it was all that he could do to keep himself from falling upon his knees.

All that night and all next day he thought about the young man with his face tilted to the stars, and at the end of the second night he knew that his own eyes had been blinded for ever to the gross glare of tawdry coins and the gaudy pattern of bank notes. The only change that others could see in him was that his yellow overall was getting a bit short in the sleeves.

One night soon afterwards Barney's father was wakened in
the night, and he thought that he heard rats down below in
the shop. He came down in his nightshirt with a spluttering
candle stuck in a bottleneck. The counters were piled with
carefully weighed bags of whiting and weed-killer, red lead,
tacks, and grass seed.   There was enough weighed out to last
all winter, and when his father asked Barney why he had weighed
out so much he was almost relieved at hearing the answer,
because he had thought, when he first looked around at the laden
counters, that his son's sudden interest in business had sent him
out of his mind.

Next evening Barney took an old fibre suitcase belonging to his
mother, put a few things in it, and tied it to the back of the
bicycle.

" I'll send one of the boys up to bring back the bicycle."

" You can take back the case too," said Barney. " I won't
need it after to-day."

His mother wiped her eyes on the corner of the tea cloth that
she held in her hand.

"Are you sure you'll be contented, Barney, inside those big
walls ? "

" Remember there's only seven acres, all told, timber and
pasture, inside those walls," said his father. " It's a small place
to pass the whole of your days."

But Barney had a vision before his mind of the great starry
expanse of sky over the walled garden, and he thought of the
shivering elms, and the deep grasses where the wind raced ; and
it seemed that the monastery garden was as wide and spacious
as the world because there men had time to meditate and dwell
on the beauties the Lord had laid open to their eyes.

The evening that he arrived he found out that the monastery
itself was as big as a city, and that it took five or ten minutes
to go from one end of it to another, and that three lengths of
the corridor were equal to half a mile. He was shown over the
whole place by a young lay brother recently joined himself,
and when they came back to the place where they had started
out from, the arches of his instep were aching and he could
hardly believe that it was nine o'clock.

Nine o'clock would have seemed a ridiculous hour to retire
at, but Barney was so tired, and his feet ached so much he was

glad to lie down. He meant to get up later in the evening and
look out of the thin pointed windows of his cell, at the dark
garden where the birds defied the silence with their song.

In the middle of the night Barney sat up in bed when there
was a knocking on the door, and he sprang to the floor when
he saw the light of a licking flame through the great windy
cracks in the door. He dashed to the door and he opened it
wide, to rush out; but a dash of holy water, chill and sudden,
cooled his fright, and he saw that the flame was from a candle
in the lay brother's hand.

Dominus vobiscum . . .

The young Brother Boniface joined the thronging feet that
went down the stone steps to the chapel; and the knocking of
the wooden rosary beads, and the sliding of the sandals from
step to step, and the jostling movement of the heavy worsted
habits made him forget that it was night and gave every appearance of daytime.

When the real daytime came at last and the birds began to
fly out from under the chapel eaves, Brother Boniface was set the
task that always fell to the latest member of the order, and
that was peeling potatoes. It took a lot of potatoes to feed seventy-
two monks, specially when they didn't eat meat with them.
But it didn't take long to eat them. Brother Boniface was used
to eating quickly, and so he would have been finished as soon as
anyone, but he was so interested in the gospel story that the
Brother Lector was reading during the meal that he had to
hurry at the end in order not to be last.

There was community prayer after the midday meal, and
after that there was recreation, but on that particular day
there was an important visitor coming to see the monastery,
and the Abbot wanted all the community to be present in the
hall to receive her. She didn't arrive at the time she had arranged.
In fact she came so late that they had only seventeen minutes
for supper; and they had a great rush to make up the time,
and clear away the meal and lay the table for breakfast, before
the great bell rang out the hour of evening prayers. And that
night an old monk died. He had lingered longer than anyone
could have imagined, and even at the end his soul lingered
among the candle flames and candle shadows while the monks
knelt around him in prayer. Boniface had never seen anyone

dying before. Death made a great impression on him. That night he had a few minutes of freedom and he went out into the cool garden that was dampened with rain, but afterwards when he tried to remember whether the stars had come out or not, and whether the birds had been singing or not, he could not remember anything about the time he had been in the garden. He had been thinking of death, and the shadows it cast upon life.

There was a very wet week after that, and during wet weather there were a great many things to be done indoors. Corridors were waxed and passageways were distempered, and the benches and pews were carefully examined to see that they were free from wood-lice. But on the evening of the seventh day there was a bright starry sky and Brother Boniface went out for a few minutes. He walked away to the right a few paces and then he saw that he was getting near the sycamore tree that stood by the gate. He remembered the young monk he had seen standing under it with his head tilted to the stars that pricked the dark greenery with their thin light. The monk was there. Brother Boniface had not yet made his acquaintance. He stepped into the damp grass and went across to the tree. But as he drew near he saw that the young monk's eyes were closed and that his lips were moving. And Boniface knew that he was saying his office, and not looking at the stars at all. And he remembered that he himself had not said his office yet, and he raised his eyes to heaven and began to say it, where he stood, under the sycamore tree, in the damp evening grasses, with the stars blazing brightly above all. But he soon found that he could not pray with open eyes. The stars distracted him too much. He closed his eyes, and when he opened them again the curfew bell was ringing and the sky was overcast.

The year went flashing by, and Boniface did not feel it passing. When his father came up the avenue to see him he was often hoeing in a field and did not see him, so intent was he on his work. And when his father called out his name—" Barney ! Barney ! "—the other monks had to pluck him by the sleeve and tell him that someone was calling him, because Brother Boniface had almost forgotten that he had once answered to the name of Barney.

Life went flashing by the monastery, leaves and petals were

blown past the uncurtained windows, trees tossed in the wind, and webs of rain were spun across the glass. The skies shook out their gay confetti of stars. Brother Boniface stepped into his sandals some twenty thousand mornings, and the days slipped by so fast that one fine morning he was eighty years old.

On the morning that Brother Boniface was eighty he was coming out of the bakehouse with a trough of dough that he had kneaded for Brother Breadmaker, and he met the monastery doctor in the middle of the courtyard.

" Good morning, Brother Boniface. You get younger every day," said the young doctor, looking at him closely and watching after him when he went on his way. The doctor turned his feet and went back to the Abbot's room.

" I met Brother Boniface in the yard," he said, to the young monk who was Abbot, and who was a personal friend of his, " and I didn't like the way the veins on his forehead were swollen. He was carrying a heavy tray of dough. He does too much for a man of his age."

" He loves work," said the Abbot.

" That is the kind of person who needs rest most. He must be forced to take life easier."

" I will see that he is released from some of his duties," said the Abbot.

" That is not enough," said the doctor. " He must be freed from all of his duties. He must sit out there in the sun, and remain as quiet as possible."

" Poor Boniface," said the young men, both together, as they stood at the low casement window of the Abbot's room and looked out at Brother Boniface, who was going across the grass with a saucer of milk, followed by five cats who ran in front of him and circled around him and lifted themselves up on their hind legs to caress him with the back of their necks.

" You can't call that hard work ? " said the Abbot.

"Any work that never ceases is hard work," said the doctor. " I'll send him out to-morrow morning to sit in the sun and I won't let him inside the door till night-time, except for his meals and prayers."

Brother Boniface took the sun like the monastery cats. He sat on the sunny seat, and smoothed down the folds of his warm brown habit. He smiled and he followed the ballet of the butterflies. The cats sometimes slit open their lazy eyes and gazed into the grass, where glossy jet insects ran up the green blades and bent them with their weight.

Brother Boniface sat in the sun and thanked the Lord that he had been led into the shade of life so safely. And he began to wonder how he had merited such happy anchorage. He tried to remember what it was that had first turned his mind to the cloister. He remembered the shop where he scattered tea leaves to keep down the dust. He remembered that he wore a yellow coat and that it got too short in the sleeves. He remembered stealing into the centres of the fields and breathing the fragrance of the trodden grass. He remembered riding in a black and yellow brake, under rustling poplar trees, while voices volleyed in the valley and the stars showered down through the sky. But for a long time he could not remember why he had left his home and come to the cloister. Then suddenly he slapped his hand on his knee and he laughed so loud the cats sprang up and arched their backs. When they saw they had nothing to fear they relaxed again, but they walked away to a more quiet place with disdainful hips and fastidious paws.

Brother Boniface continued to laugh, in short indolent chuckles. He realised that he had entered the monastery in order to have more time to meditate upon the glories of the earth, and that his life had circled round, from matin to lauds, from daylight to starlight, with greater speed than it could possibly have sped by in the world. It had gone by so fast that he could hardly tell what colour the trees were and whether the stars were blue or green. And he looked up and kept looking up till his eyes ached from the brilliance of the blue sky, because he was filled with joy to think that now, at the end of his days, having earned his leisure honestly, he would at last be able to spend long hours in appreciation. He stared upwards again. The leaves of the elms spread out wide over him till he fancied the sky was green. Just then there was the sound of a snapping stem and Brother Boniface looked down. The grey cat sprang out of the flower bed when she saw him move, but a great yellow dahlia lay broken on the grass. Brother Boniface clapped his hands at the cat and went over to the flowers, but at the same time there was a light step on the gravel and the young Abbot came down the path with an agile gait and flowing sleeves and a cowl that filled up with wind as he walked and gave him the weighty appearance of an elderly man, although he was the youngest Abbot that had ever been chosen.

" Good morning, Brother Boniface," he said, as he stooped and lifted up the broken dahlia. " What will we do with those cats ? The feast of Corpus Christi is only a few days away and we must have every single flower we can get. I wish we could dispense with the cats, but there are unfortunately too many mice for that. Did you hear them behind the wainscoting in the chapel this morning ? " He bent and examined the stems of one or two blossoms that seemed a little lopsided.

" What will we do ? " he said, and he straightened up and looked around the garden thoughtfully. Then he snapped his fingers. " I know what we'll do," he said, and he ran across the grass to the low casement window of the refectory, and he brushed aside the strands of ivy and opened the window.

" Brother Almoner ! " he called out, in a clear gay voice. " Hand me out a paper bag."

Brother Almoner could be heard shuffling around on the tiles, and pulling out drawers and opening cupboards, and then he came to the window and handed out a stiff tinfoil tea-bag, open at the mouth.

The young Abbot came striding back across the grass, and when he reached the gravel path where the stone seat was set he bent down and gathered up a handful of pebbles. He threw them into the tinfoil tea-bag and nimbly bent to gather up another handful, and another. Then, when the bag was filled to the top with smooth grey pebbles, he set it down on the rough stone seat beside Brother Boniface. " Here is a little job for you, Brother," he said. " You can do it without standing up, without moving an inch. Every time you see the cats going near the flowers, all you have to do is take up a little pebble and throw it at them to frighten them away. We must have a gorgeous blaze of flowers on the altar for Corpus Christi. Isn't that right ? "

Brother Boniface took up the tea-bag full of stones.

" I'll keep it in my lap," he said.

" I'm delighted that we have you out here," said the Abbot. " Now I need not worry about the flowers. I know I can depend on you, Brother Boniface," he said, and he strode away again.

Brother Boniface sat in the sun. The Abbot's footsteps died away. There was no sound in Brother Boniface's ears but the bells of silence ringing. A brilliant red insect crawled up a blade of grass. The blade bent. Boniface watched him. The blade was weighted down till the insect was almost on a level with the ground. He put out a feeler and caught at another blade of grass that was short and stiff and seemed to stab the air, it went up so straight. The insect began to crawl upwards. The blade began to bend. Boniface bent down. He wondered where the insect was heading for that he took such a dangerous and devious path. And he felt the full luxury of indolence in realising the triviality of his occupation. He was excited. He clasped his hands and bent closer to the grass.

Just then there was a sound of dry stems snapping, and Brother Boniface looked up in dismay. The young grey cat was in among the blossoms once more. The blossoms were breaking and falling to the gound. Three white butterflies flew among the leaves and the young cat sprang at each of them in turn.

" Pussy ! Pussy ! Pussy ! " shouted Brother Boniface.

" Pussy ! Pussy ! Pussy ! Come out of that at once ! " And he groped for a pebble in his tinfoil bag, and stamped his feet at the grey and gold cat.

" Pussy ! Pussy ! Pussy ! Come out of that at once ! "

And years and years after, when Brother Boniface was laid away in the close and secretive clay, the young monks who entered the monastery were told about his industry. They were told that he was never, never idle for a moment. They were very impressed, and they strove to follow his example. And they in turn told younger men when they themselves were old. And the part of the story that the old monks liked best to tell, and the young monks liked best to hear, was about the last days of Brother Boniface, when he was so old he couldn't even hear the bells for silence in his ears. Because then he was busiest of all. Day long, and day long, his voice could be heard, as he guarded the flowers for the feast of Corpus Christi by keeping the cats from breaking their stems.

" Pussy ! Pussy ! Pussy ! Come out of that at once ! "

— Tales from Bective Bridge

Glossary

brake—wagonette.

blazonry—literally means the painted devices on shields, banners and coats of arms. Here used metaphorically to describe the splendour of the heavens.

goodlihead—excellence.

Explorations

1. 'It's true for your father,' she said. 'You must be getting soft in the head.' Is this comment by his mother justified? Is it understandable?

2. What sort of people are Barney's parents? Are they cruel? Are they stupid? What means does the author use to let us know the sort of people they are?

3. Why does the author give Barney this sort of parents?

4. In what way does Barney change and in what way does he remain the same?

5. What does Barney learn from the man putting in the seed, the monk who took the can from him, the monk standing under the tree?

6. There is an important scene early in the story where the boy fails to keep cattle from his father's window and another at the end where he fails to keep cats off the flower-bed. In what way are these incidents alike? In what way are they different? Try to account for the difference, remembering that there is a lifetime between them.

7. There are frequent and very beautiful descriptions of natural things in the story. Why are these so plentiful? Examine a few of them carefully and try to decide why the author put them there and what they do to advance the action.

8. How do the stars appear to Barney's father? What do the words used tell us about the kind of man he is? How do the banknotes appear to Barney? Is there any similarity? What is the writer trying to tell us in passages like these? Can you find other examples of the same thing?

9. The author rarely describes a detail merely for its own sake. For instance when Barney finds himself in the monastery hall he notices a difference—there are no curtains on the windows. This is what is called a 'significant detail'. Can you find three other examples of the same thing? Having found them try to suggest what they contribute to the story.

10. What is Barney looking for when he decides to enter the monastery ? What does he find there ? Is this what he had expected to find ?

Exercises

1. Do you understand Barney's attitude towards nature ? If any aspect of nature affects you similarly write about it in a few careful paragraphs.

2. Brother Boniface is a man who was exceptionally good, almost by nature. Have you known anyone like that ? If so, describe him or her, using, if possible, a few significant examples of his behaviour.

3. When the father comes home from one of his visits to the monastery he probably discusses it with his wife. Write one of these conversations, taking in the question of the vocation, the shop, and their own feelings about their son.

14

THE STORY OF THE WIDOW'S SON

This is the story of a widow's son, but it is a story that has two endings.

There was once a widow, living in a small neglected village at the foot of a steep hill. She had only one son, but he was the meaning of her life. She lived for his sake. She wore herself out working for him. Every day she made a hundred sacrifices in order to keep him at a good school in the town, four miles away, because there was a better teacher there than the village dullard that had taught herself.

She made great plans for Packy, but she did not tell him about her plans. Instead she threatened him, day and night, that if he didn't turn out well, she would put him to work on the roads, or in the quarry under the hill.

But as the years went by, everyone in the village, and even Packy himself, could tell by the way she watched him out of sight in the morning, and watched to see him come into sight in the evening, that he was the beat of her heart, and that her gruff words were only a cover for her pride and her joy in him.

It was for Packy's sake that she walked for hours along the road, letting her cow graze the long acre of the wayside grass, in order to spare the few poor blades that pushed up through the stones in her own field. It was for his sake she walked back and forth to the town to sell a few cabbages as soon as ever they were fit. It was for his sake that she got up in the cold dawning hours to gather mushrooms that would take the place of foods that had to be bought with money. She bent her back daily to make every penny she could, and as often happens, she made more by industry, out of her few bald acres, than many of the farmers around her made out of their great bearded meadows. Out of the money she made by selling eggs alone, she paid for Packy's clothes and for the great number of his books.

When Packy was fourteen, he was in the last class in the school, and the master had great hopes of his winning a scholarship to a big college in the city. He was getting to be a tall lad, and his features were beginning to take a strong cast. His character was strengthening too, under his mother's sharp tongue. The people of the village were beginning to give him the same respect they gave to the sons of the farmers who came from their fine colleges in the summer, with blue suits and bright ties. And whenever they spoke to the widow they praised him up to the skies.

One day in June, when the air was so heavy the scent that rose up from the grass was imprisoned under the low clouds and hung in the air, the widow was waiting at the gate for Packy. There had been no rain for some days and the hens and chickens were pecking irritably at the dry ground and wandering up and down the road in bewilderment.

A neighbour passed.

" Waiting for Packy ? " said the neighbour, pleasantly, and he stood for a minute to take off his hat and wipe the sweat of the day from his face. He was an old man.

" It's a hot day ! " he said. " It will be a hard push for Packy on that battered old bike of his. I wouldn't like to have to face into four miles on a day like this ! "

" Packy would travel three times that distance if there was a book at the other end of the road ! " said the widow, with the pride of those who cannot read more than a line or two without wearying.

The minutes went by slowly. The widow kept looking up at the sun.

" I suppose the heat is better than the rain ! " she said, at last.

" The heat can do a lot of harm, too, though," said the neighbour, absent-mindedly, as he pulled a long blade of grass from between the stones of the wall and began to chew the end of it. " You could get sunstroke on a day like this ! " He looked up at the sun. " The sun is a terror," he said. " It could cause you to drop down dead like a stone ! "

The widow strained out further over the gate. She looked up the hill in the direction of the town.

" He will have a good cool breeze on his face coming down the hill, at any rate," she said.

The man looked up the hill. " That's true. On the hottest day of the year you would get a cool breeze coming down that hill on a bicycle. You would feel the air streaming past your cheeks like silk. And in the winter it's like two knives flashing to either side of you, and peeling off your skin like you'd peel the bark off a sally-rod." He chewed the grass meditatively. "That must be one of the steepest hills in Ireland," he said. "That hill is a hill worthy of the name of a hill." He took the grass out of his mouth. "It's my belief," he said, earnestly, looking at the widow—"it's my belief that that hill is to be found marked with a name in the Ordnance Survey map!"

"If that's the case," said the widow, "Packy will be able to tell you all about it. When it isn't a book he has in his hand it's a map."

"Is that so?" said the man. "That's interesting. A map is a great thing. A map is not an ordinary thing. It isn't everyone can make out a map."

The widow wasn't listening.

"I think I see Packy!" she said, and she opened the wooden gate and stepped out into the roadway.

At the top of the hill there was a glitter of spokes as a bicycle came into sight. Then there was a flash of blue jersey as Packy came flying downward, gripping the handlebars of the bike, with his bright hair blown back from his forehead. The hill was so steep, and he came down so fast, that it seemed to the man and woman at the bottom of the hill that he was not moving at all, but that it was the bright trees and bushes, the bright ditches and wayside grasses that were streaming away to either side of him.

The hens and chickens clucked and squawked and ran along the road looking for a safe place in the ditches. They ran to either side with feminine fuss and chatter. Packy waved to his mother. He came nearer and nearer. They could see the freckles on his face.

"Shoo!" cried Packy, at the squawking hens that had not yet left the roadway. They ran with their long necks straining forward.

"Shoo!" said Packy's mother, lifting her apron and flapping it in the air to frighten them out of his way.

It was only afterwards, when the harm was done, that the widow began to think that it might, perhaps, have been the flapping of her own apron that frightened the old clucking

hen, and sent her flying out over the garden wall into the middle
of the road.

The old hen appeared suddenly on top of the grassy ditch
and looked with a distraught eye at the hens and chickens as
they ran to right and left. Her own feathers began to stand out
from her. She craned her neck forward and gave a distracted
squawk, and fluttered down into the middle of the hot dusty road.

Packy jammed on the brakes. The widow screamed. There
was a flurry of white feathers and a spurt of blood. The bicycle
swerved and fell. Packy was thrown over the handlebars.

It was such a simple accident that, although the widow
screamed, and although the old man looked around to see if
there was help near, neither of them thought that Packy was very
badly hurt, but when they ran over and lifted his head, and saw
that he could not speak, they wiped the blood from his face and
looked around, desperately, to measure the distance they would
have to carry him.

It was only a few yards to the door of the cottage, but Packy
was dead before they got him across the threshold.

" He's only in a weakness ! " screamed the widow, and she
urged the crowd that had gathered outside the door to do something for him. " Get a doctor ! " she cried, pushing a young
labourer towards the door. " Hurry ! Hurry ! The doctor will
bring him around."

But the neighbours that kept coming in the door, quickly,
from all sides, were crossing themselves, one after another, and
falling on their knees, as soon as they laid eyes on the boy,
stretched out flat on the bed, with the dust and dirt and the sweat
marks of life on his dead face.

When at last the widow was convinced that her son was
dead, the other women had to hold her down. She waved
her arms and cried out aloud, and wrestled to get free. She
wanted to wring the neck of every hen in the yard.

" I'll kill every one of them. What good are they to me,
now ? All the hens in the world aren't worth one drop of human
blood. That old clucking hen wasn't worth more than six shillings,
at the very most. What is six shillings ? Is it worth poor Packy's
life ? "

But after a time she stopped raving, and looked from one
face to another.

" Why didn't he ride over the old hen ? " she asked. " Why did he try to save an old hen that wasn't worth more than six shillings ? Didn't he know he was worth more to his mother than an old hen that would be going into the pot one of these days ? Why did he do it ? Why did he put on the brakes going down one of the worst hills in the country ? Why ? Why ? "

The neighbours patted her arm.

" There now ! " they said. " There now ! " and that was all they could think of saying, and they said it over and over again. " There now ! There now ! "

And years afterwards, whenever the widow spoke of her son Packy to the neighbours who dropped in to keep her company for an hour or two, she always had the same question to ask ; the same tireless question.

" Why did he put the price of an old clucking hen above the price of his own life ? "

And the people always gave the same answer.

" There now ! " they said. " There now ! " And they sat as silently as the widow herself, looking into the fire.

But surely some of those neighbours must have been stirred to wonder what would have happened had Packy not yielded to his impulse of fear, and had, instead, ridden boldly over the old clucking hen ? And surely some of them must have stared into the flames and pictured the scene of the accident again, altering a detail here and there as they did so, and giving the story a different end. For these people knew the widow, and they knew Packy, and when you know people well it is as easy to guess what they would say and do in certain circumstances as it is to remember what they actually did say and do in other circumstances. In fact it is sometimes easier to invent than to remember accurately, and were this not so two great branches of creative art would wither in an hour : the art of the story-teller and the art of the gossip. So, perhaps, if I try to tell you what I myself think might have happened had Packy killed that cackling old hen, you will not accuse me of abusing my privileges as a writer. After all, what I am about to tell you is no more of a fiction than what I have already told, and I lean no heavier now upon your credulity than, with your full consent, I did in the first instance.

And moreover, in many respects the new story is the same as the old.

It begins in the same way, too. There is the widow grazing
her cow by the wayside, and walking the long roads to the town,
weighed down with sacks of cabbages that will pay for Packy's
schooling. There she is, fussing over Packy in the mornings in
case he would be late for school. There she is in the evening
watching the battered clock on the dresser for the hour when he
will appear on the top of the hill at his return. And there too, on
a hot day in June, is the old labouring man coming up the road,
and pausing to talk to her, as she stood at the door. There he is
dragging a blade of grass from between the stones of the wall, and
putting it between his teeth to chew, before he opens his mouth.

And when he opens his mouth at last it is to utter the same
remark.

" Waiting for Packy ? " said the old man, and then he took
off his hat and wiped the sweat from his forehead. It will be
remembered that he was an old man. " It's a hot day," he said.

" It's very hot," said the widow, looking anxiously up the hill.
" It's a hot day to push a bicycle four miles along a bad road
with the dust rising to choke you, and sun striking spikes off the
handlebars."

" The heat is better than the rain, all the same," said the
old man.

" I suppose it is," said the widow. "All the same, there were
days when Packy came home with the rain dried into his clothes
so bad they stood up stiff like boards when he took them off.
They stood up stiff like boards against the wall, for all the world
as if he was still standing in them ! "

" Is that so ? " said the old man. " You may be sure he got a
good petting on those days. There is no son like a widow's son.
A ewe lamb ! "

" Is it Packy ? " said the widow, in disgust. " Packy never
got a day's petting since the day he was born. I made up my
mind from the first that I'd never make a soft one out of him."

The widow looked up the hill again, and set herself to raking
the gravel outside the gate as if she were in the road for no other
purpose. Then she gave another look up the hill.

" Here he is now ! " she said, and she raised such a cloud
of dust with the rake that they could hardly see the glitter of
the bicycle spokes, and the flash of blue jersey as Packy came
down the hill at a breakneck speed.

Nearer and nearer he came, faster and faster, waving his hand to the widow, shouting at the hens to leave the way !

The hens ran for the ditches, stretching their necks in gawky terror. And then, as the last hen squawked into the ditch, the way was clear for a moment before the whirling silver spokes.

Then, unexpectedly, up from nowhere it seemed, came an old clucking hen and, clucking despairingly, it stood for a moment on the top of the wall and then rose into the air with the clumsy flight of a ground fowl.

Packy stopped whistling. The widow screamed. Packy yelled and the widow flapped her apron. Then Packy swerved the bicycle, and a cloud of dust rose from the braked wheel.

For a minute it could not be seen what exactly had happened, but Packy put his foot down and dragged it along the ground in the dust till he brought the bicycle to a sharp stop. He threw the bicycle down with a clatter on the hard road and ran back. The widow could not bear to look. She threw her apron over her head.

" He's killed the clucking hen ! " she said. " He's killed her ! He's killed her ! " and then she let the apron fall back into place, and began to run up the hill herself. The old man spat out the blade of grass that he had been chewing and ran after the woman.

" Did you kill it ? " screamed the widow, and as she got near enough to see the blood and feathers she raised her arm over her head, and her fist was clenched till the knuckles shone white. Packy cowered down over the carcass of the fowl and hunched up his shoulders as if to shield himself from a blow. His legs were spattered with blood, and the brown and white feathers of the dead hen were stuck to his hands, and stuck to his clothes, and they were strewn all over the road. Some of the short white inner feathers were still swirling with the dust in the air.

" I couldn't help it, Mother. I couldn't help it. I didn't see her till it was too late ! "

The widow caught up the hen and examined it all over, holding it by the bone of the breast, and letting the long neck dangle. Then, catching it by the leg, she raised it suddenly above her head, and brought down the bleeding body on the boy's back, in blow after blow, spattering the blood all over his face and his hands, over his clothes and over the white dust of the road around him.

" How dare you lie to me ! " she screamed, gaspingly, between the blows. " You saw the hen. I know you saw it. You stopped whistling ! You called out ! We were watching you. We saw." She turned upon the old man. " Isn't that right ? " she demanded. " He saw the hen, didn't he ? He saw it ? "

" It looked that way," said the old man, uncertainly, his eye on the dangling fowl in the widow's hand.

" There you are ! " said the widow. She threw the hen down on the road. " You saw the hen in front of you on the road, as plain as you see it now," she accused, " but you wouldn't stop to save it because you were in too big a hurry home to fill your belly ! Isn't that so ? "

" No, Mother. No ! I saw her all right but it was too late to do anything."

" He admits now that he saw it," said the widow, turning and nodding triumphantly at the onlookers who had gathered at the sound of the shouting.

" I never denied seeing it ! " said the boy, appealing to the onlookers as to his judges.

" He doesn't deny it ! " screamed the widow. " He stands there as brazen as you like, and admits for all the world to hear that he saw the hen as plain as the nose on his face, and he rode over it without a thought ! "

" But what else could I do ? " said the boy, throwing out his hand ; appealing to the crowd now, and now appealing to the widow. " If I'd put on the brakes going down the hill at such a speed I would have been put over the handlebars ! "

"And what harm would that have done you ? " screamed the widow. " I often saw you taking a toss when you were wrestling with Jimmy Mack and I heard no complaints after- wards, although your elbows and knees would be running blood, and your face scraped like a gridiron ! " She turned to the crowd. " That's as true as God. I often saw him come in with his nose spouting blood like a pump, and one eye closed as tight as the eye of a corpse. My hand was often stiff for a week from sopping out wet cloths to put poultices on him and try to bring his face back to rights again." She swung back to Packy again. " You're not afraid of a fall when you go climbing trees, are you ? You're not afraid to go up on the roof after a cat, are you ? Oh, there's more in this than you want me to know. I can see that. You killed that hen on purpose—that's what I believe ! You're tired of going to school. You want to get out of going away to college. That's it ! You think if you kill the few poor hens we have there will be no money in the box when the time comes to pay for books and classes. That's it ! " Packy began to redden.

" It's late in the day for me to be thinking of things like that," he said. " It's long ago I should have started those tricks if that was the way I felt. But it's not true. I want to go to college. The reason I was coming down the hill so fast was to tell you that I got the scholarship. The teacher told me as I was leaving the schoolhouse. That's why I was pedalling so hard. That's why I was whistling. That's why I was waving my hand. Didn't you see me waving my hand from once I came in sight at the top of the hill ? "

The widow's hands fell to her sides. The wind of words died down within her and left her flat and limp. She didn't know what to say. She could feel the neighbours staring at her. She wished that they were gone away about their business. She wanted to throw out her arms to the boy, to drag him against her heart and hug him like a small child. But she thought of how the crowd would look at each other and nod and snigger. A ewe lamb ! She didn't want to satisfy them. If she gave in to her feelings now they would know how much she had been counting on his getting the scholarship. She wouldn't please them ! She wouldn't satisfy them !

She looked at Packy, and when she saw him standing there before her, spattered with the furious feathers and crude blood of the dead hen, she felt a fierce disappointment for the boy's own disappointment, and a fierce resentment against him for killing the hen on this day of all days, and spoiling the great news of his success.

Her mind was in confusion. She stared at the blood on his face, and all at once it seemed as if the blood was a bad omen of the future that was for him. Disappointment, fear, resentment, and above all defiance, raised themselves within her like screeching animals. She looked from Packy to the onlookers.

" Scholarship ! Scholarship ! " she sneered, putting as much derision as she could into her voice and expression.

" I suppose you think you are a great fellow now ? I suppose you think you are independent now? I suppose you think you can go off with yourself now, and look down on your poor slave of a mother who scraped and sweated for you with her cabbages and her hens? I suppose you think to yourself that it doesn't matter now whether the hens are alive or dead? Is that the way? Well, let me tell you this! You're not as independent as you think. The scholarship may pay for your books and your teacher's fees but who will pay for your clothes? Ah-ha, you forgot that, didn't you?" She put her hands on her hips. Packy hung his head. He no longer appealed to the gawking neighbours. They might have been able to save him from blows but he knew enough about life to know that no one could save him from shame.

The widow's heart burned at sight of his shamed face, as her heart burned with grief, but her temper too burned fiercer and fiercer, and she came to a point at which nothing could quell the blaze till it had burned itself out. "Who'll buy your suits?" she yelled. "Who'll buy your boots?" She paused to think of more humiliating accusations. "Who'll buy your breeches?" She paused again and her teeth bit against each other. What would wound deepest? What shame could she drag upon him? "Who'll buy your nightshirts or will you sleep in your skin?"

The neighbours laughed at that, and the tension was broken. The widow herself laughed. She held her sides and laughed, and as she laughed everything seemed to take on a newer and simpler significance. Things were not as bad as they seemed a moment before. She wanted Packy to laugh too. She looked at him. But as she looked at Packy her heart turned cold with a strange new fear.

"Get into the house!" she said, giving him a push ahead of her. She wanted him safe under her own roof. She wanted to get him away from the gaping neighbours. She hated them, man, woman and child. She felt that if they had not been there things would have been different. And she wanted to get away from the sight of the blood on the road. She wanted to mash a few potatoes and make a bit of potato cake for Packy. That would comfort him. He loved that.

Packy hardly touched the food. And even after he had washed and scrubbed himself there were stains of blood turning up in the most unexpected places : behind his ears, under his finger-nails, inside the cuff of his sleeve.

" Put on your good clothes," said the widow, making a great effort to be gentle, but her manners had become as twisted and as hard as the branches of the trees across the road from her, and even the kindly offers she made sounded harsh. The boy sat on the chair in a slumped position that kept her nerves on edge and set up a further conflict of irritation and love in her heart. She hated to see him slumping there in the chair, not asking to go outside the door, but still she was uneasy whenever he as much as looked in the direction of the door. She felt safe while he was under the roof; inside the lintel ; under her eyes.

Next day she went in to wake him for school, but his room was empty ; his bed had not been slept in, and when she ran out into the yard and called him everywhere there was no answer. She ran up and down. She called at the houses of the neighbours but he was not in any house. And she thought she could hear sniggering behind her in each house that she left, as she ran to another one. He wasn't in the village. He wasn't in the town. The master of the school said that she should let the police have a description of him. He said he never met a boy as sensitive as Packy. A boy like that took strange notions into his head from time to time.

The police did their best but there was no news of Packy that night. A few days later there was a letter saying that he was well. He asked his mother to notify the master that he would not be coming back, so that some other boy could claim the scholarship. He said that he would send the price of the hen as soon as he made some money.

Another letter in a few weeks said that he had got a job on a trawler, and that he would not be able to write very often but that he would put aside some of his pay every week and send it to his mother whenever he got into port. He said that he wanted to pay her back for all she had done for him. He gave no address. He kept his promise about the money but he never gave any address when he wrote.

. . . And so the people may have let their thoughts run on, as they sat by the fire with the widow, many a night, listening to her complaining voice saying the same thing over and over. " Why did he put the price of an old hen above the price of his own life ? " And it is possible that their version of the story has a certain element of truth about it, too. Perhaps all our actions have this double quality about them, this possibility of alternative, and that it is only by careful watching and absolute sincerity that we follow the path that is destined for us, and, no matter how tragic that may be, it is better than the tragedy we bring upon ourselves.

— The Stories of Mary Lavin

Explorations

1. Does the story justify the moral contained in the last sentence ? Give reasons for your answer.

2. Is there any other moral that you might draw from either or both of the stories ? Set it down carefully and justify it with reference to the text.

3. Notice that the author gives us very little detailed information about anything except the widow's devotion to her task—the town is not named, nor the college in the city, nor the village. Why is it so bare of such details ? Does it compare in this respect with any other parable you have read or heard ? Discuss.

4. There is a touch of irony in the sentence—'His character was strengthening too, under his mother's sharp tongue'. Can you point out other examples of irony in the story ?

5. The author sets herself frankly to decide how certain people would behave if certain things happened. Is the behaviour of the widow, the neighbours and son well presented ? Examine the behaviour detail by detail.

6. What do you think of the author's use of dialogue ?

7. What do you honestly think of the story ?

Exercises

1. Devise a third ending to the story, working parallel to the author's method.

2. Write a similar parable to illustrate the statements : (a) Blood is thicker than water ; (b) Money is the root of all evil.

3. Tell in the first person the second version of the story as experienced by Packy, from the point where he begins to descend the hill.

4. Imagine the farmer, who saw the accident, in the local store with some friends—including the postman—a year later. The widow comes in for messages. Write dialogue for the men when she has left.

15

THE HOLY KISS

In certain parts of the country the first kiss of a child on his First Communion morning is considered a great treasure. This kiss is called the Holy Kiss and it is generally reserved for the child's mother. If it so happens that on that morning the mother is confined to bed through childbirth or illness, the aunt, or whoever accompanies the boy or girl to the church, is careful to hoard the kiss on the road home lest indeed its preciousness should be filched by a sentimental neighbour or an inconsequential relative. Arrived home, the guardian of the treasure leads the child to the mother's bedside and says : " Here, Mother, take your Holy Kiss ! "

And how eagerly the kiss is taken ! The bare arms leap out on the child, twine about the child, and the kiss is snatched with a passion far outmatching the marriage kiss which it exceeds by the same measure as the spirit transcends the body. It is as if the mother were to say : " Here, Glory be to God, I have reaped the first of conscious purity. I am greedy to snatch the lips that have held the Lord. Here is the reward of travail."

Little Tommy Donoghue lived with his grandmother, Mary Donoghue, in a cottage outside the town. Just Tommy and his grandmother. Tommy was six and his grandmother seventy-six. Despite the disparity of age the two understood one another perfectly. Mary Donoghue had the great brown eyes of Grandmother Wolf. She had a ditch-apple face ; the knob of a cyst was a landmark on one of her russet temples. The wisps of white hair sticking out from under her black shawl were tufts of bleached hay sticking out of a hayshed. She was lean, hardy, and comparatively agile for her years. Little Tommy was a funny bit of a thing with steel-rimmed spectacles balanced on a comical nose. The child's father, Tom Donoghue, had been killed felling a tree in a neighbouring demesne. Tom had been old Mary's only child, and she had cried bitterly at his death, a good deal more bitterly than Tom's wife, Bridie. Still the old woman had the comfort of little Tommy—after a time Tommy and Tom seemed one and the same person to her. She ceased to mourn the father, for it seemed as if suddenly and surprisingly Tom had somehow shrunken down into Tommy, and the pleasures and apprehensions of his youth were hers to experience anew. Bridie Donoghue, Tom's wife and Tommy's mother, had lived with the old woman for a few years after the accident. Then the young widow had married hurriedly and secretly, without informing her mother-in-law of her intention to do so, and had gone to live with her husband in a cottage about seven miles away. Tongues began to prattle at the sudden wedding, not without justification it must be admitted. Afterwards old Mary could not bear to hear her daughter-in-law's name mentioned, and it became the predominant terror of her life that some day she would return and claim little Tommy. The old woman resorted to unusual subterfuges to ensure that the boy should forget his mother. The news that Bridie had given birth to a child, afterwards to a second child, pleased the old woman greatly—she hoped that those new links would bind Bridie more closely to her new home. But old Mary's sense of security was shaken when the child returned from town one day with a bag of sweets that he said had been given to him by his mother. The old woman put the big bag of sweets on the mantelpiece. She was very silent for the rest of the day.

When Tommy came of age to make his First Communion the old woman was all ado. She took to standing at the school gate during playtime to pick out Tommy from the hundred other roaring boys. She burrowed deep in the red check bag in the cupboard of her room and took out a small hoard of banknotes tied with string. She bought black patent-leather shoes for the boy and kept polishing the toe-caps with an assiduous sleeve. She bought white socks and kept smoothing and smoothing them and putting her head sideways to look at them. She bought a grey-green tweed suit (he had only worn jerseys up to this) and a mustard-coloured tie and a white silk shirt. She gave him *My First Prayer Book* which had a long gilt-embossed cross on its snow-white cover. She bought a small white rosary in a little white bag. The old bones took to creaking loudly as she rushed hither and thither. The boy practised his first Confession on her a few times and she heard him out solemnly. He asked her if she knew when midnight was, and his little comical face grew infinitely more comical when she pretended not to know. When the First Communion morning came she polished him up wondrously till he shone. Then she led him to church.

Clouds scudded across the May sky; now and again the morning sun smouldered through the high smoke of heaven. The breeze had the remembrance of winter's sharpness in it. The children with their mothers huddled outside the church gate. The mothers were holding heavier coats for the little ones and they all looked hither and thither as they waited for the teacher to give them the signal to enter the church and take up their allotted places. Now and again the wind lifted the girls' veils and revealed shy downcast faces. At last the teacher came to the church door and signed to the children to enter. They all filed in and took their places—the boys at the Gospel side and the girls at the Epistle side.

The priest read the Mass delicately and clearly, as delicately and clearly as he had read his very first Mass. At times during the Mass the children sang hymns. When the Communion bell rang, the children filed up to the altar, each child walking slowly as if bearing a brimming vessel of liquid. The first file stood against the rails, and as the priest moved from child to child the teacher moved with him behind each Communicant to ensure that the Host was swallowed before the boy or girl left the rails. As the children received, the voices of the choir moved caressingly over them. The priest intoned leisurely, cutting the edges of his words clean. Old Mary Donoghue had been kneeling with the mothers at the rear, her eyes fixed firmly on Tommy as he walked up to the altar. Then to her chagrin she noticed that Tommy was first in the second line of boys and had moved far away to the altar's end out of her sight behind a pillar. If she remained where she was, the old woman realised, she would miss the memorable sight of the Host touching the child's lips for the first time. So, moving urgently, she clambered out of her place, walked up the passage, and with mouth agape peered affectionately to the extremity of the rail where Tommy was standing. When she had seen what she had gone out to see, she turned, widened her hands suddenly in a touching movement of thanksgiving, and thumped back into her seat. Her old mouth twitched

as she walked. The mothers were watching her through slitted
eyes. But they did not glance at one another amusedly.

Then the sun leaped down from the high windows on its
long legs and brought the gilt gate of the sanctuary to finest gold.
Through the low stained-glass windows a different, a more sober
sun filtered and drew swaths of red and purple and blue among the
varnished pews. Here and there amid the mosaics on the sanctuary walls arbitrary squares began winking. Then the wind rose
and the church drained of colour.

When the Mass was ended the bright and dark flood of children
broke upon mothers whose affections had multiplied. Everyone,
young and old, was smiling, and the warmth of comradeship
flowed freely among them. Old Mary squeezed Tommy's hand
till it must have hurt, but the child did not squeak—he laughed
up through his spectacles at his proud grandmother. The old
woman braced herself and then suddenly stooped and looked
about her. But no mother was kissing her child there in the
House of God. Mary tightened her shawl about her with one
hand, grasped the boy with the other and began to hurry out of
the little church.

Suddenly the old woman's face, that had been set in joy,
began to splinter and break. She stopped short and her grasp
on the boy's hand tightened. Below at the doorway she saw the
child's mother standing beside a pillar, her eager features pivoting
this way and that to find her son among the well-dressed children.
Old Mary at first grew terrified, then she grew fierce. The intolerable pressure on his hand made the boy turn his face upwards
to his grandmother's, and when the old mouth came down
exultantly upon him his lips ripened up for the Holy Kiss. But,
inexplicably, his grandmother's face stopped short of his, and her
mouth began twitching furiously. The child was puzzled at the
denial and he put his comical head askew. Then he saw his mother
by the pillar, and sunlight streamed into his face. His grandmother began mumbling brokenly : " Hadn't I Tom's, alanna ?
Hadn't I Tom's ? An' shouldn't that be enough for me ? " Then
she snuffled and wiped her eyes in a corner of her shawl. She
thrust the boy forward through the press of people towards his
mother. The mother came away from the pillar, spread out her
arms to receive her son, then bent fiercely and snatched the
Holy Kiss.

Mother and grandmother each took one of the boy's hands. Without speaking they walked out into the windy street. Whenever the sun caught their faces the women's eyes began to glitter like breaking glass.

— *The Lion Tamer*

Explorations

1. When Old Mary behaves oddly in church, the other mothers ' did not glance at one another amusedly.' Why should they ? Why did they not ? Why does the author make a point of it ?

2. The author makes it very clear that the Holy Kiss meant a great deal to everyone concerned. How does he convey this ?

3. Was the old woman selfish in wanting the Holy Kiss ? Was she generous in letting the mother have it ? Did she gain or lose, would you say, by sacrificing it ? What did it mean to the happiness of all three of them ? Explain.

4. Bryan MacMahon uses metaphor a good deal in his writing. In what way does his style gain from this ? Quote some metaphorical phrases that you find particularly effective. Do any of the comparisons puzzle you ? Name them and try to guess their meaning.

5. The author goes to some pains to catch the atmosphere of the church. Examine the writing here and point to some sentences or phrases that you find particularly evocative of atmosphere. Using one sentence and no more than four adjectives, describe the sort of atmosphere he conjures up.

Exercises

1. Try to reconstruct the movements and the thoughts of Tommy's mother on the morning of the ceremony up to the moment when he gave her the kiss. Use the first or third person as you wish.

2. Describe Tommy's feelings from the moment when he turns to come back from the rails.

3. Try to write dialogue for the two women and the child as they walk back to the old woman's cottage.

16

THE WINDOWS OF WONDER

The young woman wheeling the bicycle came up the roadway out of the bogland valley. Behind her, bulk on bulk outthrown across all exits, the mountains squatted. Beyond the valley a headland had thrust itself out into the sea. Over the scene hung the clarity that was a promise of rain.

On the crest of the gap the woman turned her bicycle. Placing her forearms on the handlebars, she eased her body, and looked steadfastly down into the valley she had just left. She saw the dark floor of low-lying land. She saw the ranked ricks of turf and beside them the glitter of white shirts. She saw the bright cabins and the scrawl of a hidden stream. Last of all she saw the tiny school in its cluster of windwhipt trees.

The woman's eyes became filled with a remote smouldering. Her breath came forcefully through her nostrils.

Six months before she had seen this valley for the first time. Her friends had tried to dissuade her from acting as substitute teacher in the valley school. "A queer clannish crowd—a place of appalling feuds and astonishing whims." "When the place gets you, you'll start clawing the walls," and "The children will eat you with their big brown eyes."

The woman shifted her gaze from the valley to the distant sea. Out there the white-caps were lighting and quenching in the angry water.

Perversity had made her take the post. She remembered her first day—her first week in the valley. The ominous faces at the cottage windows as she rode past . . . The solemn principal who was flesh and blood of the valley . . . She taught the junior division—he the senior boys and girls. The school-children sitting in grave rows consumed her with their large brown eyes and afforded her the traditional minimum of co-operation. Sometimes she felt afraid. Sometimes she was tempted to scream aloud, to abandon herself to welcome hysteria, to use her nails as God had intended they should be used. But day after day had found her counselling herself to the patience necessary for the finding of the keys to the children's natures.

She had tried laughter : they had turned their heads sideways as if they were looking at an insane person. She had tried music : the music she was acquainted with was so wholly apart from their own grace-noted plaints that, on realising her mistake, she had stopped suddenly. She had tried the unorthodox—leaping, grimacing and mimicry : one day she discovered in midantic that the principal was glaring at her through the glass partition. After this she yielded herself up to despair. Then, when she wasn't endeavouring, she stumbled on the secret.

It was a reading lesson. She had begun to explain the word " legend " which appeared in the text. "A legend is a tale of some event that happened so long ago that we have no means of telling whether it is true or not. You remember, children, the story of the Children of Lir ? "

There was no sudden light in the children's eyes. Could it be that . . . ? Mastering her emotion, she asked : " Hands up, the children who know the story of the Children of Lir ? "

No hand moved. It wasn't possible ! Was this the sole valley in Ireland that had let legend die ? Still, the children were obedient and dutiful. If they had heard the tale they would have . . .

" Of Deirdre of the Sorrows ? Of the Fairy Palace of the Quicken Trees ? Of the Fate of the Sons of Usna ? Of Diarmuid and Grainne ? Surely, some child . . . ? "

The children's eyes grew browner and rounder and wider. The girls stolidly planted their stout-soled boots beneath them while the bare toes of the boys squirmed on the boarded floor.

The woman was afraid to trust herself to words lest she should break into uncovered tears. She looked left, then right. She felt trapped and crushed. She looked at the wee ones and the ones that were not so wee. " Oh, children . . . " she began.

Briskly she gathered them in a ring around her.

" Listen, children," she said. " I don't know if you can understand me or not. But you must try. It's the only way. Someone has robbed you of a very precious thing. I will not have you cheated. This thing I speak of is neither gold nor silver, neither a red nor a green jewel. It is something a great deal more valuable. The other things I teach you—the figures, the words, the lines

and the letters—are not so important—as yet. Please try to understand ! How shall I begin to tell you of the treasure you have
lost ? Your minds are like rooms that are dark or brown. But
somewhere in the rooms, if only you can pull aside the heavy
curtains, you will find windows—these are the windows of
wonder. Through these you can see the yellow sunlight or the
silver stars or the many-coloured wheel of the rainbow. You've
all seen a rainbow ? " (The heads nodded). " Isn't it beautiful ? "
(The heads nodded vigorously).

" The windows I speak of are the legends of our people. Each
little legend is a window of wonder. Each time you hear a story
or ponder upon a story or dream yourself into a story or break or
remake a story, you are opening a window of wonder. Children,
please, please try to understand.

" Perhaps I had better begin with the story I myself like
best : ' Oisin in the Land of the Ever-Young.' Are you ready,
children ? " The solemn heads nodded in affirmation. " Long,
long ago, there lived . . . "

The woman on the hill-top sighed and looked across the
northern rim of the valley. A Martello tower stood black against
the livid northern sky. In the air between, the clean gulls were
moving inland. The whimper of the nearing rain was in the chill
wind that blew from the left hand.

She remembered the complaints of the parents, the semi-
deputations, the cabin growlings and the slow contemptuous
stares of elders from over the half-doors. Most keenly of all she
recalled the stern rebuke of the principal—at the apparent waste
of teaching time. Then she began to dissemble, for she had felt
the children's imaginations coming alive under her care : she
knew that something precious was being born in them. Already
they were fusing warmly into her nature : the stir of their new
life was implicit in the bright cries they uttered as they played
along the valley. Now she and the children were conspirators —
while she pretended to be reading from a text-book she was telling
yet another tale, opening up another window of wonder. By now
the children had begun to demand the stories. Their eyes that
had been dull were ready to leap and frolic on small provocation.
Now there was comradeship between the teacher and the taught.

And then the old mistress had returned. The young teacher's
stay in the school was abruptly ended.

The evening smoke had begun to drift low from the chimneys of the valley. The watcher sighed and turned away.

It was then that she noticed the old russet-faced man. He was standing inside a rough timber gate on the roadside, resting his elbows on the top spar. His fists were securely clenched. A russet man with a russet face and merry blue eyes under a black caubeen. The young woman changed colour. Turning the bicycle, she faced it for the distant town. She had her right foot on the off pedal and was hopping with her left foot when he addressed her :

" Wait ! Wait ! "

One leg on the ground, one leg on the pedal, she waited.

" Come hether, woman ! "

After a moment of puzzled delay she obeyed. The old man and the young woman looked at one another. His eyes were the bluest she had ever seen.

" You're the school-missis ? "

" I am ... I was ! "

" I heard the children talkin' about yeh. So you're leavin' us ? "

" I am ! "

"Ah ! " Slyly : " With no one to say good-bye to yeh only me. An' they have me down for bein' half-cracked. There's a lone bird like me in every parish in Ireland."

He laughed. It was a half-regretful but lovely laugh.

A warmth flowed between them. She looked first at his face, then at his clenched fists. She was dreaming his face young when he apprised her red-handed and, narrowing his eyes, said half-fooling, all in earnest :

" If I was fifty years younger, I'd chance me luck with yeh, my lovely woman. An' I'm not so sure that I'd fail ! An' why do I say that ? Because I know your mind the same as I know me own mind. You're a woman to whom I could talk about the grandeur of a lark, the swingin' of a caravan or the Resurrection of Our Lord. Together, me an' you, we'd open up many an' many a window of wonder. Then we'd be . . . "

He made to place his palms together and interlace his fingers. When he found his fists clenched he laughed at his small folly. Smilingly he held out the two fists : "A present I have for yeh an' yeh goin'. A token to remember us by. Look ! "

She watched the gnarled fists unlock. Clinging to the coarse palms were two butterflies—two Red Admirals—one on each palm. The blades of the butterflies' wings swung slowly from side to side to reveal their full beauty.

Her laughter and his laughter cancelled the disparity of years between them. She was bright-eyed ; he was sure and old. Her breath came faster. The old man wore a smile of confidence and satisfaction.

Carefully and with a movement that reminded her of a conjurer he removed the butterflies from each palm with the thumb and forefinger of the other hand. The butterflies began to beat and thrum for freedom.

The old man tossed them into the air. At first, the butterflies flew wide apart ; then the craziness of their flight begot a pattern. At last they found one another and began to lock and frolic and entwine their flights as they climbed higher and higher into the dark heavens.

The old man turned away, then strode slowly up the field. The young woman mounted her bicycle and began to pedal down into the town valley.

— The Red Petticoat

Explorations

1. Though this is a very short story it takes in a good deal of territory : the teacher's decision to go to the valley, her friends' warnings, her first day, her various attempts to break through to the class, her clashes with the headmaster, her final success, and now, her departure. Why do you think the author chooses this moment as his vantage point in time—see quotation from Frank O'Connor on page 6 of the Introduction—to unfold the whole story ?

2. Why does the writer introduce the figure of the old man ?

3. What does he really mean by ' the windows of wonder ' ? Does the phrase or the idea mean anything to you personally ? Have you ever seen through a window of wonder ? If so, describe the sensation as best you can.

4. For a present the old man gives her two butterflies and then lets them loose into the air. Was this an appropriate present ? Why ?

5. The old man has very blue eyes. Is this significant ?

6. The author suggests that the children were made brighter and happier at their play as a result of the wonder tales. Do you find this believable ?

7. Has a story ever affected the manner of your games as a child? If so, try to describe the experiences involved.

8. What sort of woman was the new teacher? Examine the story carefully. Does the author give us any early indications as to her character? What are they? The author writes ' Perversity had made her take the post.' Take account of this statement when answering.

9. One critic has suggested that there is a sharp change in the quality of the story once the old man enters. Do you agree? Is it a change for better or worse? Explain.

Exercises

1. When the old mistress came back she very probably asked the headmaster what sort of girl had replaced her for the six months. Write the dialogue that may have taken place between them during the following day's lunchtime break.

2. Try to put yourself into the shoes of one of the brighter girls or boys in the room when the teacher tells the first story. Then describe how the pupil relates the incident at home that evening, and the parents' reaction.

3. Is it important to tell children their country's legends? Give your considered opinion and argue your case carefully. Ought such legends form part of school courses? Discuss the matter honestly; try to think clearly and then write clearly.

4. What, if any, is your favourite legend? Try to explain what appeals to you in it.

5. When the girl got back to her friends she told them, no doubt, about her experiences. Try to tell, in her own words, what she said about the old man.

17

AMONG THE RUINS

There was no doubt about it, Joe thought as he sat in the car and waited for his wife and children to join him : Margo was simply wonderful. She had had an early lunch for them ; she had so cleverly primed the children—who usually detested these organised outings with their parents—that they were still curious about the destination, and eager to be off. The whole idea of going back to Corradinna had been hers, and although it was early summer and the weather would probably have been good anyhow, she had managed to choose the best Sunday of the year so far. Yes, Margo was simply wonderful.

When she had first mentioned her plan to him the previous Friday night, he felt unaccountably stubborn. " Corradinna ? What the hell would take us there ? There's nothing there now but the ruins of the old place."

" You still must have some curiosity about it," she had urged. " Even if it's only to see if you have lost the feel of the place."

" Feel ? " he had said, deliberately misunderstanding her. " You know me—I'm not sentimental that way."

"And for the children's sake, too. I would like them to see where you lived when you were their age. It would be good for them."

" I don't see the point," he had said. " I don't see the point at all. "

But she had persisted, and that night and the next day his stubbornness gave way to a stirring of memory and then to a surprising excitement that revealed itself in his silence and his foolish grin. And now that they were about to set off, there was added a great surge of gratitude to her for tapping this forgotten source of joy in him. She knew and understood him so well.

Mary and Peter sat impatiently on the edge of the back seat. She was her mother in miniature.

" Now, Mammy ! Where ? Where ? " she begged. " You promised you would tell us now."

Margo turned to watch their faces. " We are going to Donegal——- "

" I want to go to the beach," Peter broke in.

" ——to see where your daddy used to live and play when he was your age."

"Are we, Daddy ? Really ? " Mary asked.

" Looks like it," said Joe, smiling helplessly.

" I still want to go to the beach," said Peter, doggedly.

Mary caught his arm. " Can't you hear, stupid ? We're going to see where Daddy used to play when he was a little boy."

" Where's that ? " Peter asked cautiously.

"Away, away far off in Donegal," said Margo. "And if you're going to behave like that, you are going to spoil the day on all of us."

" So stop whining, boy ! " said Mary, severely, imitating her mother with unconscious accuracy.

" I'm not whining."

" You were a minute ago."

" That'll do, the both of you ! Do you want to ruin the day on your daddy ? "

" What's the name of the place ? " Mary asked.

" Corradinna," said Joe.

" Corradinna," said Peter, sampling the word. " That's a funny name." He turned to his sister, screwed up his face and said in a man's voice, " Corradinna."

" Corradinna," she piped back at him.

They fell into a fit of laughing at their private joke.

After the first hour, they became restless. They changed sides—Mary behind Margo and Peter behind Joe. Later they changed back again. Then they quarrelled over the exact position of the imaginary line down the middle of the back seat. Then Peter wanted the windows down and Mary wanted them up ; she was cold, she said. Then Margo asked Joe to pull in to the side, because Peter had to go out for a minute. Then, five miles farther on, Mary had to get out. It was the usual pattern for a Sunday afternoon outing, but today it did not irk Joe, because Margo had assumed complete control, soothing, compromising, reprimanding, keeping peace, and the children's bickering claimed only a fraction of his attention. She was allowing him the uninterrupted luxury of remembering, hearing sounds and voices and cries he thought he had forgotten.

Corradinna lay at the foot of Errigal mountain, a pyramid of granite that rose three thousand feet out of the black bog earth. Because it marked the end of their journey and was visible for the last twenty miles, Joe found himself leaning over the driving wheel, as if to see beyond the folds of hills that still lay before him.

" Easy," said Margo. " You're going too fast."

"Am I ? "

" You'll be there time enough. Do you want the children to get sick ? "

At this moment, I don't give a damn, he thought without callousness ; at this moment, with Meenalaragan and Pigeon Top on my left and Glenmakennif and Altanure on my right. Because these are my hills, and I knew them before I knew wife or children.

"Joe ! Do you hear me ? "

" Sorry," he said, slowing down. " Sorry."

Every Saturday morning, with the two Lakeland terriers, just for a walk. You got to the top of one hill and stood there with your arms opened out to the wind and watched the dogs, crazed with the scent of a fox, scramble down before you, and you ran down after them and then up the next incline and down the next and up and down and up and down, and when you got home in time for dinner, the dogs were so fatigued that they could not sleep but lay restlessly on the cold flags of the kitchen floor, staining the stone under their noses with circles of damp. It is all coming back to me, he thought.

They left the car at the side of the road and walked up the grass-covered track to the ruins of the house. The roof had fallen in, and the windows were holes in the walls. Someone had carved his initials on the doorpost : "J.M. . . . NOV. 1941." Mary, convinced that there must still be something spectacular to be seen after so long a journey, began asking petulantly, " Show us now, Mammy ! Show us now ! "

" This is it all," Margo said. " This is where your daddy used to play."

" Who did he play with ? What games did he play ? "

" He used to play around the house here. And around those fields. Why don't you and Peter go exploring for yourselves, while your daddy and I look around here ? "

" I have seen everything," said Peter.

" You couldn't have," said Margo. " Go on, off with the pair of you ! Your daddy and I will be around here somewhere. And if you get tired walking, go and sit in the car."

When they had gone, she said to Joe, " Was that the garden ? "

" Yes," he said, and walked away from her. She followed him.

The garden, the path, the gooseberry tree. And the chestnut. That is our swing. Our father ties the ropes across that branch, and we soar up and out over the laneway. And Mother cries, " Careful, Joe ! Careful ! " and Susan, my sister, squeals, " Higher ! Higher ! " and Father comes round the side of the house and says, " Is the cow not in yet, boy ? " and Susan says, " I'll get it. Joe's busy swinging." Off she runs like a fairy thing, and because she is gone, the boy who is I jumps down and runs after her, and when he catches up with her, they dawdle along the bank of the river—river ? What river ? This trickle of water ? Where did the river go ?—and he says, " Dare you to jump the river." " How much ? " " Half the hazelnuts under my bed." " It's a bet." And she grips her lips between her teeth and takes a wild, gangling leap and lands in the middle of the water. They laugh and take off her shoes and wring out her socks and, the wetting suddenly forgotten, stroll across the fields to the wood— but where is the wood ? It couldn't be this sad little cluster of oaks !—until they come to the bluebell patch. " We'll bring home bluebells to Mother." Susan's arms are out. " Fill them," she says. " No. These will do." " Fill them. Fill them." " We forgot the cow." " The cow ! Quick. The cow ! " Another race across the meadow, through the gap in the hedge, clean over the river this time, because there is no bet to tighten your legs. And home, home, back past the barn. The barn, with its treasures—parts of bicycles, bits of beehives, a tea chest of old clothes, the drumsticks. Susan sings, and he accompanies her with the drumsticks on a cigar box. She dresses up in a long, tan-coloured silk frock, strap-over shoes, a huge picture hat—all her mother's. She sings, " Red sails in the sunset," over and over again, because the first line is the only one she knows.

" Susan ! Joe ! Teatime ! "

Hide ! Hide ! Down to the bower at the foot of the garden !
Oh, the laughing in that bower ! Laughing till they are sore.
And then, as soon as they sober up, one of them pulls a face,
and they are off again. Oh, God, the pain of that laughing !
" What do you two laugh at ? " Father says. " You would think
to look at you that you were a pair of half-wits. What *do* you
laugh at, anyhow ? "   And that makes them worse, because
Susan twitches her eyes or shrugs her shoulders, and if they
were to be killed, they couldn't stop now at all.

"Joe ? " Margo's voice at his elbow. " What are you smiling
at, Joe ? "

Suddenly he was alert, wary. " Remembering," he said.

" Remembering what ? "

" The bower. Susan and myself in the bower."

" What was it ? "

"A place . . . a sort of hideout at the foot of the garden there.
It's gone now. I looked."

" What did you do there ? "

" Laugh. Laugh, mostly."

Clouds had come up from the west and hidden the sun, and
the air was cold.

" What did you laugh at ? "

" I don't know. We just laughed. We called it the laughing
house."

" But you must have been laughing *at* something," she persisted. " Did you make jokes for one another ? "

" No, no, no. No jokes. Not laughing like that. Just—just
silly laughing."

" Still there must have been something to laugh at, even
for silly laughing, as you call it. What sort of silly things used
you laugh at ? "

" What did we laugh at ? " An explanation was necessary.
We must have laughed at something. There must have been
something that triggered it off.

"Are you not going to tell me ? " Margo's face had sharpened.
She stood before him, insisting on a revelation.

" Susan and I—— " he mumbled.

" I know," she said quickly. " Susan and you in the bower.

Once you got in there together, you laughed your heads off. And I want to know what you laughed *at*."

" She would make up a word—any word, any silly-sounding word—and that would set us off," he said clutching at the first faint memory that occurred to him. " Some silly word like— like ' sligalog,' or ' skookalook.' That sort of thing."

" ' Skookalook.' What's funny about that ? "

" I don't know if that was one of them. I meant any made-up word at all. In there, in the bower, somehow it seemed to sound— so funny."

" And that's all ? "

" That was all," he said limply.

Relenting, now that he had admitted her to these privacies, she put her arm through his and rubbed her cheek against his sleeve. " Poor Joe," she said. " Poor silly, simple Joe. Come on, let's go for a walk. It will soon be time to head home again."

Later, when they got back to the car, they found Mary sitting alone in the back seat. " What kept you two ? " the child demanded in the stern voice they used to laugh at a few years ago.

" Where's Peter ? " Margo asked.

" I don't know. We're not speaking," said Mary primly. " He has been gone for over half an hour."

" I'll get him," Joe volunteered. " He won't be far away."

" Will I go with you ? "

" No. I'll be quicker alone," said Joe. He felt that Margo knew he was glad of the opportunity to have a last look around by himself. " Start the motor and turn on the heater," he called back. " There is a dew falling."

He did not look for the boy. He walked slowly up the path to the remains of the house and walked round them once, twice, three times. He tried to move without making any sound, so that the stillness in his mind would not be disturbed. He knew he was waiting for something. But nothing came from the past—no voice, no cry, no laugh, not even the bark of a dog. He was suddenly angry. He charged down the garden and through the hedge. " Peter ! " he shouted. " Peter ! Peter ! "

The echoes of his voice mocked him.

" Peter ! Peter ! "

Now panic gripped him. The child had had an accident! He broke into a run, crossed the lower meadow, leaped the stream, and ran up the incline to the cluster of trees. " Peter! Peter ! "

Peter was so engrossed in his play that he was not aware of his father until Joe caught him by the shoulder and shook him. He was on his knees at the mouth of a rabbit hole, sticking small twigs into the soft earth.

" Peter ! What the hell ! "

" Look, Daddy. Look ! I'm donging the tower ! "

" Did you not hear me shouting ? Are you deaf? "

" Let me stay, Daddy. I'll have the tower donged in another five minutes."

" Come on ! " Joe dragged him away. " Your mother will think we're both lost. Such a fright I got ! Calling all over the place. Hurry up ! "

" Please, Daddy, let me stay for—— "

" Now, I said ! It will be long past your bedtime when we get back."

• Until they got to the road, Peter had to trot to keep up with him. " Here he is ! " Joe announced. " Playing games by himself in the wood ! " Margo and Mary were listening to the radio. " Let's get started," said Margo. " I'm sleepy."

" Calling and calling, and the little blighter wouldn't even answer me ! "

" Your feet are wet," said Margo.

" That won't kill me," said Joe gruffly.

Margo said something, but he pressed the starter and revved up the engine so that her voice was drowned.

On the way home, a sense of aloneness crept over him. Once he gave in to the temptation to glance in the mirror, but it was already dark outside, and Errigal was just part of the blackness behind them. He should never have gone back, he knew ; at least, he should never have gone back with Margo and the children. Because the past is a mirage—a soft illusion into which one steps in order to escape the present. Like hiding in the bower. How could he have told Margo that the bower had been their retreat, Susan's and his, their laughing house ? That dank little den that smelled of damp and decay, which let in no sunlight and kept out no rain ? Was that their retreat ? And, if it came to that, how often had they laughed there? Did they not bicker and fight all the time, like Peter and Mary? " I'll tell on you, boy. I'll tell Mammy on you." Susan's petulant voice came back to him now, clearer and harsher than the other memories.

" Go and tell, then, old telltale."

" I'm going now. I'm going now. And you'll get a beating, boy, when you come in for your tea."

" Telltale ! "

" Bully ! "

How sharply he remembered : walking alone and desolate along the bottom of the meadow, imagining the stories Susan was telling their father and mother in the house, knowing that eventually he would have to go up and face the accusation and his father's hard eyes and his mother's hard mouth, how he would stammer out his side of the story, and then take his beating and then be sent to bed. Was that his childhood? Why, Joe wondered, had he been so excited about the trip that morning? What had he expected to find at Corradinna—a restoration of innocence? A dream confirmed? He could not remember. All he knew now was that the visit had been a mistake. It had robbed him of a precious thing, his illusions of his past, and in their place now there was nothing—nothing at all but the truth.

"Aow ! Aow ! Peter nipped me ! Peter nipped me ! " Mary's cry shattered the sleepy quiet in the car.

" What's the matter with you ? " asked Margo.

" Peter, Mammy. He nipped me in the arm ! Ah, my arm ! My arm ! " She made no effort to control her tears.

" She kicked me first," said Peter. " She kicked my ankle."

" I didn't, Mammy ! I didn't. Ah-ah-ah-ah ! It's bleeding ! I can feel it ! "

" Stop the car," said Margo.

Joe brought the car to a stop, and Margo switched on the light. " Now," she said briskly. " What happened ? Show me your arm."

" There, Mammy. Above the elbow. It's all purple."

" There's no blood," said Margo. " But it is red. Why did you do that, Peter ? "

" I didn't touch her until she kicked me first."

" I was asleep, Mammy. I couldn't have kicked him."

" Mary was asleep, Peter. Why did you nip her ? "

" She's a liar ! " said Peter in desperation.

The sharp smack of Margo's hand across his cheek startled them all. " How dare you ! " Margo cried. " You know very well I do not allow you to use that word. It's a horrible thing to say about your sister ! I've told you over and over again—it's a word I won't allow. I just won't have it ! " She looked quickly at Joe and turned away again. " Never let me hear you use that word again ! Never ! "

She had to shout her last remarks to make herself heard above the noise of Peter's howling. The crying stopped his breath, and he spluttered and choked with his face pressed against the upholstery of the seat. Mary sat timidly in her corner. Margo, uncertain what to do next, turned around, facing the windscreen.

" There, now. There, there, there, son," Joe began. " You're all right."

" I—I—I—" Peter stammered, breathing in.

" I know, I know, son. It's all right now. It's all over."

He tried to catch Margo's eyes for permission to lean over and console the child. Her reluctance to look at him was sufficient. He stretched across the seat and lifted the shuddering boy in his arms and placed him gently on his knees. " Now," he said, softly. " That's better, isn't it ? Much better. It's a good thing for a man to cry like that sometimes."

The crying stopped, but the light body still shook when a sob took it.

" You go to sleep there on my knee, and before you know it we'll be home again. O.K. ? " He switched off the light and started up the engine. The child was warm against his body. Soon the boy slept.

Silence filled the car. Through the mesmerism of motor, fleeing hedges, shadows flying from the headlights, three words swam into Joe's head. " Donging the tower." What did Peter mean, he wondered dreamily ; what game was he playing, donging the tower ? He recalled the child's face, engrossed, earnest with happiness, as he squatted on the ground by the rabbit hole. A made-up game, Joe supposed, already forgotten. He would ask him in the morning, but Peter would not know. Just out of curiosity, he would ask him, not that it mattered .

And then a flutter of excitement stirred in him. Yes, yes, it did matter. Not the words, not the game, but the fact that he had seen his son, on the first good day of summer, busily, intently happy in solitude, donging the tower. The fact that Peter would never remember it was of no importance ; it was his own possession now, his own happiness, this knowledge of a child's private joy.

Then, as he turned the car into the road that led to their house, a strange, extravagant thought struck him. He must have had moments of his own like Peter's, alone, back in Corradinna, donging his own towers. And, just as surely, his own father must have stumbled on him, and must have recognised himself in his son. And his father before that, and his father before that. Generations of fathers stretching back and back, all finding magic and sustenance in the brief, quickly destroyed happiness of their children. The past did have meaning. It was neither reality nor dreams, neither today's patchy oaks nor the great woods of his boyhood. It was simply continuance, life repeating itself and surviving.

—The Saucer of Larks

Explorations

1. When Margo suggests the visit to her husband he is not in favour of it. He feels ' unaccountably stubborn.' Can you suggest why this was his first reaction ?

2. Then he feels ' a surprising excitement ' at the idea. The writer does not state the reasons for his change of mind. Can you suggest them ?

3. As he sets out for home Joe reflects bitterly that ' he should never have gone back.' Again he does not state the reasons except by suggestion. What, do you think, were his reasons ?

4. Margo says at the beginning that it would be good for the children to see their father's home. Was it, in fact, good for them ? Was the visit good for anyone ? Explain.

5. There is a constant contrast between dreams and reality in this story. How is this contrast built up ? Point out a place in the story where you think it is done particularly well.

6. Joe first remembers the happy side of his childhood. Later he is forced to recall the less happy side. What causes the change ?

Exercises

1. Have you any such pleasant memories of your early childhood ? Try to put them into words.

2. If you have any particularly wretched glimpses of the past describe them as accurately as you can.

3. Tell the story as seen through the eyes of young Peter, or Mary.

4. Imagine Joe telling the story to a friend the next day and try to write the dialogue. Begin

Joe : ' I took the wife and kids up to the home place yesterday.'

5. For other Friel stories dealing with the same theme of illusion and reality read ' The Wee Lake Beyond,' ' The Illusionists ' and ' The Gold in the Sea,' from his second collection entitled *The Gold in the Sea*.

6. Read Benedict Kiely's story ' The Dogs in the Great Glen ' and show how it deals with a similar theme.

18

A MAN'S WORLD

I had five maiden aunts and they doted on me. I was their only nephew, the child of their youngest sister, Christina, who alone of the whole family of twelve left home while she was still in her teens to work in the nearest town of Strabane and married a town man. The others stayed together, grew into men and women, buried Grandfather and Grandmother (whom I never knew) and the six brothers (whom I never knew either) who must have died long before their time. When I first became aware of them, they were settled women whose ages ranged from about forty-five to fifty, each with her role in the running of their doll's house. Aunt Kate and Aunt Maggie were the breadwinners, teachers in the village school ; Aunt Agnes was the housekeeper ; Aunt Sarah looked after the cow and the chickens and the precise garden ; and Aunt Rose—well, as the others used to say with gentle tolerance, " Rose will always be Rose." That was good enough for me.

Every year on August first, we went to Donegal to visit them. The journey itself was an adventure in a mad scarlet rail-bus which plunged along a narrow-gauge track pulling a dancing wagon of luggage behind it and emitted a throaty toot-toot now and again just for the sheer joy of it. It was a two-and-a-half hour trip through hills and between mountains, past lakes and streams, between high banks glowing with sun-yellow whins and flat boglands of purple and brown and russet. Inside the bus, country women, anonymous in black head shawls, and great, unshaven country men chatted volubly to one another, and the atmosphere took body with the pungent smoke of their pipes. Then at the end of the line, run to earth at the foot of grey mountains, the village of Ardara itself, a hamlet of about four hundred people. The line stopped abruptly half a mile short of the village, although why, after battling across impossible terrain for the previous sixty miles, it could not tackle the last soggy stretch, used to puzzle me. But that was its unpredictable way and we had no reason to complain because mother's home was only a stone's throw away from the terminus.

For days before we would leave home, Father would be quiet and moody and I never remember a holiday that was not overshadowed by his cold withdrawal from our enthusiastic preparations. But once we were on our way, he thawed slowly, partly because of the whiskey flask he carried in his hip pocket and partly because of Mother's watchful attentions to him. So that by the time the rail-bus stuttered to a halt, he had arrived at a state of garrulous good humour. And there on the platform would be the five aunts, smiling, happy, nervous, welcoming, one or two of them very often in slippers and aprons if the rail-bus caught them unawares, bobbing up and down in the golden heat of an August afternoon.

Of course I got their first attention. Invariably, I had got bigger and fatter and healthier and more manly and cleverer—that on a second's observation—and before we had left the station, but not before I had been handled by each aunt in turn, it was unanimous that I was " more a caution than ever." Mother came next. Less said now but five pairs of eyes quickly noted the shoulders gathering flesh and the new line at the edge of the mouth and there were tentative, casual-sounding questions about how she was eating and sleeping. Lastly Father. They did love him, I believe now, because he was Christina's husband and the father of her child. But he was a man—more, a town man—and since they had no experience of men, they had nothing spontaneous to say to him and had to improvise with formalities. To tide the situation over Father usually busied himself by passing me from one to the other.

The first few days of the holiday were never enjoyable : I had to go over every song and recitation and mime and imitation that I had done in previous summers (every detail had to be perfect, too) and then bring them up to date with the latest additions to my repertoire, not once but half a dozen times until Aunt Sarah or Aunt Agnes would insist that the others were tiring me and Aunt Kate and Aunt Maggie would finally agree to release me. If I were singing, Mother would accompany me on the yellow-keyed piano, half of whose notes were mute and her eyes would rove restlessly round the five naked faces, smiling brightly if a sister's eyes met hers or just moving from one to the other as if she were somehow playing them and not the piano. At last I would be set free, out to the fields and the Atlantic wind and to Aunt Rose.

It was always a relief to get away from them and yet when I would run round to the back of the house and stand looking across the valley towards the hazel wood where the witch with the red eyes lived, I was neither surprised nor disappointed to find Aunt Rose there before me, waiting for me. I know now, after almost thirty years, that she was a plain-looking woman. Her face was too white, her cheeks too flat, her mouth permanently open, her head shot forward. But at five or six years of age, I saw only a mild woman who always smiled and seldom spoke and knew exactly what would delight a boy of my age. There would be a black rabbit in the warren or a pigeon's nest in the wood or a hedgehog along the path beside the burn or a rose tree, sudden and inexplicable, in the lower meadow. Or she had spotted an early crop of nuts and had guarded it for me by her silence. Or she had a sick hen in the byre with a ludicrous bandage of cotton-wool tied round its head or a trunkful of mysteries sent home from Kenya by some granduncle who had a wandering foot. And all these things she would reveal to me, not exultantly but almost coyly, like a fresh girl wooing her first youth. Unless we were far out of earshot of the house, away beyond the hazel wood, for example, where the boglands stretched out before us and we had to raise our voices to be heard above the wind or in the sweet-smelling secrecy of the byre where a whisper would do : in those places she talked, wildly, carelessly, senselessly it seemed to me a lot of the time, telling me about Grandfather and Grandmother and about her schooldays and about a necklace she once bought with egg money and about a fortuneteller who promised great things for her. Sometimes, too, she would talk about her dead brothers. I was too young to invest their unexplained passing with mystery and too incurious to ask questions about them. I knew only the details Aunt Kate or Aunt Maggie had volunteered—that the family had stopped keeping bees when Uncle John died or that the good bedroom could not be used for displaying mother's wedding gifts because Uncle Joe was lying there in his last illness. So that I had accepted these men as shadowy backgrounds to memorable events in the family. But Aunt Rose talked about them, giving them girth and height and colouring, made me laugh at Uncle Peter's attempt to train a sheep dog or Uncle Pat's efforts at changing the course of the burn. And once, I remember, after she had led me through Uncle Jim's career as a fighting patriot and I, hoping for a dramatic conclusion to the tale, had asked her how did he die, the question genuinely puzzled her. She thought for a moment and said, " I don't know . . . I just suppose he died." The problem interested her as much as it interested me, no more, no less.

When she and I would get back to the house again, we would find Mother and the other four basking in the sun at the gable. Aunt Kate would say, "And where has Rose been hiding our young man ? Eh ? Keeping him to herself, I'll bet. Aye, Rose is a deep one." And there would be a sympathetic laugh.

Father spent most of his day in the village. After a late breakfast, he would say, " I think I'll go out and stretch my legs and leave you women to your gossiping." We would not see him again until lunch time when he would sit at the head of the table and make laborious jokes about men in the village who, he said, had asked him to " put in a good word with the girls." Mother would tell him sharply to shut up. But he would persist. With the best of good humour, he would point out the many advantages of a match between Aunt Maggie, for example, and Jimmy the Post who owned one of the best-cared-for farms in the locality. " It's a proposition," he would say, slapping the table with his finger tips. " Turn it over. Give it a thought." Occasionally when he continued his schemes after lunch, Mother would accuse him of being drunk. He would then go sullenly to bed for the remainder of the afternoon and a silence would fall on the house. Only Aunt Rose seemed to be unaware of the undercurrents which even I was beginning to understand.

On the eve of my eighth birthday, Father was sacked from his job in the civil service. His Christmas binge had extended too far into January and his superiors had no patience left. However, as a return for twenty years' service, they promised him the first offer of any substitute work which might arise during the year through illness. When our meagre savings were exhausted three weeks after Father's dismissal, there was nothing for us but appeal to the aunts. Mother wrote to them and by return post came

an enthusiastic invitation to us to come and stay as long
as we wished. The following afternoon we set off.

Never before had I travelled to Ardara in the winter and
the journey was a series of disappointments. Darkness caught up
with us before we were halfway and snow began to fall. The
red rail-bus was cold and feebly lit and the other passengers
hugged themselves in silence in scattered seats. A cattle dealer
behind me smoked a dirty clay pipe whose fumes sickened me.
Mother sat upright beside me, her hands up her sleeves, hissing
a rosary to herself and Father slept heavily somewhere at the rear.
Only the happiness that I knew lay ahead kept me from whining.

The five aunts were on the platform to meet us and everything
was suddenly right again. They were friendlier than ever and
even more talkative. Although it was only five months since
they had last seen me, they agreed that I had got bigger and firmer
and when they hugged me in turn, each of them held on to me
protectively for a second longer than usual. Indeed they scarcely
looked at Mother at all, so concentrated were they on me. But
to Father they were as welcoming and as polite as ever. They
told him he was looking very well and said that January was a
good time for a rest. All bundled together, all talking at the same
time, the eight of us walked the short distance to the house.

That night and for the next three days, snow kept falling.
Gradually paths, roadways, hedges became one. The village
school was closed and Aunt Kate and Aunt Maggie were at home
all day. Only Father ventured out, beating an unsteady path for
himself to the town. In the house, talk became thin. There would
be hours of quiet and then from upstairs would come the sharp
voices raised in anger of two of the aunts. Sometimes they snapped
at one another when we were all together and on those occasions,
Mother would tell me to go to the sitting room and " keep up with
your lessons." I noticed that she had begun doing most of the
heavy housework ; never before had she been allowed to lift a
finger.

Ardara was turning sour for me. I could not go outside because
of the snow drifts and inside I was either forgotten about or the
object of everybody's attention. Perhaps for a whole morning
I would moon about, unseen, and then suddenly a couple of the
women would decide that my education was being neglected.
Aunt Kate and Mother would lead me to the sitting room, set

me between them and begin teaching me. These lessons frequently ended in tears. Aunt Kate would call me stubborn and obstinate and spoiled and Mother would defend me ; or Aunt Kate would stump off in disgust and Mother would suddenly slap my cheeks with her open hand, something she used never to do. To get away from them all, I would creep into Father's bed and lie beside him, warm and snoring. When he would awaken and dress himself fumblingly for the village, I would move into the part of the bed warmed by his body and wait until he came back again. Sometimes in his sleep, he would throw his hand across my chest and I would lie motionless beneath it, admiring its roughness.

By the end of two weeks, I knew I hated my five aunts, Rose especially, because she had disappointed me the most. I had expected her to provide some entertainment, to have something of interest tucked away. But she had nothing ; the snow had covered all her resources. Yet she kept haunting me. Wherever I went in the small house, she followed me, watching me with her diluted blue eyes, her head shot forward, her mouth never closed, silent. When I would look back arrogantly at her, the flat cheeks would rise in a smile and her head would bob up and down in greeting but she had nothing to say. Even when I thought she was out in the byre or bringing in turf for the fire, I would discover her pale face pressed against the window, peering in at me. I began to ignore her ; but that made no difference. At last, in desperation one day, I called her " cow face," the most hurtful nickname I could concoct, and that rid me of her. From then on, she stopped following me but whenever we were together in the kitchen or the sitting room, I could feel her eyes on me.

It was one of the railway men who found Father lying un- conscious in a drift of snow at the side of the signal box. He carried him on his shoulders to the house and then went for the doctor. I was in Father's bed, waiting for him to come back when the dark bulk of the two men passed the window. The house became suddenly quick with talk again. Mother was purposeful and competent and organised the aunts who were racing around in near-hysteria. They laid him in his bed and loaded him with blankets. His lips were blue, I remember, and one eye open and one shut in a grotesque wink. If he dies, I thought, I want to die too ; I don't want to be the only man left in this house. But mother did not let him die. Until the doctor came, hours later, she sat beside him, pouring drops of brandy into his mouth, rubbing his feet and legs and cheeks with her strong hands, talking to him with quiet intensity, calling him back to life. When the doctor arrived and I was chased out of the way, I went out to the byre to lie down and die, too.

Aunt Rose interrupted me. I should have locked the door from the inside. " Is it you ? " she said, peering into the dark corner where I lay on damp straw.

" Why ? "

" I just thought it was you." She came over to me and squatted down beside me. " What are you doing here ? "

" Nothing."

" It's the snow," she said, half to herself. " The snow."

The cold was seeping through my clothes. My lips must be darkening by now.

" I'll take you over to the brook and show you McHugh's new lambs."

" No."

" We'll go to the village—no one will miss us now—and buy a poke of sweets."

" Go away."

" You never saw Uncle John's sun helmet. It's up in the loft. Come on up and we'll look at it."

" Go away. Go away." I closed one eye and waited for death to take me.

" I'll show you something," she said softly, " if you promise to tell no one."

" I don't want to see anything."

" No one knows about this. No one in the whole world except me."

I sat up interested. I could die later. " Tell me what it is first."

" Promise ? "

" Promise."

She rose to her feet. Her face, now robbed of its perpetual smile, seemed strange, almost intelligent. She went over to the door and bolted it. Then her fingers groped along the lintel above the window, found a loose stone and removed it.

From the hole, she brought out a scrap of paper. I got up and stood behind her.

" There," she said. " Read that." It was a letter. Her hands were trembling.

The byre was dark and the handwriting spidery but I made it out. The letter was headed by an address in Boston and dated 1906. " Dear Rose," it said, " I have now made enough money for your passage. If you will come out and marry me, I will send it to you. Please make up your mind and reply by return. In haste, Bill Sweeney."

" Is that the whole surprise ? " I asked, disappointed.

She took the letter from me, folded it and put it back in its hiding place. " Bald Billy they called him," she said. " Because even then, he hadn't a stab of hair on his head." She drew back the bolt on the door and stood looking across the stunted hedge into the snow-covered meadow. The smile was creeping back into her face as she went out into the crisp air.

Father was out of his bed of pneumonia within a fortnight and well enough to accept a temporary post in early March. The fright did him good. We left Ardara when spring was imminent and as I sat waiting impatiently for the rail-bus to pull out of the station, the five faces of the aunts smiled and nodded in at us as if nothing had happened. But I knew then that this was a man's world and I was determined to go camping with the boys next August. There was nothing to bring me back there any more, nothing to interest me, not even Aunt Rose.

— *The Saucer of Larks*

Explorations

1.   There are obvious differences of character and outlook between the boy's mother and her sisters. Can you define these differences ? What did they come from ? How does the author suggest them to us ?

2.   Aunt Rose ' always smiled.' Why ? What causes her to stop smiling ?

3.   In the beginning the little boy is happy in the company of Aunt Rose. Why ?

4.   By the end of the story why has he turned against her ?

5. The author never states that there is any great bond of love between the boy and his father. Yet, when the father is sick the boy declares to himself : ' If he dies . . . I want to die too.' Can you explain this ?

6. There are several shifts of loyalties in the story as it proceeds : for instance the father begins as the odd-man-out in a world of women and children : can you trace the main shifts in this situation as the story proceeds ?

7. Is it cruel of the boy to reject Aunt Rose and her sisters as he does ? Is it wise ? Was it inevitable ? Explain.

8. What character in the story do you admire most ? Why ?

9. What has the child learned about the world by the end of the story ?

10. How would you describe the author's style in this story ?

11. Where would you place the climax ?

Exercises

1. As the mother, father and son go back on the rail-bus they probably discuss the aunts. Write your idea of their dialogue.

2. As the father gets well in the aunts' house there are, no doubt, several whispered conversations between him and his wife—conversations about his drinking, his accident, the changes in the aunts' attitude and so on. Try to imagine one such conversation and write it down.

3. Write a brief character sketch of Aunt Rose, basing your portrait on the evidence of the story.

19

THE POTATO GATHERERS

November frost had starched the flat countryside into silent rigidity. The " rat-tat-tat " of the tractor's exhaust drilled into the clean, hard air but did not penetrate it ; each staccato sound broke off as if it had been nipped. Hunched over the driver's wheel sat Kelly, the owner, a rock of a man with a huge head and broken fingernails, and in the trailer behind were his four potato gatherers—two young men, permanent farm hands, and the two boys he had hired for the day. At six o'clock in the morning, they were the only living things in that part of County Tyrone.

The boys chatted incessantly. They stood at the front of the trailer, legs apart, hands in their pockets, their faces pressed forward into the icy rush of air, their senses edged for perception. Joe, the elder of the two — he was thirteen and had worked for Kelly on two previous occasions—might have been quieter, but his brother's excitement was infectious. For this was Philly's first job, his first time to take a day off from school to earn money, his first opportunity to prove that he was a man at twelve years of age. His energy was a burden to him. Behind them, on the floor of the trailer, the two farm hands lay sprawled in half sleep.

Twice the boys had to cheer. The first time was when they were passing Dicey O'Donnell's house, and Philly, who was in the same class as Dicey, called across to the thatched, smokeless building, " Remember me to all the boys, Dicey ! " The second time was when they came to the school itself. It was then that Kelly turned to them and growled to them to shut up.

" Do you want the whole county to know you're taking the day off ? " he said. " Save your breath for your work."

When Kelly faced back to the road ahead, Philly stuck his thumbs in his ears, put out his tongue, and wriggled his fingers at the back of Kelly's head. Then, suddenly forgetting him, he said, " Tell me, Joe, what are you going to buy ? "

" Buy ? "

" With the money we get today. I know what I'm getting—
a shotgun. Bang ! Bang ! Bang ! Right there, mistah. Jist
you put your two hands up above your head and I reckon you'll
live a little longer." He menaced Kelly's neck.

"Agh ! " said Joe derisively.

" True as God, Joe. I can get it for seven shillings—an old
one that's lying in Tom Tracy's father's barn. Tom told me he
would sell it for seven shillings."

" Who would sell it ? "

" Tom."

" Steal it, you mean. From his old fella."

" His old fella has a new one. This one's not wanted." He
sighted along an imaginary barrel and picked out an unsuspecting
sparrow in the hedge. " Bang ! Never knew what hit you, did
you ? What are you going to buy, Joe ? "

" I don't know. There won't be much to buy with. Maybe
—naw, I don't know. Depends on what Ma gives us back."

"A bicycle, Joe. What about a bike ? Quinn would give
his away for a packet of cigarettes. You up on the saddle, Joe,
and me on the crossbar. Out to the millrace every evening. Me
shooting all the rabbits along the way. Bang ! Bang ! Bang !
What about a bike, Joe ? "

" I don't know. I don't know."

" What did she give you back the last time ? "

" I can't remember."

" Ten shillings ? More ? What did you buy then ? A leather
belt ? A set of rabbit snares ? "

" I don't think I got anything back. Maybe a shilling. I
don't remember."

"A shilling ! One lousy shilling out of fourteen ! Do you
know what I'm going to buy ? " He hunched his shoulders
and lowered his head between them. One eye closed in a huge
wink. " Tell no one ? Promise ? "

" What ? "

"A gaff. See ? "

" What about the gun ? "

" It can wait until next year. But a gaff, Joe. See ? Old
Philly down there beside the Black Pool. A big salmon. A

beaut. Flat on my belly, and—*phwist!*—there he is on the bank, the gaff stuck in his guts." He clasped his middle and writhed in agony, imitating the fish. Then his act switched suddenly back to cowboys and he drew from both holsters at a cat sneaking home along the hedge. " Bang ! Bang ! That sure settled you, boy. Where *is* this potato territory, mistah ? Ah want to show you hombres what work is. What's a-keeping this old tractor-buggy ? "

" We're jist about there, Mistah Philly, sir," said Joe. "Ah reckon you'll show us, O.K. You'll show us."

The field was a two-acre rectangle bordered by a low hedge. The ridges of potatoes stretched lengthwise in straight, black lines. Kelly unfastened the trailer and hooked up the mechanical digger. The two labourers stood with their hands in their pockets and scowled around them, cigarettes hanging from their lips.

" You two take the far side," Kelly told them. "And Joe, you and—— " He could not remember the name. " You and the lad there, you two take this side. You show him what to do, Joe." He climbed up on the tractor seat. "And remember," he called over his shoulder, " if the school-attendance officer appears, it's up to you to run. I never seen you. I never heard of you."

The tractor moved forward into the first ridges, throwing up a spray of brown earth behind it as it went.

" Right," said Joe. " What we do is this, Philly. When the digger passes, we gather the spuds into these buckets and then carry the buckets to the sacks and fill them. Then back again to fill the buckets. And back to the sacks. O.K., mistah ? "

" O.K., mistah. Child's play. What does he want four of us for ? I could do the whole field myself—one hand tied behind my back."

Joe smiled at him. " Come on, then. Let's see you."

"Just you watch," said Philly. He grabbed a bucket and ran stumbling across the broken ground. His small frame bent over the clay and his thin arms worked madly. Before Joe had begun gathering, Philly's voice called to him. "Joe ! Look ! Full already ! Not bad, eh ? "

" Take your time," Joe called back.

"And look, Joe! Look!" Philly held his hands out for his brother's inspection. They were coated with earth. "How's that, Joe? They'll soon be as hard as Kelly's!"

Joe laughed. "Take it easy, Philly. No rush."

But Philly was already stooped again over his work, and when Joe was emptying his first bucket into the sack, Philly was emptying his third. He gave Joe the huge wink again and raced off.

Kelly turned at the bottom of the field and came back up. Philly was standing waiting for him.

"What you need is a double digger, Mr. Kelly!" he called as the tractor passed. But Kelly's eyes never left the ridges in front of him. A flock of seagulls swooped and dipped behind the tractor, fluttering down to catch worms in the newly turned earth. The boy raced off with his bucket.

"How's it going?" shouted Joe after another twenty minutes. Philly was too busy to answer.

A pale sun appeared about eight-thirty. It was not strong enough to soften the earth, but it loosened sounds—cars along the road, birds in the naked trees, cattle let out for the day. The clay became damp under it but did not thaw. The tractor exulted in its new freedom and its splutterings filled the countryside.

"I've been thinking," said Philly when he met Joe at a sack. "Do you know what I'm going to get, Joe? A scout knife with one of those leather scabbards. Four shillings in Byrne's shop. Great for skinning a rabbit." He held his hands out from his sides now, because they were raw in places. "Yeah. A scout knife with a leather scabbard."

"A scout knife," Joe repeated.

"You always have to carry a scout knife in case your gun won't fire or your powder gets wet. And when you're swimming underwater, you can always carry a knife between your teeth."

"We'll have near twenty ridges done before noon," said Joe.

"He should have a double digger. I told him that. Too slow, mistah. Too doggone slow. Tell me, Joe, have you made up your mind yet?"

"What about?"

"What you're going to buy, stupid."

"Aw, naw. Naw . . . I don't know yet."

Philly turned to his work again and was about to begin, when the school bell rang. He dropped his bucket and danced back to his brother. " Listen ! Joe ! Listen ! " He caught fistfuls of his hair and tugged his head from side to side. " Listen ! Listen ! Ha, ha, ha ! Ho, ho, ho ! Come on, you fat, silly, silly scholars and get to your lessons ! Come on, come on, come on ! No dallying ! Speed it up ! Get a move on ! Hurry ! Hurry ! Hurry ! 'And where are the O'Boyle brothers today ? Eh ? Where are they ? Gathering potatoes ? What's that I hear ? What ? What ? ' "

" Look out, lad ! " roared Kelly.

The tractor passed within inches of Philly's legs. He jumped out of its way in time, but a fountain of clay fell on his head and shoulders. Joe ran to his side.

"Are you all right, Philly ? Are you O.K. ? "

" Tried to get me, that's what he did, the dirty cattle thief. Tried to get me."

" You O.K., mistah ? Reckon you'll live ? "

" Sure, mistah. Take more'n that ole coyote to scare me. Come on, mistah. We'll show him what men we really are." He shook his jacket and hair and hitched up his trousers. " Would you swap now, Joe ? "

" Swap what ? "

" Swap places with those poor eejits back there ? " He jerked his thumb in the direction of the school.

" No sir," said Joe. " Not me."

" Nor me neither, mistah. Meet you in the saloon." He swaggered off, holding his hands as if they were delicate things, not part of him.

They broke for lunch at noon. By then, the sun was high and brave but still of little use. With the engine of the tractor cut off, for a brief time there was a self-conscious silence, which became relaxed and natural when the sparrows, now audible, began to chirp. The seagulls squabbled over the latest turned earth and a cautious puff of wind stirred the branches of the tall trees. Kelly adjusted the digger while he ate. On the far side of the field, the two labourers stretched themselves on sacks and conversed in monosyllables. Joe and Philly sat on upturned buckets. For lunch they each had half a scone of home-made soda bread, cut into thick slices and skimmed with butter. They washed it down with mouthfuls of cold tea from a bottle. After they had eaten, Joe threw the crusts to the gulls, gathered up the newspapers in which the bread had been wrapped, emptied out the remains of the tea, and put the bottle and the papers into his jacket pocket. Then he stood up and stretched himself.

" My back's getting stiff," he said.

Philly sat with his elbows on his knees and studied the palms of his hands.

" Sore ? " asked Joe.

" What ? "

" Your hands. Are they hurting you ? "

" They're O.K.", said Philly. " Tough as leather. But the clay's sore. Gets right into every cut and away up your nails." He held his arms out. " They're shaking," he said. " Look."

" That's the way they go," said Joe. " But they'll—Listen ! Do you hear ? "

" Hear what ? "

" Lunchtime at school. They must be playing football in the playground."

The sounds of high, delighted squealing came intermittently when the wind sighed. They listened to it with their heads uplifted, their faces broadening with memory.

" We'll get a hammering tomorrow," said Joe. " Six on each hand."

" It's going to be a scout knife," Philly said. " I've decided on that."

" She mightn't give us anything back. Depends on how much she needs herself."

" She said she would. She promised. Have you decided yet ? "

" I'm still thinking," said Joe.

The tractor roared suddenly, scattering every other sound.

" Come on, mistah," said the older one. " Four more hours to go. Saddle up your horse."

" Coming. Coming," Philly replied. His voice was sharp with irritation.

The sun was a failure. It held its position in the sky and flooded the countryside with light but could not warm it. Even before it had begun to slip to the west, the damp ground had become glossy again, and before the afternoon was spent, patches of white frost were appearing on higher ground. Now the boys were working automatically, their minds acquiescing in what their bodies did. They no longer straightened up ; the world was their feet and the hard clay and the potatoes and their hands and the buckets and the sacks. Their ears told them where the tractor was, at the bottom of the field, turning, approaching. Their muscles had become adjusted to their stooped position, and as long as the boys kept within the established pattern of movement their arms and hands and legs and shoulders seemed to float as if they were free of gravity. But if something new was expected from the limbs —a piece of glass to be thrown into the hedge, a quick stepping back to avoid the digger—then their bodies shuddered with pain and the tall trees reeled and the hedges rose to the sky.

Dicey O'Donnell gave them a shout from the road on his way home from school. " Hi ! Joe ! Philly ! "

They did not hear him. He waited until the tractor turned. " Hi ! Hi ! Philly ! Philly ! Joe ! "

" Hello," Joe called back.

" Youse are for it the morrow. I'm telling youse. He knows where youse are. He says he's going to beat the scruff out of youse the morrow. Youse are in for it, all right. Blue murder ! Bloody hell ! True as God ! "

" Get lost ! " Joe called back.

"Aye, and he's going to report youse to the attendance officer, and your old fella'll be fined. Youse are ruined ! Destroyed ! Blue murder ! "

" Will I put a bullet in him, mistah ? " said Joe to Philly.

Philly did not answer. He thought he was going to fall, and his greatest fear was that he might fall in front of the tractor, because now the tractor's exhaust had only one sound, fixed forever in his head, and unless he saw the machine he could not tell whether it was near him or far away. The " rat-tat-tat " was a finger tapping in his head, drumming at the back of his eyes.

" Vamoose, O'Donnell ! " called Joe. " You annoy us. Vamoose."

O'Donnell said something more about the reception they could expect the next day, but he got tired of calling to two stooped backs and he went off home.

The last pair of ridges was turned when the sky had veiled itself for dusk. The two brothers and the two labourers worked on until they met in the middle. Now the field was all brown, all flat, except for the filled sacks that patterned it. Kelly was satisfied ; his lips formed an O and he blew through them as if he were trying to whistle. He detached the digger and hooked up the trailer. "All aboard ! " he shouted, in an effort at levity.

On the way home, the labourers seemed to be fully awake, for the first time since morning. They stood in the trailer where the boys had stood at dawn, behind Kelly's head and facing the road before them. They chatted and guffawed and made plans for a dance that night. When they met people they knew along the way, they saluted extravagantly. At the crossroads, they began to wrestle, and Kelly had to tell them to watch out or they would fall over the side. But he did not sound angry.

Joe sat on the floor, his legs straight out before him, his back resting against the side of the trailer. Philly lay flat out, his head cushioned on his brother's lap. Above him, the sky spread out, grey, motionless, enigmatic. The warmth from Joe's body made him drowsy. He wished the journey home to go on forever, the sound of the tractor engine to anaesthetise his mind forever. He knew that if the movement and the sound were to cease, the pain of his body would be unbearable.

" We're nearly there," said Joe quietly. "Are you asleep ? " Philly did not answer. " Mistah ! Are you asleep, mistah ? "
" No."

Darkness came quickly, and when the last trace of light disappeared the countryside became taut with frost. The head lamps of the tractor glowed yellow in the cold air.

" Philly ? Are you awake, mistah ? "
" What ? "
" I've been thinking," said Joe slowly. "And do you know what I think ? I think I've made up my mind now."

One of the labourers burst into song.

" If I were a blackbird, I'd whistle and sing, and I'd follow the ship that my true love sails in."

His mate joined him at the second line and their voices exploded in the still night.

" Do you know what I'm going to buy ? " Joe said, speaking more loudly. " If she gives us something back, that is. Mistah ! Mistah Philly ! Are you listening ? I'm going to buy a pair of red silk socks."

He waited for approval from Philly. When none came, he shook his brother's head. "Do you hear, mistah? Red silk socks—the kind Jojo Teague wears. What about that, eh? What do you think?"

Philly stirred and half raised his head from his brother's lap. "I think you're daft," he said in an exhausted, sullen voice. "Ma won't give us back enough to buy anything much. No more than a shilling. You knew it all the time." He lay down again and in a moment he was fast asleep.

Joe held his brother's head against the motion of the trailer and repeated the words "red silk socks" to himself again and again, nodding each time at the wisdom of his decision.

— *The Saucer of Larks*

Explorations

1. Do you find this a very real story? Say what parts of it strike you as particularly true to life, and why.

2. The effect of the story depends on a series of contrasts between people. Explain how the contrast is made between (a) the children and Kelly, (b) Joe and Philly, (c) the farm-boys and the young children. Are any of these particularly well done? Explain.

3. A good deal depends on the contrast between different moods. Point out where these contrasts are made. What do you think of the author's skill in making them?

4. When the children set out in the morning they are full of excitement about the money they will make and the things they will buy with it. At the end the younger of them says, 'Ma won't give us back enough to buy anything much. No more than a shilling. You knew it all the time.' Did Joe know it all the time? Did Philly know it all the time? If so, why their early optimism? What does the author mean to convey by Joe's repeated mention of the 'red silk socks'?

5. What does the writer convey to us by making Dicey O'Donnell appear when he does?

6. Has Philly learned anything about life from his day's work? If so, what? Has Joe learned anything? What is the difference between what they may have learned?

Exercises

1. The children at the beginning of the story imagine themselves as cowboys. Most children have fantasies and day dreams of this kind. Write down with as much honesty and accuracy as you can manage three of your own private visions. Having done so, read ' The Secret Life of Walter Mitty ' and see how they compare with those of an alleged adult.

2. Examine the passages in which the writer conveys the sense of growing exhaustion in the limbs and minds of the children. What words and phrases there strike you as particularly vivid ? If you have ever experienced similar exhaustion (at games, work, walking, cycling) try to find the right words to describe it in a few paragraphs.

3. Examine the structure of the story with a special eye to time and action. For instance, as time advances, the morale of the children rises and falls. The morale of the adults follows a different pattern. Try to devise a graph or table that will show these changes throughout the day.

20

THE WEB

WHEN the Black and Tan lorry left the strand road to swing instead towards the centre of the town, the Dummy was lounging at the corner house. All evening he had stood there in the mild warmth of the October sunlight, and though he was startled he did not move. But when the lorry passed close to him, his eyes narrowed and his head inclined slightly towards the wide strand on his left. He counted the turns. The engine slowed, revved, dropped again. It was going towards Freddie's house. By the time it stopped completely he was hammering loudly at one of the small cottages which faced the strand. There was no answer. He sucked his thumb and looked over his shoulder. About half a mile out in the centre of the pool-pocked sands two men were digging for bait. Their bent figures were diminutive with distance. Beyond them he could see the first foamy ridge of water and then the barracks at the extreme end of the breakwater towards which the lorry should normally have gone. He began to force the part-open window. Niall was standing at the foot of a disordered bed. He held a revolver which pointed at the window. The skin over his cheek-bones and about his mouth was tight, and he held his gun steadily.

" I heard them," he said. " Tell Waxer."

The Dummy nodded and went swiftly through the hallway. In the kitchen he passed Mrs. Ryan. She had a loaf and a knife in her hands and her face was white. She followed him with wide eyes and moaned when his boots scraped on the wall of the small yard at the back.

When he returned she was with Niall in her husband's bedroom. It was disordered because Ryan had been cranky that evening and would let no one disturb him. His tea was cold and untouched beside his bed, and the buttered bread fouled with cigarette ash. Only his head was visible, a narrowed egg of a head and a face sunken and yellow.

" I'm a dyin' man, Waxer," he whined, " a dyin' man."

" We're all dyin' men," Waxer said. " You're not dyin' when it comes to finding your way to Tobin's of a Saturday."

He beckoned Niall and strode to the window.

" The stuff," he snapped without turning around. Niall bent over his father.

" Dad," he pleaded, " will you get up ? Did you not hear them ? "

"Am I ever hearin' anythin' else ? They're goin' to the barracks."

" They're not," Niall said urgently. " They're goin' to Freddie's house."

His father shrank into an obstinate ball in the bed. His thin hands gripped the clothes tightly about his neck.

" What curse is over me ? " he asked. " What possessed yiz to come in ? There's no more guns goin' in here. I'm black and blue with the lumps under me mattress."

Niall gripped him by the shoulders and swung him to the floor. While the mattress was rolled back he stood bent and shivering by his bed. His left hand clutched the neck of his nightshirt, and when a fit of coughing seized him, his right pulled the bottom downwards for decency.

" Waxer," he pleaded, " am I to spend me latter days lyin' on a bloody magazine ? "

" Come on, come on," Waxer snorted. " Get the stuff out of that."

He leaned forward to peer through the window. There were lorries about the block and the room quivered sometimes with the trundling of them. Suddenly he stiffened.

" Dummy," he breathed, " get the manhole open."

Niall's mother crossed herself. The Dummy went out quickly to the back. The boots of soldiers grew loud on the pavement outside, while another lorry thundered in from the strand road. They were surrounding the house. Waxer motioned and Niall's mother followed them to the backyard.

" You'll have to put back the cover," Waxer said to her. " Lift it slowly and don't fuss. Then put your stool and the bath-tub over it. Splash the water about as though you'd been washing."

Niall and she exchanged looks. She bit her lip.

" I will, Mr. Brannigan," she said, " I will."

The sun lay warmly on the little yard and the bin in the corner cast a long shadow. Waxer let Niall and the Dummy down first. Then he followed nimbly. Niall's shoulder brushed

against the green ooze of the wall and the Dummy's nose wrinkled
in disgust. Then the trap above was eased into position and the
square of light narrowed and went out. They began to shuffle
forward warily in the smelling darkness.

When the lorry pulled up outside Freddie's house the street
was deserted except for a child with a white milk jug who stood
to watch. The old men who used to sit on the low window sills
were gone, and their dogs and their gossip. From an arc of
wetness around a half-scrubbed doorstep, steam still rose lightly,
and here and there a furtive curtain moved. The child went
demurely up the street. She found Freddie with Phil Tobin in
the back bar.

" Well ? " he said.

" The soldiers are at the house," she panted. " I ran."

" Did they see you ? "

" No," she said, " they didn't mind me. I was fetchin' milk."

Phil Tobin was twisting his white apron with his hands. He
had fat stubby fingers. The apron was like a handkerchief
against the width of his stomach. Freddie put his hand on her
head.

" Good child," he said gently, " get the milk and bring it
back and say nothing."

He became anxious.

" Remember," he insisted quietly, " nothing."

She nodded and slipped out.

Phil tugged at his sleeve.

" For God's sake make a move," he said. " They'll be in on
top of us."

" That's right," Freddie answered. " They waste no time."

They picked their way through a tortuous passage and down
stone steps.

When they were in the cellar Phil said : " I knew it. Someone informed."

" What makes you think that ? "

" I'm no man's fool," said Phil Tobin.

" Unless we were seen, only yourself and the Ryans could
know."

" People can talk," said Phil.

Freddie glanced round at the barrels which littered the cellar,
and at the grating which opened into the lane above. There

was a mattress in the corner and a roll of blankets. He stooped
and took out a revolver. Phil crumpled his apron in his hands.
The apple-red of his lusty face was wrinkled and perturbed.

" I don't know in the name of God what prompted youse to
come in," he declared.

" Orders," Freddie said, straightening. " Don't ask me why."
He settled himself facing the door.

" You'd best get back to the shop," he said. " If they find me,
tell them I came in through the grating."

Phil closed the door and went off with a nervous jangling
of keys, and Freddie sat down to wait.

The soldiers searched his house. They swore at his mother
because she would not answer them. They took his father,
struggling, with them. Other houses were ransacked also. But
when the night came and they were spread watchfully throughout the town, nothing had been found.

When they reached the mouth of the tunnel the sun was
down and the smell of the sea stronger because it was night.
From the fern-grown opening of the disused drain they could
see the whole wide expanse of the strand ; the lighthouse which
stood beside the barracks at the extreme end of the breakwater,
two miles of inkiness between, then the stringing of lamps along
the coast road on their right, smears of blurred light through
the misting rain. On the right, too, lay the Terrace and the
house they had come from, Niall's house. The light was in his
father's bedroom. He could single it out from all the lights along
the strand road. When he was a child and night had overtaken
his playing he had often walked to it in a straight line across the
ebbed strand.

Niall stared for a long time at the light while they crouched
in misery and felt the air damp about them.

" Somebody told," he said with sudden bitterness, " some
rat."

" I know," Waxer said smoothly, " but who ? "

" I don't know," Niall said, " someone."

He stared back into the darkness.

" They went to Freddie's house ; I counted the turns."

" For all his smart talk," Waxer said, " Freddie is only a child ;
he wanted to be with his mother."

" He's got his bellyful now," Niall said. " You might as well talk to the wall." Waxer's mouth was closed tightly and his eyes looked to the right at nothing. He was thinking of several things at once.

But Niall's eyes moved restlessly, surveying the dripping walls, scanning the darkness.

" If they come to search here we're cornered. We can't get out."

Waxer smiled coldly. " We can get out the way we got in. You can always do that."

" No damn fear," Niall said, " not back through the house. I'm damned if we go that way."

" Who's giving orders ? "

" To hell with orders," Niall said with heat. " That's one order you won't give." Waxer's mouth thinned.

" Who said so ? " he asked evenly.

" I did. The mother is there and the da is a sick man, he's dyin'. If there was any trouble it would kill him."

Waxer smiled coldly. He sucked in his cheeks until the skin across the massive cheek-bones was white. He let the matter rest.

" Until we know what's outside," he said, " we'll stay put."

The tunnel was dismally cold about them and the rain spun thinly across the dark sands. Sound travelled easily across the open space, but tonight the familiar noises were hushed. The darkness of narrow streets echoed now and then as a lorry moved off or changed its position, and that was all. Niall crouched and looked back along the tunnel which ran right under his home. He wondered if the soldiers had stayed in his house, and what his father and mother were doing. He had a long sallow face which at the moment was strained and apprehensive, and eyes that were at all times wide and lustrous. Opposite to him crouched the stocky figure of Waxer. It was Waxer who had brought both Niall and the Dummy into the movement. At the language-revival classes Niall had more aptitude than Waxer, but when it came to military action Waxer was officer. It was Waxer who had thought of exploring the almost forgotten tunnel and had arranged with H.Q. for using it as a dump. He was checking the barrel of the revolver which was his sole certificate for scholarship.

Niall watched the house-lights on the shore go out one by one. He started at any unusual sound.

" All the same," he said later, " we shouldn't have come in. We were safe in the hills."

Waxer did not answer.

" Safer than here. It was bloody foolish to order four men——"

" Cut that out," Waxer said coldly. " Cut it out."

" I don't see——."

" Drop it," Waxer snarled.

The Dummy looked up mildly. He had taken possession of the bomb and was playing idly with it. Though he was young enough to wear knickerbockers, the legs beneath his black stockings were muscular. His lips were turned up and slightly parted, as though smiling at his thoughts.

" When you've knocked off four officers," Waxer said grimly, " you're safe nowhere." He spat into the darkness. He looked at the Dummy and then lay back against the tunnel-wall once more.

" Yer a good soldier," he said drily, " you don't answer back."

The Dummy grinned and continued to play idly with the bomb. A long time later, when they were chilled and cramped and everyone had forgotten the context, Waxer said :

". . . Nowhere."

When Ryan walked up the plots the following morning there were fewer men than usual. They looked at him sympathetically and let him pass when he showed little inclination to linger. Nothing more had happened during the night. He had been wakened early by his wife. It was a clear morning of sunshine and light white clouds. The sun was on the front of the house and had filled the bedroom as he raised himself on his elbow to lean over the breakfast tray.

" Nuthin' happened ? " he had asked, screwing up his eyes.

She glanced covertly at the soldier who sat in the window.

" What could happen," she had said indifferently, " and them miles away."

" That's right," he said, " of course."

He grunted uneasily.

"It's bright out, d'yeh think ? "

" Like a summer's morning—thank God. You could take your walk."

" I will," he decided, " I'll take a turn down to the Bakery." It was his habit when Saturday was fine. He would walk down to the Bakery for his pension and then up the strand road for a pipe and a chat.

He showed improvement, the men sometimes said to him. It pleased him and made him feel better. " It's the dry weather," he would say ; " the doctor says I should go to a sanatorium. It'd cure me, he says."

But that morning he went by without a word. He shuffled moodily past them and stopped some distance away at the strand wall. They saw him hobble with his hands deep in his pockets, staring and staring at the bright pools which flashed in the wake of the tide.

One of the men said : " The soldiers were in the house all night. Isn't it a queer thing they should let him out ? " and another : " He's waitin' for the band to play. They can't be hidin' for ever."

Phil was with Freddie on and off during the day. There was little doing in the shop. The soldiers were still in the streets and people did not go out without necessity. When he was taking away the remains of Freddie's dinner he said : " I sent that note you gave out. The youngster took it."

" Good," Freddie said. " If an answer comes, bring it immediately. Was there anything else ? "

" Ryan was out and about."

" He goes down for the pension," Freddie said.

Phil said meaningly, " The soldiers are in his house."

" What about it ? " Freddie asked irritably.

" Nothing," Phil answered mildly, " except that it's funny they should let him out."

Freddie ran his hands quickly through his hair.

He said, " No man would split on his own son." There were dark circles under his eyes and his face was pinched. His eyes were quick and nervous.

" Men do queer things, especially sick men."

Freddie shook his head. He looked around at the dust-encrusted walls, at the barrels tilted about the floor and the cobwebs which stretched like threadbare rags across every corner of the low ceiling. He began to pace restlessly.

" I wish to God I could get away from here," he said at last. Then : " Will Ryan be here tonight ? "

" Always on a Saturday."

" Watch him," Freddie said, " and if an answer comes, let me know." The keys jangled and the beat of feet on the stone stairway dwindled once more into silence. There was still light in the cellar, and on the grating above loud feet clanged on occasion and passed. But there were long silences, during which he crouched in a corner from which he could command the door, smoking cigarettes, watching a spider spreading its dexterous web between two barrels. It stopped occasionally as though to stare at him. Now and then he blew smoke from his cigarette in a gentle stream towards the web. This would send it scurrying out of sight. His eyes narrowed as he considered the spider. Once he laughed suddenly. Then his mood changed. He broke the web in sudden disgust. It retired altogether for a time, but later came back and began to spin once more. It was inexorable. The streets grew hushed as the light failed and the cellar echoed not at all. The dust, smelling more strongly, foretold rain.

It began that night when the men in Tobin's were beginning to glance at the yellow-faced clock. At first, but for the diminutive drops which flecked the windows, it was hardly noticeable. But later it grew fierce. They sat and heard the wind rise and the rain sweeping over streets and little houses, over limp ropes and hanging nets and the dreary stretches of sand. There was little conversation. A stranger stood for a time at the bar, had some words with Phil and, when the rain was beginning, left. Ryan was there also. He sat nearer the right-hand end of the counter and lingered over his drinks. His overcoat was too big for him and pieces of fluff clung to it because of his habit of throwing it on the foot of the bed. He spoke to no one except Phil. He stared miserably into space and tapped absently at his chin with a bony finger.

Whenever Phil stood before him he took out a purse and fumbled awkwardly as he paid.

" It's a poor night," he said and looked down at his drink.

" It is," Phil answered, " for a man on his keeping."

When the men were leaving, Phil went down and stood before him with his hands resting on the counter. He looked down steadily at him.

" The sergeant is in the snug," Phil said levelly. " They were round at the house looking for you."

" Lookin' ? " Ryan repeated.

" They want to question you."

" Question, Phil. They'd have your soul damned into hell with their questions. They'd have you tormented." He looked right and left quickly. He reached out with bony fingers to caress Phil's arm.

" Phil," he asked, " have you word of Niall, do you know where they are . "

" Where ? "

" I'm askin' you, Phil, you that knew them." He leaned forward. "Are they in the tunnel—I know there's a tunnel. Are they there ? "

" You seem to know more than I do," Phil said.

Ryan looked down at his drink. His face was old and yellow-lined like a rotten apple. His eyes, like Niall's, swam with odd lustre, but they were sunken and peeped from a distance.

" I don't, Phil," he breathed, " I know nuthin'. I didn't even know they were coming back. But if they're in the tunnel it's not safe. I have word, I—I heard them talking last night in the bedroom——".

" You're keepin' the sergeant," said Phil coldly.

" Maybe I am, Phil, but I swear before God Niall is a good boy and I played fair by him. He'd tell you that. I reared him and I put the clothes on his back. I worked when I should have been at home in me bed. The doctor said a sanatorium would cure me, but it meant money and I couldn't see him hungry. There was nuthin' he had that didn't come from me." Phil's eyes mocked him.

" I wouldn't harm a hair on his head," he said almost to himself, " nor let others do it." A hand was laid on his shoulder. He turned around.

" There's a couple of questions I'd like to ask," said the sergeant, " so finish your business——".

Phil came in with the note and held the candle so that Freddie could read. The flame quivered and the grease dripped over

and stung his fingers. The shadows retreated from the flame.
They huddled in a ring about the two of them. Outside the rain
ran in rivulets down channels, and the soldiers, scattered at their
stations throughout the town, crouched miserably and swore.
They looked up at the skies and wished for something to happen.
Freddie stuck the note into the flame. They watched in silence
while it burned.

" I've got to go," Freddie said. " I've got to find the rest."

" You'll find no one tonight, are you mad ? "

" I'll find them all right. Put out the candle and help me to
raise the grating."

" I won't," Phil said backing away. " Why can't you bide
your time ? "

" Quickly," Freddie said, " there isn't any time."

He listened acutely. There was no sound but the monotonous beat of the rain. He snuffed the candle and caught Phil
by the arm. They began to build a pyramid of crates directly
under the grating. When they had finished Phil's face ran with
sweat. They eased up the gate cautiously. There was no creaking
on account of the rain. Freddie let himself through. He crouched
for a moment to listen. Phil stood by while the gate was lowered.
Freddie signed to him, straightened quickly, and strode away.

He went casually through the darkened town, his shoulders
hunched and his head down against the rain. Nobody passed ;
the streets were deserted ; lorries stood here and there by the
side of the road, vacant and dead beneath the swollen skies,
like derelict ships.

But when he reached the strand there were soldiers at intervals along the wall. One was so near that he could hear the
crunch of his boots and the irritable clank of equipment. He
stopped dead. He was intensely aware of the web that had been
built around him, a web which for months had been growing
about him, a web he must break from or perish in. The spider
was spinning. His eyes narrowed as each sense became suddenly
sharpened. After a while he dropped to his knees and made
with painful slowness towards the wall.

They crouched in the darkness, each withdrawn into himself, so that they were three beings, three isolated points of life

in a vast solitude. The great ferns which cluttered the mouth
of the tunnel were swaying and dripping, but when the wind
dropped they could hear sounds on the beach, lost sounds that
were lonely like eternity. Niall shuddered and when a fit of
coughing seized him he would bury his mouth in his cap in
order to stifle it. When shots rang out he licked his lips and
glanced through the darkness at Waxer and the Dummy.

His face was grey. The smell of the tunnel and the strain of
waiting had made him sick. His limbs were cramped and stiff
with waiting. He was fascinated when either of the others
moved or betrayed signs of life.

" Who the hell are they firing at ? " he asked, his voice rising.

" Maybe they're jittery," said Waxer, " shootin' their
shadows."

" We should have shifted last night, Waxer. We could have
made it."

" We waited for word."

" How could they send it ? "

" If I know anythin' about it," said Waxer, " they'll find a
way. They won't let the dump go."

" If Freddie was caught——."

" Hush," Waxer said, " we've got to listen."

Niall hunched miserably. He squirmed and became uneasy,
chafing at his helplessness. He drew his knees up to his chin,
then stretched them full length ; he turned on one side. Then
he shifted again, rubbed a cramped leg, crouched once more
over his knees. Sometimes he sighed. But Waxer and the Dummy
sat unmoved.

They were silent until the Dummy half rose and grunted.

" What ? " Waxer snapped, and Niall jerked forward with
his hand going automatically to his pocket. The Dummy jabbed
his thumb towards the strand. They listened. Somebody slid
down the embankment some distance away. A tin can clinked
and then rolled noisily, and shots rang out.

" Christ," Niall said, panicking. He scrambled forward on his
hands and knees towards the tunnel entrance.

" Back," Waxer growled, " you bloody fool, back towards the
house."

The Dummy sat rigid, his mouth and eyes narrow lines,
Niall still went forward.

" Them's orders," Waxer hissed, " and put that revolver away."

" Go to hell," Niall said. Waxer swore and pounced. Feet slithered on the embankment below and someone fell forward into the tunnel. Waxer flung sideways and came to grips.

" Who is it ? " he snarled, and his fingers slipped swiftly upwards.

" Me," Freddie said simply.

Waxer loosened his grip. He felt his hands sticky.

" You're hit."

" Left shoulder," Freddie said. " They caught me when I'd crossed the wall."

" We'd better shift. Is it bad ? "

" I can't say," Freddie answered. " I had a message from Cassidy. I burned it and came straight."

" Good work," Waxer said. He looked quickly behind him and then back at Freddie.

" Do you know how things are ? "

But Freddie had slumped back against the wall. He was quite young, almost as young as the Dummy. His face beneath the shock of dark curls was pale. It was scratched and streaked with sand where he had fallen when the bullets struck him. His nose still bled slightly. Waxer and the Dummy looked on while Niall wiped away the sand with his handkerchief.

" See to his shoulder," said Waxer, " and bring him round. We don't want him on our hands."

" I don't want to strip his shoulder," Niall answered. " I think it might be dangerous in this atmosphere."

" That's right," grumbled Waxer, " do nuthin' you're told." But he made no move himself. He lay back and watched while Niall bent in silence over Freddie. The Dummy shaded a small torch with his body.

" He's bleeding like hell," Niall whispered in sudden terror. " Why don't you do something ? "

" Wake him up," demanded Waxer. " I want to know all I can."

Niall shook Freddie.

" Freddie," he pleaded, " Freddie, don't sleep now. Do you hear me ? We've got to get away from here."

Freddie murmured and twisted his head from side to side.

" What's he say ? "

" He's wandering," Niall answered, frightened. " Something about spiders . . ."

Waxer grunted.

After a while Freddie sighed with his whole body and opened his eyes. Waxer leaned forward.

" There's a first-aid kit in the bend by the dump," he said to Niall. " You'll get bandages there." He nodded to the Dummy. " Show him," he added.

When they had gone he spoke to Freddie. " Now," he said.

" Cassidy sent word by Phil. I was in the cellar . . . watching the . . . They're coming for the dump tonight."

"Are you sure of that ? "

" Intelligence says so. You've to lay a fuse if you can and then get out. They'll have a car outside the Ivy Church——"

" The Ivy Church," Waxer said ironically, " that's a bloody good one."

" Someone informed——" Freddie added.

" Who ? " demanded Waxer.

Freddie moved weakly and looked straight at Waxer. He hesitated.

" Niall's father," he said.

Waxer slid forward to the mouth of the tunnel. Here and there on the strand lights moved. They jerked in nervous bars in the blackness. He thought they were coming nearer, but very slowly. When he got back Niall was leaning once more over Freddie.

" They're coming," he said.

Niall looked quickly over his shoulder. Then he went on with his bandaging.

" Do you know who split ? " he asked between clenched teeth. Freddie looked queerly at him.

" No, Niall," he said, " I don't know."

There was a short silence during which the Dummy's eyes turned with half understanding from Waxer to Freddie. Freddie looked away and Waxer's eyes focussed on the ground between his feet.

" We've got to move quickly," Waxer said after a pause. " Can you make it, Freddie ? "

Freddie nodded.

" Very well. We'll go back by the house."

Niall bit his lip. He seemed on the point of tears.

" Waxer," he said, " it'll kill me da, it'll be the death of him."

Waxer swore.

" Waxer," Niall appealed.   " Supposin' they're still in the yard——"

" It's dark. If we go out shooting there's a chance. You and I will go first. Then while we cover them the Dummy will help Freddie through. Is that clear ? "

Niall bowed his head. They nodded. There were noises from the strand as the ring drew nearer. They could feel the ring tightening on them. Waxer gestured with the revolver.

"All right," he said, " move."

He betrayed no emotion.

They followed, crouched, through the darkness. Once Freddie fell, and the Dummy helped him to his feet. They passed the opening of a tunnel on their right. It was at right angles to the main tunnel but had been blocked up about twenty yards from the opening. It contained the dump. There were bandages scattered here and there from Niall's searching. The Dummy paused but Waxer said, " There isn't time."

When they were crouching under the manhole which opened into Niall's back yard there were loud reports and shots ricochetted through the tunnel.

" Quick," Waxer said.

Niall went to his side and pressed his hands against the manhole. He took the strain with his wrists. Then he rose slowly and bent his arms. Waxer grunted and they pushed violently. The cover lifted with the sudden pressure. It went skidding across the yard. Then the rain was wet on their faces.

Waxer fired into the darkness, covering the scullery door and the opposite wall. Freddie gained the yard but the bin tripped him and he fell. He rose painfully, firing while Niall and Waxer broke for the back wall. " Freddie!" Niall screamed, beckoning, " Freddie!" But Freddie did not attempt the wall. He turned instead towards the house. After a while he was alone in the yard. He was dimly aware of lights and a kitchen table, and further away, like a long dark tunnel, the hallway and an open door. Beyond the door were soldiers. They opened fire.

He shouted and lunged savagely forward. They closed around the hall door. They shot solidly until he reeled against the bedroom door. It swung inwards and he pitched headlong into the room. He moaned and breathed painfully . . .

The Dummy lay back along the tunnel. They had followed him, forcing him slowly yard by yard back to the dump. He was not quite dead. But though the bomb had rolled away from him, the pin which he had withdrawn was still clutched in his hand. It was intensely dark. In front of him and behind him, at about twenty yards' distance, were bars of light and cautiously approaching feet. . . . .

When Freddie opened his eyes there was no one besides Ryan in the room. At first Freddie did not see him. He was watching the spider. It fascinated him. It crept across the floor, now stopping, now moving forward. It grew giant-like and after diminished ; it became three spiders, and then ten, all marching or floating in a serried line. Sometimes they wavered and dissolved, sometimes all were spinning furiously. It became one again. Then slowly he was aware of a voice from the bed, an incoherent mumbling. He saw a head above the bedclothes and a thin hand which clutched rosary beads. He stretched his arm along the floor towards the revolver.

He said, " Why did you do it ? "

The hand tightened.

Ryan sat up. He looked in terror at Freddie. He had been crying. He shuddered and said, " I didn't know youse were comin' back—I swear—youse told me nuthin'—what are you doin' with the gun ? "

" It's not for you," Freddie answered, " it's for the spider." Ryan saw no spider. His eyes searched. His jaw fell open.

" Why ? "

The spider, Freddie knew, had caused the trouble. The spider had made a web. It must be found. He raised himself painfully on his elbow.

Ryan yelled in alarm.

" Freddie—for the love of God—I didn't know youse were coming back. I only knew about the dump. There wasn't badness in that, not just about the dump."

" Why . . . ? " Freddie breathed.

He hardly knew he asked the question. He had found the

spider. It was crawling slowly over the bedclothes towards the beads and the hand. As Ryan sank back against the pillow Freddie raised the revolver. He levelled at the spider, lost sight of it, then levelled again.

Ryan moaned and said, " How could I know youse were coming back ? "

Then he closed his eyes. His voice, tired and almost inaudible, murmured : " I wanted the money. I wanted it for a sanatorium."

Freddie fired twice at the spider. It disappeared. He stared and saw the stain of blood growing on the sheets. Then suddenly his elbow gave under him and he pitched forward. His eyes were still open. When the explosion shook the room a moment later he neither moved nor heard.

But Waxer and Niall heard. They lay flat in the rain and the darkness. The little garden shuddered with the noise of lorries and about them they could feel the inexorable closing-in of the search. They looked sideways at one another.

Two blocks away, aeons away, looming over low roofs and intersecting walls, rose the Ivy Church.

— *The Trusting and the Maimed*

Explorations

1. On the evidence of the story what do you think of Waxer as a soldier ? What do you think of him as a human being ?

2. There is tension and disagreement between Niall and Waxer as they wait at the end of the tunnel. Is this due to their different temperaments ? Or is it due to something else ? Or both ?

3. What use does the author make of irony in the story ? In answering, take account of the spider, the movements of the characters in the story, the relationships and associations of the people with each other.

4. There is considerable suspense and terror in the story. Show some of the ways in which this atmosphere is built up and sustained.

5. Would it have been as good a story had the author left the spider out altogether ? In answering, consider why the spider appears so alarmingly on Mr. Ryan's bed at the end.

6. A short story writer has not the same leisure to describe character as a novelist. Normally he can give only enough information about the

character to make his actions meaningful in the context of the story. Discuss the characterisation of Freddie, Mr. Ryan, Niall and the Dummy in the light of this statement.

7. As the manhole is closed after the descent of the guerillas the author states that ' the trap was eased into position.' Is there a deliberate ambiguity in the word ' trap ' ? Are there other examples of this use of language throughout the story ? Examine the text carefully in answering.

Exercises

1. Tell the story as seen through Niall's eyes from the moment when Waxer ' smiled coldly.' Try to follow his thoughts as well as his actions.

2. Tell the story as seen through the eyes of Phil Tobin, or of Waxer.

3. Read O'Connor's ' Guests of the Nation ' so that you can compare the stories in next day's class discussion. Give particular attention to both theme and structure. Which of them, for instance, best achieves that unique and single effect that Poe mentions? See p. 6 of Introduction.

21

JANEY MARY

When Janey Mary turned the corner into Nicholas Street that morning, she leaned wearily against a shop-front to rest. Her small head was bowed and the hair which was so nondescript and unclean covered her face. Her small hands gripped one another for warmth across the faded bodice of her frock. Around the corner lay Canning Cottages with their tiny, frost-gleaming gardens, and gates that were noisy and freezing to touch. She had tried each of them in turn. Her timid knock was well known to the people who lived in Canning Cottages. That morning some of them said : " It's that little 'Carthy one, never mind opening. Twice in the last week she's been around—it's too much of a good thing." Those who did answer her had been dour. They poked cross and harassed faces around half-open doors. Tell her mammy, they said, it's at school she should have her, and not out worrying poor people the likes of them. They had the mouths of their own to feed and the bellies of their own to fill, and God knows that took doing.

The school was in Nicholas Street and children with satchels were already passing. Occasionally Janey Mary could see a few paper books peeping from an open flap, and beside them a child's lunch and a bottle of milk. In the schoolroom was a scrawled and incomprehensible blackboard, and rows of staring faces which sniggered when Janey Mary was stupid in her answers.

Sometimes Father Benedict would visit the school. He asked questions in Catechism and gave the children sweets. He was a huge man who had more intuition than intellect, more genuine affection for children than for learning. One day he found Janey Mary sitting by herself in the back desk. She felt him, giant-like above her, bending over her. Some wrapped sweets were put on her desk.

"And what's your name, little girl ? "

" Janey Mary 'Carthy, Father."

" I'm Father Benedict of the Augustinians. Where do you live ? " Father Benedict had pushed his way and shoved his way until he was sitting in the desk beside her. Quite suddenly Janey Mary had felt safe and warm. She said easily, " I lives in Canning Cottages."

He talked to her while the teacher continued self-consciously with her lesson.

" So, your daddy works in the meat factory ? "

" No, Father, my daddy's dead."

Father Benedict nodded and patted her shoulder. " You and I must be better friends, Janey," he said. " We must tell your mammy to send you to school more often."

" Yes, Father."

" Because we must see more of one another, mustn't we ? "

" Yes, Father."

" Would you always come ? "

" I'd like to come, Father."

Father Benedict had talked with her for some time like that, the pair of them crushed clumsily in the desk and their heads close together. When he was leaving he gave her more sweets. Later the teacher took them from her as a punishment and gave them out again as little prizes for neatness.

She thought of Father Benedict until an old beggar who was passing said to her : " Are you whingin', child ? Is there anything up with you ? "

She lifted her head and looked stupidly at him, her mouth open and her eyes quite dry. He was a humpbacked man with broken boots and a bulbous nose. The street about him was a moving forest of feet ; the stolid tread of workmen and the pious shuffle of middle-aged women on their way from Mass.

" You look a bit shook, kid," he said. "Are you after taking a turn ? "

" No, mister," she said, wondering. " I'm only going for to look for bread at St. Nicholas's. My mammy told me."

" Your mammy left it a bit late. They'll be going in for to pray." As though awakened by his words, the bell of the Augustinian Friary rang three times. It rang out with long, resounding strokes across the quivering street, and people paused to uncover their heads and to bless themselves.

Janey Mary looked up quickly. The steeple of the church

rose clear and gleaming above the tall houses, and the golden slimness of its cross raced swiftly against the blue and gold of the sky.

Her mother had said : " Look till you find, my lady, and you won't lose your labour. This is the day of the Blessed Bread and if you get it nowhere else they'll be giving it out at St. Nicholas's."

She turned suddenly and ran quickly up the length of the street. But when she reached the priory the doors were closed and the waiting queue had broken into small knots. She stopped uncertainly and stared for some time.

The priests, the people said, had gone in to pray. They would be back in an hour.

She was glad to turn homewards. She was tired and her bare feet moved reluctantly on the ice-cold pavement. Johnny might have been given some bread on his round with the sticks, or her mother might have had some hidden away. Her mother sometimes did that so that Janey Mary would try very hard to get some.

Picking her way amongst the debris-littered wasteland upon which houses had once stood, she watched her shadow bobbing and growing with the uneven rippling of the ground. The light of the wintry sun rested wanly on everything and the sky was dizzily blue and fluffed a little with white cloud. There were rust-eaten tin-cans lying neglected on the waste, and fragments of coloured delf which she could have gathered to play chaneys had she had the time. The children often went there to play shop ; they marked out their pitches with a file of pebbles in the form of an open square. When Janey Mary stood in one of the squares for a moment she was no longer Janey Mary. The waste-land became a busy street and the tracery of pebbles glittering stores. Her face would grow grave. It was that serene gravity of a child at play. But when she stepped out of the magic square she was again Janey Mary, a Janey Mary who was cold and hungry and whose mother was waiting impatiently for bread that had not been found.

" There was none," she said, looking up at her mother's face. " Nobody would give it and the man said the priests wouldn't be back for an hour." She looked around hopefully as she spoke, but there were only a few crumbs on the table. They littered its grease-fouled and flower-patterned covering. An enamel jug stood in the centre and about it the slopped ugliness of used cups. Now that she was home she realised how endless the morning's trudging had been. She realised how every door had been closed against her. Her mother's voice rose.

" Then you can do without. Are you after looking at all, you little trollop ? Two hours to go the length of the street and around to the holy priests, and us all in a wakeness with the hunger. And Johnny going out with the sticks and him famished but for the little bit I had left away. Are you after looking at all ? "

The enamel of the jug was broken in three places. The breaks were spidery, like the blobs of ink which used to fall so dis-hearteningly on her copy-books. Down the side of each cup clung the yellow residue of dribbled tea. The whole table shifted suddenly and went back again, and her mother's voice seemed far away. Janey Mary wanted to sit down.

" Gallivanting," her mother said, " off gallivanting with your pals. I'll gallivant you. But you can go back again. There's nothing in the house. Back with you to the priests' house and wait like any Christian for what's going. And take the bag with you. You don't do a hand's turn till you do that."

Janey Mary stood with her hands clasped in front of her and looked up at her mother. The thought of going back again filled her with misery.

" I asked," she said. " I asked everywhere."

" Then you can ask again," said her mother. " You can ask till you find," and swung away. Janey Mary went wearily to the corner to fetch the bag. The kitchen trembled and became dark when she bent to pick it up. As she went out of the door her mother said :

" Put a bit of hurry on yourself and don't be slingeing. It's certain you'll never die with the beating of your heart. The world and its wife would get something and mine'd be left."

Once more she was out in the ancient crookedness of streets, picking her way amidst the trundling of wheels and the count-less feet. Tiny and lost beneath the steepness of houses, she went slowly, her bare feet dragging and dirty. At this hour the shops in Nicholas Street were crowded with women who haggled over halfpennies. White-coated assistants leaned quickly over marble-topped counters with heads cocked to one side and pencils raised in readiness, or dashed from counters to shelves

and back again, banging things on the scales and then licking
pencil stubs while they frowned over figures. Sometimes Janey
Mary used to stand and watch them, but now she went by
without interest. When a tram went grinding past her, her lips
trembled, and though the rails after it and before it gleamed in
the sunlight, it was a pale cold gleaming. There was no friendly
heat in the sunlight. There was nothing friendly. There were
only trundling trams and the tramp of feet, and once again the
slim cross on the spire of St. Nicholas's.

On the Feast of the Blessed Bread it was the custom of the
priests to erect a wooden counter on the high steps before the
door of the priory. Here two of the brothers stood to watch the
forming of the queue. Janey Mary looked hard through the
veil which blurred occasionally in front of her eyes, but could
catch no sign of Father Benedict. No bread had yet appeared
though the queue was growing. She took her place and kept
close to the wall. In near the wall she found it easier to hold
her position. It was very cold at first, but after a while more
people came and the air grew warmer. They came, as she had
known they would, with baskets and shawls, with torn shopping
bags and ragged coats, and gathered thickly about her. There
were men there too, old pensioners and men who had not worked
for years.

" There won't be much going," they said. " There was a
shocking crowd here this morning."

" Take your bloody hour," they said. " Who d'you think
you're pushing ? "

"Aisy, aisy, mind the chisler."

They talked like that for a long time. At first they argued
furiously with one another. But later they became dour with
impatience. They shuffled uncomfortably. They spat frequently
and heaved long sighs.

After a while it became frightening to be in there so close
to the wall, to be so small that everyone towered over you.
Janey Mary felt weak and wanted to get out. When she glanced
sideways or ahead of her she could see nothing but tightly packed
bodies, and when she looked down there were feet, but no ground.
She tried to look upwards, but could not. An hour passed before
Father Benedict appeared on the steps.

" Father Benedict, God bless him," they said. " It'll be coming soon when he's here."

Janey Mary was lifted clear off the ground by the movement of the crowd and lost her place. Now she was behind a stoop-backed man with a threadbare coat and heavily nailed boots. His collar was flaked and greasy with dandruff and his coat was foul smelling, but it was the boots which held Janey Mary's attention. They clattered unsteadily on the pavement very close to her bare feet. There were diamond-shaped nails in double rings about the heels of them. She bent to keep her eyes fixed on the boots and wriggled to avoid them. Her attention became fixed on them. To a man near her she said, " I want to get out, mister, let me get out," but even if he had heard her he could not have helped her now. She tried to attract attention, but they had forgotten her. They kept telling one another over and over again what each of them already knew.

" It's coming," they said, pressing forward, " it's coming." And after a while the murmuring changed and the queue surged.

" Look," they shouted, " it's here."

Janey Mary was lifted once more. Once more her feet were clear of the ground and her breathing stifled by the pressure of those around her. She was in danger now and clawed whimpering at the dandruff-flaked collar. Through a whirl of arms and shoulders she had a view of Father Benedict, his broad shoulders tall and firm above the press of bodies. She tried to call out to him.

" The chisler," someone said, noticing. " For God's sake quit pushing. Look at the chisler." A man threw out his hand to grip her, but a movement of the crowd twisted him suddenly aside. She saw his hand grabbing futilely to her left. As the crowd parted she began to slip.

" Father Benedict," she called faintly, " Father Benedict." Then the man in front stumbled and the nailed boots crushed heavily on her feet.

When her eyes opened again she was on the sofa in the visitors' parlour. Father Benedict and one of the lay brothers were bending over her. Someone had put a rug about her. An electric fire glowed warmly against the opposite wall, and over it hung a gold-framed picture of the Sacred Heart. Her feet felt numb and heavy and the picture swam before her eyes. But it was warm in the parlour and the morning's searching was over. Then she remembered the bread and her mother's words. She moved suddenly, but when she tried to speak her ears were filled with noise. The lay brother had turned to Father Benedict.

" You were very quick," he was saying. " Is she badly hurt ? "

Father Benedict, answering him, said in a strange voice :

" Only her feet . . . You can see the print of the nails . . . "

— *The Trusting and the Maimed*

Explorations

1.   Jim Larkin, for whom James Plunkett once worked, used to vow that ' Christ will no longer be crucified in the streets of Dublin ' ! Does this story help you to see what he meant ? Explain.

2.   The author makes use of symbols, especially religious symbols, in the course of the story. The ' print of the nails ' is an example . . . See can you find other symbols of this kind and discuss their part in the story.

3.   Throughout the story there are hints of Janey Mary's final collapse : one feels it coming. Where are these hints to be found ? Do you find them vivid and convincing or otherwise ? Why ?

4.   You have probably noticed that James Plunkett takes great care in describing objects—as, for instance, the cups on the table of Janey Mary's home. Point out other descriptions that you find particularly vivid. Do they contribute anything to the total meaning of the story ?

5.   Why does Father Benedict mean so much to Janey Mary ? What makes him different from other people in the story—her mother, the teacher ?

6.   People are indifferent and cruel to Janey Mary. Do you find this true to life ? Is this how people treat poor children ? Discuss.

7.   Consider the author's use of words throughout the story. For instance, he refers to Janey Mary's ' small ' hands several times. Would it have made any difference had he written ' little ' hands instead ? Why does he say ' unclean ' instead of ' dirty ' hair ? The people poked ' cross and harassed faces around half-open doors ' : what is the effect of the word ' harassed ' ?

8.   The passage beginning ' Picking her way amongst the debris-littered wasteland . . . ' introduces a change of mood and atmosphere. What is the nature of this change ? How long does it last ? What does it add to our understanding of Janey Mary's predicament ?

Exercises

1.   Have you ever felt real hunger or have you ever been really frightened in a crowd ? If so, try and describe the circumstances and how you felt.

2.   The children in ' The Lumber Room,' ' First Confession ' and ' The Confirmation Suit,' suffer various kinds of persecution. Read these stories and be ready to discuss them in next day's class.

3.   James Plunkett has another story in *The Trusting and the Maimed* entitled ' Weep for our Pride.' Read it for comparison with ' Janey Mary.'

4.   Tell, as best you can imagine it, the story of Johnny going round trying to sell bundles of sticks from door to door.

5.   Write a paragraph or two on a poor person you know.

22

THE WILD DUCK'S NEST

The sun was setting, spilling gold light on the low western hills of Rathlin Island. A small boy walked jauntily along a hoof-printed path that wriggled between the folds of these hills and opened out into a crater-like valley on the cliff-top. Presently he stopped as if remembering something, then suddenly he left the path, and began running up one of the hills. When he reached the top he was out of breath and stood watching streaks of light radiating from golden-edged clouds, the scene reminding him of a picture he had seen of the Transfiguration. A short distance below him was the cow standing at the edge of a reedy lake. Colm ran down to meet her waving his stick in the air, and the wind rumbling in his ears made him give an exultant whoop which splashed upon the hills in a shower of echoed sound. A flock of gulls lying on the short grass near the lake rose up languidly, drifting like blown snowflakes over the rim of the cliff.

The lake faced west and was fed by a stream, the drainings of the semi-circling hills. One side was open to the winds from the sea and in winter a little outlet trickled over the cliffs making a black vein in their grey sides. The boy lifted stones and began throwing them into the lake, weaving web after web on its calm surface. Then he skimmed the water with flat stones, some of them jumping the surface and coming to rest on the other side. He was delighted with himself and after listening to his echoing shouts of delight he ran to fetch his cow. Gently he tapped her on the side and reluctantly she went towards the brown-mudded path that led out of the valley. The boy was about to throw a final stone into the lake when a bird flew low over his head, its neck a-strain, and its orange-coloured legs clear in the soft light. It was a wild duck. It circled the lake twice, thrice, coming lower each time and then with a nervous flapping of wings it skidded along the surface, its legs breaking the water into a series of silvery arcs. Its wings closed, it lit silently, gave a slight shiver, and began pecking indifferently at the water.

Colm, with dilated eyes, eagerly watched it making for the

farther end of the lake. It meandered between tall bulrushes, its body black and solid as stone against the greying water. Then as if it had sunk it was gone. The boy ran stealthily along the bank looking away from the lake, pretending indifference. When he came opposite to where he had last seen the bird he stopped and peered through the sighing reeds whose shadows streaked the water in a maze of black strokes. In front of him was a soddy islet guarded by the spears of sedge and separated from the bank by a narrow channel of water. The water wasn't too deep—he could wade across with care.

Rolling up his short trousers he began to wade, his arms outstretched, and his legs brown and stunted in the mountain water. As he drew near the islet, his feet sank in the cold mud and bubbles winked up at him. He went more carefully and nervously. Then one trouser leg fell and dipped into the water ; the boy dropped his hands to roll it up, he unbalanced, made a splashing sound, and the bird arose with a squawk and whirred away over the cliffs. For a moment the boy stood frightened. Then he clambered on to the wet-soaked sod of land, which was spattered with seagulls' feathers and bits of wind-blown rushes.

Into each hummock he looked, pulling back the long grass. At last he came on the nest, facing seawards. Two flat rocks dimpled the face of the water and between them was a neck of land matted with coarse grass containing the nest. It was untidily built of dried rushes, straw and feathers, and in it lay one solitary egg. Colm was delighted. He looked around and saw no one. The nest was his. He lifted the egg, smooth and green as the sky, with a faint tinge of yellow like the reflected light from a buttercup ; and then he felt he had done wrong. He put it back. He knew he shouldn't have touched it and he wondered would the bird forsake the nest. A vague sadness stole over him and he felt in his heart he had sinned. Carefully smoothing out his footprints he hurriedly left the islet and ran after his cow. The sun had now set and the cold shiver of evening enveloped him, chilling his body and saddening his mind.

In the morning he was up and away to school. He took the grass rut that edged the road for it was softer on the bare feet. His house was the last on the western headland and after a mile or so he was joined by Paddy McFall ; both boys, dressed in similar hand-knitted blue jerseys and grey trousers, carried home-made school bags. Colm was full of the nest and as soon as he joined his companion he said eagerly : " Paddy, I've a nest— a wild duck's with one egg."

"And how do you know it's a wild duck's ? " asked Paddy, slightly jealous.

" Sure I saw her with my own two eyes, her brown speckled back with a crow's patch on it, and her yellow legs—— "

" Where is it ? " interrupted Paddy, in a challenging tone.

" I'm not going to tell you, for you'd rob it ! "

"Aach ! I suppose it's a tame duck's you have or maybe an old gull's."

Colm put out his tongue at him. "A lot you know ! " he said, " for a gull's egg has spots and this one is greenish-white, for I had it in my hand."

And then the words he didn't want to hear rushed from Paddy in a mocking chant, " You had it in your hand ! . . . She'll forsake it ! She'll forsake it ! She'll forsake it ! " he said, skipping along the road before him.

Colm felt as if he would choke or cry with vexation.

His mind told him that Paddy was right, but somehow he couldn't give in to it and he replied : " She'll not forsake it ! She'll not ! I know she'll not ! "

But in school his faith wavered. Through the windows he could see moving sheets of rain—rain that dribbled down the panes filling his mind with thoughts of the lake creased and chilled by wind ; the nest sodden and black with wetness ; and the egg cold as a cave stone. He shivered from the thoughts and fidgeted with the inkwell cover, sliding it backwards and forwards mechanically. The mischievous look had gone from his eyes and the school day dragged on interminably. But at last they were out in the rain, Colm rushing home as fast as he could.

He was no time at all at his dinner of potatoes and salted fish until he was out in the valley now smoky with drifts of slanting rain. Opposite the islet he entered the water. The wind was blowing into his face, rustling noisily the rushes heavy with the dust of rain. A moss-cheeper, swaying on a reed like a mouse, filled the air with light cries of loneliness.

The boy reached the islet, his heart thumping with excitement, wondering did the bird forsake. He went slowly, quietly, on to the strip of land that led to the nest. He rose on his toes, looking over the ledge to see if he could see her. And then every muscle tautened. She was on, her shoulders hunched up, and her bill lying on her breast as if she were asleep. Colm's heart hammered wildly in his ears. She hadn't forsaken. He was about to turn stealthily away. Something happened. The bird moved, her neck straightened, twitching nervously from side to side. The boy's head swam with lightness. He stood transfixed. The wild duck with a panicky flapping, rose heavily, and flew off towards the sea . . . A guilty silence enveloped the boy . . . He turned to go away, hesitated, and glanced back at the bare nest ; it'd be no harm to have a look. Timidly he approached it, standing straight, and gazing over the edge. There in the nest lay two eggs. He drew in his breath with delight, splashed quickly from the island, and ran off whistling in the rain.

— *The Gamecock and Other Stories*

Explorations

1. Colm has a very deep love of natural beauty and of wild creatures. Point out some of the ways in which this is shown.

2. The author has a sharp eye for natural detail. Point out some touches that you find particularly effective.

3. 'A vague sadness stole over him and he felt in his heart he had sinned'. Why was the sadness vague ? Had he really sinned ? The next day he suffered in his mind for what he had done. Did he deserve to suffer so much ? Why ?

4. A good storyteller should involve the reader in the plight of his characters. Does Michael McLaverty succeed in this ? How ?

5. Is there anything about this story that you particularly liked ? Explain.

6. Little Michael in ' Three Lambs ' is in many ways similar to Colm : in what ways ?

7. If Colm had Little Jimmy (from ' The Wren's Nest ') with him when he found the wild duck's nest would he have behaved as Little Michael did ? Give your opinion and your reasons for it.

Exercises

1. Tell the story from the viewpoint of the wild duck. You may find it helpful to read O'Flaherty's ' His First Flight.'

2. Have you ever felt very happy walking through the countryside ? If so, try, on looking back, to describe your mood and its causes.

3. Tell of the second visit to the nest as Colm might have done in a school composition.

23

THE ROAD TO THE SHORE

" 'Tis going to be a lovely day, thanks be to God," sighed Sister Paul to herself, as she rubbed her wrinkled hands together and looked out at the thrushes hopping across the lawn. "And it was a lovely day last year and the year before," she mused, and in her mind saw the fresh face of the sea where, in an hour or two, she and the rest of the community would be enjoying their annual trip to the shore. "And God knows it may be my last trip," she said resignedly, and gazed abstractedly at a butterfly that was purring its wings against the sunny pane. She opened the window and watched the butterfly swing out into the sweet air, zigzagging down to a cushion of flowers that bordered the lawn. " Isn't it well Sister Clare wasn't here," she said to herself, " for she'd be pestering the very soul out of me with her questions about butterflies and birds and flowers and the fall of dew ? " She gave her girdle of beads a slight rattle. Wasn't it lovely to think of the pleasure that little butterfly would have when it found the free air under its wings again and its little feet pressing on the soft petals of the flowers and not on the hard pane ? She always maintained it was better to enjoy Nature without searching and probing and chattering about the what and the where and the wherefore. But Sister Clare !—what she got out of it all, goodness only knew, for she'd give nobody a minute's peace—not a moment's peace would she give to a saint, living or dead. " How long would that butterfly live in the air of a class-room ? " she'd be asking. " Do you think it would use up much of the active part of the air—the oxygen part, I mean ? . . . What family would that butterfly belong to ? . . . You know it's wrong to say that a butterfly lives only a day . . . When I am teaching my little pupils I always try to be accurate. I don't believe in stuffing their heads with fantastical nonsense, however pleasurable it may be . . . " Sister Paul turned round as if someone had suddenly walked into the room, and she was relieved when she saw nothing only the quiet vacancy of the room, the varnished desks with the sun on them and their reflections on the parquet floor.

She hoped she wouldn't be sitting beside Clare in the car today! She'd have no peace with her—not a bit of peace to look out at the countryside and see what changes had taken place inside twelve months. But Reverend Mother, she knew, would arrange all that—and if it'd be her misfortune to be parked beside Clare she'd have to accept it with resignation; yes, with resignation, and in that case her journey to the sea would be like a pilgrimage.

At that moment a large limousine drove up the gravel path, and as it swung round to the convent door she saw the flowers flow across its polished sides in a blur of colour. She hurried out of the room and down the stairs. In the hall Sister Clare and Sister Benignus were standing beside two baskets and Reverend Mother was staring at the stairs. "Where were you, Sister Paul?" she said with mild reproof. "We searched the whole building for you . . . We're all ready this ages . . . And Sister Francis has gone to put out the cat. Do you remember last year it had been in all the time we were at the shore and it ate the bacon?" As she spoke a door closed at the end of the corridor and Sister Francis came along, polishing her specs with the corner of her veil. Reverend Mother glanced away from her; that continual polishing of the spectacles irritated her; and then that empty expression on Sister Francis's face when the spectacles were off—vacuous, that's what it was!

"All ready now," Reverend Mother tried to say without any trace of perturbation. Sister Clare and Sister Benignus lifted two baskets at their feet, Reverend Mother opened the hall-door, and they all glided out into the flat sunlight.

The doors of the car were wide open, the engine purring gently, and a perfume of new leather fingering the air. The chauffeur, a young man, touched his cap and stood deferentially to the side. Reverend Mother surveyed him quickly, noting his clean-bright face and white collar. "I think there'll be room for us all in the back," she said.

"There's a seat in the front, Sister," the young man said, touching his cap again.

"Just put the baskets on it, if you please," said Reverend Mother. And Sister Clare who, at that moment, was smiling at her own grotesque reflection in the back of the car came forward with her basket, Sister Benignus following. Sister Paul sighed audibly and fingered her girdle of beads.

" Now, Sister Paul, you take one of the corner seats. Sister Clare, you sit beside her, and Sister Benignus and Sister Francis on the spring-up seats facing them—they were just made for you, the tiny tots ! " And they all laughed, a brittle laugh that emphasised the loveliness of the day.

When they were all seated, Reverend Mother made sure that the hall-door was locked, glanced at the fastened windows, and then stood for a minute watching the gardener who was pushing his lawn-mower with unusual vigour and concentration. He stopped abruptly when her shadow fell across his path. "And, Jack," she said, as if continuing a conversation that had been interrupted, " you'll have that lawn finished today ? "

" Yes, Mother," and he took off his hat and held it in front of his breast. " To be sure I'll have it finished today. Sure what'd prevent me to finish it, and this the grandest day God sent this many a long month—a wholesome day ! "

"And, Jack, I noticed some pebbles on the lawn yesterday—white ones."

" I remarked them myself, Mother. A strange terrier disporting himself in the garden done it."

" Did it."

" Yes, Mother, he did it with his two front paws, scratching at the edge of the lawn like it was a rabbit burrow. He done it yesterday, and when I clodded him off the grounds he'd the impertinence to go out a different way than he came in. But I've now his entrances and exits all blocked and barricaded and I'm afraid he'll have to find some other constituency to disport himself. Dogs is a holy terror for bad habits."

" Be sure and finish it all today," she said with some impatience. She turned to go away, hesitated, and turned back. " By the way, Jack, if there are any drips of oil made by the car on the gravel you'll scuffle fresh pebbles over them."

" I'll do that. But you need have no fear of oil from her engine," and he glanced over at the limousine. " She'll be as clean as a Swiss clock. 'Tis them grocery vans that leak—top, tail and middle."

Crossing to the car, she heard with a feeling of pleasure the surge of the lawn-mower over the grass. Presently the car swung out of the gate on to a tree-lined road at the edge of the town. The nuns relaxed, settled themselves more comfortably in their seats and chatted about the groups on bicycles that were all heading for the shore.

" We will go to the same quiet strip as last year," said Reverend Mother, and then as she glanced out of the window a villa on top of a hill drew her attention. " There's a house that has been built since last year," she said.

" No, no," said Sister Francis. " It's more than a year old for I remember seeing it last year," and she peered at it through her spectacles.

Reverend Mother spoke through the speaking-tube to the driver : " Is that villa on the hill newly built ? " she asked.

He stopped the car. "A doctor by the name of McGrath built it two years ago," he said. " He's married to a daughter of Solicitor O'Kane."

" Oh, thank you," said Reverend Mother ; and the car proceeded slowly up the long hill above the town.

Sister Francis took off her spectacles, blew her breath on them, rubbed them with her handkerchief. She took another look at the villa and said with obvious pride : " A fine site, indeed. I remember last year that they had that little gadget over the door."

" The architrave," said Sister Clare importantly.

"Aye," said Sister Paul, and she looked out at the trees and below them the black river with its strings of froth moving through the valley. How lovely it would be, she thought, to sit on the edge of that river, dabble her parched feet in it and send bubbles out into the race of the current. She had often done that when she was a child, and now that river and its trees, which she only saw once in a year, brought her childhood back to her. She sighed and opened the window so as to hear the mumble of the river far below them. The breeze whorled in, and as it lifted their veils they all smiled, invigorated by the fresh loveliness of the air. A bumble bee flew in and crawled up the pane at Reverend Mother's side of the car. She opened the window and assisted the bee towards the opening with the tip of her fountain-pen, but the bee clung to the pen and as she tried to shake it free the wind carried it in again. " Like everything else it hates to leave you," said Sister Benignus. Reverend Mother smiled and the bee flew up to the roof of the car and then alighted on the window beside Sister Paul. Sister Paul swept the bee to safety with the back of her hand.

" You weren't one bit afraid of it," said Sister Clare. "And if it had stung you, you would in a way have been responsible for its death. If it had been a Queen bee—though Queens wouldn't be flying at this time of the year—you would have been responsible for the death of potential thousands. A Queen bumble bee lays over two thousand eggs in one season ! "

" 'Tis a great pity we haven't a hen like that," put in Sister Francis, and they all laughed except Sister Clare. Sister Francis laughed till her eyes watered and, once more, she took off her spectacles. Reverend Mother fidgeted slightly and, in order to control her annoyance, she fixed her gaze on Sister Clare and asked her to continue her interesting account of the life of bumble bees. Sister Paul put her hands in her sleeves and sought distraction in the combings of cloud that streaked the sky.

Reverend Mother pressed her toe on the floor of the car and, instead of listening to Sister Clare, she was glaring unconsciously at Sister Francis who was tapping her spectacles on the palm of her hand and giving an odd laugh.

" Your spectacles are giving you much trouble today," she broke in, unable any longer to restrain herself. " Perhaps you would like to sit in the middle. It may provide your poor eyes with some rest."

" No, thank you," said Sister Francis, " I like watching the crowds of cyclists passing on the road. But sometimes the sun glints on their handlebars and blinds me for a moment and makes me feel that a tiny thread or two has congregated on my lenses. It's my imagination of course."

" Maybe you would care to have a look at *St. Anthony's Annals*," and Reverend Mother handed her the magazine.

" Thank you, Mother. I'll keep it until we reach the shore, for the doctor told me not to read in moving vehicles." .

The car rolled on slowly and when it reached the top of a hill, where there was a long descent of five miles to the sea, a strange silence came over the nuns, and each became absorbed in her own premeditation on the advancing day. " Go slowly down the hill," Reverend Mother ordered the driver.

Boys sailed past them on bicycles, and when some did so with their hands off the handlebars a little cry of amazement would break from Sister Francis and she would discuss with Sister Clare the reckless irresponsibility of boys and the worry they must bring to their parents.

Suddenly at a bend on the hill they all looked at Sister Paul for she was excitedly drawing their attention to a line of young poplars. " Look, look ! " she was saying. " Look at the way their leaves are dancing and not a flicker out of the other trees. And to think I never noticed them before ! "

" I think they are aspens," said Sister Clare, " and anyway they are not indigenous to this country."

" We had four poplars in our garden when I was growing up—black poplars, my father called them," said Sister Paul, lost in her own memory.

" What family did they belong to ?   There's *angustifolia*, *laurifolia*, and *balsamifera* and others among the poplar family."

" I don't know what family they belonged to," Sister Paul went on, quietly. " I only know they were beautiful—beautiful in very early spring when every tree and twig around them would still be bleak—and there they were bursting into leaf, a brilliant yellow leaf like a flake of sunshine. My father, God be good to his kindly soul, planted four of them when I was young, for there were four in our family, all girls, and one of the trees my father called Kathleen, another Teresa, another Eileen, and lastly my own, Maura. And I remember how he used to stand at the dining-room window gazing out at the young poplars with the frost white and hard around them. ' I see a leaf or two coming on Maura,' he used to say, and we would all rush to the window and gaze into the garden, each of us fastening her eye on her own tree and then measuring its growth of leaf with the others. And to the one whose tree was first in leaf he used to give a book or a pair of rosary beads . . . Poor Father," she sighed, and fumbled in her sleeve for her handkerchief.

" Can you not think of what special name those trees had ? " pressed Clare. " Did their leaves tremble furiously—*tremula*, *tremuloides* ? "

" They didn't quiver very much," said Sister Paul, her head bowed. " My father didn't plant aspens, I remember. He told us it was from an aspen that Our Saviour's rood was made, and because their leaves remember the Crucifixion they are always trembling . . . But our poplars had a lovely warm perfume when they were leafing and that perfume always reminded my father of autumn. Wasn't that strange ? " she addressed the whole car, " a tree coming into leaf and it reminding my poor father of autumn."

" I know its family now," said Clare, clapping her hands together. " *Balsamifera*—that's the family it belonged to—it's a native of Northern Italy."

"And I remember," said Paul, folding and unfolding her handkerchief on her lap, " how my poor father had no gum once to wrap up a newspaper that he was posting. It was in winter and he went out to the poplars and dabbed his finger here and there on the sticky buds and smeared it on the edge of the wrapping paper."

" That was enough to kill the buds," said Clare. " The gum, as you call it, is their only protective against frost."

" It was himself he killed," said Paul. " He had gone out from a warm fire in his slippers, out into the bleak air and got his death."

"And what happened to the poplars ? " said Clare. But Sister Paul had turned her head to the window again and was trying to stifle the tears that were rising to her eyes.

" What other trees grew in your neighbourhood ? " continued Clare. Sister Paul didn't seem to hear her, but when the question was repeated she turned and said slowly : " I'm sorry that I don't know their names. But my father, Lord have mercy on him, used to say that a bird could leap from branch to branch for ten miles around without using its wings."

Sister Clare smiled and Reverend Mother nudged her with her elbow, signing to her to keep quiet ; and when she, herself, glanced at Paul she saw the sun shining through the fabric of her veil and a handkerchief held furtively to her eyes.

There was silence now in the sun-filled car while outside cyclists continued to pass them, free-wheeling down the long hill. Presently there was a rustle of paper in the car as Sister Francis drew forth from her deep pocket a bag of soft peppermints, stuck together by the heat. Carefully she peeled the bits of paper off the sweets, and as she held out the bag to Reverend Mother she said : " Excuse my fingers." But Reverend Mother shook her head, and Clare and Benignus, seeing that she had refused, felt it would be improper for them to accept. Francis shook the bag towards Paul but since she had her eyes closed, as if in prayer, she neither saw nor heard what was being offered to her. " *In somno pacis,*" said Francis, popping two peppermints into her own mouth and hiding the bag in her wide sleeve. " A peppermint is soothing and cool on a hot day like this," she added with apologetic good nature.

A hot smell of peppermint drifted around the car. Reverend Mother lowered her window to its full length, and though the air rushed in in soft folds around her face it was unable to quench the flaming odour. Somehow, for Reverend Mother, the day, that had hardly begun yet, was spoiled by an old nun with foolish habits and by a young nun unwise enough not to know when to stop questioning. Everything was going wrong, and it would not surprise her that before evening clouds of rain would blow in from the sea and blot out completely the soft loveliness of the sunny day. Once more she looked at Paul, and, seeing her head bowed in thought, she knew that there was some aspect of the countryside, some shape in cloud or bush, that brought back to Paul a sweet but sombre childhood. For herself she had no such memories—there was nothing in her own life, she thought, only a mechanical ordering, a following of routine, that may have brought some pleasure into other people's lives but none to her own. However, she'd do her best to make the day pleasant for them ; after all, it was only one day in the year and if the eating of peppermints gave Sister Francis some satisfaction it was not right to thwart her.

She smiled sweetly then at Francis, and as Francis offered the sweets once more, and she was stretching forward to take one there was a sudden dunt to the back of the car and a crash of something falling on the road. The car stopped and the nuns looked at one another, their heads bobbing in consternation. They saw the driver raise himself slowly from his seat, walk back the road, and return again with a touch of his cap at the window.

"A slight accident, Sister," he said, addressing Reverend Mother. "A cyclist crashed into our back wheel. But it's nothing serious, I think."

Reverend Mother went out leaving the door open, and through it there came the free sunlight, the cool air, and the hum of people talking. She was back again in a few minutes with her handkerchief dabbed with blood, and collected other handkerchiefs from the nuns, who followed her out on to the road. Sister Paul stood back and saw amongst the bunch of people a young man reclining on the bank of the road, a hand to his head. " I can't stand the sight of blood," she said to herself, her fingers clutching her rosary beads. She beckoned to a lad who was resting on his bicycle : " Is he badly hurt, lad ? He'll not die, will he ? "

" Not a bit of him, Sister. He had his coat folded over the handlebars and the sleeve of it caught in the wheel and flung him against the car."

" Go up, like a decent boy, and have a good look at him again."

But before the lad had reached the group the chauffeur had assisted the injured man to his feet and was leading him to the car. The handkerchiefs were tied like a turban about his head, his trousers were torn at the knee, and a holy medal was pinned to his braces.

" Put his coat on or he'll catch cold," Reverend Mother was saying.

" Och, Sister, don't worry about me," the man was saying. " Sure it was my own fault. Ye weren't to blame at all. I'll go back again on my own bicycle—I'm fit enough."

Reverend Mother consulted the chauffeur and whatever advice he gave her the injured man was put into the back of the car. Sister Francis was ordered into the vacant seat beside the driver, the baskets were handed to Paul and Clare, and when the man's bicycle was tied to the carrier they drove off for the hospital in the town.

The young man, sitting between Reverend Mother and Sister Paul, shut his eyes in embarrassment, and when the blood oozed through the pile of handkerchiefs Reverend Mother took the serviettes from the baskets and tied them round his head and under his chin, and all the time the man kept repeating : " I'm a sore trouble to you, indeed. And sure it was my own fault." She told him to button his coat or he would catch cold, and when he had done so she noticed a Total Abstinence badge in the lapel.

"A good clean-living man," she thought, and to think that he was the one to meet with an injury while many an old drunkard

could travel the roads of Ireland on a bicycle and arrive home
without pain or scratch or cough.

" 'Tis a blessing of God you weren't killed," she said, with a
rush of protectiveness, and she reached for the thermos flask from
the basket and handed the man a cup of tea.

Now and again Sister Paul would steal a glance at him, but
the sight of his pale face and the cup trembling in his hand and
rattling on the saucer made her turn to the window where she
tried to lose herself in contemplation. But all her previous mood
was now scattered from her mind, and she could think of nothing
only the greatness of Reverend Mother and the cool way she took
command of an incident that would have left the rest of them weak
and confused.

" How are you feeling now ? " she could hear Reverend
Mother asking. " Would you like another sandwich ? "

" No, thank you, Sister ; sure I had my good breakfast in
me before I left the house. I'm a labouring man and since
I'm out of work this past three months my wife told me to go off
on the bike and have a swim with myself. I was going to take one
of the youngsters on the bar of the bike but my wife wouldn't let
me."

" She had God's grace about her," said Reverend Mother.
" That should be a lesson to you," and as she refilled his cup
from the thermos flask she thought that if the young man had
been killed they, in a way, would have had to provide his widow
and children with some help. "And we were only travelling
slowly," she found herself saying aloud.

" Sure, Sister, no one knows that better than myself. You
were keeping well in to your own side of the road and when I
was ready to sail past you on the hill my coat caught in the front
wheel and my head hit the back of your car."

" S-s-s," and the nuns drew in their breath with shrinking
solicitude.

They drove up to the hospital, and after Reverend Mother
had consulted the doctor and was told that the wound was only a
slight abrasion and contusion she returned light-heartedly to the
car. Sister Clare made no remark when she heard the news but
as the wheels of the car rose and fell on the road they seemed to

echo what was in her mind : *abrasion and contusion, abrasion and contusion.* "Abrasion and contusion of what ? " she asked herself. " Surely the doctor wouldn't say ' head '—abrasion and contusion of the head ? " No, there must be some medical term that Reverend Mother had withheld from them, and as she was about to probe Reverend Mother for the answer the car swung unexpectedly into the convent avenue. " Oh," she said with disappointment, and when alighting from the car and seeing Sister Francis give the remains of her sweets to the chauffeur she knew that for her, too, the day was at an end.

They all passed inside except Reverend Mother who stood on the steps at the door noting the quiet silence of the grounds and the heat-shadows flickering above the flower-beds. With a mocking smile she saw the lawnmower at rest on the uncut lawn and found herself mimicking the gardener : " I'll have it all finished today, Sister, I'll have it all finished today." She put a hand to her throbbing head and crossed the gravel path to look for him, and there in the clump of laurel bushes she found him fast asleep, his hat over his face to keep off the flies, and three empty porter bottles beside him. She tiptoed away from him. " He has had a better day than we have had," she said to herself, " so let him sleep it out, for it's the last he'll have at my expense . . . Oh, drink is a curse," and she thought of the injury that had befallen the young man with the Abstinence Badge and he as sober as any judge. Then she drew up suddenly as something quick and urgent came into her mind : " Of course !—he would take the job as gardener, and he unemployed this past three months ! " With head erect she sped quickly across the grass and into the convent. Sister Paul was still in the corridor when she saw Reverend Mother lift the 'phone and ring up the hospital : " Is he still there ? . . . He's all right ? . . . That's good . . . Would you tell him to call to see me sometime this afternoon ? " There was a transfigured look on her face as she put down the receiver, and strode across to Sister Paul. " Sister Paul," she said, " you may tell the other Sisters that on tomorrow we will set out again for the shore." Sister Paul smiled and whisked away down the corridor : " Isn't Reverend Mother great the way she can handle things ? " she said to herself. "And to think that on tomorrow I'll be able to see the poplars again."

—*The Gamecock and Other Stories*

Explorations

1.   Each of the nuns in this story is worried about something. Are these important worries ?   Compare them with the problems of the man who is knocked down.

2.   There is little evidence that any of the nuns—except perhaps the Reverend Mother — is deeply affected by this accident which might have caused the death of a young married man. Do you find this credible ?

3.   Why is the Reverend Mother's face 'transfigured' at the end of the story ? Why does she decide to set out on the same expedition the next day ?

4.   The author makes frequent use of character contrast in the story.   Point out some examples of it.

5.   Do you honestly like this story ?   Give your reasons.

Exercises

1.   Tell the entire story in the words of Sister Clare, bearing in mind her relationship with Sister Paul.

2.   Have you ever witnessed an accident ? If so try to remember the behaviour of the onlookers and the people who were involved in it. Try to describe your own feelings on the occasion.

3.   With which of the four nuns would you like to spend an evening in conversation ?   Explain your reasons in a few paragraphs.

4.   Read Mary Lavin's story, ' Brother Boniface ' ; compare and contrast the monk in his old age with Sister Paul : be alert to the differences as well as the similarities.

24

THE POTEEN MAKER

When he taught me some years ago, he was an old man near his retirement, and when he would pass through the streets of the little town on his way from school, you would hear the women talking about him as they stood at their doors knitting or nursing their babies : " Poor man, he's done. . . . Killing himself. . ., . Digging his own grave ! " With my bag of books under my arm I could hear them, but I could never understand why they said he was digging his own grave, and when I would ask my mother, she would scold me : " Take your dinner like a good boy, and don't be listening to the hard back-biters of this town. Your father has always a good word for Master Craig—so that should be enough for you ! "

" But why do they say he's killing himself ? "

" Why do who say ? Didn't I tell you to take your dinner and not be repeating what the idle gossips of this town are saying ? Listen to me, son ! Master Craig is a decent, good-living man— a kindly man that would go out of his way to do you a good turn. If Master Craig was in any other town, he'd have got a place in the new school at the Square instead of being stuck for ever in that wee poky bit of a school at the edge of the town ! "

It was true that the school was small—a two-roomed ramshackle of a place that lay at the edge of the town beyond the last street lamp. We all loved it. Around it grew a few trees, their trunks hacked with boys' names and pierced with nibs and rusty drawing-pins. In summer, when the windows were open we could hear the leaves rubbing together and in winter, see the raindrops hanging on the bare twigs.

It was a draughty place and the master was always complaining of the cold, and even in the early autumn he would wear his overcoat in the classroom and rub his hands together : " Boys, it's very cold today. Do you feel it cold ? " And to please him, we would answer : " Yes, sir, 'tis very cold." He would continue to rub his hands, and he would look out at the old trees

221

casting their leaves or at the broken spout that flung its tail of
rain against the window. He always kept his hands clean and
three times a day he would wash them in a basin and wipe them
on a roller towel affixed to the inside of his press. He had a
hanger for his coat and a brush to brush away the chalk that
accumulated on the collar in the course of the day.

In the wet, windy month of November, three buckets were
placed on the top of the desks to catch the drips that plopped
here and there from the ceiling, and those drops made different
music according to the direction of the wind. When the buckets
were filled, the master always called me to empty them, and I
would take them one at a time and swirl them into the drain at
the street and stand for a minute gazing down at the wet roofs
of the town or listen to the rain pecking at the lunch-papers
scattered about on the cinders.

" What's it like outside ? " he always asked when I came in
with the empty buckets.

" Sir, 'tis very bad."

He would write sums on the board and tell me to keep an eye
on the class, and out to the porch he would go and stand in grim
silence watching the rain nibbling at the puddles. Sometimes
he would come in and I would see him sneak his hat from the
press and disappear for five or ten minutes. We would fight then
with rulers or paper-darts till our noise would disturb the mistress
next door and in she would come and stand with her lips com-
pressed, her finger in her book. There was silence as she up-
braided us : " Mean, low, good-for-nothing corner boys. Wait'll
Mister Craig comes back and I'll let him know the angels he has.
And I'll give him special news about *you* ! "—and she shakes her
book at me : "An altar boy on Sunday and a corner boy for the
rest of the week ! " We would let her barge away, the buckets
plink-plonking as they filled up with rain and her own class
beginning to hum, now that she was away from them.

When Mr. Craig came back he would look at us and ask if we
disturbed Miss Lagan. Our silence or our tossed hair always
gave him the answer. He would correct the sums on the board,
flivell the pages of a book with his thumb, and listen to us reading ;
and occasionally he would glance out of the side-window at the
river that flowed through the town and, above it, the bedraggled
row of houses whose tumbling yardwalls sheered to the water's

edge. "The loveliest county in Ireland is County Down!"
he used to say, with a sweep of his arm to the river and the tin
cans and the chalked walls of the houses.

During that December he was ill for two weeks and when he
came back amongst us, he was greatly failed. To keep out the
draughts he nailed perforated plywood over the ventilators and
stuffed blotting paper between the wide crevices at the jambs
of the door. There were muddy marks of a ball on one of the
windows and on one pane a long crack with fangs at the end of
it : "So someone has drawn the River Ganges while I was
away," he said ; and whenever he came to the geography of
India, he would refer to the Ganges delta by pointing to the
cracks on the pane.

When our ration of coal for the fire was used up, he would
send me into the town with a bucket, a coat over my head to
keep off the rain, and the money in my fist to buy a stone of coal.
He always gave me a penny to buy sweets for myself, and I can
always remember that he kept his money in a waistcoat pocket.
Back again I would come with the coal and he would give me
disused exercise books to light the fire. "Chief stoker!" he
called me, and the name has stuck to me to this day.

It was at this time that the first snow had fallen, and someone
by using empty potato bags had climbed over the glass-topped
wall and stolen the school coal, and for some reason Mr. Craig
did not send me with the bucket to buy more. The floor was
continually wet from our boots, and our breaths frosted the
windows. Whenever the door opened, a cold draught would
rush in and gulp down the breath-warmed air in the room. We
would jig our feet and sit on our hands to warm them. Every
half-hour Mr. Craig would make us stand and while he lilted
O'Donnell Abu, we did a series of physical exercises which he had
taught us, and in the excitement and the exaltation, we forgot
about our sponging boots and the snow that pelted against the
windows. It was then that he did his lessons on Science ; and
we were delighted to see the bunsen burner attached to the gas
bracket which hung like an inverted T from the middle of the
ceiling. The snoring bunsen seemed to heat up the room and we
all gathered round it, pressing in on top of it till he scattered us
back to our places with the cane : "Sit down!" he would shout.
"There's no call to stand. Everybody will be able to see!"

The cold spell remained, and over and over again he repeated one lesson in Science, which he called : *Evaporation and Condensation.*

" I'll show you how to purify the dirtiest of water," he had told us. " Even the filthiest water from the old river could be made fit for drinking purposes." In a glass trough he had a dark brown liquid and when I got his back turned, I dipped my finger in it and it tasted like treacle or burnt candy, and then I remembered about packets of brown sugar and tins of treacle I had seen in his press.

He placed some of the brown liquid in a glass retort and held it aloft to the class : " In the retort I have water which I have discoloured and made impure. In a few minutes I'll produce from it the clearest of spring water." And his weary eyes twinkled, and although we could see nothing funny in that, we smiled because he smiled.

The glass retort was set up with the flaming bunsen underneath, and as the liquid was boiling, the steam was trapped in a long-necked flask on which I sponged cold water. With our eyes we followed the bubbling mixture and the steam turning into drops and dripping rapidly into the flask. The air was filled with a biscuity smell, and the only sound was the snore of the bunsen. Outside was the cold air and the falling snow. Presently the master turned out the gas and held up the flask containing clear water.

"As pure as crystal ! " he said, and we watched him pour some of it into a tumbler, hold it in his delicate fingers, and put it to his lips. With wonder we watched him drink it and then our eyes travelled to the dirty, cakey scum that had congealed on the glass sides of the retort. He pointed at this with his ruler : "The impurities are sifted out and the purest of pure water remains." And for some reason he gave his roguish smile. He filled up the retort again with the dirty brown liquid and repeated the experiment until he had a large bottle filled with the purest of pure water.

The following day it was still snowing and very cold. The master filled up the retort with the clear liquid which he had stored in the bottle : " I'll boil this again to show you that there are no impurities left." So once again we watched the water bubbling, turning to steam, and then to shining drops. Mr.

Craig filled up his tumbler : "As pure as crystal," he said, and then the door opened and in walked the Inspector. He was muffled to the ears and snow covered his hat and his attaché case. We all stared at him—he was the old, kind man whom we had seen before. He glanced at the bare firegrate and at the closed windows with their sashes edged with snow. The water continued to bubble in the retort, giving out its pleasant smell.

The Inspector shook hands with Mr. Craig and they talked and smiled together, the Inspector now and again looking towards the empty grate and shaking his head. He unrolled his scarf and flicked the snow from off his shoulders and from his attaché case. He sniffed the air, rubbed his frozen hands together, and took a black notebook from his case. The snow ploofed against the windows and the wind hummed under the door.

" Now, boys," Mr. Craig continued, holding up the tumbler of water from which a thread of steam wriggled in the air. He talked to us in a strange voice and told us about the experiment as if we were seeing it for the first time. Then the Inspector took the warm tumbler and questioned us on our lesson. " It should be perfectly pure water," he said, and he sipped at it. He tasted its flavour. He sipped at it again. He turned to Mr. Craig. They whispered together, the Inspector looking towards the retort which was still bubbling and sending out its twirls of steam to be condensed to water of purest crystal. He laughed loudly, and we smiled when he again put the tumbler to his lips and this time drank it all. Then he asked us more questions and told us how, if we were shipwrecked, we could make pure water from the salt sea water.

Mr. Craig turned off the bunsen and the Inspector spoke to him. The master filled up the Inspector's tumbler and poured out some for himself in a cup. Then the Inspector made jokes with us, listened to us singing, and told us we were the best class in Ireland. Then he gave us a few sums to do in our books. He put his hands in his pockets and jingled his money, rubbed a little peep-hole in the breath-covered window and peered out at the loveliest sight in Ireland. He spoke to Mr. Craig again and Mr. Craig shook hands with him and they both laughed. The Inspector looked at his watch. Our class was let out early, and while I remained behind to tidy up the Science apparatus the master gave me an empty treacle tin to throw in the bin and told me to carry the Inspector's case up to the station. I remember that day well as I walked behind them through the snow, carrying the attaché case, and how loudly they talked and laughed as the snow whirled cold from the river. I remember how they crouched together to light their cigarettes, how match after match was thrown on the road, and how they walked off with the unlighted cigarettes still in their mouths. At the station, Mr. Craig took a penny from his waistcoat pocket and as he handed it to me, it dropped on the snow. I lifted it and he told me I was the best boy in Ireland. . . .

When I was coming from his funeral last week—God have mercy on him—I recalled that wintry day and the feel of the cold penny and how much more I know now about Mr. Craig than I did then. On my way out of the town—I don't live there now—I passed the school and saw a patch of new slates on the roof and an ugly iron barrier near the door to keep the home-going children from rushing headlong on to the road. I knew if I had looked at the trees I'd have seen rusty drawing-pins stuck into their rough flesh. But I passed by. I heard there was a young teacher in the school now, with an array of coloured pencils in his breast pocket.

— The Game-cock and Other Stories

Explorations

1. There are two opinions of Master Craig put forward in the first paragraph of the story. What are they ?

2. What did the neighbours mean when they said he was 'digging his own grave'? What did the mother think of the master ?

3. On the evidence of the story what sort of man would you say he was ? Would you have liked to have been in his class ? Give your reasons, taking into account the condition of the school.

4. There are two points of view in this story : the child's view and the adult's view. For instance, when the master is about to start the experiment the author states that 'his weary eyes twinkled, and although we could see nothing funny in that, we smiled because he smiled'. Examine how the author keeps the two points of view before the reader's eyes throughout the story.

5. The school as described was unusually dismal. Yet the author says 'We all loved it'. Why?

6. What sort of man was the inspector? In answering, consider what little information the author, in fact, gives us about him.

7. Examine the many references to weather in the story. Why, in your opinion, does the author make such a point of it?

Exercises

1. The author describes very accurately the school in which the pupils studied. Try to describe with similar accuracy the primary school you attended.

2. You may have some vivid memories of your national or primary school teacher. Write them as carefully, accurately and economically as you can.

3. Tell the story from the inspector's point of view, taking particular care with the private thoughts that may have crossed his mind when he entered that unheated classroom.

25

THE DOGS IN THE GREAT GLEN

The professor had come over from America to search out his origins and I met him in Dublin on the way to Kerry where his grandfather had come from and where he had relations, including a grand-uncle, still living.

" But the trouble is," he said, " that I've lost the address my mother gave me. She wrote to tell them I was coming to Europe. That's all they know. All I remember is a name out of my dead father's memories : the great Glen of Kanareen."

" You could write to your mother."

" That would take time. She'd be slow to answer. And I feel impelled right away to find the place my grandfather told my father about.

" You wouldn't understand," he said. " Your origins are all around you."

" You can say that again, professor. My origins crop up like the bones of rock in thin sour soil. They come unwanted like the mushroom of merulius lacrimans on the walls of a decaying house."

" It's no laughing matter," he said.

" It isn't for me. This island's too small to afford a place in which to hide from one's origins. Or from anything else. During the war a young fellow in Dublin said to me : ' Mister, even if I ran away to sea I wouldn't get beyond the three-mile limit.' "

He said, " But it's large enough to lose a valley in. I couldn't find the valley of Kanareen marked on any map or mentioned in any directory."

" I have a middling knowledge of the Kerry mountains," I said. " I could join you in the search."

" It's not marked on the half-inch ordnance survey map."

" There are more things in Kerry than were ever dreamt of by the Ordnance Survey. The place could have another official name. At the back of my head I feel that once in the town of Kenmare in Kerry I heard a man mention the name of Kanareen."

We set off two days later in a battered, rattly Ford Prefect. Haste, he said, would be dangerous because Kanareen might not be there at all, but if we idled from place to place in the lackadaisical Irish summer we might, when the sentries were sleeping and the glen unguarded, slip secretly as thieves into the land whose legends were part of his rearing.

" Until I met you," the professor said, " I was afraid the valley might have been a dream world my grandfather imagined to dull the edge of the first nights in a new land. I could see how he might have come to believe in it himself and told my father— and then, of course, my father told me."

One of his grandfather's relatives had been a Cistercian monk in Mount Melleray, and we went there hoping to see the evidence of a name in a book and to kneel, perhaps, under the high arched roof of the chapel close to where that monk had knelt. But, when we had traversed the corkscrew road over the purple Knockmealdowns and gone up to the mountain monastery through the forest the monks had made in the wilderness, it was late evening and the doors were closed. The birds sang vespers. The great silence affected us with something between awe and a painful, intolerable shyness. We hadn't the heart to ring a doorbell or to promise ourselves to return in the morning. Not speaking to each other we retreated, the rattle of the Ford Prefect as irreverent as dicing on the altar-steps. Half a mile down the road the mute, single-file procession of a group of women exercitants walking back to the female guest-house underlined the holy, unreal, unanswering stillness that had closed us out. It could easily have been that his grandfather never had a relative a monk in Mount Melleray.

A cousin of his mother's mother had, he had been told, been a cooper in Lady Gregory's Gort in the County Galway. But when we crossed the country westwards to Gort, it produced nothing except the information that apart from the big breweries, where they survived like birds or bison in a sanctuary, the coopers had gone, leaving behind them not a hoop or a stave. So we visited the woods of Coole, close to Gort, where Lady Gregory's house had once stood, and on the brimming lake-water among the stones, we saw by a happy poetic accident the number of swans the poet had seen.

Afterwards in Galway City there was, as there always is in Galway City, a night's hard drinking that was like a fit of jovial hysteria, and a giggling ninny of a woman in the bar who kept saying, " You're the nicest American I ever met. You don't look like an American. You don't even carry a camera. You look like a Kerryman."

And in the end, we came to Kenmare in Kerry, and in another bar we met a talkative Kerryman who could tell us all about the prowess of the Kerry team, about the heroic feats of John Joe Sheehy or Paddy Bawn Brosnan. He knew so much, that man, yet he couldn't tell us where in the wilderness of mountains we might find the Glen of Kanareen. Nor could anybody else in the bar be of the least help to us, not even the postman who could only say that wherever it was, that is if it was at all, it wasn't in his district.

" It could of course," he said, " be east over the mountain."

Murmuring sympathetically, the entire bar assented. The rest of the world was east over the mountain.

With the resigned air of men washing their hands of a helpless, hopeless case the postman and the football savant directed us to a roadside post office twelve miles away where, in a high-hedged garden before an old grey-stone house with latticed windows and an incongruous, green, official post office sign there was a child, quite naked, playing with a coloured, musical spinning-top as big as itself, and an old half-deaf man sunning himself and swaying in a rocking-chair, a straw hat tilted forwards to shade his eyes. Like Oisin remembering the Fenians, he told us he had known once of a young woman who married a man from a place called Kanareen, but there had been contention about the match and her people had kept up no correspondence with her. But the day she left home with her husband that was the way she went. He pointed. The way went inland and up and up. We followed it.

" That young woman could have been a relation of mine," the professor said.

On a rock-strewn slope, and silhouetted on a saw-toothed ridge where you'd think only a chamois could get by without broken legs, small black cows, accurate and active as goats, rasped good milk from the grass between the stones. His grandfather had told his father about those athletic, legendary cows and about the proverb that said : Kerry cows know Sunday. For in famine times, a century since, mountain people bled the cows once a week to mix the blood into yellow maize meal and provide a meat dish, a special Sunday dinner.

The road twisted on across moorland that on our left sloped dizzily to the sea, as if the solid ground might easily slip and slide into the depths. Mountain shadows melted like purple dust into a green bay. Across a ravine set quite alone on a long, slanting, brown knife-blade of a mountain, was a white house with a red door. The rattle of our pathetic little car affronted the vast stillness. We were free to moralise on the extent of all space in relation to the trivial area that limited our ordinary daily lives.

The two old druids of men resting from work on the leeward side of a turf-bank listened to our enquiry with the same attentive, half-conscious patience they gave to bird-cries or the sound of wind in the heather. Then they waved us ahead towards a narrow cleft in the distant wall of mountains as if they doubted the ability of ourselves and our conveyance to negotiate the Gap and find the Glen. They offered us strong tea and a drop out of a bottle. They watched us with kind irony as we drove away. Until the Gap swallowed us and the hazardous, twisting track absorbed all our attention we could look back and still see them, motionless, waiting with indifference for the landslide that would end it all.

By a roadside pool where water-beetles lived their vicious secretive lives, we sat and rested, with the pass and the cliffs, overhung with heather, behind us and another ridge ahead. Brazenly the sheer rocks reflected the sun and semaphored at us. Below us, in the dry summer, the bed of a stream held only a trickle of water twisting painfully around piles of round black stones. Touch a beetle with a stalk of dry grass and the creature either dived like a shot or, angry at invasion, savagely grappled with the stalk.

" That silly woman in Galway," the professor said.

He dropped a stone into the pool and the beetles submerged to weather the storm.

" That day by the lake at Lady Gregory's Coole. The exact number of swans Yeats saw when the poem came to him. Upon the brimming water among the stones are nine and fifty swans. Since I don't carry a camera nobody will ever believe me. But you saw them. You counted them."

" Now that I am so far," he said, " I'm half-afraid to finish the journey. What will they be like ? What will they think of me ? Will I go over that ridge there to find my grandfather's brother living in a cave ? "

Poking at and tormenting the beetles on the black mirror of the pool, I told him, " Once I went from Dublin to near Shannon Pot, where the river rises, to help an American woman find the house where her dead woman friend had been reared. On her death-bed the friend had written it all out on a sheet of note-paper : ' Cross the river at Battle Bridge. Go straight through the village with the ruined castle on the right. Go on a mile to the cross-roads and the labourer's cottage with the lovely snap-dragons in the flower garden. Take the road to the right there, and then the second boreen on the left beyond the schoolhouse. Then stop at the third house on that boreen. You can see the river from the flagstone at the door.'

"Apart from the snapdragons it was exactly as she had written it down. The dead woman had walked that boreen as a bare-footed schoolgirl. Not able to revisit it herself she entrusted the mission as her dying wish to her dearest friend. We found the house. Her people were long gone from it but the new tenants remembered them. They welcomed us with melodeon and fiddle and all the neighbours came in and collated the long memories of the townland. They feasted us with cold ham and chicken, porter and whiskey, until I had cramps for a week."

" My only grip on identity," he said, " is that a silly woman told me I looked like a Kerryman. My grandfather was a Kerry-man. What do Kerrymen look like ? "

" Big," I said.

"And this is the heart of Kerry. And what my grandfather said about the black cows was true. With a camera I could have taken a picture of those climbing cows. And up that hill trail and over that ridge is Kanareen."

" We hope," I said.

The tired cooling engine coughed apologetically when we abandoned it and put city-shod feet to the last ascent.

" If that was the mountain my grandfather walked over in the naked dawn coming home from an all-night card-playing then, by God, he was a better man than me," said the professor.

He folded his arms and looked hard at the razor-cut edges of stone on the side of the mountain.

" Short of too much drink and the danger of mugging," he said, " getting home at night in New York is a simpler operation than crawling over that hunk of miniature Mount Everest. Like walking up the side of a house."

He was as proud as Punch of the climbing prowess of his grandfather.

" My father told me," he said, " that one night coming home from the card-playing my grandfather slipped down fifteen feet of rock and the only damage done was the ruin of one of two bottles of whiskey he had in the tail-pockets of his greatcoat. The second bottle was unharmed."

The men who surfaced the track we were walking on had been catering for horses and narrow iron-hooped wheels. After five minutes of agonised slipping and sliding, wisdom came to us and we took to the cushioned grass and heather. As we ascended, the professor told me what his grandfather had told his father about the market town he used to go to when he was a boy. It was a small town where even on market days the dogs would sit no-where except exactly in the middle of the street. They were lazy town dogs, not active, loyal and intelligent like the dogs the grandfather had known in the great glen. The way the old man had described it, the town's five streets grasped the ground of Ireland as the hand of a strong swimmer might grasp a ledge of rock to hoist himself out of the water. On one side was the sea. On the other side a shoulder of mountain rose so steeply that the Gaelic name of it meant the gable of the house.

When the old man went as a boy to the town on a market day it was his custom to climb that mountain, up through furze and following goat tracks, leaving his shiny boots, that he only put on, anyway, when he entered the town, securely in hiding behind a furze bush. The way he remembered that mountain it would seem that twenty minutes active climbing brought him halfways to heaven. The little town was far below him, and the bay and the islands. The unkempt coastline tumbled and sprawled to left and right, and westwards the ocean went on for ever. The sounds of market-day, voices, carts, dogs barking, musicians on the streets, came up to him as faint, silvery whispers. On the tip of one island two tall aerials marked the place where, he was told, messages went down into the sea to travel all the way to America by cable. That was a great marvel for a boy from the mountains to hear about : the ghostly, shrill, undersea voices ; the words of people in every tongue of Europe far down among monstrous fish and shapeless sea-serpents that never saw the light of the sun. He closed his eyes one day and it seemed to him that the sounds of the little town were the voices of Europe setting out on their submarine travels. That was the time he knew that when he was old enough he would leave the Glen of Kanareen and go with the voices westwards to America.

" Or so he said. Or so he told my father," said the professor.

Another fifty yards and we would be on top of the ridge. We kept our eyes on the ground, fearful of the moment of vision and, for good or ill, revelation. Beyond the ridge there might be nothing but a void to prove that his grandfather had been a dreamer or a liar. Rapidly, nervously, he tried to talk down his fears.

" He would tell stories for ever, my father said, about ghosts and the good people. There was one case of an old woman whose people buried her—when she died, of course—against her will, across the water, which meant on the far side of the lake in the glen. Her dying wish was to be buried in another graveyard, nearer home. And there she was, sitting in her own chair in the chimney corner, waiting for them, when they came home from the funeral. To ease her spirit they replanted her."

To ease the nervous moment I said, " There was a poltergeist once in a farmhouse in these mountains, and the police decided to investigate the queer happenings, and didn't an ass's collar come flying across the room to settle around the sergeant's neck. Due to subsequent ridicule the poor man had to be transferred to Dublin."

Laughing, we looked at the brown infant runnel that went parallel to the path. It flowed with us : we were over the water-shed. So we raised our heads slowly and saw the great Glen of Kanareen. It was what Cortez saw, and all the rest of it. It was a discovery. It was a new world. It gathered the sunshine into a gigantic coloured bowl. We accepted it detail by detail.

" It was there all the time," he said. " It was no dream. It was no lie."

The first thing we realised was the lake. The runnel leaped down to join the lake, and we looked down on it through ash trees regularly spaced on a steep, smooth, green slope. Grasping from tree to tree you could descend to the pebbled, lapping edge of the water.

" That was the way," the professor said, " the boys in his time climbed down to fish or swim. Black, bull-headed mountain trout. Cannibal trout. There was one place where they could dive off sheer rock into seventy feet of water. Rolling like a gentle sea : that was how he described it. They gathered kindling, too, on the slopes under the ash trees."

Then, after the lake, we realised the guardian mountain ; not rigidly chiselled into ridges of rock like the mountain behind us but soft and gently curving, protective and, above all, noble, a monarch of mountains, an antlered stag holding a proud horned head up to the highest point of the blue sky. Green fields swathed its base. Sharp lines of stone walls, dividing wide areas of moor-land sheep-grazing, marked man's grip for a thousand feet or so above sea-level, then gave up the struggle and left the mountain alone and untainted. Halfways up one snow-white cloud rested as if it had hooked itself on a snagged rock and there it stayed motionless, as step by step we went down into the Glen. Below the cloud a long cataract made a thin, white, forked-lightning line, and, in the heart of the glen, the river that the cataract became, sprawled on a brown and green and golden patchwork bed.

" It must be some one of those houses," he said, pointing ahead and down to the white houses of Kanareen.

" Take a blind pick," I said. " I see at least fifty."

They were scattered over the glen in five or six clusters.

" From what I heard it should be over in that direction," he said.

Small rich fields were ripe in the sun. This was a glen of plenty, a gold-field in the middle of a desert, a happy laughing mockery of the arid surrounding moors and mountains. Five hundred yards away a dozen people were working at the hay. They didn't look up or give any sign that they had seen two strangers cross the high threshold of their kingdom but, as we went down, stepping like grenadier guards, the black-and-white sheepdogs detached themselves from the haymaking and moved silently across to intercept our path. Five of them I counted. My step faltered.

" This could be it," I suggested with hollow joviality. " I feel a little like an early Christian."

The professor said nothing. We went on down, deserting the comfort of the grass and heather at the side of the track. It seemed to me that our feet on the loose pebbles made a tearing, crackling, grinding noise that shook echoes even out of the imperturbable mountain. The white cloud had not moved. The haymakers had not honoured us with a glance.

" We could," I said, " make ourselves known to them in a civil fashion. We could ask the way to your grand-uncle's house. We could have a formal introduction to those slinking beasts."

" No, let me," he said. " Give me my head. Let me try to remember what I was told."

" The hearts of these highland people, I've heard, are made of pure gold," I said. " But they're inclined to be the tiniest bit suspicious of town-dressed strangers. As sure as God made smells and shotguns they think we're inspectors from some government department : weeds, or warble-fly, or horror of horrors, rates and taxes. With equanimity they'd see us eaten."

He laughed. His stride had a new elasticity in it. He was another man. The melancholy of the monastic summer dusk at Mount Melleray was gone. He was somebody else coming home. The white cloud had not moved. The silent dogs came closer. The unheeding people went on with their work.

" The office of rates collector is not sought after in these parts," I said. " Shotguns are still used to settle vexed questions of land title. Only a general threat of excommunication can settle a major feud."

" This was the way he'd come home from the gambling cabin," the professor said, " his pockets clinking with winnings. That night he fell he'd won the two bottles of whiskey. He was only eighteen when he went away. But he was the tallest man in the Glen. So he said. And lucky at cards."

The dogs were twenty yards away, silent, fanning out like soldiers cautiously circling a point of attack.

" He was an infant prodigy," I said. " He was a peerless grand-father for a man to have. He also had one great advantage over us—he knew the names of these taciturn dogs and they knew his smell."

He took off his white hat and waved at the workers. One man at a haycock raised a pitchfork—in salute or in threat ? Nobody else paid the least attention. The dogs were now at our heels, suiting their pace politely to ours. They didn't even sniff. They had impeccable manners.

" This sure is the right glen," he said. " The old man was never done talking about the dogs. They were all black-and-white in his day, too."

He stopped to look at them. They stopped. They didn't look up at us. They didn't snarl. They had broad shaggy backs. Even for their breed they were big dogs. Their long tails were rigid. Fixing my eyes on the white cloud I walked on.

" Let's establish contact," I said, " before we're casually eaten. All I ever heard about the dogs in these mountains is that their family tree is as old as the Red Branch Knights. That they're the best sheepdogs in Ireland and better than anything in the Highlands of Scotland. They also savage you first and bark afterwards."

Noses down, they padded along behind us. Their quiet breath was hot on my calves. High up and far away the nesting white cloud had the security of heaven.

" Only strangers who act suspiciously," the professor said.

" What else are we ? I'd say we smell bad to them."

" Not me," he said. " Not me. The old man told a story about a stranger who came to Kanareen when most of the people were away at the market. The house he came to visit was empty except for two dogs. So he sat all day at the door of the house and the dogs lay and watched him and said and did nothing. Only once, he felt thirsty and went into the kitchen of the house and lifted a bowl to go to the well for water. Then there was a low duet of a snarl that froze his blood. So he went thirsty and the dogs lay quiet."

" Hospitable people."

" The secret is touch nothing, lay no hand on property and you're safe."

" So help me God," I said, " I wouldn't deprive them of a bone or a blade of grass."

Twice in my life I had been bitten by dogs. Once, walking to
school along a sidestreet on a sunny morning and simultaneously
reading in *The Boy's Magazine* about a soccer centre forward, the
flower of the flock, called Fiery Cross the Shooting Star—he
was redheaded and his surname was Cross—I had stepped on a
sleeping Irish terrier. In retaliation, the startled brute had bitten
me. Nor could I find it in my heart to blame him, so that, in my
subconscious, dogs took on the awful heaven-appointed dignity
of avenging angels. The other time—and this was an even more
disquieting experience—a mongrel dog had come up softly
behind me while I was walking on the fairgreen in the town I
was reared in and bitten the calf of my leg so as to draw spurts of
blood. I kicked him but not resenting the kick, he had walked
away as if it was the most natural, legitimate thing in heaven and
earth for a dog to bite me and be kicked in return. Third time, I
thought, it will be rabies. So as we walked and the silent watchers
of the valley padded at our heels, I enlivened the way with brave
and trivial chatter. I recited my story of the four wild brothers of
Adrigole.

" Once upon a time," I said, " there lived four brothers in a
rocky corner of Adrigole in West Cork, under the mountain
called Hungry Hill. Daphne du Maurier wrote a book called after
the mountain, but divil a word in it about the four brothers of
Adrigole. They lived, I heard tell, according to instinct and never
laced their boots and came out only once a year to visit the
nearest town which was Castletownberehaven on the side of
Bantry Bay. They'd stand there, backs to the wall, smoking,
saying nothing, contemplating the giddy market-day throng.
One day they ran out of tobacco and went into the local branch
of the Bank of Ireland to buy it and raised havoc because the
teller refused to satisfy their needs. To pacify them the manager
and the teller had to disgorge their own supplies. So they went
back to Adrigole to live happily without lacing their boots, and
ever after they thought that in towns and cities the bank was the
place where you bought tobacco.

" That," said I with a hollow laugh, " is my moral tale about
the four brothers of Adrigole."

On a level with the stream that came from the lake and went
down to join the valley's main river, we walked towards a group

of four whitewashed, thatched farmhouses that were shining and scrupulously clean. The track looped to the left. Through a small triangular meadow a short-cut went straight towards the houses. In the heart of the meadow, by the side of the short-cut, there was a spring well of clear water, the stones that lined its sides and the roof cupped over it all white and cleansed with lime. He went down three stone steps and looked at the water. For good luck there was a tiny brown trout imprisoned in the well. He said quietly, " That was the way my grandfather described it. But it could hardly be the self-same fish."

He stooped to the clear water. He filled his cupped hands and drank. He stooped again, and again filled his cupped hands and slowly, carefully, not spilling a drop, came up the moist, cool steps. Then, with the air of a priest, scattering hyssop, he sprinkled the five dogs with the spring-water. They backed away from him, thoughtfully. They didn't snarl or show teeth. He had them puzzled. He laughed with warm good nature at their obvious perplexity. He was making his own of them. He licked his wet hands. Like good pupils attentively studying a teacher, the dogs watched him.

" Elixir," he said. " He told my father that the sweetest drink he ever had was out of this well when he was on his way back from a drag hunt in the next glen. He was a great hunter."

" He was Nimrod," I said. " He was everything. He was the universal Kerryman."

" No kidding," he said. " Through a thorn hedge six feet thick and down a precipice and across a stream to make sure of a wounded bird. Or all night long waist deep in an icy swamp waiting for the wild geese. And the day of this drag hunt. What he most remembered about it was the way they sold the porter to the hunting crowd in the pub at the crossroads. To meet the huntsmen halfways they moved the bar out to the farmyard. With hounds and cows and geese and chickens it was like having a drink in Noah's Ark. The pint tumblers were set on doors lifted off their hinges and laid flat on hurdles. The beer was in wooden tubs and all the barmaids had to do was dip and there was the pint. They didn't bother to rinse the tumblers. He said it was the quickest-served and the flattest pint of porter he ever saw or tasted. Bitter and black as bog water. Completely devoid of the creamy clerical collar that should grace a good pint. On

the way home he spent an hour here rinsing his mouth and the
well-water tasted as sweet, he said, as silver."

The white cloud was gone from the mountain.

" Where did it go ? " I said. " Where could it vanish to ? "

In all the wide sky there wasn't a speck of cloud. The mountain
was changing colour, deepening to purple with the approaching
evening.

He grasped me by the elbow, urging me forwards. He said,
" Step on it. We're almost home."

We crossed a crude wooden stile and followed the short-cut
through a walled garden of bright-green heads of cabbage and
black and red currant bushes. Startled, fruit-thieving birds
rustled away from us and on a rowan tree a sated, impudent
blackbird opened his throat and sang.

" Don't touch a currant," I said, " or a head of cabbage.
Don't ride your luck too hard."

He laughed like a boy half hysterical with happiness. He said,
" Luck. Me and these dogs, we know each other. We've been
formally introduced."

" Glad to know you dogs," he said to them over his shoulder.

They trotted behind us. We crossed a second stile and followed
the short-cut through a haggard, and underfoot the ground was
velvety with chipped straw. We opened a five-barred iron gate,
and to me it seemed that the noise of its creaking hinges must
be audible from end to end of the Glen. While I paused to rebolt
it he and the dogs had gone on, the dogs trotting in the lead.
I ran after them. I was the stranger who had once been the
guide. We passed three houses as if they didn't exist. They
were empty. The people who lived in them were above at the
hay. Towards the fourth thatched house of the group we walked
along a green boreen, lined with hazels and an occasional mountain ash. The guardian mountain was by now so purple that the
sky behind it seemed, by contrast, as silvery as the scales of a
fish. From unknown lands behind the lines of hazels two more
black-and-white dogs ran, barking with excitement, to join our
escort. Where the hazels ended there was a house fronted by a
low stone wall and a profusion of fuchsia. An old man sat on the
wall and around him clustered the children of the four houses.

He was a tall, broad-shouldered old man with copious white hair and dark side whiskers and a clear prominent profile. He was dressed in good grey with long, old-fashioned skirts to his coat — formally dressed as if for some formal event — and his wide-brimmed black hat rested on the wall beside him, and his joined hands rested on the curved handle of a strong ash plant. He stood up as we approached. The stick fell to the ground. He stepped over it and came towards us. He was as tall or, without the slight stoop of age, taller than the professor. He put out his two hands and rested them on the professor's shoulders. It wasn't an embrace. It was an appraisal, a salute, a sign of recognition.

He said, " Kevin, well and truly we knew you'd come if you were in the neighbourhood at all. I watched you walking down. I knew you from the top of the Glen. You have the same gait my brother had, the heavens be his bed. My brother that was your grandfather."

" They say a grandson often walks like the grandfather," said the professor.

His voice was shaken and there were tears on his face. So, a stranger in the place myself, I walked away a bit and looked back up the Glen. The sunlight was slanting now and shadows were lengthening on mountain slopes and across the small fields. From where I stood the lake was invisible, but the ashwood on the slope above it was dark as ink. Through sunlight and shadow the happy haymakers came running down towards us ; and barking, playing, frisking over each other, the seven black-and-white dogs, messengers of good news, ran to meet them. The great Glen, all happy echoes, was opening out and singing to welcome its true son.

Under the hazels, as I watched the running haymakers, the children came shyly around me to show me that I also was welcome. Beyond the high ridge, the hard mountain the card-players used to cross to the cabin of the gambling stood up gaunt and arrogant and leaned over towards us as if it were listening.

It was moonlight, I thought, not sunlight, over the great Glen. From house to house, the dogs were barking, not baying the moon, but to welcome home the young men from the card-playing over the mountain. The edges of rock glistened like quartz. The tall young gambler came laughing down the Glen, greatcoat swinging open, waving in his hand the one bottle of whiskey that hadn't been broken when he tumbled down the spink. The ghosts of his own dogs laughed and leaped and frolicked at his heels.

— A Journey to the Seven Streams

Explorations

1. This story of a quest rises to a fine climax at the end when the old man addresses the professor by his christian name. See if there are any minor climaxes leading up to this moment ?

2. There is a mounting sense of excitement as the story proceeds. How does the writer build it up and sustain it ? What means does he use to relieve it occasionally ?

3. ' It was there all the time,' he said, ' It was no dream. It was no lie.' How do you think the professor felt as he said this ?

4. As they proceed down the glen the narrator remarks : ' I was the stranger who had once been the guide.' How did this reversal of roles come about ? Is the whole meaning of the story, in a sense, contained in these words ? Develop your opinions on this point, taking into account such things as the attitude of both men towards the dogs.

5. What sort of man is the narrator ? In answering, take into account his willingness to take part in the search, his yielding to the professor when he wants to be given his 'head,' his standing aside when they meet the old man.

6. The author makes use of contrast between the two characters, especially when they enter the great glen. How does this help the story ? Support your opinions with precise reference.

7. Why, do you think, is it so important for the professor to find the glen ?

8. Frequently the author pauses to describe scenery. What do you think of these descriptions as descriptions ? Are they in any other way important to the story ? Explain.

9. Do you get a feeling of enchantment from this story ? If so seek out some passages and phrases in which it is notably present. You might start, for instance, with the sentence which begins ' Haste ' he said, ' would be dangerous. . . '

10. Look up the word ' semaphore ' in your dictionary and try to decide what the author means by it in the story. Is the word correctly used ?

Exercises

1. Write a note on the character of the professor, basing your judgements on the evidence of the story.

2. Have you seen a relative of yours or friend of your parents return to his ancestral home ? If so, try to describe what you recall of the experience.

3. Read Brian Friel's 'Among the Ruins' and be ready to compare the two stories in the next day's class.

26

THE CONFIRMATION SUIT

For weeks it was nothing but simony and sacrilege, and the sins crying to heaven for vengeance, the big green Catechism in our hands, walking home along the North Circular Road. And after tea, at the back of the brewery wall, with a butt too, to help our wits, what is a pure spirit, and don't kill that, Billser has to get a drag out of it yet, what do I mean by apostate, and hell and heaven and despair and presumption and hope. The big fellows, who were now thirteen and the veterans of last year's Confirmation, frightened us, and said the Bishop would fire us out of the chapel if we didn't answer his questions, and we'd be left wandering around the streets, in a new suit and top-coat with nothing to show for it, all dressed up and nowhere to go. The big people said not to mind them ; they were only getting it up for us, jealous because they were over their Confirmation, and could never make it again. At school we were in a special room to ourselves, for the last few days, and went round, a special class of people. There were worrying times too, that the Bishop would light on you, and you wouldn't be able to answer his questions. Or you might hear the women complaining about the price of boys' clothes.

" Twenty-two and sixpence for tweed, I'd expect a share in the shop for that. I've a good mind to let him go in jersey and pants for that."

" Quite right, ma'am," says one to another, backing one another up, " I always say what matter if they are good and pure." What had that got to do with it, if you had to go into the Chapel in a jersey and pants, and every other kid in a new suit, kid gloves and tan shoes and a scoil cap. The Cowan brothers were terrified. They were twins, and twelve years old, and every one in the street seemed to be wishing a jersey and pants on them, and saying their poor mother couldn't be expected to do for two in the one year, and she ought to go down to Sister Monica and tell her to put one back. If it came to that, the Cowans agreed to fight it out, at the back of the brewery wall, whoever got best, the other would be put back.

I wasn't so worried about this. My old fellow was a tradesman, and made money most of the time. Besides, my grandmother, who lived at the top of the next house, was a lady of capernosity and function. She had money and lay in bed all day, drinking porter or malt, and taking pinches of snuff, and talking to the neighbours that would call up to tell her the news of the day. She only left her bed to go down one flight of stairs and visit the lady in the back drawing-room, Miss McCann.

Miss McCann worked a sewing-machine, making habits for the dead. Sometimes girls from our quarter got her to make dresses and costumes, but mostly she stuck to the habits. They were a steady line, she said, and you didn't have to be always buying patterns, for the fashions didn't change, not even from summer to winter. They were like a long brown shirt, and a hood attached, that was closed over the person's face before the coffin lid was screwn down. A sort of little banner hung out of one arm, made of the same material, and four silk rosettes in each corner, and in the middle, the letters I.H.S., which mean, Miss McCann said : " I have Suffered."

My grandmother and Miss McCann liked me more than any other kid they knew. I like being liked, and could only admire their taste.

My Aunt Jack, who was my father's aunt as well as mine, sometimes came down from where she lived, up near the Basin, where the water came from before they started getting it from Wicklow. My Aunt Jack said it was much better water, at that. Miss McCann said she ought to be a good judge. For Aunt Jack was funny. She didn't drink porter or malt, or take snuff, and my father said she never thought much about men, either. She was also very strict about washing yourself very often. My grandmother took a bath every year, whether she was dirty or not, but she was in no way bigoted in the washing line in between times.

Aunt Jack made terrible raids on us now and again, to stop snuff and drink, and make my grandmother get up in the morning, and wash herself, and cook meals and take food with them. My grandmother was a gilder by trade, and served her time in one of the best shops in the city, and was getting a man's wages at sixteen. She liked stuff out of the pork butchers, and out of cans, but didn't like boiling potatoes, for she said she was no skivvy, and the chip man was better at it. When she was left alone it was a pleasure to eat with her. She always had cans of lovely things and spicy meat and brawn, and plenty of seasoning, fresh out of the German man's shop up the road. But after a visit from Aunt Jack, she would have to get up and wash for a week, and she would have to go and make stews and boil cabbage and pig's cheeks. Aunt Jack was very much up for sheep's heads, too. They were so cheap and nourishing.

But my grandmother only tried it once. She had been a first-class gilder in Eustace Street, but never had anything to do with sheep's heads before. When she took it out of the pot, and laid it on the plate, she and I sat looking at it, in fear and trembling. It was bad enough going into the pot, but with the soup streaming from its eyes, and its big teeth clenched in a very bad temper, it would put the heart crossways in you. My grandmother asked me, in a whisper, if I ever thought sheep could look so vindictive, but that it was more like the head of an old man, and would I for God's sake take it up and throw it out of the window. The sheep kept glaring at us, but I came the far side of it, and rushed over to the window and threw it out in a flash. My grandmother had to drink a Baby Power whiskey, for she wasn't the better of herself.

Afterwards she kept what she called her stock-pot on the gas. A heap of bones, and as she said herself, any old muck that would come in handy, to have boiling there, night and day, on a glimmer. She and I ate happily of cooked ham and California pineapple and sock-eye salmon, and the pot of good nourishing soup was always on the gas even if Aunt Jack came down the chimney, like the Holy Souls at midnight. My grandmother said she didn't begrudge the money for the gas. Not when she remembered the looks that sheep's head was giving her. And all she had to do with the stock-pot was to throw in another sup of water, now and again, and a handful of old rubbish the pork butcher would send over, in the way of lights or bones. My Aunt Jack thought a lot about barley, too, so we had a package of that lying beside the gas, and threw a sprinkle in any time her foot was heard on the stairs. The stock-pot bubbled away on the gas for years after, and only when my grandmother was dead did someone notice it. They tasted it, and spat it out just as quick, and wondered what it was. Some said it was paste, and more that it was gold size, and there were other people and they maintained that it was glue. They all agreed on one thing, that it was dangerous tack to leave lying around, where there might be young children, and in the heel of the reel, it went out the same window as the sheep's head.

Miss McCann told my grandmother not to mind Aunt Jack but to sleep as long as she liked in the morning. They came to an arrangement that Miss McCann would cover the landing and keep an eye out. She would call Aunt Jack in for a minute, and give the signal by banging the grate, letting on to poke the fire, and have a bit of a conversation with Aunt Jack about dresses and costumes, and hats and habits. One of these mornings, and Miss McCann delaying a fighting action, to give my grandmother time to hurl herself out of bed and into her clothes and give her face the rub of a towel, the chat between Miss McCann and Aunt Jack came to my Confirmation suit.

When I made my first Communion, my grandmother dug deep under the mattress, and myself and Aunt Jack were sent round expensive shops, and I came back with a rig that would take the sight of your eye. This time, however, Miss McCann said there wasn't much stirring in the habit line, on account of the mild winter, and she would be delighted to make the suit, if Aunt Jack would get the material. I nearly wept, for terror of what these old women would have me got up in, but I had to let on to be delighted, Miss McCann was so set on it. She asked Aunt Jack did she remember my father's Confirmation suit. He did. He said he would never forget it. They sent him out in a velvet suit, of plum colour, with a lace collar. My blood ran cold when he told me.

The stuff they got for my suit was blue serge, and that was not so bad. They got as far as the pants, and that passed off very civil. You can't do much to a boy's pants, one pair is like the next, though I had to ask them not to trouble themselves putting three little buttons on either side of the legs. The waistcoat was all right, and anyway the coat would cover it. But the coat itself, that was where Aughrim was lost.

The lapels were little wee things, like what you'd see in pictures
like *Ring* magazine of John L. Sullivan, or Gentleman Jim, and
the buttons were the size of saucers, or within the hawl of an ass of
it, and I nearly cried when I saw them being put on, and ran down
to my mother, and begged her to get me any sort of a suit, even a
jersey and pants, than have me set up before the people in this
get-up. My mother said it was very kind of Aunt Jack and Miss
McCann to go to all this trouble and expense, and I was very
ungrateful not to appreciate it. My father said that Miss McCann
was such a good tailor that people were dying to get into her
creations, and her handiwork was to be found in all the best
cemeteries. He laughed himself sick at this, and said if it was
good enough for him to be sent down to North William Street in
plum-coloured velvet and lace, I needn't be getting the needle
over a couple of big buttons and little lapels. He asked me not to
forget to get up early the morning of my Confirmation, and let
him see me, before he went to work : a bit of a laugh started the
day well. My mother told him to give over and let me alone, and
said she was sure it would be a lovely suit, and that Aunt Jack
would never buy poor material, but stuff that would last forever.
That nearly finished me altogether, and I ran through the hall
up to the corner, fit to cry my eyes out, only I wasn't much of a
hand at crying. I went more for cursing, and I cursed all belonging to me, and was hard at it on my father, and wondering why
his lace collar hadn't choked him, when I remembered that it
was a sin to go on like that, and I going up for Confirmation, and
I had to simmer down, and live in fear of the day I'd put on that
jacket.

The days passed, and I was fitted and refitted, and every old one
in the house came up to look at the suit, and took a pinch of snuff,
and a sup out of the jug, and wished me long life and the health to
wear and tear it, and they spent that much time viewing it round,
back, belly and sides, that Miss McCann hadn't time to make the
overcoat, and like an answer to a prayer, I was brought down to
Talbot Street, and dressed out in a dinging overcoat, belted, like
a grown-up man's. And my shoes and gloves were dear and
dandy, and I said to myself that there was no need to let anyone
see the suit with its little lapels and big buttons. I could keep the
topcoat on all day, in the chapel, and going round afterwards.

The night before Confirmation day, Miss McCann handed over

the suit to my mother, and kissed me, and said not to bother thanking her. She would do more than that for me, and she and my grandmother cried and had a drink on the strength of my having grown to be a big fellow, in the space of twelve years, which they didn't seem to consider a great deal of time. My father said to my mother, and I getting bathed before the fire, that since I was born Miss McCann thought the world of me. When my mother was in hospital, she took me into her place till my mother came out, and it near broke her heart to give me back.

In the morning I got up, and Mrs. Rooney in the next room shouted in to my mother that her Liam was still stalling, and not making any move to get out of it, and she thought she was cursed ; Christmas or Easter, Communion or Confirmation, it would drive a body into Riddleys, which is the mad part of Grangegorman, and she wondered she wasn't driven out of her mind, and above in the puzzle factory years ago. So she shouted again at Liam to get up, and washed and dressed. And my mother shouted at me, though I was already knotting my tie, but you might as well be out of the world, as out of fashion, and they kept it up like a pair of mad women, until at last Liam and I were ready and he came in to show my mother his clothes. She handselled him a tanner, which he put in his pocket and Mrs. Rooney called me in to show her my clothes. I just stood at her door, and didn't open my coat, but just grabbed the sixpence out of her hand, and ran up the stairs like the hammers of hell. She shouted at me to hold on a minute, she hadn't seen my suit, but I muttered something about it not being lucky to keep a Bishop waiting, and ran on.

The Church was crowded, boys on one side and the girls on the other, and the altar ablaze with lights and flowers, and a throne for the Bishop to sit on when he wasn't confirming. There was a cheering crowd outside, drums rolled, trumpeters from Jim Larkin's band sounded the Salute. The Bishop came in and the door was shut. In short order I joined the queue to the rails, knelt and was whispered over, and touched on the cheek. I had my overcoat on the whole time, though it was warm, and I was in a lather of sweat waiting for the hymns and the sermon.

The lights grew brighter and I got warmer, was carried out

fainting. But though I didn't mind them loosening my tie, I clenched firmly my overcoat, and nobody saw the jacket with the big buttons and the little lapels. When I went home, I got into bed, and my father said I went into a sickness just as the Bishop was giving us the pledge. He said this was a master stroke, and showed real presence of mind.

Sunday after Sunday, my mother fought over the suit. She said I was a liar and a hypocrite, putting it on for a few minutes every week, and running into Miss McCann's and out again, letting her think I wore it every week-end. In a passionate temper my mother said she would show me up, and tell Miss McCann, and up like a shot with her, for my mother was always slim, and light on her feet as a feather, and in next door. When she came back she said nothing, but sat at the fire looking into it. I didn't really believe she would tell Miss McCann. And I put on the suit and thought I would go in and tell her I was wearing it this week-night, because I was going to the Queen's with my brothers. I ran next door and upstairs, and every step was more certain and easy that my mother hadn't told her. I ran, shoved in the door, saying : " Miss Mc., Miss Mc., Rory and Sean and I are going to the Queen's . . . " She was bent over the sewing-machine and all I could see was the top of her old grey head, and the rest of her shaking with crying, and her arms folded under her head, on a bit of habit where she had been finishing the I.H.S. I ran down the stairs and back into our place, and my mother was sitting at the fire, sad and sorry, but saying nothing.

I needn't have worried about the suit lasting forever. Miss McCann didn't. The next winter was not so mild, and she was whipped before the year was out. At her wake people said how she was in a habit of her own making, and my father said she would look queer in anything else, seeing as she supplied the dead of the whole quarter for forty years, without one complaint from a customer.

At the funeral, I left my topcoat in the carriage and got out and walked in the spills of rain after her coffin. People said I would get my end, but I went on till we reached the graveside, and I stood in my Confirmation suit drenched to the skin. I thought this was the least I could do.

— Brendan Behan's Island

Glossary

scoil cap—a Dublin usage for ' school cap.'

a lady of capernosity and function—extensive research in Dublin North-side pubs has convinced the editor that the word 'capernosity' is one of Behan's personal coinages. It may be a portmanteau word made up of 'capability' and 'generosity.' *Function*—seems to mean usefulness.

I.H.S.—an abbreviation of the Greek word for Jesus.

malt—a widely used Irish euphemism for whiskey.

Basin—the North Blessington St. Basin from which the north side of the city got its water supply until the construction of the Vartry Reservoir in Co. Wicklow.

in no way bigoted—not very particular or meticulous.

chip man—the man at the fish and chip shop.

. . . even if Aunt Jack came down the chimney on Holy Souls' Night.—There is a superstition that Holy Souls come down the chimney on All Souls' Night.

gold size—a gelatinous substance used by gilders for glazing purposes.

Aughrim—a battle in 1689 where the Irish were defeated.

hanselled—gave him a present of sixpence on the occasion of his new suit.

Jim Larkin's band—Jim Larkin was founder of the Irish Transport and General Workers' Union. The trades union band frequently attended ceremonial occasions in Dublin city.

pledge—confirmation pledge against alcoholic drink.

Explorations

1. Why, do you think, did Brendan have such a horror of wearing the confirmation suit ? Is there any evidence in the story to suggest that he was the kind of boy who would particularly hate to wear such a stylish outfit ? Search the story carefully for such evidence—the dialogue, the narrative, the background descriptions.

2. Why is Miss McCann so very hurt when she discovers that Brendan has been deceiving her ?

3. Had Brendan any intention of hurting Miss McCann ?

4. His mother calls him ' a liar and a hypocrite.' Are these charges just ?

5. In your opinion was the mother wise in giving the game away to Miss McCann ? Give reasons for your opinion.

6. When Brendan comes back from Miss McCann he finds his mother sitting by the fire ' sad and sorry, but saying nothing.' Why do you think she was sad and sorry ?

7. Does Brendan take confirmation seriously ? Cite your evidencé.

8. Was Brendan's behaviour typical of boys anywhere ? How would you have behaved in the circumstances ?

9. What sort of man was Brendan's father ? Where is the evidence for your opinion ?

10. Is there a contrast in the story between the male and the female point of view ? If so, how is this contrast managed ?

11. The young boy is, in a sense, persecuted. Do his tormentors realize the torture he is going through ? If they did, would they, in your opinion, have carried on with it ? Give this question some thought and view it in relation to your own personal experience.

12. Why does Brendan feel that the least he can do is wear the suit to Miss McCann's funeral ?

13. In what sort of English is this story written ? Produce four typical sentences from the story and comment on their expressiveness.

14. Is the style appropriate to the material ? In what ways ? Give examples of the style working at its best and at its worst.

15. Behan uses many means of portraying character : (a) by direct description ; (b) by getting the character to speak ; (c) by getting a second character to comment ; (d) by describing the character's behaviour. Give one example of each of these methods, pointing out what trait of character it lights up.

16. Consider the structure of the story. Is the material of the story well organised ? Are there gaps in the narrative or is there unnecessary padding ?

Exercises

1. Translate the first four paragraphs into normal grammatical English.

2. Tell the entire story in the words of the mother.

3. Tell the story in day-to-day snatches as the father might retail it to his friends at work.

4. Try to reconstruct in dialogue the conversation that went on between Brendan's mother and Miss McCann when the former went up to reveal Brendan's ' hypocrisy.'

5. Try to recall your feelings and experiences on your first communion or confirmation day. Try to reproduce them with honest exactitude.

6. For comparison read Saki's 'The Lumber Room' and O'Connor's 'First Confession' so that you can discuss them in next day's class.

SHORT STORIES

BY

OTHER AUTHORS

27

THE LUMBER-ROOM

The children were to be driven, as a special treat, to the sands at Jagborough. Nicholas was not to be of the party; he was in disgrace. Only that morning he had refused to eat his wholesome bread-and-milk on the seemingly frivolous ground that there was a frog in it. Older and wiser and better people had told him that there could not possibly be a frog in his bread-and-milk and that he was not to talk nonsense; he continued, nevertheless, to talk what seemed the veriest nonsense, and described with much detail the colouration and markings of the alleged frog. The dramatic part of the incident was that there really was a frog in Nicholas' basin of bread-and-milk; he had put it there himself, so he felt entitled to know something about it. The sin of taking a frog from the garden and putting it into a bowl of wholesome bread-and-milk was enlarged on at great length, but the fact that stood out clearest in the whole affair, as it presented itself to the mind of Nicholas, was that the older, wiser, and better people had been proved to be profoundly in error in matters about which they had expressed the utmost assurance.

"You said there couldn't possibly be a frog in my bread-and-milk; there *was* a frog in my bread-and-milk," he repeated, with the insistence of a skilled tactician who does not intend to shift from favourable ground.

So his boy-cousin and girl-cousin and his quite uninteresting younger brother were to be taken to Jagborough sands that afternoon and he was to stay at home. His cousins' aunt, who insisted, by an unwarranted stretch of imagination, in styling herself his aunt also, had hastily invented the Jagborough expedition in order to impress on Nicholas the delights that he had justly forfeited by his disgraceful conduct at the breakfast-table. It was her habit, whenever one of the children fell from grace, to improvise something of a festival nature from which the offender would be rigorously debarred; if all the children sinned collectively they were suddenly informed of a circus in a neigh-

bouring town, a circus of unrivalled merit and uncounted ele-
phants, to which, but for their depravity, they would have been
taken that very day.

A few decent tears were looked for on the part of Nicholas
when the moment for the departure of the expedition arrived.
As a matter of fact, however, all the crying was done by his
girl-cousin, who scraped her knee rather painfully against the
step of the carriage as she was scrambling in.

"How she did howl!" said Nicholas cheerfully, as the party
drove off without any of the elation of high spirits that should
have characterised it.

"She'll soon get over that," said the *soi-disant* aunt; "it will
be a glorious afternoon for racing about over those beautiful
sands. How they will enjoy themselves!"

"Bobby won't enjoy himself much, and he won't race much
either," said Nicholas with a grim chuckle; "his boots are
hurting him. They're too tight."

"Why didn't he tell me they were hurting?" asked the aunt
with some asperity.

"He told you twice, but you weren't listening. You often
don't listen when we tell you important things."

"You are not to go into the gooseberry garden," said the
aunt, changing the subject.

"Why not?" demanded Nicholas.

"Because you are in disgrace," said the aunt loftily.

Nicholas did not admit the flawlessness of the reasoning; he
felt perfectly capable of being in disgrace and in a gooseberry
garden at the same moment. His face took on an expression of
considerable obstinacy. It was clear to his aunt that he was
determined to get into the gooseberry garden, "only," as she
remarked to herself, "because I have told him he is not to."

Now the gooseberry garden had two doors by which it might be
entered, and once a small person like Nicholas could slip in
there he could effectually disappear from view amid the masking
growth of artichokes, raspberry canes, and fruit bushes. The
aunt had many other things to do that afternoon, but she spent
an hour or two in trivial gardening operations among flower beds
and shrubberies, whence she could keep a watchful eye on the
two doors that led to the forbidden paradise. She was a woman
of few ideas, with immense powers of concentration.

Nicholas made one or two sorties into the front garden, wriggling his way with obvious stealth of purpose towards one or other of the doors, but never able for a moment to evade the aunt's watchful eye. As a matter of fact, he had no intention of trying to get into the gooseberry garden, but it was extremely convenient for him that his aunt should believe that he had ; it was a belief that would keep her on self-imposed sentry-duty for the greater part of the afternoon. Having thoroughly confirmed and fortified her suspicions, Nicholas slipped back into the house and rapidly put into execution a plan of action that had long germinated in his brain. By standing on a chair in the library, one could reach a shelf on which reposed a fat, important-looking key. The key was as important as it looked ; it was the instrument which kept the mysteries of the lumber-room secure from unauthorised intrusion, which opened a way only for aunts and suchlike privileged persons. Nicholas had not had much experience of the art of fitting keys into keyholes and turning locks, but for some days past he had practised with the key of the schoolroom door ; he did not believe in trusting too much to luck and accident. The key turned stiffly in the lock, but it turned. The door opened, and Nicholas was in an unknown land, compared with which the gooseberry garden was a stale delight, a mere material pleasure.

Often and often Nicholas had pictured to himself what the lumber-room might be like, that region that was so carefully sealed from youthful eyes and concerning which no questions were ever answered. It came up to his expectations. In the first place it was large and dimly lit, one high window opening on to the forbidden garden being its only source of illumination. In the second place it was a storehouse of unimagined treasures. The aunt-by-assertion was one of those people who think that things spoil by use and consign them to dust and damp by way of preserving them. Such parts of the house as Nicholas knew best were rather bare and cheerless, but here there were wonderful things for the eye to feast on. First and foremost there was a piece of framed tapestry that was evidently meant to be a fire-screen. To Nicholas it was a living, breathing story ; he sat down on a roll of Indian hangings, glowing in wonderful colours beneath a layer of dust, and took in all the details of the tapestry picture. A man, dressed in the hunting costume of some remote

period, had just transfixed a stag with an arrow ; it could not
have been a difficult shot because the stag was only one or two`
paces away from him ; in the thickly growing vegetation that
the picture suggested it would not have been difficult to creep
up to a feeding stag, and the two spotted dogs that were springing
forward to join in the chase had evidently been trained to keep
to heel till the arrow was discharged. That part of the picture
was simple, if interesting, but did the huntsman see, what
Nicholas saw, that four galloping wolves were coming in his
direction through the wood ? There might be more than four
of them hidden behind the trees, and in any case would the man
and his dogs be able to cope with the four wolves if they made an
attack ? The man had only two arrows left in his quiver, and he
might miss with one or both of them ; all one knew about his
skill in shooting was that he could hit a large stag at a ridiculously
short range. Nicholas sat for many golden minutes revolving the
possibilities of the scene ; he was inclined to think that there
were more than four wolves and that the man and his dogs were
in a tight corner.

But there were other objects of delight and interest claiming his
instant attention : there were quaint twisted candlesticks in the
shape of snakes, and a teapot fashioned like a china duck, out
of whose open beak the tea was supposed to come. How dull and
shapeless the nursery teapot seemed in comparison ! And there
was a carved sandal-wood box packed tight with aromatic
cotton-wool, and between the layers of cotton-wool were little
brass figures, hump-necked bulls, and peacocks and goblins,
delightful to see and to handle. Less promising in appearance
was a large square book with plain black covers ; Nicholas
peeped into it, and, behold, it was full of coloured pictures of
birds. And such birds ! In the garden, and in the lanes when he
went for a walk, Nicholas came across a few birds, of which the
largest were an occasional magpie or wood-pigeon ; here were
herons and bustards, kites, toucans, tiger-bitterns, brush turkeys,
ibises, golden pheasants, a whole portrait gallery of undreamed-of
creatures. And as he was admiring the colouring of the mandarin
duck and assigning a life-history to it, the voice of his aunt in
shrill vociferation of his name came from the gooseberry garden
without. She had grown suspicious at his long disappearance,

and had leapt to the conclusion that he had climbed over the
wall behind the sheltering screen of the lilac bushes; she was now
engaged in energetic and rather hopeless search for him among
the artichokes and raspberry canes.

"Nicholas, Nicholas!" she screamed, "you are to come out
of this at once. It's no use trying to hide there; I can see you
all the time."

It was probably the first time for twenty years that any one had
smiled in that lumber-room.

Presently the angry repetitions of Nicholas's name gave way
to a shriek, and a cry for somebody to come quickly. Nicholas
shut the book, restored it carefully to its place in a corner, and
shook some dust from a neighbouring pile of newspapers over
it. Then he crept from the room, locked the door and replaced
the key exactly where he had found it. His aunt was still calling
his name when he sauntered into the front garden.

"Who's calling?" he asked.

"Me," came the answer from the other side of the wall;
"didn't you hear me? I've been looking for you in the gooseberry garden, and I've slipped into the rain-water tank. Luckily
there's no water in it, but the sides are slippery and I can't get
out. Fetch the little ladder from under the cherry tree—"

"I was told I wasn't to go into the gooseberry garden," said
Nicholas promptly.

"I told you not to, and now I tell you that you may," came the
voice from the rain-water tank, rather impatiently.

"Your voice doesn't sound like aunt's," objected Nicholas;
"you may be the Evil One tempting me to be disobedient. Aunt
often tells me that the Evil One tempts me and that I always
yield. This time I'm not going to yield."

"Don't talk nonsense," said the prisoner in the tank; "go
and fetch the ladder."

"Will there be strawberry jam for tea?" asked Nicholas
innocently.

"Certainly there will be," said the aunt, privately resolving
that Nicholas should have none of it.

"Now I know that you are the Evil One and not aunt,"
shouted Nicholas gleefully; "when we asked aunt for strawberry jam yesterday she said there wasn't any. I know there
are four jars of it in the store cupboard, because I looked, and

of course you know it's there, but *she* doesn't, because she said there wasn't any. Oh, Devil, you *have* sold yourself!"

There was an unusual sense of luxury in being able to talk to an aunt as though one was talking to the Evil One, but Nicholas knew, with childish discernment, that such luxuries were not to be over-indulged in. He walked noisily away, and it was a kitchenmaid, in search of parsley, who eventually rescued the aunt from the rain-water tank.

Tea that evening was partaken of in a fearsome silence. The tide had been at its highest when the children had arrived at Jagborough Cove, so there had been no sands to play on—a circumstance that the aunt had overlooked in the haste of organising her punitive expedition. The tightness of Bobby's boots had had a disastrous effect on his temper the whole of the afternoon, and altogether the children could not have been said to have enjoyed themselves. The aunt maintained the frozen muteness of one who has suffered undignified and unmerited detention in a rain-water tank for thirty-five minutes. As for Nicholas, he, too, was silent, in the absorption of one who has much to think about; it was just possible, he considered, that the huntsman would escape with his hounds, while the wolves feasted on the stricken stag.

— The Bodley Head Saki

Glossary

soi-disant—self-styled.

Explorations

1. Saki apparently sets out to tell the story of a visit to a lumber-room. Why does he begin with the story of a frog in the bread-and-milk?

2. In this story of a war between Nicholas and his aunt, on whose side is the author? How does he indicate his loyalty? In answering this, examine the various adjectives he uses to describe the aunt and comment on their effectiveness.

3. Humour is a primary ingredient of the story. Point out five humorous touches that particularly amused you and say what you found funny in them.

4. The aunt proves no match for Nicholas. What has he got that she lacks as a cold war tactician?

5. ' Such parts of the house as Nicholas knew best were rather bare and cheerless, but here there were wonderful things for the eye to feast on.' What does this sentence suggest to us about the aunt, Nicholas, the children's daily life and education ? Is there any sense in which this might be the key sentence of the story ? Explain.

6. Is Nicholas an evil boy ? Is he a naughty boy ? In answering name all the things in which he takes pleasure.

7. Is the aunt cruel or simply misguided ? Explain.

8. How would you describe the tone of the story ? Before answering, examine the last sentence in the first paragraph.

Exercises

1. Did you ever outwit a parent, teacher or guardian ? If so, describe how you did so.

2. The aunt, perhaps, related her misfortunes to someone like the vicar's wife the next day. Try to write their conversation.

3. Nicholas probably got Bobby to describe the Jagborough trip in the presence of the aunt. Try to write the conversation.

4. Re-read the first paragraph carefully and re-write it as dialogue. Begin : ' I can't eat my bread and milk,' said Nicholas distinctly, ' there's a frog in it.'

5. Compare and contrast the characters of Nicholas and the hero of ' First Confession.'

28

AN OCCURRENCE AT OWL CREEK BRIDGE

I

A man stood upon a railroad bridge in Northern Alabama, looking down into the swift waters twenty feet below. The man's hands were behind his back, the wrists bound with a cord. A rope loosely encircled his neck. It was attached to a stout cross-timber above his head, and the slack fell to the level of his knees. Some loose boards laid upon the sleepers supporting the metals of the railway supplied a footing for him and his executioners—two private soldiers of the Federal army, directed by a sergeant, who in civil life may have been a deputy sheriff. At a short remove upon the same temporary platform was an officer in the uniform of his rank, armed. He was a captain. A sentinel at each end of the bridge stood with his rifle in the position known as " support," that is to say, vertical in front of the left shoulder, the hammer resting on the forearm thrown straight across the chest—a formal and unnatural position, enforcing an erect carriage of the body. It did not appear to be the duty of these two men to know what was occurring at the centre of the bridge ; they merely blockaded the two ends of the foot plank which traversed it.

Beyond one of the sentinels nobody was in sight ; the railroad ran straight away into a forest for a hundred yards, then, curving, was lost to view. Doubtless there was an outpost further along. The other bank of the stream was open ground—a gentle acclivity crowned with a stockade of vertical tree trunks, loop-holed for rifles, with a single embrasure through which protruded the muzzle of a brass cannon commanding the bridge. Midway of the slope between bridge and fort were the spectators—a single company of infantry in line, at " parade rest," the butts of the rifles on the ground, the barrels inclining slightly backward against the right shoulder, the hands crossed upon the stock. A lieutenant stood at the right of the line, the point of his sword upon the ground, his left hand resting upon his right. Excepting the group of four at the centre of the bridge, not a man moved. The company faced the bridge, staring stonily, motionless. The sentinels, facing the banks of the stream, might have been statues to adorn the bridge. The captain stood with folded arms, silent, observing the work of his subordinates but making no sign. Death is a dignitary who, when he comes announced, is to be received with formal manifestations of respect, even by those most familiar with him. In the code of military etiquette, silence and fixity are forms of deference.

The man who was engaged in being hanged was apparently about thirty-five years of age. He was a civilian, if one might judge by his dress, which was that of a planter. His features were good—a straight nose, firm mouth, broad forehead, from which his long, dark hair was combed straight back, falling behind his ears to the collar of his well-fitting frock coat. He wore a moustache and pointed beard, but no whiskers; his eyes were large and dark grey and had a kindly expression which one would hardly have expected in one whose neck was in the hemp. Evidently this was no vulgar assassin. The liberal military code makes provision for hanging many kinds of people, and gentlemen are not excluded.

The preparations being complete, the two private soldiers stepped aside and each drew away the plank upon which he had been standing. The sergeant turned to the captain, saluted and placed himself immediately behind that officer, who in turn moved apart one pace. These movements left the condemned man and the sergeant standing on the two ends of the same plank, which spanned three of the cross-ties of the bridge. The end upon which the civilian stood almost, but not quite, reached a fourth. This plank had been held in place by the weight of the captain; it was now held by that of the sergeant. At a signal from the former, the latter would step aside, the plank would tilt and the condemned man go down between two ties. The arrangement commended itself to his judgment as simple and effective. His face had not been covered, nor his eyes bandaged. He looked a moment at his " unsteadfast footing," then let his gaze wander to the swirling water of the stream racing madly beneath his feet. A piece of dancing driftwood caught his attention and his eyes followed it down the current. How slowly it appeared to move. What a sluggish stream !

He closed his eyes in order to fix his last thoughts upon his wife and children. The water, touched to gold by the early sun, the brooding mists under the banks at some distance down the stream, the fort, the soldiers, the piece of drift—all had distracted him. And now he became conscious of a new disturbance. Striking through the thought of his dear ones was a sound which he could neither ignore nor understand, a sharp, distinct, metallic percussion like the stroke of a blacksmith's hammer upon the anvil ; it had the same ringing quality. He wondered what it was, and whether immeasurably distant or near by—it seemed both. Its recurrence was regular, but as slow as the tolling of a death knell. He awaited each stroke with impatience and—he knew not why—apprehension. The intervals of silence grew progressively longer ; the delays became maddening. With their greater infrequency the sounds increased in strength and sharpness. They hurt his ear like the thrust of a knife ; he feared he would shriek. What he heard was the ticking of his watch.

He unclosed his eyes and saw again the water below him. " If I could free my hands," he thought, " I might throw off the noose and spring into the stream. By diving, I could evade the bullets, and, swimming vigorously, reach the bank, take to the woods, and get away home. My home, thank God, is as yet outside their lines ; my wife and little ones are still beyond the invader's farthest advance."

As these thoughts, which have here to be set down in words, were flashed into the doomed man's brain rather than evolved from it, the captain nodded to the sergeant. The sergeant stepped aside.

II

Peyton Farquhar was a well-to-do planter, of an old and highly respected Alabama family. Being a slave owner, and, like other slave owners, a politician, he was naturally an original secessionist and ardently devoted to the Southern cause. Circumstances of an imperious nature which it is unnecessary to relate here, had prevented him from taking service with the gallant army which had fought the disastrous campaigns ending with the fall of Corinth, and he chafed under the inglorious restraint, longing for the release of his energies, the larger life of the soldier, the

.opportunity for distinction. That opportunity, he felt, would come, as it comes to all in war time. Meanwhile he did what he could. No service was too humble for him to perform in aid of the South, no adventure too perilous for him to undertake if consistent with the character of a civilian who was at heart a soldier, and who in good faith and without too much qualification assented to at least a part of the frankly villainous dictum that all is fair in love and war.

One evening while Farquhar and his wife were sitting on a rustic bench near the entrance to his grounds, a grey-clad soldier rode up to the gate and asked for a drink of water. Mrs. Farquhar was only too happy to serve him with her own white hands. While she was gone to fetch the water, her husband approached the dusty horseman and inquired eagerly for news from the front.

" The Yanks are repairing the railroads," said the man, " and are getting ready for another advance. They have reached the Owl Creek bridge, put it in order, and built a stockade on the other bank. The commandant has issued an order, which is posted everywhere, declaring that any civilian caught interfering with the railroad, its bridges, tunnels, or trains will be summarily hanged. I saw the order."

" How far is it to the Owl Creek bridge ? " Farquhar asked. "About thirty miles."

" Is there no force on this side of the creek ? "

" Only a picket post half a mile out, on the railroad, and only a single sentinel at this end of the bridge."

" Suppose a man—a civilian and student of hanging—should elude the picket post and perhaps get the better of the sentinel," said Farquhar, smiling, " what could he accomplish ? "

The soldier reflected. " I was there a month ago," he replied. " I observed that the flood of last winter had lodged a great quantity of driftwood against the wooden pier at this end of the bridge. It is now dry and would burn like tow."

The lady had now brought the water, which the soldier drank. He thanked her ceremoniously, bowed to her husband, and rode away. An hour later, after nightfall, he repassed the plantation, going northward in the direction from which he had come. He was a Federal scout.

III

As Peyton Farquhar fell straight downward through the bridge, he lost consciousness and was as one already dead. From this state he was awakened—ages later, it seemed to him—by the pain of a sharp pressure upon his throat, followed by a sense of suffocation. Keen, poignant agonies seemed to shoot from his neck downwards through every fibre of his body and limbs. These pains appeared to flash along well-defined lines of ramification, and to beat with an inconceivably rapid periodicity. They seemed like streams of pulsating fire heating him to an intolerable temperature. As to his head, he was conscious of nothing but a feeling of fullness—of congestion. These sensations were unaccompanied by thought. The intellectual part of his nature was already effaced ; he had power only to feel, and feeling was torment. He was conscious of motion. Encompassed in a luminous cloud, of which he was now merely the fiery heart, without material substance, he swung through unthinkable arcs of oscillation, like a vast pendulum. Then all at once, with terrible suddenness, the light about him shot upward with the noise of a loud plash ; a frightful roaring was in his ears, and all was cold and dark. The power of thought was restored ; he knew that the rope had broken and he had fallen into the stream. There was no additional strangulation ; the noose about his neck was already suffocating him, and kept the water from his lungs. To die of hanging at the bottom of a river !—the idea seemed to him ludicrous. He opened his eyes in the blackness and saw above him a gleam of light, but how distant, how inaccessible ! He was still sinking, for the light became fainter and fainter until it was a mere glimmer. Then it began to grow and brighten, and he knew that he was rising towards the surface —knew it with reluctance, for he was now very comfortable. " To be hanged and drowned," he thought, " that is not so bad ; but I do not wish to be shot. No ; I will not be shot ; that is not fair."

He was not conscious of an effort, but a sharp pain in his wrists apprised him that he was trying to free his hands. He gave the struggle his attention, as an idler might observe the feat of a juggler, without interest in the outcome. What splendid effort !— what magnificent, what superhuman strength ! Ah, that was a fine endeavour ! Bravo ! The cord fell away ; his arms parted and floated upward, the hands dimly seen on each side in the growing light. He watched them with a new interest as first one and then the other pounced upon the noose at his neck. They tore it away and thrust it fiercely aside, its undulations resembling those of a water-snake. " Put it back, put it back ! " He thought he shouted these words to his hands, for the undoing of the noose had been succeeded by the direst pang which he had yet experienced. His neck ached horribly ; his brain was on fire ; his heart, which had been fluttering faintly, gave a great leap, trying to force itself out at his mouth. His whole body was racked and wrenched with an insupportable anguish ! But his disobedient hands gave no heed to the command. They beat the water vigorously with quick, downward strokes, forcing him to the surface. He felt his head emerge ; his eyes were blinded by the sunlight ; his chest expanded convulsively, and with a supreme and crowning agony his lungs engulfed a great draught of air, which instantly he expelled in a shriek !

He was now in full possession of his physical senses. They were, indeed, preternaturally keen and alert. Something in the awful disturbance of his organic system had so exalted and refined them that they made record of things never before perceived. He felt the ripples upon his face and heard their separate sounds as they struck. He looked at the forest on the bank of the stream, saw the individual trees, the leaves and the veining of each leaf— saw the very insects upon them, the locusts, the brilliant-bodied flies, the grey spiders stretching their webs from twig to twig. He noted the prismatic colours in all the dewdrops upon the million blades of grass. The humming of the gnats that danced above the eddies of the stream, the beating of the dragon-flies' wings, the strokes of the water spiders' legs, like oars which had lifted their boat—all these made audible music. A fish slid along beneath his eyes and he heard the rush of its body parting the water.

He had come to the surface facing down the stream ; in a moment the visible world seemed to wheel slowly round, himself the pivotal point, and he saw the bridge, the fort, the soldiers upon the bridge, the captain, the sergeant, the two privates, his executioners. They were in silhouette against the blue sky. They shouted and gesticulated, pointing at him ; the captain had drawn his pistol, but did not fire ; the others were unarmed.

Their movements were grotesque and horrible, their forms gigantic.

Suddenly he heard a sharp report and something struck the water smartly within a few inches of his head, spattering his face with spray. He heard a second report, and saw one of the sentinels with his rifle at his shoulder, a light cloud of blue smoke rising from the muzzle. The man in the water saw the eye of the man on the bridge gazing into his own through the sights of the rifle. He observed that it was a grey eye, and remembered having read that grey eyes were keenest, and that all famous marksmen had them. Nevertheless, this one had missed.

A counter swirl had caught Farquhar and turned him half round ; he was again looking into the forest on the bank opposite the fort. The sound of a clear, high voice in a monotonous singsong now rang out behind him and came across the water with a distinctness that pierced and subdued all other sounds, even the beating of the ripples in his ears. Although no soldier, he had frequented camps enough to know the dread significance of that deliberate, drawling, aspirated chant ; the lieutenant on shore was taking a part in the morning's work. How coldly and pitilessly—with what an even, calm intonation presaging and enforcing tranquillity in the men—with what accurately measured intervals fell those cruel words :

"Attention company. . . . Shoulder arms. . . . Ready. . . . Aim. . . . Fire."

Farquhar dived—dived as deeply as he could. The water roared in his ears like the voice of Niagara, yet he heard the dulled thunder of the volley, and rising again towards the surface met shining bits of metal, singularly flattened, oscillating slowly downward. Some of them touched him on the face and hands, then fell away, continuing their descent. One lodged between his collar and neck ; it was uncomfortably warm, and he snatched it out.

As he rose to the surface, gasping for breath, he saw that he had been a long time under water ; he was perceptibly farther down stream—nearer to safety. The soldiers had almost finished reloading ; the metal ramrods flashed all at once in the sunshine as they were drawn from the barrels, turned in the air, and thrust into their sockets. The two sentinels fired again, independently and ineffectually.

The hunted man saw all this over his shoulder; he was now swimming vigorously with the current. His brain was as energetic as his arms and legs; he thought with the rapidity of lightning.

"The officer," he reasoned, "will not make that martinet's error a second time. It is as easy to dodge a volley as a single shot. He has probably given the command to fire at will. God help me, I cannot dodge them all!"

An appalling plash within two yards of him, followed by a loud rushing sound, *diminuendo*, which seemed to travel back through the air to the fort and died in an explosion which stirred the very river to its deeps! A rising sheet of water, which curved over him, fell down upon him, blinded him, strangled him! The cannon had taken a hand in the game. As he shook his head free from the commotion of the smitten water, he heard the deflected shot humming through the air ahead, and in an instant it was cracking and smashing the branches in the forest beyond.

"They will not do that again," he thought; "the next time they will use a charge of grape. I must keep my eye upon the gun; the smoke will apprise me—the report arrives too late; it lags behind the missile. It is a good gun."

Suddenly he felt himself whirled round and round—spinning like a top. The water, the banks, the forest, the now distant bridge, fort and men—all were commingled and blurred. Objects were represented by their colours only; circular horizontal streaks of colour—that was all he saw. He had been caught in a vortex and was being whirled on with a velocity of advance and gyration which made him giddy and sick. In a few moments he was flung upon the gravel at the foot of the left bank of the stream—the southern bank—and behind a projecting point which concealed him from his enemies. The sudden arrest of his motion, the abrasion of one of his hands on the gravel, restored him and he wept with delight. He dug his fingers into the sand, threw it over himself in handfuls and audibly blessed it. It looked like gold, like diamonds, rubies, emeralds; he could think of nothing beautiful which it did not resemble. The trees upon the bank were giant garden plants; he noted a definite order in their arrangement, inhaled the fragrance of their blooms. A strange, roseate light shone through the spaces among their trunks, and the wind made in their branches the music of aeolian harps. He had no wish to perfect his escape, was content to remain in that enchanting spot until retaken.

A whiz and rattle of grapeshot among the branches high above his head roused him from his dream. The baffled cannoneer had fired him a random farewell. He sprang to his feet, rushed up the sloping bank, and plunged into the forest.

All that day he travelled, laying his course by the rounding sun. The forest seemed interminable ; nowhere did he discover a break in it, not even a woodman's road. He had not known that he lived in so wild a region. There was something uncanny in the revelation.

By nightfall he was fatigued, footsore, famishing. The thought of his wife and children urged him on. At last he found a road which led him in what he knew to be the right direction. It was as wide and straight as a city street, yet it seemed untravelled. No fields bordered it, no dwelling anywhere. Not so much as the barking of a dog suggested human habitation. The black bodies of the great trees formed a straight wall on both sides, terminating on the horizon in a point, like a diagram in a lesson in perspective. Overhead, as he looked up through this rift in the wood, shone great golden stars looking unfamiliar and grouped in strange constellations. He was sure they were arranged in some order which had a secret and malign significance. The wood on either side was full of singular noises, among which— once, twice, and again—he distinctly heard whispers in an unknown tongue.

His neck was in pain, and, lifting his hand to it, he found it horribly swollen. He knew that it had a circle of black where the rope had bruised it. His eyes felt congested ; he could no longer close them. His tongue was swollen with thirst ; he relieved its fever by thrusting it forward from between his teeth into the cool air. How softly the turf had carpeted the un- travelled avenue ! He could no longer feel the roadway beneath his feet !

Doubtless, despite his suffering, he fell asleep while walking, for now he sees another scene—perhaps he has merely recovered from a delirium. He stands at the gate of his own home. All is as he left it, and all bright and beautiful in the morning sun- shine. He must have travelled the entire night. As he pushes open the gate and passes up the wide white walk, he sees a flutter of female garments ; his wife, looking fresh and cool and sweet, steps down from the verandah to meet him. At the bottom of the steps she stands waiting, with a smile of ineffable joy, an attitude of matchless grace and dignity. Ah, how beautiful she is ! He springs forward with extended arms. As he is about to clasp her, he feels a stunning blow upon the back of the neck ; a blinding white light blazes all about him, with a sound like the shock of a cannon—then all is darkness and silence !

Peyton Farquhar was dead ; his body, with a broken neck, swung gently from side to side beneath the timbers of the Owl Creek bridge.

— In the Midst of Life

Glossary

The Civil War (1861-1865) was fought between the Federal states of the North and the Confederate (Secessionist) slave-owning states of the South. The Confederates wore grey uniforms, the Federals blue.

acclivity—a slope upwards, opposite of declivity.

fall of Corinth—the town of Corinth was taken by the Federal forces under the command of Rosecrans in the autumn of 1862.

the Yanks—the Northern Federal troops.

diminuendo—term in music for gradual decrease in volume.

Explorations

1. Look again at the presentation of the Federal soldiers in the opening of the story. Clearly Bierce wishes us to see them as dehumanized figures. How does he achieve this ? Why does he represent them in this way ?

2. In what respects does Farquhar differ from them ?

3. What is the tone of the story : angry, cynical, compassionate, romantic ? In answering this you might examine such a key sentence as 'In the code of military etiquette silence and fixity are forms of deference' and refer to any others that might help you towards a decision.

4. One critic of this story has said 'The dry, mechanical, precise prose hammers at the reader and creates a special, inhuman effect of its own'. See can you find examples of this kind of writing in the story.

5. The writer chooses to re-arrange the sequence of events in the story, making particular use of flashback. Do you think that this device was necessary? Can you think of any other time arrangement that the writer might have used?

6. Read the first three paragraphs carefully. At what point do we begin to see through Farquhar's eyes? Do we ever get outside him again? Where?

7. Would you regard the story as (a) an indictment of the Federal soldiers? (b) a celebration of the Southern virtues? (c) an indictment of war? (d) or something else?

8. In the story some things are dwelt on at great length and some are dismissed rather casually. Why, for instance, is the effort of the soldiers to shoot Farquhar so intense and extended while the visit of the scout—on which the entire action hinges— is handled with such apparent casualness? In answering bear in mind the author's overall intention in writing the story.

9. In his imagination Farquhar seems to be responding to nature and to the beauty of his home with unusual sensitivity. Point out some phrases and passages in which this is evident. Why is Bierce so anxious to emphasise this theme?

10. Were you surprised by the ending? Can you find the paragraph in which the writer prepares us for the ending?

Exercises

1. Tell the story from the viewpoint of the Federal Scout.

2. Has the story altered, in any way, your attitude towards war? Explain in a few paragraphs.

3. Without going beyond the evidence of the story itself write a brief character sketch of Farquhar. In summing up try to decide whether Bierce wished us to see him—or his wife—as an individual or as a type.

4. For comparison read ' Guests of the Nation ' and ' The Web ' and be able to discuss them in the next day's class.

29

THE GREEN DOOR

Suppose you should be walking down Broadway after dinner with
the ten minutes allotted to the consummation of your cigar while
you are choosing between a diverting tragedy and something
serious in the way of vaudeville. Suddenly a hand is laid upon
your arm. You turn to look into the thrilling eyes of a beautiful
woman, wonderful in diamonds and Russian sables. She thrusts
hurriedly into your hand an extremely hot buttered roll, flashes
out a tiny pair of scissors, snips off the second button of your
overcoat, meaningly ejaculates the one word " parallelogram ! "
and swiftly flies down a cross-street, looking back fearfully over
her shoulder.

That would be pure adventure. Would you accept it? Not
you. You would flush with embarrassment; you would
sheepishly drop the roll and continue down Broadway, fumbling
feebly for the missing button. This you would do unless you are
one of the blessed few in whom the pure spirit of adventure is
not dead.

True adventurers have never been plentiful. They who are
set down in print as such have been mostly business men with
newly invented methods. They have been out after the things
they wanted—golden fleeces, holy grails, lady-loves, treasure,
crowns and fame. The true adventurer goes forth aimless and
uncalculating to meet and greet unknown fate. A fine example
was the Prodigal Son—when he started back home.

Half-adventurers—brave and splendid figures—have been
numerous. From the Crusades to the Palisades they have en-
riched the arts of history and fiction and the trade of historical
fiction. But each of them had a prize to win, a goal to kick, an
axe to grind, a race to run, a new thrust in tierce to deliver, a
name to carve, a crow to pick—so they were not followers of true
adventure.

In the big city the twin spirits Romance and Adventure are
always abroad seeking worthy wooers. As we roam the streets
they slyly peep at us and challenge us in twenty different guises.

Without knowing why, we look up suddenly to see in a window a face that seems to belong to our gallery of intimate portraits ; in a sleeping thoroughfare we hear a cry of agony and fear coming from an empty and shuttered house ; instead of at our familiar curb a cab-driver deposits us before a strange door, which one, with a smile, opens for us and bids us enter ; a slip of paper, written upon, flutters down to our feet from the high lattices of Chance ; we exchange glances of instantaneous hate, affection and fear with hurrying strangers in the passing crowds ; a sudden souse of rain—and our umbrella may be sheltering the daughter of the Full Moon and first cousin of the Sidereal System ; at every corner handkerchiefs drop, fingers beckon, eyes besiege, and the lost, the lonely, the rapturous, the mysterious, the perilous, changing clues of adventure are slipped into our fingers. But few of us are willing to hold and follow them. We are grown stiff with the ramrod of convention down our backs. We pass on ; and some day we come, at the end of a very dull life, to reflect that our romance has been a pallid thing of a marriage or two, a satin rosette kept in a safe-deposit drawer, and a lifelong feud with a steam radiator.

Rudolf Steiner was a true adventurer. Few are the evenings on which he did not go forth from his hall bedchamber in search of the unexpected and the egregious. The most interesting thing in life seemed to him to be what might lie just around the next corner. Sometimes his willingness to tempt fate led him into strange paths. Twice he had spent the night in a station-house ; again and again he had found himself the dupe of ingenious and mercenary tricksters ; his watch and money had been the price of one flattering allurement. But with undiminished ardour he picked up every glove cast before him into the merry lists of adventure.

One evening Rudolf was strolling along a cross-town street in the older central part of the city. Two streams of people filled the sidewalks—the home-hurrying, and that restless contingent that abandons home for the specious welcome of the thousand-candle-power table d'hôte.

The young adventurer was of pleasing presence, and moved serenely and watchfully. By daylight he was a salesman in a piano store. He wore his tie drawn through a topaz ring instead of fastened with a stick pin ; and once he had written to the editor of a magazine that *Junie's Love Test*, by Miss Libbey, had been the book that had most influenced his life.

During his walk a violent chattering of teeth in a glass case on the sidewalk seemed at first to draw his attention (with a qualm) to a restaurant before which it was set ; but a second glance revealed the electric letters of a dentist's sign high above the next door. A giant negro, fantastically dressed in a red embroidered coat, yellow trousers and a military cap, discreetly distributed cards to those of the passing crowd who consented to take them.

This mode of dentistic advertising was a common sight to Rudolf. Usually he passed the dispenser of the dentist's cards without reducing his store ; but to-night the African slipped one into his hands so deftly that he retained it there, smiling a little at the successful feat.

When he had travelled a few yards further he glanced at the card indifferently. Surprised, he turned it over and looked again with interest. One side of the card was blank ; on the other was written in ink three words, " The Green Door." And then Rudolf saw, three steps in front of him, a man throw down the card the negro had given him as he passed. Rudolf picked it up. It was printed with the dentist's name and address and the usual schedule of " plate work " and " bridge work " and " crowns," and specious promises of " painless " operations.

The adventurous piano salesman halted at the corner and considered. Then he crossed the street, walked down a block, recrossed and joined the upward current of people again. Without seeming to notice the negro as he passed the second time, he carelessly took the card that was handed him. Ten steps away he inspected it. In the same handwriting that appeared on the first card " The Green Door " was inscribed upon it. Three or four cards were tossed to the pavement by pedestrians both following and leading him. These fell blank side up. Rudolf turned them over. Every one bore the printed legend of the dental " parlours."

Rarely did the arch-sprite Adventure need to beckon twice to Rudolf Steiner, his true follower. But twice it had been done, and the quest was on.

Rudolf walked slowly back to where the giant negro stood by the case of rattling teeth. This time as he passed he received no card. In spite of his gaudy and ridiculous garb, the Ethiopian displayed a natural barbaric dignity as he stood offering the cards suavely to some, allowing others to pass unmolested. Every half-minute he chanted a harsh, unintelligible phrase akin to the jabber of car conductors and grand opera. And not only did he withhold a card this time, but it seemed to Rudolf that he received from the shining and massive black countenance a look of cold, almost contemptuous disdain.

The look stung the adventurer. He read in it a silent accusation that he had been found wanting. Whatever the mysterious written words on the cards might mean, the black had selected him twice from the throng for their recipient ; and now seemed to have condemned him as deficient in the wit and spirit to engage the enigma.

Standing aside from the rush, the young man made a rapid estimate of the building in which he conceived that his adventure must lie. Five stories high it rose. A small restaurant occupied the basement.

The first floor, now closed, seemed to house millinery or furs. The second floor, by the winking electric letters, was the dentist's. Above this a polyglot babel of signs struggled to indicate the abode of palmists, dressmakers, musicians and doctors. Still higher up draped curtains and milk bottles white on the window-sills proclaimed the regions of domesticity.

After concluding his survey, Rudolf walked briskly up the high flight of stone steps into the house. Up two flights of the carpeted stairway he continued ; and at its top paused. The hallway there was dimly lighted by two pale jets of gas—one far to his right, the other nearer, to his left. He looked toward the nearer light and saw, within its wan halo, a green door. For one moment he hesitated ; then he seemed to see the contumelious sneer of the African juggler of cards ; and then he walked straight to the green door and knocked against it.

Moments like those that passed before his knock was answered measure the quick breath of true adventure. What might not be behind those green panels ! Gamesters at play ; cunning rogues baiting their traps with subtle skill ; beauty in love with courage, and thus planning to be sought by it ; danger, death, love, disappointment, ridicule—any of these might respond to that temerarious rap.

A faint rustle was heard inside, and the door slowly opened. A girl not yet twenty stood there, white-faced and tottering. She loosed the knob and swayed weakly, groping with one hand. Rudolf caught her and laid her on a faded couch that stood against the wall. He closed the door and took a swift glance around the room by the light of a flickering gas-jet. Neat but extreme poverty was the story that he read.

The girl lay still, as if in a faint. Rudolf looked around the room excitedly for a barrel. People must be rolled upon a barrel who—no, no ; that was for drowned persons. He began to fan her with his hat. That was successful, for he struck her nose with the brim of his derby and she opened her eyes. And then the young man saw that hers, indeed, was the one missing face from his heart's gallery of intimate portraits. The frank grey eyes, the little nose, turning pertly outward ; the chestnut hair, curling like the tendrils of a pea vine, seemed the right end and reward of all his wonderful adventures. But the face was woefully thin and pale.

The girl looked at him calmly, and then smiled.

" Fainted, didn't I ? " she asked weakly. " Well, who wouldn't ? You try going without anything to eat for three days and see ! "

" Himmel ! " exclaimed Rudolf, jumping up. " Wait till I come back."

He dashed out the green door and down the stairs. In twenty minutes he was back again, kicking at the door with his toe for her to open it. With both arms he hugged an array of wares from the grocery and the restaurant. On the table he laid them— bread and butter, cold meats, cakes, pies, pickles, oysters, a roasted chicken, a bottle of milk and one of red-hot tea.

" This is ridiculous," said Rudolf blusteringly, " to go without eating. You must quit making election bets of this kind. Supper is ready." He helped her to a chair at the table and asked : " Is there a cup for the tea ? " " On the shelf by the window," she answered. When he turned again with the cup he saw her, with eyes shining rapturously, beginning upon a huge Dill pickle that she had rooted out from the paper bags with a woman's unerring instinct. He took it from her, laughingly, and poured the cup full of milk. " Drink that first," he ordered, " and then you shall have some tea, and then a chicken wing.

If you are very good, you shall have a pickle to-morrow. And, now, if you'll allow me to be your guest, we'll have supper."

He drew up the other chair. The tea brightened the girl and brought back some of her colour. She began to eat with a sort of dainty ferocity like some starved wild animal. She seemed to regard the young man's presence and the aid he had rendered her as a natural thing—not as though she undervalued the conventions ; but as one whose great stress gave her the right to put aside the artificial for the human. But gradually, with the return of strength and comfort, came also a sense of the little conventions that belong ; and she began to tell him her little story. It was one of a thousand such as the city yawns at every day—the shop-girl's story of insufficient wages, further reduced by " fines " that go to swell the store's profits ; of time lost through illness ; and then of lost positions, lost hope, and—the knock of the adventurer upon the green door.

But to Rudolf the history sounded as big as the Iliad or the crisis in *Junie's Love Test.*

" To think of you going through all that ! " he exclaimed.

" It was something fierce," said the girl solemnly.

" And you have no relatives or friends in the city ? "

" None whatever."

" I am all alone in the world, too," said Rudolf, after a pause.

" I am glad of that," said the girl promptly ; and somehow it pleased the young man to hear that she approved of his bereft condition.

Very suddenly her eyelids dropped and she sighed deeply.

" I'm awfully sleepy," she said, " and I feel so good."

Rudolf rose and took his hat.

" Then I'll say good night. A long night's sleep will be fine for you."

He held out his hand, and she took it and said " good night." But her eyes asked a question so eloquently, so frankly and pathetically, that he answered it with words.

" Oh, I'm coming back to-morrow to see how you are getting along. You can't get rid of me so easily."

Then, at the door, as though the way of his coming had been so much less important than the fact that he had come, she asked : " How did you come to knock at my door ? "

He looked at her for a moment, remembering the cards, and

felt a sudden jealous pain. What if they had fallen into other hands as adventurous as his ? Quickly he decided that she must never know the truth. He would never let her know that he was aware of the strange expedient to which she had been driven by her great distress.

" One of our piano tuners lives in this house," he said. " I knocked at your door by mistake."

The last thing he saw in the room before the green door closed was her smile.

At the head of the stairway he paused and looked curiously about him. And then he went along the hallway to its other end ; and, coming back, ascended to the floor above and continued his puzzled explorations. Every door that he found in the house was painted green.

Wondering, he descended to the sidewalk. The fantastic African was still there. Rudolf confronted him with his two cards in his hand.

" Will you tell me why you gave me these cards and what they mean ? " he asked.

In a broad, good-natured grin the negro exhibited a splendid advertisement of his master's profession.

" Dar it is, boss," he said, pointing down the street. " But I 'spect you is a little late for de fust act."

Looking the way he pointed, Rudolf saw above the entrance to a 'theatre the blazing electric sign of its new play, " The Green Door."

" I'm informed dat it's a fust-rate show, sah," said the negro. " De agent what represents it pussented me with a dollar, sah, to distribute a few of his cards along with de doctah's. May I offer you one of de doctah's cards, sah ? "

At the corner of the block in which he lived, Rudolf stopped for a glass of beer and a cigar. When he had come out with his lighted weed, he buttoned his coat, pushed back his hat, and said, stoutly, to the lamp-post on the corner :

"All the same, I believe it was the hand of Fate that doped out the way for me to find her."

Which conclusion, under the circumstances, certainly admits Rudolf Steiner to the ranks of the true followers of Romance and Adventure.

— *The Four Million*

Explorations

1. The author ends by electing Rudolf Steiner one of ' the true followers of Romance and Adventure.' What does he mean by this description ? In view of Rudolf's performance does he, in your opinion, deserve the description ?

2. This is, among other things, the story of a starving girl. Is it a sad story ? Is the author's attitude to the events sad or jocular ? Can you describe the tone of the writing ? Take as your point of departure phrases like ' the consummation of your cigar,' ' a diverting tragedy and something serious in the way of vaudeville.'

3. A great city like New York can be a gloomy, sinister and lonely place. Is it such to O. Henry ? Explain.

4. Do you find Rudolf's conversation with the girl believable in the circumstances ? Give reasons.

5. O. Henry was a most prolific writer : are there any signs of carelessness in ' The Green Door '?—any hint that it might have been written against time ?

6. Do you wish to read the story again ? Give your reasons. Do you wish to read more of O. Henry ? Why ?

Exercises

1. The author uses a long preamble and goes on to tell the story in a highly individual style and language. It is reasonable to assume that you would tell it somewhat differently. Take up the narrative at the moment when Rudolf gets the card and carry it through to the end. Use first person narrative if you wish.

2. Develop the story about the woman in Russian sables, using, if you like, your home place as a setting.

3. Compose a story from your own imagination with some sort of whip-crack ending. If possible use your own home place for background.

4. 'Louise', 'A Fly in the Ointment' and 'Vanity' have variations on the whip-crack ending. Choose one of them and compare it with 'The Green Door' from the point of view of characterization, dialogue, plausibility.

30

LOUISE

I could never understand why Louise bothered with me. She disliked me and I knew that behind my back, in that gentle way of hers, she seldom lost the opportunity of saying a disagreeable thing about me. She had too much delicacy ever to make a direct statement, but with a hint and a sigh and a little flutter of her beautiful hands she was able to make her meaning plain. She was a mistress of cold praise. It was true that we had known one another almost intimately, for five-and-twenty years, but it was impossible for me to believe that she could be affected by the claims of old association. She thought me a coarse, brutal, cynical, and vulgar fellow. I was puzzled at her not taking the obvious course and dropping me. She did nothing of the kind ; indeed, she would not leave me alone ; she was constantly asking me to lunch and dine with her and once or twice a year invited me to spend a week-end at her house in the country. At last I thought that I had discovered her motive. She had an uneasy suspicion that I did not believe in her ; and if that was why she did not like me, it was also why she sought my acquaintance : it galled her that I alone should look upon her as a comic figure and she could not rest till I acknowledged myself mistaken and defeated. Perhaps she had an inkling that I saw the face behind the mask and because I alone held out was determined that sooner or later I too should take the mask for the face. I was never quite certain that she was a complete humbug. I wondered whether she fooled herself as thoroughly as she fooled the world or whether there was some spark of humour at the bottom of her heart. If there was it might be that she was attracted to me, as a pair of crooks might be attracted to one another, by the knowledge that we shared a secret that was hidden from everybody else.

I knew Louise before she married. She was then a frail, delicate girl with large and melancholy eyes. Her father and mother worshipped her with an anxious adoration, for some illness, scarlet fever, I think, left her with a weak heart and she had to take the greatest care of herself. When Tom Maitland proposed to her they were dismayed, for they were convinced that she was much too delicate for the strenuous state of marriage. But they were not too well off and Tom Maitland was rich. He promised to do everything in the world for Louise and finally they entrusted her to him as a sacred charge. Tom Maitland was a big, husky fellow, very good-looking, and a fine athlete. He doted on Louise. With her weak heart he could not hope to keep her with him long and he made up his mind to do everything he could to make her few years on earth happy. He gave up the games he excelled in, not because she wished him to—she was glad that he should play golf and hunt—but because by a coincidence she had a heart attack whenever he proposed to leave her for a day. If they had a difference of opinion she gave into him at once, for she was the most submissive wife a man could have, but her heart failed her and she would be laid up, sweet and uncomplaining, for a week. He could not be such a brute as to cross her. Then they would have a quiet little tussle about which should yield and it was only with difficulty that at last he persuaded her to have her own way. On one occasion seeing her walk eight miles on an expedition that she particularly wanted to make, I suggested to Tom Maitland that she was stronger than one would have thought. He shook his head and sighed.

" No, no, she's dreadfully delicate. She's been to all the best heart specialists in the world, and they all say that her life hangs on a thread. But she has an unconquerable spirit."

He told her that I had remarked on her endurance.

" I shall pay for it tomorrow," she said to me in her plaintive way. " I shall be at death's door."

" I sometimes think that you're quite strong enough to do the things you want to," I murmured.

I had noticed that if a party was amusing she could dance till five in the morning, but if it was dull she felt very poorly and Tom had to take her home early. I am afraid she did not like my reply, for though she gave me a pathetic little smile I saw no amusement in her large blue eyes.

" You can't very well expect me to fall down dead just to please you," she answered.

Louise outlived her husband. He caught his death of cold one day when they were sailing and Louise needed all the rugs there were to keep her warm. He left her a comfortable fortune and a daughter. Louise was inconsolable. It was wonderful that she managed to survive the shock. Her friends expected her speedily to follow poor Tom Maitland to the grave. Indeed they already felt dreadfully sorry for Iris, her daughter, who would be left an orphan. They redoubled their attentions towards Louise. They would not let her stir a finger ; they insisted on doing everything in the world to save her trouble. They had to, because if she was called upon to do anything tiresome or inconvenient her heart went back on her and there she was at death's door. She was entirely lost without a man to take care of her, she said, and she did not know how, with her delicate health, she was going to bring up her dear Iris. Her friends asked why she did not marry again. Oh, with her heart it was out of the question, though of course she knew that dear Tom would have wished her to, and perhaps it would be the best thing for Iris if she did ; but who would want to be bothered with a wretched invalid like herself ? Oddly enough more than one young man showed himself quite ready to undertake the charge and a year after Tom's death she allowed George Hobhouse to lead her to the altar. He was a fine, upstanding fellow, and he was not at all badly off. I never saw any one so grateful as he for the privilege of being allowed to take care of this frail little thing.

" I shan't live to trouble you long," she said.

He was a soldier and an ambitious one, but he resigned his commission. Louise's health forced her to spend the winter at Monte Carlo and the summer at Deauville. He hesitated a little at throwing up his career, and Louise at first would not hear of it ; but at last she yielded as she always yielded, and he prepared to make his wife's last few years as happy as might be.

" It can't be very long now," she said. " I'll try not to be troublesome."

For the next two or three years Louise managed, notwithstanding her weak heart, to go beautifully dressed to all the most lively parties, to gamble very heavily, to dance and even to flirt with tall, slim young men. But George Hobhouse had not the stamina of Louise's first husband and he had to brace himself now and then with a stiff drink for his day's work as Louise's second husband. It is possible that the habit would have grown on him, which Louise would not have liked at all, but very fortunately (for her) the war broke out. He rejoined his regiment and three months later was killed. It was a great shock to Louise. She felt, however, that in such a crisis she must not give way to private grief; and if she had a heart attack nobody heard of it. In order to distract her mind, she turned her villa at Monte Carlo into a hospital for convalescent officers. Her friends told her that she would never survive the strain.

" Of course it will kill me," she said, " I know that. But what does it matter ? I must do my bit."

It didn't kill her. She had the time of her life. There was no convalescent home in France that was more popular. I met her by chance in Paris. She was lunching at the Ritz with a tall and very handsome Frenchman. She explained that she was there on business connected with the hospital. She told me that the officers were too charming to her. They knew how delicate she was and they wouldn't let her do a single thing. They took care of her, well—as though they were all her husbands. She sighed.

" Poor George, who would ever have thought that I, with my heart, should survive him ? "

"And poor Tom ! " I said.

I don't know why she didn't like my saying that. She gave me her plaintive smile and her beautiful eyes filled with tears.

" You always speak as though you grudged me the few years that I can expect to live."

" By the way, your heart's much better, isn't it ? "

" It'll never be better. I saw a specialist this morning and he said I must be prepared for the worst."

" Oh, well, you've been prepared for that for nearly twenty years now, haven't you ? "

When the war came to an end Louise settled in London. She was now a woman of over forty, thin and frail still, with large eyes and pale cheeks, but she did not look a day more than twenty-five. Iris, who had been at school and was now grown up, came to live with her.

" She'll take care of me," said Louise. " Of course it'll be hard on her to live with such a great invalid as I am, but it can only be for such a little while, I'm sure she won't mind."

Iris was a nice girl. She had been brought up with the knowledge that her mother's health was precarious. As a child she had never been allowed to make a noise. She had always realised that her mother must on no account be upset. And though Louise told her now that she would not hear of her sacrificing herself for a tiresome old woman the girl simply would not listen. It wasn't a question of sacrificing herself, it was a happiness to do what she could for her poor dear mother. With a sigh her mother let her do a great deal.

" It pleases the child to think she's making herself useful," she said.

" Don't you think she ought to go out and about more ? " I asked.

" That's what I'm always telling her. I can't get her to enjoy herself. Heaven knows, I never want any one to put themselves out on my account."

And Iris, when I remonstrated with her, said : " Poor dear mother, she wants me to go and stay with friends and go to parties, but the moment I start off anywhere she has one of her heart attacks, so I much prefer to stay at home."

But presently she fell in love. A young friend of mine, a very good lad, asked her to marry him and she consented. I liked the child and was glad that she was to be given the chance to lead a life of her own. She had never seemed to suspect that such a thing was possible. But one day the young man came to me in great distress and told me that his marriage was indefinitely postponed. Iris felt that she could not desert her mother. Of course it was really no business of mine, but I made the opportunity to go and see Louise. She was always glad to receive her friends at tea-time and now that she was older she cultivated the society of painters and writers.

" Well, I hear that Iris isn't going to be married," I said after a while.

" I don't know about that. She's not going to be married quite as soon as I could have wished. I've begged her on my bended knees not to consider me, but she absolutely refuses to leave me."

" Don't you think it's rather hard on her ? "

" Dreadfully. Of course it can only be for a few months, but I hate the thought of any one sacrificing themselves for me."

" My dear Louise, you've buried two husbands. I can't see the least reason why you shouldn't bury at least two more."

" Do you think that's funny ? " she asked me in a tone that she made as offensive as she could.

" I suppose it's never struck you as strange that you're always strong enough to do anything you want to and that your weak heart only prevents you from doing things that bore you ? "

" Oh, I know, I know what you've always thought of me. You've never believed that I had anything the matter with me, have you ? "

I looked at her full and square.

" Never. I think you've carried out for twenty-five years a stupendous bluff. I think you're the most selfish and monstrous woman I have ever known. You ruined the lives of those two wretched men you married and now you're going to ruin the life of your daughter."

I should not have been surprised if Louise had had a heart attack then. I fully expected her to fly into a passion. She merely gave me a gentle smile.

" My poor friend, one of these days you'll be so dreadfully sorry you said this to me."

" Have you quite determined that Iris shall not marry this boy ? "

" I've begged her to marry him. I know it'll kill me, but I don't mind. Nobody cares for me. I'm just a burden to everybody."

" Did you tell her it would kill you ? "

" She made me."

"As if any one ever made you do anything that you were not yourself quite determined to do."

" She can marry her young man tomorrow if she likes. If it kills me, it kills me."

" Well, let's risk it, shall we ? "

" Haven't you got any compassion for me ? "

" One can't pity any one who amuses one as much as you amuse me," I answered.

A faint spot of colour appeared on Louise's pale cheeks and though she smiled still her eyes were hard and angry.

" Iris shall marry in a month's time," she said, " and if anything happens to me I hope you and she will be able to forgive yourselves."

Louise was as good as her word. A date was fixed, a trousseau of great magnificence was ordered, and invitations were issued. Iris and the very good lad were radiant. On the wedding-day, at ten o'clock in the morning, Louise, that devilish woman, had one of her heart attacks—and died. She died gently forgiving Iris for having killed her.

— *Cosmopolitans*

Explorations

1. At one stage in the story the heroine remarks to the hero : 'You can't very well expect me to fall down dead just to please you.' Explain the irony of this remark having regard to the story as a whole.

2. There are other examples of verbal irony in the story : for instance, the narrator remarks in the third sentence that Louise 'had too much delicacy to make a direct statement' against him. Can you find other examples of this sort of ironical use of words in the story ?

3. When the war takes her husband from her, Louise sets up 'a hospital for convalescent officers.' Is it significant that it was not just a hospital for ordinary soldiers ? In view of the story as a whole, how significant ?

4. Even though Louise proves that she had a heart condition by actually dying, the narrator insists on still referring to her as 'that devilish woman.' Do you think the description is justified ? Explain.

5. Towards the end of the first paragraph the narrator gives a few possible reasons why Louise keeps him as a friend. Which of them do you find the most convincing ?

6. If the narrator despises Louise so much, why does he keep accepting her invitations ? Think hard on this one and develop your thought a little on it.

7. Is it possible, after all, that he misjudged Louise ? State your views briefly and stay within the evidence of the story for your proof.

8. Is Maugham's style suited to the story ? Explain.

9. Almost a lifetime passes in the course of this story. How does Maugham manage to treat it in such a short space ? Answer in detail.

Exercises

1. There must have been a long conversation between Iris and her mother before she decided to postpone the marriage indefinitely. Try to write the dialogue for the conversation. Begin something like this :

' The young girl's eyes were shining with excitement as she burst into the room. " Mother," she said, " you'll never believe it ! Harry has asked me to marry him!"

2. If the narrator is right Louise is thinking very harsh things of him when she is speaking so gently ; try to write down the thoughts — ungrammatically if you find it better — that she has while she is conversing with him.

3. Do you know anyone like Louise ? If so describe her—or him—and if possible give examples of how she behaved at certain revealing moments.

4. Have you ever played the martyr either to get your own way or to punish someone else ? If so, describe the experience (or experiences) with as much honesty and precision as you can manage.

31

BILLY THE KID

On the first day, Lily, my nurse, took me to school. We went hand-in-hand through the churchyard, down the Town Hall steps, and along the south side of the High Street. The school was at the bottom of an alley ; two rooms, one downstairs and one upstairs, a staircase, a place for hanging coats, and a lavatory. " Miss " kept the school—handsome, good-tempered Miss, whom I liked so much. Miss used the lower room for prayers and singing and drill and meetings, and the upper one for all the rest. Lily hung my coat up, took me upstairs and deposited me among a score or so of children who ranged in age from five to eleven. The boys were neatly dressed, and the girls over-dressed if anything. Miss taught in the old-fashioned way, catering for all ages at once.

I was difficult.

No one had suggested, before this time, that anything mattered outside myself. I was used to being adored, for I was an attractive child in an Anglo-Saxon sort of way. Indeed, my mother, in her rare moments of lyricism, would declare that I had " eyes like cornflowers and hair like a field of ripe corn." I had known no one outside my own family—nothing but walks with Lily or my parents, and long holidays by a Cornish sea. I had read much for my age but saw no point in figures. I had a passion for words in themselves, and collected them like stamps or birds' eggs. I had also a clear picture of what school was to bring me. It was to bring me fights. I lacked opposition, and yearned to be victorious. Achilles, Lancelot and Æneas should have given me a sense of human nobility but they gave me instead a desire to be a successful bruiser.

It did not occur to me that school might have discipline or that numbers might be necessary. While, therefore, I was supposed to be writing out my tables, or even dividing four oranges between two poor boys, I was more likely to be scrawling a list of words, butt (barrel), butter, butt (see goat). While I was supposed to be learning my Collect, I was likely to be chanting

inside my head a list of delightful words which I had picked up
God knows where—deebriss and Skirmishar, creskant and
sweeside. On this first day, when Miss taxed me with my apparent
inactivity, I smiled and said nothing, but nothing, until she went
away.

At the end of the week she came to see my mother. I stuck my
field of ripe corn round the dining-room door and listened to
them as they came out of the drawing-room.

My mother was laughing gaily and talking in her front-door
voice.

" He's just a little butterfly, you know—just a butterfly ! "
Miss replied judiciously.

" We had better let that go for a while."

So let go it was. I looked at books or pictures, and made up
words, dongbulla for a carthorse ; drew ships, and aeroplanes
with all their strings, and waited for the bell.

I had quickly narrowed my interest in school to the quarter of
an hour between eleven and fifteen minutes past. This was Break,
when our society at last lived up to my expectations. While Miss
sat at her desk and drank tea, we spent the Break playing and
fighting in the space between the desks and the door. The noise
rose slowly in shrillness and intensity, so that I could soon assess
the exact note at which Miss would ring a handbell and send us
back to our books. If we were dull and listless, Break might be
extended by as much as ten minutes ; so there was a constant
conflict in my mind—a desire to be rowdy, and a leader in
rowdiness, together with the knowledge that success would send
us back to our desks. The games were numerous and varied
with our sex. The girls played with dolls or at weddings. Most
of the time they played Postman's Knock among themselves—
played it seriously, like a kind of innocent apprenticeship.

Tap ! Tap !
" Who's there ? "
"A letter for Mary."

We boys ignored them with a contempt of inexpressible
depth. We did not kiss each other, not we. We played tag or
fought in knots and clusters, while Miss drank tea and smiled
indulgently and watched our innocent apprenticeship.

Fighting proved to be just as delightful as I had thought.
I was chunky and zestful and enjoyed hurting people. I exulted

in victory, in the complete subjugation of my adversary, and thought that they should enjoy it too—or at least be glad to suffer for my sake. For this reason, I was puzzled when the supply of opponents diminished. Soon, I had to corner victims before I could get a fight at all.

Imperceptibly the gay picture altered. Once back in our desks, where the boys were safe from me, they laughed at me, and sniggered. I became the tinder to a catch word. Amazed, behind my eager fists, I watched them and saw they were—but what were they? Appearances must lie ; for of course they could not drive themselves from behind those aimed eyes, could not persuade themselves that I, ego Billy, whom everyone loved and cherished, as by nature, could not persuade themselves that I was not uniquely woven of precious fabric—

Could it be ?

Nonsense ! Sky, fly, pie, soup, hoop, croup—geourgeous.

But there were whisperings in corners and on the stairs. There were cabals and meetings. There were conversations which ceased when I came near. Suddenly in Break, when I tried to fight, the opposition fled with screams of hysterical laughter, then combined in democratic strength and hurled itself on my back. As for the little girls, they no longer played Postman's Knock, but danced on the skirts of the scrum, and screamed encouragement to the just majority.

That Break ended early. When we were back at our desks, I found my rubber was gone, and no one would lend me another. But I needed a rubber, so I chewed up a piece of paper and used that. Miss detected my fault and cried out in mixed horror and amusement. Now the stigma of dirt was added to the others.

At the end of the morning I was left disconsolate in my desk. The other boys and girls clamoured out purposefully. I wandered after them, puzzled at a changing world. But they had not gone far. They were grouped on the cobbles of the alley, outside the door. The boys stood warily in a semi-circle, their satchels swinging loose like inconvenient shillelaghs. The girls were ranged behind them, ready to send their men into the firing line. The girls were excited and giggling, but the boys were pale and grim.

" Go on ! " shouted the girls, " go on ! "

The boys took cautious steps forward.

Now I saw what was to happen—felt shame, and the bitterest of all my seven beings. Humiliation gave me strength. A rolled-up exercise book became an epic sword. I went mad. With what felt like a roar, but must really have been a pig-squeal, I leapt at the nearest boy and hit him squarely on the nose. Then I was round the semi-circle, hewing and thumping like Achilles in the river bed. The screams of the little girls went needle sharp. A second or two later, they and the boys were broken and running up the alley, piling through the narrow entry, erupting into the street.

I stood alone on the cobbles and a wave of passionate sorrow engulfed me. Indignation and affront, shame and frustration took command of my muscles and my lungs. My voice rose in a sustained howl, for all the world as though I had been the loser, and they had chased Achilles back to his tent. I began to zigzag up the alley, head back, my voice serenading a vast sorrow in the sky. My feet found their way along the High Street, and my sorrow went before me like a brass band. Past the Antique Shoppe, the International Stores, Barclay's Bank; past the tobacconist's and the Green Dragon, with head back, and grief as shrill and steady as a siren——

How can one record and not invent? Is there any point in understanding the nature of a small boy crying? Yet if I am to tell the small, the unimportant truth, it is a fact that my sorrows diminished unexpectedly and woefully up the street. What had been universal, became an army with banners, became soon so small that I could carry it before me, as it were, in two hands. Still indignant, still humiliated, still moving zigzag, with little running impulses and moments of pause, I had my grief where I could hold it out and see it—look! Some complexity of nature added three persons to my seven devils—or perhaps brought three of the seven to my notice. There was Billy grieving, smitten to the heart; there was Billy who felt the unfairness of having to get this grief all the way home where his mother could inspect it; and there was scientific Billy, who was rapidly acquiring know-how.

I suspected that my reservoirs were not sufficient for the waters of lamentation, suspected that my voice would disappear, and that I was incapable of a half-mile's sustained emotion. I began to run, therefore, so that my sorrow would last. When suspicion turned to certainty, I cut my crying to a whimper and settled to the business of getting it home. Past the Aylesbury Arms, across the London Road, through Oxford Street by the Wesleyan Chapel, turn left for the last climb in the Green—and there my feelings inflated like a balloon, so that I did the last twenty yards as tragically as I could have wished, swimming through an ocean of sorrow, all, paradoxically enough, quite, quite genuine—swung on the front door knob, stumbled in, staggered to my mother—

" Why, Billy ! Whatever's the matter ? "

—balloon burst, floods, tempests, hurricanes, rage and anguish —a monstrous yell—

" THEY DON'T LIKE ME ! "

My mother administered consolation and the hesitant suggestion that perhaps some of the transaction had been my fault. But I was beyond the reach of such footling ideas. She comforted, my father and Lily hovered, until at last I was quiet enough to eat. My mother put on her enormous hat and went out with an expression of grim purpose. When she came back, she said she thought everything would be all right. I continued to eat and sniff and hiccup. I brooded righteously on what was going to happen to my school-fellows now that my mother had taken a hand. They were, I thought, probably being sent to bed without anything to eat, and it would serve them right and teach them to like me and not be cruel. After lunch, I enjoyed myself darkly (scaffole, birk, rake), inventing possible punishments for them —lovely punishments.

Miss called later and had a long talk with my mother in the drawing-room. As she left, I stuck my field of ripe corn round the dining-room door again and saw them.

" Bring him along a quarter of an hour late," said Miss. "That's all I shall need."

My mother inclined her stately head.

" I know the children don't really mean any harm—but Billy is so sensitive."

We were back to normal again, then. That night, I suffered my usual terrors ; but the morning came and I forgot them again in the infinite promise of day. Lily took me to school a quarter

of an hour later than usual. We went right in, right upstairs.
Everyone was seated and you could have stuck a fork into the
air of noiseless excitement. I sat in my desk, Lily went, and
school began. Wherever I looked there were faces that smiled
shyly at me. I inspected them for signs of damage but no one
seemed to have suffered any crippling torment. I reached for a
rubber, and a girl in pink and plaits leaned over.

" Borrow mine."

A boy offered me a handkerchief. Another passed me a note
with " wil you jine my ggang " written on it. I was in. We began
to say our tables and I only had to pause for breath before giving
an answer to six sevens for a gale of whispers to suggest sums
varying from thirty-nine to forty-five. Dear Miss had done her
work well, and today I should enjoy hearing her fifteen minutes'
homily on brotherly love. Indeed, school seemed likely to come
to a full stop from sheer excess of charity ; so Miss, smiling
remotely, said we would have an extra long break. My heart
leapt, because I thought that now we could get on with some
really fierce, friendly fighting, with even a bloody nose. But
Miss produced a train set. When the older boys got down to
fixing rails, the girls, inexpressibly moved by the homily, seized
me in posse. I never stood a chance against those excited arms,
those tough, silken chests, those bird-whistling mouths, that
mass of satin and serge and wool and pigtails and ribbons.
Before I knew where I was, I found myself, my cornflowers
popping out of my head, playing Postman's Knock.

The first girl to go outside set the pattern.

"A parcel for Billy Golding ! "

In and out I went like a weaver's shuttle, pecked, pushed,
hugged, mouthed and mauled, in and out from fair to dark to
red, from Eunice who had had fever and a crop, to big Martha
who could sit on her hair.

I kissed the lot.

This was, I suppose, my first lesson ; and I cannot think it was
successful. For I did not know about the homily, I merely felt
that the boys and girls who tried to do democratic justice on me
had been shown to be wrong. I was, and now they knew it, a
thoroughly likable character.   I was unique and precious after
all ; and I still wondered what punishments their parents had
found for them which had forced them to realise the truth.

I still refused to do my lessons, confronting Miss with an impenetrable placidity. I still enjoyed fighting if I was given the chance. I still had no suspicion that Billy was anything but perfect. At the end of term, when I went down to Cornwall, I sat in a crowded carriage with my prize book open on my knees for six hours (keroube, serrap, konfeederul), so that passengers could read the inscription. I am reading it now :

BILLY GOLDING

1919

PRIZE FOR

GENERAL IMPROVEMENT

— The Hot Gates

Glossary

Eunice who had had fever and a crop—whose hair had been cropped or cut short in the course of her illness.

Explorations

1. At a point in the middle of the story the author speaks of the difficulty of 'recording' his memory of the incidents without 'inventing' anything. Would you say it is a faithful record of a childhood experience ? Or is there any element of invention in it ? It might help to compare it with Behan's ' Confirmation Suit ' in this respect.

2. What was Billy's opinion of himself ? What led him to hold this opinion ? Does he change it at any stage ? Explain.

3. The author, looking back, decides that he learned nothing about himself from the experience described. Is this altogether true ? Think about the matter a little before answering.

4. Is there any indication in the story that Billy will turn out to be a writer ? Are there any other indications for Billy's future ?

5. Examine all of Billy's strange words and write notes on each of them. For instance, 'skirmishar' is probably a 'portmanteau' word for 'skirmish' and 'scimitar', meaning a guerilla fighter armed with a scimitar.

6. Say what details of the story strike you as particularly vivid or true and explain why.

Exercises

1.   Can you remember a school bully from your primary school days ? Describe him as he appeared to you then. Does he appear any differently to you on looking back ?

2.   Was there any moment in your own childhood when it struck you that people might not like you as much as you liked yourself? If so, describe it in detail.

3.   Write out what you think Miss told the children before Billy arrived a quarter of an hour late.

4.   Try to write the dialogue between the mother and Miss on the latter's two visits to Billy's home.

5.   Write a brief character study of Billy's mother without going beyond the evidence of the story. In doing so note how economically the author conveys her character—or that aspect of her character that is relevant to the story.

6.   What parts of the story struck you as funny ? Say why.

7.   Compare and contrast the characters of Billy and the hero of 'The Lumber-room'.

32

THE FLY IN THE OINTMENT

It was the dead hour of a November afternoon. Under the ceiling of level mud-coloured cloud, the latest office buildings of the city stood out alarmingly like new tombstones, among the mass of older buildings. And along the streets the few cars and the few people appeared and disappeared slowly as if they were not following the roadway or the pavement but some inner, personal route. Along the road to the main station, at intervals of two hundred yards or so, unemployed men and one or two beggars were dribbling slowly past the desert of public buildings to the next patch of shop fronts.

Presently a taxi stopped outside one of the underground stations and a man of thirty-five paid his fare and made off down one of the small streets.

Better not arrive in a taxi, he was thinking. The old man will wonder where I got the money.

He was going to see his father. It was his father's last day at his factory, the last day of thirty years' work and life among these streets, building a business out of nothing, and then, after a few years of prosperity, letting it go to pieces in a chafer of rumour, idleness, quarrels, accusations and, at last, bankruptcy.

Suddenly all the money quarrels of the family, which nagged in the young man's mind, had been dissolved. His dread of being involved in them vanished. He was overcome by the sadness of his father's situation. Thirty years of your life come to an end. I must see him. I must help him. All the same, knowing his father, he had paid off the taxi and walked the last quarter of a mile.

It was a shock to see the name of the firm, newly painted too, on the sign outside the factory and on the brass of the office entrance, newly polished. He pressed the bell at the office window inside and it was a long time before he heard footsteps cross the empty room and saw a shadow cloud the frosted glass of the window.

" It's Harold, Father," the young man said. The door was opened.

" Hullo, old chap. This is very nice of you, Harold," said the old man shyly, stepping back from the door to let his son in, and lowering his pleased, blue eyes for a second's modesty.

" Naturally I had to come," said the son, shyly also. And then the father, filled out with assurance again and taking his son's arm, walked him across the floor of the empty workroom.

" Hardly recognise it, do you ? When were you here last ? " said the father.

This had been the machine-room, before the machines had gone. Through another door was what had been the showroom, where the son remembered seeing his father, then a dark-haired man, talking in a voice he had never heard before, a quick, bland voice, to his customers. Now there were only dust-lines left by the shelves on the white brick walls, and the marks of the showroom cupboards on the floor. The place looked large and light. There was no throb of machines, no hum of voices, no sound at all, now, but the echo of their steps on the empty floors. Already, though only a month bankrupt, the firm was becoming a ghost.

The two men walked towards the glass door of the office. They were both short. The father was well-dressed in an excellent navy-blue suit. He was a vigorous, broad man with a pleased impish smile. The sunburn shone through the clipped white hair of his head and he had the simple, trim, open-air look of a snow-man. The man beside him was round-shouldered and shabby, a keen but anxious fellow in need of a hair-cut and going bald.

" Come in, Professor," said the father. This was an old family joke. He despised his son, who was, in fact, not a professor but a poorly paid lecturer at a provincial university.

" Come in," said the father, repeating himself, not with the impatience he used to have, but with the habit of age. " Come inside, into my office. If you can call it an office now," he apologised. " This used to be my room, do you remember, it used to be my office. Take a chair. We've still got a chair. The desk's gone, yes, that's gone, it was sold, fetched a good price —what was I saying ? " he turned a bewildered look to his son. " The chair. I was saying they have to leave you a table and a chair. I was just going to have a cup of tea, old boy, but—

pardon me," he apologised again, " I've only one cup. Things have been sold for the liquidators and they've cleaned out nearly everything. I found this cup and teapot upstairs in the foreman's room. Of course, he's gone, all the hands have gone, and when I looked around just now to lock up before taking the keys to the agent when I hand over today, I saw this cup. Well, there it is. I've made it. Have a cup ? "

" No, thanks," said the son, listening patiently to his father. "I have had my tea."

" You've had your tea ? Go on. Why not have another ? "

" No, really, thanks," said the son. " You drink it."

" Well," said the father, pouring out the tea and lifting the cup to his soft rosy face and blinking his eyes as he drank, " I feel badly about this. This is terrible. I feel really awful drinking this tea and you standing there watching me, but you say you've had yours—well, how are things with you? How are you ? And how is Alice ? Is she better ? And the children ? You know I've been thinking about you—you look worried. Haven't lost sixpence and found a shilling have you, because I wouldn't mind doing that ? "

" I'm all right," the son said, smiling to hide his irritation. " I'm not worried about anything, I'm just worried about you. This "—he nodded with embarrassment to the dismantled showroom, the office from which even the calendars and waste-paper-basket had gone—" this "—what was the most tactful and sympathetic word to use ?—" this is bad luck," he said.

" Bad luck ? " said the old man sternly.

" I mean," stammered his son, " I heard about the creditors' meeting. I knew it was your last day—I thought I'd come along, I . . . to see how you were."

" Very sweet of you, old boy," said the old man with zest. " Very sweet. We've cleared everything up. They got most of the machines out today. I'm just locking up and handing over. Locking up is quite a business. There are so many keys. It's tiring, really. How many keys do you think there are to a place like this ? You wouldn't believe it, if I told you."

" It must have been worrying," the son said.

" Worrying ? You keep on using that word. I'm not worrying. Things are fine," said the old man, smiling aggressively. " I feel they're fine. I *know* they're fine."

" Well, you always were an optimist," smiled his son.

" Listen to me a moment. I want you to get this idea," said his father, his warm voice going dead and rancorous and his nostrils fidgeting. His eyes went hard, too. A different man was speaking, and even a different face ; the son noticed for the first time that like all big-faced men his father had two faces. There was the outer face like a soft warm and careless daub of innocent sealing-wax and inside it, as if thumbed there by a seal, was a much smaller one, babyish, shrewd, scared and hard. Now this little inner face had gone greenish and pale and dozens of little veins were broken on the nose and cheeks. The small, drained, purplish lips of this little face were speaking. The son leaned back instinctively to get just another inch away from this little face.

" Listen to this," the father said and leaned forward on the table as his son leaned back, holding his right fist up as if he had a hammer in his hand and was auctioning his life. " I'm sixty-five. I don't know how long I shall live, but let me make this clear : if I were not an optimist I wouldn't be here. I wouldn't stay another minute." He paused, fixing his son's half-averted eyes to let the full meaning of his words bite home. " I've worked hard," the father went on. " For thirty years I built up this business from nothing. You wouldn't know it, you were a child, but many's the time coming down from the North I've slept in this office to be on the job early the next morning." He looked decided and experienced like a man of forty, but now he softened to sixty again. The ring in the hard voice began to soften into a faint whine and his thick nose sniffed. " I don't say I've always done right," he said. " You can't live your life from A to Z like that. And now I haven't a penny in the world. Not a cent. It's not easy at my time of life to begin again. What do you think I've got to live for ? There's nothing holding me back. My boy, if I wasn't an optimist I'd go right out. I'd finish it." Suddenly the father smiled and the little face was drowned in a warm flood of triumphant smiles from the bigger face. He rested his hands on his waistcoat and that seemed to be smiling too, his easy coat smiling, his legs smiling and even winks of light on the shining shoes. Then he frowned.

" Your hair's going thin," he said. " You oughtn't to be losing your hair at your age. I don't want you to think I'm criticising you, you're old enough to live your own life, but your hair you know—you ought to do something about it. If you used oil every day and rubbed it in with both hands, the thumbs and forefingers is what you want to use, it would be better. I'm often thinking about you and I don't want you to think I'm lecturing you, because I'm not, so don't get the idea this is a lecture, but I was thinking, what you want, what we all want, I say this for myself as well as you, what we all want is ideas— big ideas. We go worrying along but you just want bigger and better ideas. You ought to think big. Take your case. You're a lecturer. I wouldn't be satisfied with lecturing to a small batch of people in a university town. I'd lecture the world. You know, you're always doing yourself injustice. We all do. Think big."

" Well," said his son, still smiling, but sharply. He was very angry. " One's enough in the family. You've thought big till you bust."

He didn't mean to say this, because he hadn't really the courage, but his pride was touched.

" I mean," said the son, hurriedly covering it up in a panic, " I'm not like you . . . I . . . "

" What did you say ? " said the old man. " Don't say that." It was the smaller of the two faces speaking in a panic. " Don't say that. Don't use that expression. That's not a right idea. Don't you get a wrong idea about me. We paid sixpence in the pound," said the old man proudly.

The son began again, but his father stopped him.

" Do you know," said the bigger of his two faces, getting bigger as it spoke, " some of the oldest houses in the city are in Queer Street, some of the biggest firms in the country ? I came up this morning with Mr. Higgins, you remember Higgins ? They're in liquidation. They are. Oh yes. And Moore, he's lost everything. He's got his chauffeur, but it's his wife's money. Did you see Beltman in the trade papers ? Quarter of a million deficit. And how long are Prestons going to last ? "

The big face smiled and overflowed on the smaller one. The whole train, the old man said, was practically packed with bankrupts every morning. Thousands had gone. Thousands ? Tens of thousands. Some of the biggest men in the City were broke.

A small man himself, he was proud to be bankrupt with the big ones ; it made him feel rich.

" You've got to realise, old boy," he said gravely, " the world's changing. You've got to move with the times."

The son was silent. The November sun put a few strains of light through the frosted window and the shadow of its bars and panes was weakly placed on the wall behind his father's head. Some of the light caught the tanned scalp that showed between the white hair. So short the hair was that the father's ears protruded and, framed against that reflection of the window bars, the father suddenly took (to his son's fancy) the likeness of a convict in his cell and the son, startled, found himself asking : Were they telling the truth when they said the old man was a crook and that his balance sheets were cooked ? What about that man they had to shut up at the meeting, the little man from Birmingham, in a mackintosh . . . ?

" There's a fly in this room," said the old man suddenly, looking up in the air and getting to his feet. " I'm sorry to interrupt what you were saying, but I can hear a fly. I must get it out."

"A fly ? " said his son, listening.

" Yes, can't you hear it ? It's peculiar how you can hear everything now the machines have stopped. It took me quite a time to get used to the silence. Can you see it, old chap ? I can't stand flies, you never know where they've been. Excuse me one moment."

The old man pulled a duster out of a drawer.

" Forgive this interruption. I can't sit in a room with a fly in it," he said apologetically. They both stood up and listened. Certainly in the office was the small dying fizz of a fly, deceived beyond its strength by the autumn sun.

" Open the door, will you, old boy," said the old man with embarrassment. " I hate them."

The son opened the door and the fly flew into the light. The old man struck at it but it sailed away higher.

" There it is," he said, getting up on the chair. He struck again and the son struck too as the fly came down. The old man got on top of his table. An expression of disgust and fear was curled on his smaller face ; and an expression of apology and weakness,

" Excuse me," he said again, looking up at the ceiling.

" If we leave the door open or open the window it will go," said the son

" It may seem a fad to you," said the old man shyly. " I don't like flies. Ah, here it comes."

They missed it. They stood helplessly gaping up at the ceiling where the fly was buzzing in small circles round the cord of the electric light.

" I don't like them," the old man said.

The table creaked under his weight. The fly went on to the ceiling and stayed there. Unavailingly the old man snapped the duster at it.

" Be careful," said the son. " Don't lose your balance."

The old man looked down. Suddenly he looked tired and old, his body began to sag and a look of weakness came on to his face.

" Give me a hand, old boy," the old man said in a shaky voice. He put a heavy hand on his son's shoulder and the son felt the great helpless weight of his father's body.

" Lean on me."

Very heavily and slowly the old man got cautiously down from the table to the chair. "Just a moment, old boy," said the old man. Then, after getting his breath, he got down from the chair to the floor.

" You all right ? " his son asked.

" Yes, yes," said the old man out of breath. " It was only that fly. Do you know, you're actually more bald at the back than I thought. There's a patch there as big as my hand. I saw it just then. It gave me quite a shock. You really must do something about it. How are your teeth ? Do you have any trouble with your teeth ? That may have something to do with it. Hasn't Alice told you how bald you are ? "

" You've been doing too much. You're worried," said the son, soft with repentance and sympathy. " Sit down. You've had a bad time."

" No, nothing," said the old man shyly, breathing rather hard. "A bit. Everyone's been very nice. They came in and shook hands. The staff came in. They all came in just to shake hands. They said, ' We wish you good luck.' "

The old man turned his head away. He actually wiped a tear

from his eye. A glow of sympathy transported the younger man.
He felt as though a sun had risen.

" You know——" the father said uneasily, flitting a glance at
the fly on the ceiling as if he wanted the fly as well as his son to
listen to what he was going to say—" you know," he said, " the
world's all wrong. I've made my mistakes. I was thinking about
it before you came. You know where I went wrong ? You know
where I made my mistake ? "

The son's heart started to a panic of embarrassment. For
heaven's sake, he wanted to shout, don't ! Don't stir up the
whole business. Don't humiliate yourself before me. Don't
start telling the truth. Don't oblige me to say we know all
about it, that we have known for years the mess you've been in,
that we've seen through the plausible stories you've spread, that
we've known the people you've swindled.

" Money's been my trouble," said the old man. " I thought I
needed money. That's one thing it's taught me. I've done with
money. Absolutely done and finished with it. I never want to
see another penny as long as I live. I don't want to see or hear
of it. If you came in now and offered me a thousand pounds I
should laugh at you. We deceive ourselves. We don't want the
stuff. All I want now is just to go to a nice little cottage by the
sea," the old man said. " I feel I need air, sun, life."

The son was appalled.

" You want money even for that," the son said irritably. " You
want quite a lot of money to do that."

" Don't say I want money," the old man said vehemently.
" Don't say it. When I walk out of this place tonight I'm going
to walk into freedom. I am not going to think of money. You
never know where it will come from. You may see something.
You may meet a man. You never know. Did the children of
Israel worry about money ? No, they just went out and collected
the manna. That's what I want to do."

The son was about to speak. The father stopped him.

" Money," the father said, " isn't necessary at all."

Now, like the harvest moon in full glow, the father's face shone
up at his son.

" What I came round about was this," said the son awkwardly
and dryly. " I'm not rich. None of us is. In fact, with things as
they are we're all pretty shaky and we can't do anything. I

wish I could, but I can't. But "—after the assured beginning he began to stammer and to crinkle his eyes timidly—" but the idea of your being—you know, well short of some immediate necessity, I mean—well, if it is ever a question of—well, to be frank, *cash*, I'd raise it somehow."

He coloured. He hated to admit his own poverty, he hated to offer charity to his father. He hated to sit there knowing the things he knew about him. He was ashamed to think how he, how they all dreaded having the gregarious, optimistic, extravagant, uncontrollable, disingenuous old man on their hands. The son hated to feel he was being in some peculiar way which he could not understand, mean, cowardly and dishonest.

The father's sailing eyes came down and looked at his son's nervous, frowning face and slowly the dreaming look went from the father's face. Slowly the harvest moon came down from its rosy voyage. The little face suddenly became dominant within the outer folds of skin like a fox looking out of a hole of clay. He leaned forward brusquely on the table and somehow a silver-topped pencil was in his hand preparing to note something briskly on a writing-pad.

" Raise it ? " said the old man sharply. " Why didn't you tell me before you could raise money ? How can you raise it ? Where ? By when ? "

— *The Saint and Other Stories*

Explorations

1. Towards the end of the story the son ' hated to feel that he was being in some peculiar way which he could not understand, mean, cowardly and dishonest.' Was this feeling of guilt justified ? Was it something brought about by the outlook and attitudes of the father ? Develop your thought on the matter.

2. The author describes two distinct personalities of the father. Which of them was the real man ? Which of these personalities tries to kill flies ? Explain.

3. The author ascribes no such double personality to the son. But is there a sense in which he also appears to be two people ? In answering consider such things as his behaviour with the taxi, his mixed feelings towards lending money.

4.   The father basically ' despises ' the son, or so the author tells us.   Are there any incidents or remarks in the story that support this statement ?

5.   Does the son, in any way, despise the father ?

6.   Is the father justified in despising the son ?

7.   The father makes a fuss about the cup of tea, the son's baldness, the fly.   Is this in any way indicative of his general character and outlook ?   Explain.

8.   The son feels some kind of responsibility for the father.   Does it spring from love, or pity, or duty, or guilt, or something else ? Explain.

9.   Does the father feel any such responsibility for the son ?

10.   What do you think the writer wishes to convey by the fly incident and by the title of the story ?   There are many possible answers to this.   How many can you suggest ?

11.   Pritchett's writing sometimes has great visual power.   Point out some examples of it in the present story.

Exercises

1.   Try to continue the story for about another page as the father cross-examines the son about how money can be raised.

2.   Write a character sketch of the son based on the evidence of the story.

3.   Before he set out to visit the father, Harold must have had an anxious conversation with his wife about what they were prepared to do for the old man.   Try to write their dialogue.

4.   Compare the character of the father with that of the boss in 'The Fly'.   Can you draw any general conclusions from the two stories about the effects of big business on character ?

33

THE DIAMOND MAKER

Some business had detained me in Chancery Lane until nine in the evening, and thereafter, having some inkling of a headache, I was disinclined either for entertainment or further work. So much of the sky as the high cliffs of that narrow cañon of traffic left visible spoke of a serene night, and I determined to make my way down to the Embankment, and rest my eyes and cool my head by watching the variegated lights upon the river. Beyond comparison the night is the best time for this place ; a merciful darkness hides the dirt of the waters, and the lights of this transition age, red, glaring orange, gas-yellow, and electric white, are set in shadowy outlines of every possible shade between grey and deep purple. Through the arches of Waterloo Bridge a hundred points of light mark the sweep of the Embankment, and above its parapet rise the towers of Westminster, warm grey against the starlight. The black river goes by with only a rare ripple breaking its silence, and disturbing the reflections of the lights that swim upon its surface.

"A warm night," said a voice at my side.

I turned my head, and saw the profile of a man who was leaning over the parapet beside me. It was a refined face, not unhandsome though pinched and pale enough, and the coat collar turned up and pinned round the throat marked his status in life as sharply as a uniform. I felt I was committed to the price of a bed and breakfast if I answered him.

I looked at him curiously. Would he have anything to tell me worth the money, or was he the common incapable—incapable even of telling his own story ? There was a quality of intelligence in his forehead and eyes, and a certain tremulousness in his nether lip that decided me.

" Very warm," said I ; " but not too warm for us here."

" No," he said, still looking across the water, " it is pleasant enough here . . . just now."

" It is good," he continued after a pause, " to find anything so restful as this in London. After one has been fretting about business all day, about getting on, meeting obligations, and parrying dangers, I do not know what one would do if it were not for such pacific corners." He spoke with long pauses between the sentences. " You must know a little of the irksome labour of the world, or you would not be here. But I doubt if you can be so brain-weary and footsore as I am . . . Bah ! Sometimes I doubt if the game is worth the candle. I feel inclined to throw the whole thing over—name, wealth, and position—and take to some modest trade. But I know if I abandoned my ambition—hardly as she uses me—I should have nothing but remorse left for the rest of my days."

He became silent. I looked at him in astonishment. If ever I saw a man hopelessly hard-up it was the man in front of me. He was ragged and he was dirty, unshaven and unkempt ; he looked as though he had been left in a dust-bin for a week. And he was talking to *me* of the irksome worries of a large business. I almost laughed outright. Either he was mad or playing a sorry jest on his own poverty.

" If high aims and high positions," said I, " have their draw-backs of hard work and anxiety, they have their compensations. Influence, the power of doing good, of assisting those weaker and poorer than ourselves ; and there is even a certain gratification in display . . . "

My banter under the circumstances was in very vile taste. I spoke on the spur of the contrast of his appearance and speech. I was sorry even while I was speaking.

He turned a haggard but very composed face upon me. Said he : " I forget myself. Of course you would not understand."

He measured me for a moment. " No doubt it is very absurd. You will not believe me even when I tell you, so that it is fairly safe to tell you. And it will be a comfort to tell someone. I really have a big business in hand, a very big business. But there are troubles just now. The fact is . . . I make diamonds."

" I suppose," said I, " you are out of work just at present ? "

" I am sick of being disbelieved," he said impatiently, and suddenly unbuttoning his wretched coat he pulled out a little canvas bag that was hanging by a cord round his neck. From this he produced a brown pebble. " I wonder if you know enough to know what that is ? " He handed it to me.

Now, a year or so ago, I had occupied my leisure in taking a

London science degree, so that I have a smattering of physics and mineralogy. The thing was not unlike an uncut diamond of the darker sort, though far too large, being almost as big as the top of my thumb. I took it, and saw it had the form of a regular octahedron, with the carved faces peculiar to the most precious of minerals. I took out my penknife and tried to scratch it—vainly. Leaning forward towards the gas-lamp, I tried the thing on my watch-glass, and scored a white line across that with the greatest ease.

I looked at my interlocutor with rising curiosity. " It certainly is rather like a diamond. But, if so, it is a Behemoth of diamonds. Where did you get it ? "

" I tell you I made it," he said. " Give it back to me."

He replaced it hastily and buttoned his jacket. " I will sell it to you for one hundred pounds," he suddenly whispered eagerly. With that my suspicions returned. The thing might, after all, be merely a lump of that almost equally hard substance, corundum, with an accidental resemblance in shape to the diamond. Or if it was a diamond, how came he by it, and why should he offer it at a hundred pounds ?

We looked into one another's eyes. He seemed eager, but honestly eager. At that moment I believed it was a diamond he was trying to sell. Yet I am a poor man, a hundred pounds would leave a visible gap in my fortunes and no sane man would buy a diamond by gaslight from a ragged tramp on his personal warranty only. Still, a diamond that size conjured up a vision of many thousands of pounds. Then, thought I, such a stone could scarcely exist without being mentioned in every book on gems, and again I called to mind the stories of contraband and light-fingered Kaffirs at the Cape. I put the question of purchase on one side.

" How did you get it ? " said I.

" I made it."

I had heard something of Moissan, but I knew his artificial diamonds were very small. I shook my head.

" You seem to know something of this kind of thing. I will tell you a little about myself. Perhaps then you may think better of the purchase." He turned round with his back to the river, and put his hands in his pockets. He sighed. " I know you will not believe me."

" Diamonds," he began—and as he spoke his voice lost its faint flavour of the tramp and assumed something of the easy tone of an educated man—" are to be made by throwing carbon out of combination in a suitable flux and under a suitable pressure; the carbon crystallises out, not as black-lead or charcoal-powder, but as small diamonds. So much has been known to chemists for years, but no one yet has hit upon exactly the right flux in which to melt up the carbon, or exactly the right pressure for the best results. Consequently the diamonds made by chemists are small and dark, and worthless as jewels. Now I, you know, have given up my life to this problem—given my life to it.

" I began to work at the conditions of diamond making when I was seventeen, and now I am thirty-two. It seemed to me that it might take all the thought and energies of a man for ten years, or twenty years, but, even if it did, the game was still worth the candle. Suppose one to have at last just hit the right trick, before the secret got out and diamonds became as common as coal, one might realise millions. Millions ! "

He paused and looked for my sympathy. His eyes shone hungrily. " To think," said he, " that I am on the verge of it all, and here ! "

" I had," he proceeded, " about a thousand pounds when I was twenty-one, and this, I thought, eked out by a little teaching, would keep my researches going. A year or two was spent in study, at Berlin chiefly, and then I continued on my own account. The trouble was the secrecy. You see, if once I had let out what I was doing, other men might have been spurred on by my belief in the practicability of the idea ; and I do not pretend to be such a genius as to have been sure of coming in first, in the case of a race for the discovery. And you see it was important that if I really meant to make a pile, people should not know it was an artificial process and capable of turning out diamonds by the ton. So I had to work all alone. At first I had a little laboratory, but as my resources began to run out I had to conduct my experiments in a wretched unfurnished room in Kentish Town, where I slept at last on a straw mattress on the floor among all my apparatus. The money simply flowed away. I grudged myself everything except scientific appliances. I tried to keep things going by a little teaching, but I am not a very good teacher, and I have no university degree, not very much education except in chemistry, and I found I had to give a lot of time and labour for precious little money. But I got nearer and nearer the thing. Three years ago I settled the problem of the composition of the flux, and got near the pressure by putting this flux of mine and a certain carbon composition into a closed-up gunbarrel, filling up with water, sealing tightly, and heating."

He paused.

" Rather risky," said I.

" Yes. It burst, and smashed all my windows and a lot of my apparatus ; but I got a kind of diamond powder nevertheless. Following out the problem of getting a big pressure upon the molten mixture from which the things were to crystallise, I hit upon some researches of Daubrée's at the Paris *Laboratorie des Poudres et Salpêtres*. He exploded dynamite in a tightly screwed steel cylinder, too strong to burst, and I found he could crush rocks into a muck not unlike the South African bed in which diamonds are found. It was a tremendous strain on my resources, but I got a steel cylinder made for my purpose after his pattern. I put in all my stuff and my explosives, built up a fire in my furnace, put the whole concern in, and—went out for a walk."

I could not help laughing at his matter-of-fact manner. " Did you not think it would blow up the house ? Were there other people in the place ? "

" It was in the interest of science," he said ultimately. " There was a costermonger family on the floor below, a begging-letter writer in the room behind mine, and two flower-women were upstairs. Perhaps it was a bit thoughtless. But possibly some of them were out.

" When I came back the thing was just where I left it, among the white-hot coals. The explosive hadn't burst the case. And then I had a problem to face. You know time is an important element in crystallisation. If you hurry the process the crystals are small—it is only by prolonged standing that they grow to any size. I resolved to let this apparatus cool for two years, letting the temperature go down slowly during that time. And I was now quite out of money ; and with a big fire and the rent of my room, as well as my hunger to satisfy, I had scarcely a penny in the world.

" I can hardly tell you all the shifts I was put to while I was making the diamonds. I have sold newspapers, held horses, opened cab-doors. For many weeks I addressed envelopes. I had a place as assistant to a man who owned a barrow, and used to call down one side of the road while he called down the other. Once for a week I had absolutely nothing to do, and I begged. What a week that was! One day the fire was going out and I had eaten nothing all day, and a little chap taking his girl out, gave me sixpence—to show-off. Thank heaven for vanity! How the fish-shops smelt! But I went and spent it all on coals, and had the furnace bright red again, and then—— Well, hunger makes a fool of a man.

"At last, three weeks ago, I let the fire out. I took my cylinder and unscrewed it while it was still so hot that it punished my hands, and I scraped out the crumbling lava-like mass with a chisel, and hammered it into a powder upon an iron plate. And I found three big diamonds and five small ones. As I sat on the floor hammering, my door opened, and my neighbour, the begging-letter writer, came in. He was drunk—as he usually is. ' 'Nerchist,' said he. ' You're drunk,' said I. ' 'Structive scoundrel,' said he. ' Go to your father,' said I, meaning the Father of Lies. ' Never you mind,' said he, and gave me a cunning wink, and hiccupped, and leaning up against the door, with his other eye against the door-post, began to babble of how he had been prying in my room, and how he had gone to the police that morning, and how they had taken down everything he had to say—' 'siffiwas a ge'm,' said he. Then I suddenly realised I was in a hole. Either I should have to tell these police my little secret, and get the whole thing blown upon, or be lagged as an anarchist. So I went up to my neighbour and took him by the collar, and rolled him about a bit, and then I gathered up my diamonds and cleared out. The evening newspapers called my den the Kentish-Town Bomb Factory. And now I cannot part with the things for love or money.

" If I go into a respectable jewellers they ask me to wait, and go and whisper to a clerk to fetch a policeman, and then I say I cannot wait. And I found out a receiver of stolen goods, and he simply stuck to the one I gave him and told me to prosecute if I wanted it back. I am going about now with several hundred thousand pounds-worth of diamonds round my neck, and without either food or shelter. You are the first person I have taken into my confidence. But I like your face and I am hard-driven."

He looked into my eyes.

" It would be madness," said I, " for me to buy a diamond under the circumstances. Besides, I do not carry hundreds of pounds about in my pocket. Yet I more than half believe your story. I will, if you like, do this : come to my office tomorrow . . ."

" You think I am a thief ! " said he keenly. " You will tell the police. I am not coming into a trap."

" Somehow I am assured you are no thief. Here is my card. Take that, anyhow. You need not come to any appointment. Come when you will."

He took the card, and an earnest of my good-will.

" Think better of it and come," said I.

He shook his head doubtfully. " I will pay back your half-crown with interest some day—such interest as will amaze you," said he. "Anyhow, you will keep the secret ? . . . Don't follow me."

He crossed the road and went into the darkness towards the little steps under the archway leading into Essex Street, and I let him go. And that was the last I ever saw of him.

Afterwards I had two letters from him asking me to send bank-notes—not cheques—to certain addresses. I weighed the matter over, and took what I conceived to be the wisest course. Once he called upon me when I was out. My urchin described him as a very thin, dirty, and ragged man, with a dreadful cough. He left no message. That was the finish of him so far as my story goes. I wonder sometimes what has become of him. Was he an ingenious monomaniac, or a fraudulent dealer in pebbles, or has he really made diamonds as he asserted ? The latter is just sufficiently credible to make me think at times that I have missed the most brilliant opportunity of my life. He may of course be dead, and his diamonds carelessly thrown aside—one, I repeat, was almost as big as my thumb. Or he may be still wandering about trying to sell the things. It is just possible he may yet emerge upon society, and, passing athwart my heavens in the serene altitude sacred to the wealthy and the well-advertised, reproach me silently for my want of enterprise. I sometimes think I might at least have risked five pounds.

— *The Short Stories of H. G. Wells*

Glossary

octahedron—a shape with eight triangular, plane faces.
behemoth—an enormous creature. (see Job 40 : 15)
Kaffir—member of South African race of Bantu family many of whom worked in the diamond mines of South Africa.
costermonger—a man who sells fruit or fish off a street barrow.
"nerchist'—mispronunciation of 'anarchist'.

Explorations

1. At the end of the story the narrator says to the stranger : 'Somehow I am assured you are no thief.' What features in the man and his story would have led the listener to that conclusion ?

2. The narrator asks himself : 'Was he an ingenious monomaniac, or a fraudulent dealer in pebbles, or has he really made diamonds as he asserted ' ? Which do you think he is ? Base your answer on the evidence of the story.

3. There is a distinct impression that the tramp is genuinely suffering and has suffered. By what means does Wells convey this sense of pain ? Cite the significant details.

4. Read the first paragraph carefully and give your opinion of it as an opening for this particular story.

5. Did you find this story gripping ? If so how did the author manage to keep up the sense of suspense and excitement ?

6. Is it a short story in the modern sense or is it closer to what we referred to in the Introduction as an anecdote ? Explain. Has it anything in common with the old-fashioned tale as discussed on pages 5 and 6 of Introduction ?

7. Comment on Wells' use of words, especially in the creation of atmosphere and description of people and objects. Quote some phrases that particularly appeal to you and say why they do.

Exercises

1. From the evidence of the story write a brief character sketch of the narrator.

2. Have you ever had a strange meeting with an unusual stranger ? If so, try to describe it with complete accuracy, using the details that remain most vividly in your mind.

3. Note the skill with which Wells builds up the London night atmosphere. If ever you have been struck by the atmosphere of a place you have visited, try to recapture it in two carefully written paragraphs.

4. Read 'Brother Boniface' and 'The Breath of Life' and see if they have anything in common with this story.

34

THE QUEER FEET

If you meet a member of that select club, " The Twelve True
Fishermen," entering the Vernon Hotel for the annual club
dinner, you will observe, as he takes off his overcoat, that his
evening coat is green and not black. If (supposing that you have
the star-defying audacity to address such a being) you ask him
why, he will probably answer that he does it to avoid being
mistaken for a waiter. You will then retire crushed. But you
will leave behind you a mystery as yet unsolved and a tale worth
telling.

If (to pursue the same vein of improbable conjecture) you were
to meet a mild, hard-working little priest, named Father Brown,
and were to ask him what he thought was the most singular luck
of his life, he would probably reply that upon the whole his best
stroke was at the Vernon Hotel, where he had averted a crime
and perhaps, saved a soul, merely by listening to a few footsteps
in a passage. He is perhaps a little proud of this wild and wonderful guess of his, and it is possible that he might refer to it. But
since it is immeasurably unlikely that you will ever rise high
enough in the social world to find " The Twelve True Fishermen,"
or that you will ever sink low enough among slums and criminals
to find Father Brown, I fear you will never hear the story at all
unless you hear it from me.

The Vernon Hotel, at which The Twelve True Fishermen
held their annual dinners, was an institution such as can only
exist in an oligarchical society which has almost gone mad on
good manners. It was that topsy-turvy product—an " exclusive "
commercial enterprise. That is, it was a thing which paid, not by
attracting people, but actually by turning people away. In the
heart of a plutocracy tradesmen become cunning enough to be
more fastidious than their customers. They positively create
difficulties so that their wealthy and weary clients may spend
money and diplomacy in overcoming them. If there were a
fashionable hotel in London which no man could enter who was
under six foot, society would meekly make up parties of six-foot

men to dine in it. If there were an expensive restaurant which by a mere caprice of its proprietor was only open on Thursday afternoon, it would be crowded on Thursday afternoon. The Vernon Hotel stood, as if by accident, in the corner of a square in Belgravia. It was a small hotel ; and a very inconvenient one. But its very inconveniences were considered as walls protecting a particular class. One inconvenience, in particular, was held to be of vital importance : the fact that practically only twenty-four people could dine in the place at once. The only big dinner table was the celebrated terrace table, which stood open to the air on a sort of veranda overlooking one of the most exquisite old gardens in London. Thus it happened that even the twenty-four seats at this table could only be enjoyed in warm weather ; and this making the enjoyment yet more difficult made it yet more desired. The existing owner of the hotel was a Jew named Lever ; and he made nearly a million out of it, by making it difficult to get into. Of course he combined with this limitation in the scope of his enterprise the most careful polish in its performance. The wines and cooking were really as good as any in Europe, and the demeanour of the attendants exactly mirrored the fixed mood of the English upper class. The proprietor knew all his waiters like the fingers on his hand ; there were only fifteen of them all told. It was much easier to become a Member of Parliament than to become a waiter in that hotel. Each waiter was trained in terrible silence and smoothness, as if he were a gentleman's servant. And, indeed, there was generally at least one waiter to every gentleman who dined.

The club of The Twelve True Fishermen would not have consented to dine anywhere but in such a place, for it insisted on a luxurious privacy ; and would have been quite upset by the mere thought that any other club was even dining in the same building. On the occasion of their annual dinner the Fishermen were in the habit of exposing all their treasures, as if they were in a private house, especially the celebrated set of fish knives and forks which were, as it were, the insignia of the society, each being exquisitely wrought in silver in the form of a fish, and each loaded at the hilt with one large pearl. These were always laid out for the fish course, and the fish course was always the most magnificent in that magnificent repast. The society had a vast number of ceremonies and observances, but it had no history and no object ; that was where it was so very aristocratic. You did not have to be any-thing in order to be one of the Twelve Fishers ; unless you were already a certain sort of person, you never even heard of them. It had been in existence twelve years. Its president was Mr. Audley. Its vice-president was the Duke of Chester.

If I have in any degree conveyed the atmosphere of this appalling hotel, the reader may feel a natural wonder as to how I came to know anything about it, and may even speculate as to how so ordinary a person as my friend Father Brown came to find himself in that golden gallery. As far as that is concerned, my story is simple, or even vulgar. There is in the world a very aged rioter and demagogue who breaks into the most refined retreats with the dreadful information that all men are brothers, and wherever this leveller went on his pale horse it was Father Brown's trade to follow. One of the waiters, an Italian, had been struck down with a paralytic stroke that afternoon ; and his Jewish employer, marvelling mildly at such superstitions, had consented to send for the nearest Popish priest. With what the waiter con-fessed to Father Brown we are not concerned, for the excellent reason that the cleric kept it to himself ; but apparently it in-volved him in writing out a note or statement for the conveying of some message or the righting of some wrong. Father Brown, therefore, with a meek impudence which he would have shown equally in Buckingham Palace, asked to be provided with a room and writing materials. Mr. Lever was torn in two. He was a kind man, and had also that bad imitation of kindness, the dislike of any difficulty or scene. At the same time the presence of one unusual stranger in his hotel that evening was like a speck of dirt on something just cleaned. There was never any borderland or ante-room in the Vernon Hotel, no people waiting in the hall, no customers coming in on chance. There were fifteen waiters. There were twelve guests. It would be as startling to find a new guest in the hotel that night as to find a new brother taking breakfast or tea in one's own family. Moreover, the priest's appearance was second-rate and his clothes muddy ; a mere glimpse of him afar off might precipitate a crisis in the club. Mr. Lever at last hit on a plan to cover, since he might not obliterate, the disgrace. When you enter (as you never will) the Vernon Hotel, you pass down a short passage decorated with a few dingy but important pictures, and come to the main vestibule and

lounge which opens on your right into passages leading to the
public rooms, and on your left to a similar passage pointing to the
kitchens and offices of the hotel. Immediately on your left hand is
the corner of a glass office, which abuts upon the lounge—a house'
within a house, so to speak, like the old hotel bar which probably
once occupied its place.

In this office sat the representative of the proprietor (nobody
in this place ever appeared in person if he could help it), and just
beyond the office, on the way to the servants' quarters, was the
gentlemen's cloakroom, the last boundary of the gentlemen's
domain. But between the office and the cloak-room was a small
private room without other outlet, sometimes used by the proprietor for delicate and important matters, such as lending a
duke a thousand pounds or declining to lend him sixpence. It is a
mark of the magnificent tolerance of Mr. Lever that he permitted
this holy place to be for about half an hour profaned by a mere
priest, scribbling away on a piece of paper. The story which
Father Brown was writing down was very likely a much better
story than this one, only it will never be known. I can merely
state that it was very nearly as long, and that the last two or three
paragraphs of it were the least exciting and absorbing.

For it was by the time he had reached these that the priest
began a little to allow his thoughts to wander and his animal
senses, which were commonly keen, to awaken. The time of darkness and dinner was drawing on ; his own forgotten little room
was without a light, and perhaps the gathering gloom, as occasionally happens, sharpened the sense of sound. As Father Brown
wrote the last and least essential part of his document, he caught
himself writing to the rhythm of a recurrent noise outside, just as
one sometimes thinks to the tune of a railway train. When he
became conscious of the thing he found what it was : only the
ordinary patter of feet passing the door, which in an hotel was no
very unlikely matter. Nevertheless, he stared at the darkened
ceiling, and listened to the sound. After he had listened for a few
seconds dreamily, he got to his feet and listened intently, with his
head a little on one side. Then he sat down again and buried his
brow in his hands, now not merely listening, but listening and
thinking also.

The footsteps outside at any given moment were such as one
might hear in any hotel ; and yet, taken as a whole, there was

something very strange about them. There were no other footsteps. It was always a very silent house, for the few familiar guests
went at once to their own apartments, and the well-trained waiters
were told to be almost invisible until they were wanted. One
could not conceive any place where there was less reason to appre-
hend anything irregular. But these footsteps were so odd that one
could not decide to call them regular or irregular. Father Brown
followed them with his finger on the edge of the table, like a man
trying to learn a tune on the piano.

First, there came a long rush of rapid little steps, such as a light
man might make in winning a walking race. At a certain point
they stopped and changed to a sort of slow, swinging stamp,
numbering not a quarter of the steps, but occupying about the
same time. The moment the last echoing stamp had died away
would come again the run or ripple of light, hurrying feet, and
then again the thud of the heavier walking. It was certainly the
same pair of boots, partly because (as has been said) there were no
other boots about, and partly because they had a small but
unmistakable creak in them. Father Brown had the kind of
head that cannot help asking questions ; and on this apparently
trivial question his head almost split. He had seen men run in
order to jump. He had seen men run in order to slide. But why
on earth should a man run in order to walk ? Or, again, why
should he walk in order to run ? Yet no other description would
cover the antics of this invisible pair of legs. The man was either
walking very fast down one-half of the corridor in order to walk
very slow down the other half ; or he was walking very slow at
one end to have the rapture of walking fast at the other. Neither
suggestion seemed to make much sense. His brain was growing
darker and darker, like his room.

Yet, as he began to think steadily, the very blackness of his cell
seemed to make his thoughts more vivid ; he began to see as in a
kind of vision the fantastic feet capering along the corridor in
unnatural or symbolic attitudes. Was it a heathen religious
dance ? Or some entirely new kind of scientific exercise ? Father
Brown began to ask himself with more exactness what the steps
suggested. Taking the slow step first ; it certainly was not the
step of the proprietor. Men of his type walk with a rapid waddle
or they sit still. It could not be any servant or messenger waiting
for directions. It did not sound like it. The poorer orders (in an

oligarchy) sometimes lurch about when they are slightly drunk, but generally, and especially in such gorgeous scenes, they stand or sit in constrained attitudes. No ; that heavy yet springy step, with a kind of careless emphasis, not specially noisy, yet not caring what noise it made, belonged to only one of the animals of this earth. It was a gentleman of western Europe, and probably one who had never worked for his living.

Just as he came to this solid certainty, the step changed to the quicker one, and ran past the door as feverishly as a rat. The listener remarked that though this step was much swifter it was also much more noiseless, almost as if the man were walking on tiptoe. Yet it was not associated in his mind with secrecy, but with something else—something that he could not remember. He was maddened by one of those half-memories that make a man feel half-witted. Surely he had heard that strange, swift walking somewhere. Suddenly he sprang to his feet with a new idea in his head, and walked to the door. His room had no direct outlet on the passage, but let on one side into the glass office, and on the other into the cloak-room beyond. He tried the door into the office, and found it locked. Then he looked at the window, now a square pane full of purple cloud cleft by livid sunset, and for an instant he smelt evil as a dog smells rats.

The rational part of him (whether the wiser or not) regained its supremacy. He remembered that the proprietor had told him that he should lock the door, and would come later to release him. He told himself that twenty things he had not thought of might explain the eccentric sounds outside ; he reminded himself that there was just enough light left to finish his own proper work. Bringing his paper to the window so as to catch the last stormy evening light, he resolutely plunged once more into the almost completed record. He had written for about twenty minutes, bending closer and closer to his paper in the lessening light ; then suddenly he sat upright. He had heard the strange feet once more.

This time they had a third oddity. Previously the unknown man had walked, with levity indeed and lightning quickness, but he had walked. This time he ran. One could hear the swift, soft, bounding steps coming along the corridor, like the pads of a fleeing and leaping panther. Whoever was coming was a very strong, active man, in still yet tearing excitement. Yet, when the sound had swept up to the office like a sort of whispering whirl-wind, it suddenly changed again to the old slow, swaggering stamp.

Father Brown flung down his paper, and, knowing the office door to be locked, went at once into the cloak-room on the other side. The attendant of this place was temporarily absent, probably because the only guests were at dinner, and his office was a sine-cure. After groping through a grey forest of overcoats, he found that the dim cloak-room opened on the lighted corridor in the form of a sort of counter or half-door, like most of the counters across which we have all handed umbrellas and received tickets. There was a light immediately above the semi-circular arch of this opening. It threw little illumination on Father Brown himself, who seemed a mere dark outline against the dim sunset window behind him. But it threw an almost theatrical light on the man who stood outside the cloak-room in the corridor.

He was an elegant man in very plain evening-dress ; tall, but with an air of not taking up much room ; one felt that he could have slid along like a shadow where many smaller men would have been obvious and obstructive. His face, now flung back in the lamplight, was swarthy and vivacious, the face of a foreigner. His figure was good, his manners good-humoured and confident ; a critic could only say that his black coat was a shade below his figure and manners, and even bulged and bagged in an odd way. The moment he caught sight of Brown's black silhouette against the sunset, he tossed down a scrap of paper with a number and called out with amiable authority : " I want my hat and coat, please ; I find I have to go away at once."

Father Brown took the paper without a word, and obediently went to look for the coat ; it was not the first menial work he had done in his life. He brought it and laid it on the counter ; mean-while, the strange gentleman who had been feeling in his waist-coat pocket, said, laughing : " I haven't got any silver ; you can keep this." And he threw down half a sovereign, and caught up his coat.

Father Brown's figure remained quite dark and still ; but in that instant he had lost his head. His head was always most valuable when he had lost it. In such moments he put two and two together and made four million. Often the Catholic Church (which is wedded to common sense) did not approve of it. Often he did not approve of it himself. But it was a real inspiration—important at rare crises—when whosoever shall lose his head the same shall save it.

" I think, sir," he said civilly, " that you have some silver in your pocket."

The tall gentleman stared. " Hang it," he cried. " If I give you gold, why should you complain ? "

" Because silver is sometimes more valuable than gold," said the priest mildly ; " that is, in large quantities."

The stranger looked at him curiously. Then he looked still more curiously up the passage towards the main entrance. Then he looked back at Brown again, and then he looked very carefully at the window beyond Brown's head, still coloured with the after-glow of the storm. Then he seemed to make up his mind. He put one hand on the counter, vaulted over as easily as an acrobat and towered above the priest, putting one tremendous hand upon his collar.

" Stand still," he said, in a hacking whisper. " I don't want to threaten you, but—— "

" I do want to threaten you," said Father Brown, in a voice like a rolling drum. " I want to threaten you with the worm that dieth not, and the fire that is not quenched."

" You're a rum sort of cloak-room clerk," said the other.

" I am a priest, Monsieur Flambeau," said Brown, " and I am ready to hear your confession."

The other stood gasping for a few moments, and then staggered back into a chair.

The first two courses of the dinner of The Twelve True Fisher-men had proceeded with placid success. I do not possess a copy of the menu ; and if I did it would not convey anything to any-body. It was written in a sort of super-French employed by cooks, but quite unintelligible to Frenchmen. There was a tradition in the club that the *hors d'œuvres* should be various and manifold to the point of madness. They were taken seriously because they were avowedly useless extras, like the whole dinner and the whole club. There was also a tradition that the soup course should be light and unpretending—a sort of simple and austere vigil for the feast of fish that was to come. The talk was that strange, slight talk which governs the British Empire, which governs it in secret, and yet would scarcely enlighten an ordinary Englishman even if he could overhear it. Cabinet Ministers on both sides were alluded to by their Christian names with a sort of bored benignity. The Radical Chancellor of the Exchequer, whom the whole Tory party was supposed to be cursing for his extortions, was praised for his minor poetry, or his saddle in the hunting-field. The Tory leader, whom all Liberals were supposed to hate as a tyrant, was discussed and, on the whole, praised— as a Liberal. It seemed somehow that politicians were very important. And yet, anything seemed important about them except their politics. Mr. Audley, the chairman, was an amiable, elderly man who still wore Gladstone collars ; he was a kind of symbol of all that phantasmal and yet fixed society. He had never done anything—not even anything wrong. He was not fast ; he was not even particularly rich. He was simply in the thing ; and there was an end of it. No party could ignore him, and if he had wished to be in the Cabinet he certainly would have been put there. The Duke of Chester, the vice-president, was a young and rising politician. That is to say, he was a pleasant youth, with flat, fair hair and a freckled face, with moderate intelligence and enormous estates. In public his appearances were always success- ful and his principle was simple enough. When he thought of a joke he made it, and was called brilliant. When he could not think of a joke he said that this was no time for trifling, and was called able. In private, in a club of his own class, he was simply quite pleasantly frank and silly, like a schoolboy. Mr. Audley, never having been in politics, treated them a little more seriously. Sometimes he even embarrassed the company by phrases suggest- ing that there was some difference between a Liberal and a Conservative. He, himself, was a Conservative, even in private life. He had a roll of grey hair over the back of his collar, like certain old-fashioned statesmen, and seen from behind he looked like the man the empire wants. Seen from the front he looked like a mild, self-indulgent bachelor, with rooms in the Albany— which he was.

As has been remarked, there were twenty-four seats at the terrace table, and only twelve members of the club. Thus they could occupy the terrace in the most luxurious style of all, being ranged along the inner side of the table, with no one opposite, commanding an uninterrupted view of the garden, the colours of which were still vivid, though evening was closing in somewhat luridly for the time of year. The chairman sat in the centre of the line, and the vice-president at the right-hand end of it. When the twelve guests first trooped into their seats it was the custom (for some unknown reason) for all the fifteen waiters to stand lining the wall like troops presenting arms to the king, while the fat proprietor stood and bowed to the club with radiant surprise, as if he had never heard of them before. But before the first clink of knife and fork this army of retainers had vanished, only the one or two required to collect and distribute the plates darting about in deathly silence. Mr. Lever, the proprietor, of course had disappeared in convulsions of courtesy long before. It would be exaggerative, indeed irreverent, to say that he ever positively appeared again. But when the important course, the fish course, was being brought on, there was—how shall I put it?—a vivid shadow, a projection of his personality, which told that he was hovering near. The sacred fish course consisted (to the eyes of the vulgar) in a sort of monstrous pudding, about the size and shape of a wedding cake, in which some considerable number of interesting fishes had finally lost the shapes which God had given to them. The Twelve True Fishermen took up their celebrated fish knives and fish forks, and approached it as gravely as if every inch of the pudding cost as much as the silver fork it was eaten with. So it did, for all I know. This course was dealt with in eager and devouring silence; and it was only when his plate was nearly empty that the young duke made the ritual remark : " They can't do this anywhere but here."

" Nowhere," said Mr. Audley, in a deep bass voice, turning to the speaker and nodding his venerable head a number of times. " Nowhere, assuredly, except here. It was represented to me that at the Café Anglais—— "

Here he was interrupted and even agitated for a moment by the removal of his plate, but he recaptured the valuable thread of his thoughts. " It was represented to me that the same could be done at the Café Anglais. Nothing like it, sir," he said, shaking his head ruthlessly, like a hanging judge. " Nothing like it."

" Overrated place," said a certain Colonel Pound, speaking (by the look of him) for the first time for some months.

" Oh, I don't know," said the Duke of Chester, who was an

optimist, "it's jolly good for some things. You can't beat it at——"

A waiter came swiftly along the room, and then stopped dead. His stoppage was as silent as his tread; but all those vague and kindly gentlemen were so used to the utter smoothness of the unseen machinery which surrounded and supported their lives, that a waiter doing anything unexpected was a start and a jar. They felt as you and I would feel if the inanimate world disobeyed —if a chair ran away from us.

The waiter stood staring a few seconds, while there deepened on every face at table a strange shame which is wholly the product of our time. It is the combination of modern humanitarianism with the horrible modern abyss between the souls of the rich and the poor. A genuine historic aristocrat would have thrown things at the waiter, beginning with empty bottles, and very probably ending with money. A genuine democrat would have asked him, with a comrade-like clearness of speech, what the devil he was doing. But these modern plutocrats could not bear a poor man near to them, either as a slave or as a friend. That something had gone wrong with the servants was merely a dull, hot embarrassment. They did not want to be brutal, and they dreaded the need to be benevolent. They wanted the thing, whatever it was, to be over. It was over. The waiter, after standing for some seconds rigid, like a cataleptic, turned round and ran madly out of the room.

When he reappeared in the room, or rather in the doorway, it was in company with another waiter, with whom he whispered and gesticulated with southern fierceness. Then the first waiter went away, leaving the second waiter, and reappeared with a third waiter. By the time a fourth waiter had joined this hurried synod, Mr. Audley felt it necessary to break the silence in the interests of Tact. He used a very loud cough, instead of the presidential hammer, and said: "Splendid work young Moocher's doing in Burmah. Now, no other nation in the world could have—— "

A fifth waiter had sped towards him like an arrow, and was whispering in his ear: "So sorry. Important! Might the proprietor speak to you?"

The chairman turned in disorder, and with a dazed stare saw Mr. Lever coming towards them with his lumbering quickness.

The gait of the good proprietor was indeed his usual gait, but his face was by no means usual. Generally it was a genial copper-brown ; now it was a sickly yellow.

" You will pardon me, Mr. Audley," he said, with asthmatic breathlessness. " I have great apprehensions. Your fish-plates, they are cleared away with the knife and fork on them ! "

" Well, I hope so," said the chairman, with some warmth.

" You see him ? " panted the excited hotel keeper ; " you see the waiter who took them away ? You know him ? "

" Know the waiter ? " answered Mr. Audley indignantly. " Certainly not ! "

Mr. Lever opened his hands with a gesture of agony. " I never send him," he said. " I know not when or why he come. I send my waiter to take away the plates, and he find them already away."

Mr. Audley still looked rather too bewildered to be really the man the empire wants ; none of the company could say anything except the man of wood—Colonel Pound—who seemed galvanised into an unnatural life. He rose rigidly from his chair, leaving all the rest sitting, screwed his eyeglass into his eye, and spoke in a raucous undertone as if he had half-forgotten how to speak. " Do you mean," he said, " that somebody has stolen our silver fish service ? "

The proprietor repeated the open-handed gesture with even greater helplessness ; and in a flash all the men at the table were on their feet.

"Are all your waiters here ? " demanded the colonel, in his low, harsh accent.

" Yes ; they're all here. I noticed it myself," cried the young duke, pushing his boyish face into the inmost ring. "Always count 'em as I come in ; they look so queer standing up against the wall."

" But surely one cannot exactly remember," began Mr. Audley, with heavy hesitation.

" I remember exactly, I tell you," cried the duke excitedly. " There never have been more than fifteen waiters at this place, and there were no more than fifteen to-night, I'll swear ; no more and no less."

The proprietor turned upon him, quaking in a kind of palsy of surprise. " You say—you say," he stammered, " that you see all my fifteen waiters ? "

" As usual," assented the duke. " What is the matter with that ? "

" Nothing," said Lever, with a deepening accent, " only you did not. For one of zem is dead upstairs."

There was a shocking stillness for an instant in that room. It may be (so supernatural is the word death) that each of those idle men looked for a second at his soul, and saw it as a small dried pea. One of them—the duke, I think—even said with the idiotic kindness of wealth : " Is there anything we can do ? "

" He has had a priest," said the Jew, not untouched.

Then, as to the clang of doom, they awoke to their own position. For a few weird seconds they had really felt as if the fifteenth waiter might be the ghost of the dead man upstairs. They had been dumb under that oppression, for ghosts were to them an embarrassment, like beggars. But the remembrance of the silver broke the spell of the miraculous ; broke it abruptly and with a brutal reaction. The colonel flung over his chair and strode to the door. " If there was a fifteenth man here, friends," he said, " that fifteenth fellow was a thief. Down at once to the front and back doors and secure everything ; then we'll talk. The twenty-four pearls of the Club are worth recovering."

Mr. Audley seemed at first to hesitate about whether it was gentlemanly to be in such a hurry about anything ; but, seeing the duke dash down the stairs with youthful energy, he followed with a more mature motion.

At the same instant a sixth waiter ran into the room, and declared that he had found the pile of fish plates on a sideboard, with no trace of the silver.

The crowd of diners and attendants that tumbled helter-skelter down the passages divided into two groups. Most of the Fishermen followed the proprietor to the front room to demand news of any exit. Colonel Pound, with the Chairman, the vice-president, and one or two others, darted down the corridor leading to the servants' quarters, as the more likely line of escape. As they did so they passed the dim alcove or cavern of the cloak-room, and saw a short, black-coated figure, presumably an attendant, standing a little way back in the shadow of it.

" Hallo there ! " called out the duke. " Have you seen anyone pass ? "

The short figure did not answer the question directly, but

merely said : " Perhaps I have got what you are looking for, gentlemen."

They paused, wavering and wondering, while he quietly went to the back of the cloak-room, and came back with both hands full of shining silver, which he laid out on the counter as calmly as a salesman. It took the form of a dozen quaintly shaped forks and knives. " You——you—— " began the colonel, quite thrown off his balance at last. Then he peered into the dim little room and saw two things : first, that the short, black-clad man was dressed like a clergyman ; and, second, that the window of the room behind him was burst, as if someone had passed violently through.

" Valuable things to deposit in a cloak-room, aren't they ? " remarked the clergyman, with cheerful composure.

" Did—did you steal those things ? " stammered Mr. Audley, with staring eyes.

" If I did," said the cleric pleasantly, " at least I am bringing them back again."

" But you didn't," said Colonel Pound, still staring at the broken window.

" To make a clean breast of it, I didn't," said the other, with some humour. And he seated himself quite gravely on a stool.

" But you know who did," said the colonel.

" I don't know his real name," said the priest placidly ; " but I know something of his fighting weight, and a great deal about his spiritual difficulties. I formed the physical estimate when he was trying to throttle me, and the moral estimate when he repented."

" Oh, I say—repented ! " cried young Chester, with a sort of crow of laughter.

Father Brown got to his feet, putting his hands behind him. " Odd, isn't it," he said, " that a thief and a vagabond should repent, when so many who are rich and secure remain hard and frivolous, and without fruit for God or man ? But there, if you will excuse me, you trespass a little upon my province. If you doubt the penitence as a practical fact, there are your knives and forks. You are The Twelve True Fishers, and there are all your silver fish. But He has made me a fisher of men."

" Did you atch this man ? " asked the colonel, frowning.

Father Brown looked him full in his frowning face. " Yes,"
he said, " I caught him, with an unseen hook and an invisible
line which is long enough to let him wander to the ends of the
world, and still to bring him back with a twitch upon the thread."

There was a long silence. All the other men present drifted
away to carry the recovered silver to their comrades, or to consult
the proprietor about the queer condition of affairs. But the grim-
faced colonel still sat sideways on the counter, swinging his long,
lank legs and biting his dark moustache.

At last he said quietly to the priest : " He must have been a
clever fellow, but I think I know a cleverer."

" He was a clever fellow," answered the other, " but I am
not quite sure of what other you mean."

" I mean you," said the colonel, with a short laugh. " I
don't want to get the fellow jailed ; make yourself easy about
that. But I'd give a good many silver forks to know exactly how
you fell into this affair, and how you got the stuff out of him. I
reckon you're the most up-to-date devil of the present company."

Father Brown seemed rather to like the saturnine candour of the
soldier. " Well," he said, smiling, " I mustn't tell you anything
of the man's identity, or his own story, of course ; but there's no
particular reason why I shouldn't tell you of the mere outside
facts which I found out for myself."

He hopped over the barrier with unexpected activity, and sat
beside Colonel Pound, kicking his short legs like a little boy on a
gate. He began to tell the story as easily as if he were telling it to
an old friend by a Christmas fire.

" You see, colonel," he said, " I was shut up in that small
room there doing some writing, when I heard a pair of feet in
this passage doing a dance that was as queer as the dance of
death. First came quick, funny little steps, like a man walking on
tiptoe for a wager ; then came slow, careless, creaking steps, as of
a big man walking about with a cigar. But they were both made
by the same feet, I swear, and they came in rotation ; first the
run and then the walk, and then the run again. I wondered at
first idly, and then wildly why a man should act these two parts
at once. One walk I knew ; it was just like yours, colonel. It
was the walk of a well-fed gentleman waiting for something, who
strolls about rather because he is physically alert than because he

is mentally impatient. I knew that I knew the other walk, too, but I could not remember what it was. What wild creature had I met on my travels that tore along on tiptoe in that extraordinary style ? Then I heard a clink of plates somewhere ; and the answer stood up as plain as St. Peter's. It was the walk of a waiter —that walk with the body slanted forward, the eyes looking down, the ball of the toe spurning away the ground, the coat tails and napkin flying. Then I thought for a minute and a half more. And I believe I saw the manner of the crime, as clearly as if I were going to commit it."

Colonel Pound looked at him keenly, but the speaker's mild grey eyes were fixed upon the ceiling with almost empty wistfulness.

"A crime," he said slowly, " is like any other work of art. Don't look surprised ; crimes are by no means the only works of art that come from an infernal workshop. But every work of art, divine or diabolic, has one indispensable mark—I mean, that the centre of it is simple, however much the fulfilment may be complicated. Thus, in *Hamlet*, let us say, the grotesqueness of the grave-digger, the flowers of the mad girl, the fantastic finery of Osric, the pallor of the ghost and the grin of the skull are all oddities in a sort of tangled wreath round one plain tragic figure of a man in black. Well, this also," he said, getting slowly down from his seat with a smile, " this also is the plain tragedy of a man in black. Yes," he went on, seeing the colonel look up in some wonder, " the whole of this tale turns on a black coat. In this, as in *Hamlet*, there are the rococo excrescences—yourselves, let us say. There is the dead waiter, who was there when he could not be there. There is the invisible hand that swept your table clear of silver and melted into air. But every clever crime is founded ultimately on some one quite simple fact—some fact that is not itself mysterious. The mystification comes in covering it up, in leading men's thoughts away from it. This large and subtle and (in the ordinary course) most profitable crime, was built on the plain fact that a gentleman's evening dress is the same as a waiter's. All the rest was acting, and thundering good acting, too."

" Still," said the colonel, getting up and frowning at his boots, " I am not sure that I understand."

" Colonel," said Father Brown, " I tell you that this arch-

angel of impudence who stole your forks walked up and down
this passage twenty times in the blaze of all the lamps, in the
glare of all the eyes. He did not go and hide in dim corners
where suspicion might have searched for him. He kept constantly
on the move in the lighted corridors, and everywhere that he
went he seemed to be there by right. Don't ask me what he was
like ; you have seen him yourself six or seven times to-night. You
were waiting with all the other grand people in the reception
room at the end of the passage there, with the terrace just beyond.
Whenever he came among you gentlemen, he came in the lightning style of a waiter, with bent head, flapping napkin and flying
feet. He shot out on to the terrace, did something to the table-
cloth, and shot back again towards the office and the waiters'
quarters. By the time he had come under the eye of the office
clerk and the waiters he had become another man in every inch
of his body, in every instinctive gesture. He strolled among the
servants with the absent-minded insolence which they have all
seen in their patrons. It was no new thing to them that a swell
from the dinner party should pace all parts of the house like an
animal at the Zoo ; they know that nothing marks the Smart
Set more than a habit of walking where one chooses. When he
was magnificently weary of walking down that particular passage
he would wheel round and pace back past the office ; in the
shadow of the arch just beyond he was altered as by a blast of
magic, and went hurrying forward again among the Twelve
Fishermen, an obsequious attendant. Why should the gentlemen
look at a chance waiter ? Why should the waiters suspect a first-
rate walking gentleman ? Once or twice he played the coolest
tricks. In the proprietor's private quarters he called out breezily
for a syphon of soda water, saying he was thirsty. He said genially
that he would carry it himself, and he did ; he carried it quickly
and correctly through the thick of you, a waiter with an obvious
errand. Of course, it could not have been kept up long, but it
only had to be kept up till the end of the fish course.

" His worst moment was when the waiters stood in a row ;
but even then he contrived to lean against the wall just around
the corner in such a way that for that important instant the waiters
thought him a gentleman, while the gentlemen thought him a
waiter. The rest went like winking. If any waiter caught him
away from the table, that waiter caught a languid aristocrat. He

had only to time himself two minutes before the fish was cleared, become a swift servant, and clear it himself. He put the plates down on a sideboard, stuffed the silver in his breast pocket, giving it a bulgy look, and ran like a hare (I heard him coming) till he came to the cloak-room. There he had only to be a plutocrat again—a plutocrat called away suddenly on business. He had only to give his ticket to the cloak-room attendant, and go out again elegantly as he had come in. Only—only I happened to be the cloak-room attendant."

" What did you do to him ? " cried the colonel, with unusual intensity. " What did he tell you ? "

" I beg your pardon," said the priest immovably, " that is where the story ends."

"And the interesting story begins," muttered Pound. " I think I understand his professional trick. But I don't seem to have got hold of yours."

" I must be going," said Father Brown.

They walked together along the passage to the entrance hall, where they saw the fresh, freckled face of the Duke of Chester, who was bounding buoyantly along towards them.

" Come along, Pound," he cried breathlessly. " I've been looking for you everywhere. The dinner's going again in spanking style, and old Audley has got to make a speech in honour of the forks being saved. We want to start some new ceremony, don't you know, to commemorate the occasion. I say, you really got the goods back, what do you suggest ? "

" Why," said the colonel, eyeing him with a certain sardonic approval. " I should suggest that henceforward we wear green coats instead of black. One never knows what mistakes may arise when one looks so like a waiter."

" Oh, hang it all ! " said the young man, " a gentleman never looks like a waiter."

" Nor a waiter like a gentleman, I suppose," said Colonel Pound, with the same lowering laughter on his face. " Reverend sir, your friend must have been very smart to act the gentleman."

Father Brown buttoned up his commonplace overcoat to the neck, for the night was stormy, and took his commonplace umbrella from the stand.

" Yes," he said ; " it must be very hard work to be a

gentleman ; but, do you know, I have sometimes thought that it may be almost as laborious to be a waiter."

And saying " Good evening," he pushed open the heavy doors of that palace of pleasures. The golden gates closed behind him, and he went at a brisk walk through the damp, dark streets in search of a penny omnibus.

— The Innocence of Father Brown

Explorations

1. A good detective story normally builds up a feeling of mystery. Chesterton sets out to do this during the period when Father Brown is listening in the locked room to the sound of feet. Is it successfully done ? Does it arouse your curiosity ? Examine the passage concerned and try to discover how the writer sets about it.

2. When Father Brown confronts Flambeau he uses a scriptural turn of phrase. What does this convey to us about the priest and his attitude to crime and criminals ? Indicate other examples of the same thing.

3. Chesterton's references to ' class,' ' waiters,' 'gentlemen' and ' oligarchy ' are often ironical. Point out other examples of irony in the story and explain its general purpose.

4. Chesterton was also an essayist. Can you find any evidence of this in the story ?

5. What does the writer really think of the hotel ? How is his opinion of it conveyed ?

6. Chesterton in this—and in most of his stories—makes liberal use of coincidence. Examine the coincidences in this story and say whether they are a weakness or a strength.

7. Chesterton has frequently been praised for his ability to create atmosphere. How well does he, in your opinion, catch the atmosphere of this strange hotel ?

Exercises

1. Write out a clear explanation of how Father Brown caught the thief.

2. Choose three points in the story that you found amusing and try to explain their humour.

3. A detective story must create mystery, sustain it till the reader's curiosity is at full stretch, and then resolve it. This often involves great structural problems, especially in handling the time element. In order to appreciate the structure of this story the student might draw up two parallel lists :

    (a)   The order of events as Chesterton gives it.

    (b)   The order of events as they actually happened.

35

THE FLY

" Y'are very snug in here," piped old Mr. Woodifield, and he peered out of the great, green-leathern arm-chair by his friend the boss's desk as a baby peers out of its pram. His talk was over ; it was time for him to be off. But he did not want to go. Since he had retired, since his . . . stroke, the wife and the girls kept him boxed up in the house every day of the week except Tuesday. On Tuesday he was dressed and brushed and allowed to cut back to the City for the day. Though what he did there the wife and girls couldn't imagine. Made a nuisance of himself to his friends, they supposed . . . Well, perhaps so. All the same, we cling to our last pleasures as the tree clings to its last leaves. So there sat old Woodifield, smoking a cigar and staring almost greedily at the boss, who rolled in his office chair, stout, rosy, five years older than he, and still going strong, still at the helm. It did one good to see him.

Wistfully, admiringly, the old voice added, " It's snug in here, upon my word ! "

" Yes, it's comfortable enough," agreed the boss, and he flipped the *Financial Times* with a paper-knife. As a matter of fact he was proud of his room ; he liked to have it admired, especially by old Woodifield. It gave him a feeling of deep, solid satisfaction to be planted there in the midst of it in full view of that frail old figure in the muffler.

" I've had it done up lately," he explained, as he had explained for the past—how many ?—weeks. " New carpet," and he pointed to the bright red carpet with a pattern of large white rings. " New furniture," and he nodded towards the massive bookcase and the table with legs like twisted treacle. " Electric heating ! " He waved almost exultantly towards the five transparent, pearly sausages glowing so softly in the tilted copper pan.

But he did not draw old Woodifield's attention to the photograph over the table of a grave-looking boy in uniform standing in one of those spectral photographers' parks with photographers' stormclouds behind him. It was not new. It had been there for over six years.

" There was something I wanted to tell you," said old Woodifield, and his eyes grew dim remembering. " Now what was it ? I had it in my mind when I started out this morning." His hands began to tremble, and patches of red showed above his beard.

Poor old chap, he's on his last pins, thought the boss. And, feeling kindly, he winked at the old man, and said jokingly, " I tell you what. I've got a little drop of something here that'll do you good before you go out into the cold again. It's beautiful stuff. It wouldn't hurt a child." He took a key off his watch-chain, unlocked a cupboard below his desk, and drew forth a dark, squat bottle. " That's the medicine," said he. "And the man from whom I got it told me on the strict Q.T. it came from the cellars at Windsor Castle."

Old Woodifield's mouth fell open at the sight. He couldn't have looked more surprised if the boss had produced a rabbit.

" It's whiskey, ain't it ? " he piped feebly.

The boss turned the bottle and lovingly showed him the label. Whiskey it was.

" D'you know," said he, peering up at the boss wonderingly, " they won't let me touch it at home." And he looked as though he was going to cry.

"Ah, that's where we know a bit more than the ladies," cried the boss, swooping across for two tumblers that stood on the table with the water-bottle, and pouring a generous finger into each. " Drink it down. It'll do you good. And don't put any water with it. It's sacrilege to tamper with stuff like this. Ah ! " He tossed off his, pulled out his handkerchief, hastily wiped his moustaches and cocked an eye at old Woodifield, who was rolling his in his chaps.

The old man swallowed, was silent a moment, and then said faintly, " It's nutty ! "

But it warmed him ; it crept into his chill old brain—he remembered.

" That was it," he said, heaving himself out of his chair. " I thought you'd like to know. The girls were in Belgium last week having a look at poor Reggie's grave, and they happened to come across your boy's. They're quite near each other, it seems."

Old Woodifield paused, but the boss made no reply. Only a quiver in his eyelids showed that he heard.

" The girls were delighted with the way the place is kept," piped the old voice. " Beautifully looked after. Couldn't be better if they were at home. You've not been across, have yer ? "

" No, no ! " For various reasons the boss had not been across.

" There's miles of it," quavered old Woodifield, " and it's all as neat as a garden. Flowers growing on all the graves. Nice broad paths." It was plain from his voice how much he liked a nice broad path.

The pause came again. Then the old man brightened wonderfully.

" D'you know what the hotel made the girls pay for a pot of jam ? " he piped. " Ten francs ! Robbery, I call it. It was a little pot, so Gertrude says, no bigger than a half-crown.   And she hadn't taken more than a spoonful when they charged her ten francs. Gertrude brought the pot away with her to teach 'em a lesson. Quite right, too ; it's trading on our feelings. They think because we're over there having a look round we're ready to pay anything. That's what it is." And he turned towards the door.

" Quite right, quite right ! " cried the boss, though what was quite right he hadn't the least idea. He came round by his desk, followed the shuffling footsteps to the door, and saw the old fellow out. Woodifield was gone.

For a long moment the boss stayed, staring at nothing, while the grey-haired office messenger, watching him, dodged in and out of his cubby-hole like a dog that expects to be taken for a run. Then : " I'll see nobody for half an hour, Macey," said the boss. "Understand ? Nobody at all."

" Very good, sir."

The door shut, the firm heavy steps recrossed the bright carpet, the fat body plumped down in the spring chair, and leaning forward, the boss covered his face with his hands. He wanted, he intended, he had arranged to weep . . .

It had been a terrible shock to him when old Woodifield sprang that remark upon him about the boy's grave. It was exactly as though the earth had opened and he had seen the boy lying there with Woodifield's girls staring down at him. For it was strange. Although over six years had passed away, the boss never thought of the boy except as lying unchanged, unblemished in his uniform, asleep for ever. " My son ! " groaned the boss. But no tears came yet. In the past, in the first months and even years after the boy's death, he had only to say those words to be overcome by such grief that nothing short of a violent fit of weeping could relieve him. Time, he had declared then, he had told everybody, could make no difference. Other men perhaps might recover, might live their loss down, but not he. How was it possible ? His boy was an only son. Ever since his birth the boss had worked at building up this business for him ; it had no other meaning if it was not for the boy. Life itself had come to have no other meaning. How on earth could he have slaved, denied himself, kept going all those years without the promise for ever before him of the boy's stepping into his shoes and carrying on where he left off ?

And that promise had been so near being fulfilled. The boy had been in the office learning the ropes for a year before the war. Every morning they had started off together ; they had come back. by the same train. And what congratulations he had received as the boy's father ! No wonder ; he had taken to it marvellously. As to his popularity with the staff, every man jack of them down to old Macey couldn't make enough of the boy. And he wasn't in the least spoilt. No, he was just his bright natural self, with the right word for everybody, with that boyish look and his habit of saying, " Simply splendid ! "

But all that was over and done with as though it never had been. The day had come when Macey had handed him the telegram that brought the whole place crashing about his head. " Deeply regret to inform you . . . " And he had left the office a broken man, with his life in ruins.

Six years ago, six years . . . How quickly time passed ! It might have happened yesterday. The boss took his hands from his face ; he was puzzled. Something seemed to be wrong with him. He wasn't feeling as he wanted to feel. He decided to get up and have a look at the boy's photograph. But it wasn't a favourite photograph of his ; the expression was unnatural. It was cold, even stern-looking. The boy had never looked like that.

At that moment the boss noticed that a fly had fallen into his broad inkpot, and was trying feebly but desperately to clamber out again. Help ! help ! said those struggling legs. But the sides of the inkpot were wet and slippery ; it fell back again and began to swim. The boss took up a pen, picked the fly out of the ink, and shook it on to a piece of blotting-paper. For a fraction of a second it lay still on the dark patch that oozed round it. Then the front legs waved, took hold, and, pulling its small, sodden body up, it began the immense task of cleaning the ink from its wings. Over and under, over and under, went a leg along a wing as the stone goes over and under the scythe. Then there was a pause, while the fly, seeming to stand on the tips of its toes, tried to expand first one wing and then the other. It succeeded at last, and sitting down, it began, like a minute cat, to clean its face. Now one could imagine that the little front legs rubbed against each other lightly, joyfully. The horrible danger was over ; it had escaped ; it was ready for life again.

But just then the boss had an idea. He plunged his pen back into the ink, leaned his thick wrist on the blotting-paper, and as the fly tried its wings down came a great heavy blot. What would it make of that ? What indeed ! The little beggar seemed absolutely cowed, stunned, and afraid to move because of what would happen next. But then, as if painfully, it dragged itself forward. The front legs waved, caught hold, and, more slowly this time, the task began from the beginning.

He's a plucky little devil, thought the boss, and he felt a real admiration for the fly's courage. That was the way to tackle things ; that was the right spirit. Never say die ; it was only a question of . . . But the fly had again finished its laborious task, and the boss had just time to refill his pen, to shake fair and square on the new-cleaned body yet another dark drop. What about it this time ? A painful moment of suspense followed. But behold, the front legs were again waving ; the boss felt a rush of relief. He leaned over the fly and said to it tenderly, " You artful little b . . . " And he actually had the brilliant notion of breathing on it to help the drying process. All the same, there was something timid and weak about its efforts now, and the boss decided that this time should be the last, as he dipped the pen deep into the inkpot.

It was. The last blot fell on the soaked blotting-paper, and the draggled fly lay in it and did not stir. The back legs were stuck to the body ; the front legs were not to be seen.

" Come on," said the boss. " Look sharp ! " And he stirred it with his pen—in vain. Nothing happened or was likely to happen. The fly was dead.

The boss lifted the corpse on the end of the paper-knife and flung it into the waste-paper basket. But such a grinding feeling of wretchedness seized him that he felt positively frightened. He started forward and pressed the bell for Macey.

" Bring me some fresh blotting-paper," he said sternly, " and look sharp about it." And while the old dog padded away he fell to wondering what it was he had been thinking about before. What was it ? It was ... He took out his handkerchief and passed it inside his collar. For the life of him he could not remember.

— *Thirty-Four Short Stories*

Explorations

1. The boss likes to entertain old Woodifield generously when he comes in. Is he therefore a generous, kind-hearted man ?

2. What do we learn about Woodifield in the first paragraph ? How is the information conveyed ? As Woodifield is not a central character why does the author devote so much space to him ?

3. 'Something seemed to be wrong with him. He wasn't feeling as he wanted to feel'. How did he want to feel ? Was it natural to want to feel thus ? Did this show real grief for his son or did it show something else ? If so what ?

4. When the boss considers his loss what particular aspects of that loss does he think of ? What does this tell us about his character ?

5. What traits of character does the torturing of the fly indicate ? cruelty ? thoughtlessness ? curiosity ? delight in power ?

6. Does it help us to understand the father's relation with his son, living or dead ?

7. When the fly dies the boss is overcome by 'a grinding feeling of wretchedness.' Why ? Does this indicate a basic tenderness in his character ? Or does it indicate his desire to have things both ways ? Is there any other sense in which he likes to have things both ways ?

8. What does the author mean to convey to us by referring to the servant as the 'old dog'?

9. The struggles of the fly are described with great accuracy and vividness. Mention some phrases that particularly impress you.

10. Mention any other verbal touches in the story that appeal to you and try to explain their effectiveness.

11. What is the tone of the story ? Angry, ironical, bitter, warm, lyrical ? In answering consider, for instance, the descriptions of the furniture.

Exercises

1. Write a character sketch of the boss, basing your portrait on the evidence of the story.

2. Have you ever killed an insect as deliberately as the boss kills the fly ? If so, describe the incident as clearly and truthfully as you can and describe your feelings during and after the event.

3. Have you ever felt grief for a relative or friend ? If so, try to describe the various stages of your sorrow from its early moments to the present.

4. Very little happens in this story. Yet the events are put together in order to achieve a certain 'unique and single effect.' Trace the course of the action in brief phrases : e.g.

    (1)   Woodifield, retired, drops in on the old boss.

    (2)   Conversation about office etc.

When you have finished, try to state the central theme of the story in one sentence.

36

THE SECRET LIFE OF WALTER MITTY

" We're going through ! " The Commander's voice was like thin ice breaking. He wore his full-dress uniform, with the heavily braided white cap pulled down rakishly over one cold grey eye. " We can't make it, sir. It's spoiling for a hurricane, if you ask me." " I'm not asking you, Lieutenant Berg," said the Commander. " Throw on the power lights ! Rev her up to 8,500 ! We're going through ! " The pounding of the cylinders increased: ta-pocketa-pocketa-pocketa-*pocketa-pocketa*. The Commander stared at the ice forming on the pilot window. He walked over and twisted a row of complicated dials. " Switch on No. 8 auxiliary ! " he shouted. " Switch on No. 8 auxiliary ! " repeated Lieutenant Berg. " Full strength in No. 3 turret ! " shouted the Commander. " Full strength in No. 3 turret ! " The crew, bending to their various tasks in the huge, hurtling eight-engined Navy hydroplane, looked at each other and grinned. " The Old Man'll get us through," they said to one another. " The Old Man ain't afraid of Hell ! " . . .

" Not so fast ! You're driving too fast ! " said Mrs. Mitty. " What are you driving so fast for ? "

" Hmm ? " said Walter Mitty. He looked at his wife, in the seat beside him, with shocked astonishment. She seemed grossly unfamiliar, like a strange woman who had yelled at him in a crowd. " You were up to fifty-five," she said. " You know I don't like to go more than forty. You were up to fifty-five." Walter Mitty drove on toward Waterbury in silence, the roaring of the SN202 through the worst storm in twenty years of Navy flying fading in the remote, intimate airways of his mind. " You're tensed up again," said Mrs. Mitty. " It's one of your days. I wish you'd let Dr. Renshaw look you over."

Walter Mitty stopped the car in front of the building where his wife went to have her hair done. " Remember to get those overshoes while I'm having my hair done," she said. " I don't need overshoes," said Mitty. She put her mirror back into her

bag. " We've been all through that," she said, getting out of the
car. " You're not a young man any longer." He raced the engine
a little. " Why don't you wear your gloves ? Have you lost your
gloves ? " Walter Mitty reached in a pocket and brought out the
gloves. He put them on, but after she had turned and gone into
the building and he had driven on to a red light, he took them
off again. " Pick it up, brother ! " snapped a cop as the lights
changed, and Mitty hastily pulled on his gloves and lurched
ahead. He drove around the streets aimlessly for a time, and then
he drove past the hospital on his way to the parking lot.

.   .   .   " It's the millionaire banker, Wellington McMillan," said
the pretty nurse. " Yes ? " said Walter Mitty, removing his gloves
slowly. " Who has the case ? " " Dr. Renshaw and Dr. Benbow,
but there are two specialists here, Dr. Remington from New York
and Mr. Pritchard-Mitford from London. He flew over." A door
opened down a long, cool corridor and Dr. Renshaw came out.
He looked distraught and haggard. " Hello, Mitty," he said.
" We're having the devil's own time with McMillan, the millionaire banker and close personal friend of Roosevelt. Obstreosis of
the ductal tract. Tertiary. Wish you'd take a look at him."
" Glad to," said Mitty.

In the operating room there were whispered introductions :
" Dr. Remington, Dr. Mitty.   Mr. Pritchard-Mitford, Dr.
Mitty."   " I've read your book on streptothricosis," said
Pritchard-Mitford, shaking hands.   "A brilliant performance,
sir." " Thank you," said Walter Mitty. " Didn't know you were
in the States, Mitty," grumbled Remington. " Coals to New-
castle, bringing Mitford and me up here for a tertiary." " You
are very kind," said Mitty.   A huge, complicated machine,
connected to the operating table, with many tubes and wires,
began at this moment to go pocketa-pocketa-pocketa.   " The
new anaesthetiser is giving way ! " shouted an interne. " There is
no one in the East who knows how to fix it ! " " Quiet, man ! "
said Mitty, in a low, cool voice. He sprang to the machine, which
was now going pocketa-pocketa-queep-pocketa-queep. He began
fingering delicately a row of glistening dials. " Give me a fountain
pen ! " he snapped. Someone handed him a fountain pen. He
pulled a faulty piston out of the machine and inserted the pen in
its place. " That will hold for ten minutes," he said. " Get on
with the operation."   A nurse hurried over and whispered to

Renshaw, and Mitty saw the man turn pale. " Coreopsis has set in," said Renshaw nervously. " If you would take over, Mitty ? " Mitty looked at him and at the craven figure of Benbow, who drank, and at the grave, uncertain faces of the two great specialists. " If you wish," he said. They slipped a white gown on him ; he adjusted a mask and drew on thin gloves ; nurses handed him shining . . .

" Back it up, Mac ! Look out for that Buick ! " Walter Mitty jammed on the brakes. " Wrong lane, Mac," said the parking-lot attendant, looking at Mitty closely. " Gee. Yeh," muttered Mitty. He began cautiously to back out of the lane marked " Exit Only." " Leave her sit there," said the attendant. " I'll put her away." Mitty got out of the car. " Hey, better leave the key." " Oh," said Mitty, handing the man the ignition key. The attendant vaulted into the car, backed it up with insolent skill, and put it where it belonged.

They're so damn cocky, thought Walter Mitty, walking along Main Street ; they think they know everything. Once he had tried to take his chains off, outside New Milford, and he had got them wound around the axles. A man had had to come out in a wrecking car and unwind them, a young, grinning garageman. Since then Mrs. Mitty always made him drive to a garage to have the chains taken off. The next time, he thought, I'll wear my right arm in a sling ; they won't grin at me then. I'll have my right arm in a sling and they'll see I couldn't possibly take the chains off myself. He kicked at the slush on the sidewalk. " Overshoes," he said to himself, and he began looking for a shoe store.

When he came out into the street again, with the overshoes in a box under his arm, Walter Mitty began to wonder what the other thing was his wife had told him to get. She had told him, twice, before they set out from their house for Waterbury. In a way he hated these weekly trips to town—he was always getting something wrong. Kleenex, he thought, Squibb's, razor blades ? No. Toothpaste, toothbrush, bicarbonate, carborundum, initiative and referendum ? He gave it up. But she would remember it. " Where's the what's-its-name ? " she would ask. " Don't tell me you forgot the what's-its-name." A newsboy went by shouting something about the Waterbury trial.

. . . " Perhaps this will refresh your memory." The District Attorney suddenly thrust a heavy automatic at the quiet figure

on the witness stand. " Have you ever seen this before ? " Walter
Mitty took the gun and examined it expertly. " This is my
Webley-Vickers 50.80," he said calmly. An excited buzz ran
around the courtroom. The Judge rapped for order. " You are a
crack shot with any sort of firearms, I believe ? " said the District
Attorney, insinuatingly. " Objection ! " shouted Mitty's attorney.
" We have shown that the defendant could not have fired the
shot. We have shown that he wore his right arm in a sling on the
night of the fourteenth of July." Walter Mitty raised his hand
briefly and the bickering attorneys were stilled. " With any
known make of gun," he said evenly, " I could have killed
Gregory Fitzhurst at three hundred feet *with my left hand*." Pande-
monium broke loose in the courtroom. A woman's scream rose
above the bedlam and suddenly a lovely, dark-haired girl was in
Walter Mitty's arms. The District Attorney struck at her savagely.
Without rising from his chair, Mitty let the man have it on the
point of the chin. " You miserable cur ! " . . .

" Puppy biscuit," said Walter Mitty. He stopped walking and
the buildings of Waterbury rose up out of the misty courtroom
and surrounded him again. A woman who was passing laughed.
" He said ' Puppy Biscuit,' " she said to her companion. " That
man said ' Puppy biscuit ' to himself." Walter Mitty hurried on.
He went into an A. & P., not the first one he came to but a smaller
one farther up the street. " I want some biscuit for small, young
dogs," he said to the clerk. "Any special brand, sir ? " The
greatest pistol shot in the world thought a moment. " It says
' Puppies Bark for It ' on the box," said Walter Mitty.

His wife would be through at the hairdresser's in fifteen minutes,
Mitty saw in looking at his watch, unless they had trouble
drying it ; sometimes they had trouble drying it. She didn't like
to get to the hotel first ; she would want him to be there waiting
for her as usual. He found a big leather chair in the lobby, facing
a window, and he put the overshoes and the puppy biscuit on the
floor beside it. He picked up an old copy of *Liberty* and sank
down into the chair. " Can Germany Conquer the World
Through the Air ? " Walter Mitty looked at the pictures of
bombing planes and of ruined streets.
. . . " The cannonading has got the wind up in young Raleigh,

sir," said the sergeant. Captain Mitty looked up at him through tousled hair. " Get him to bed," he said wearily. " With the others. I'll fly alone." " But you can't, sir," said the sergeant anxiously. " It takes two men to handle that bomber and the Archies are pounding hell out of the air. Von Richtman's circus is between here and Saulier." " Somebody's got to get that ammunition dump," said Mitty. " I'm going over. Spot of brandy ? " He poured a drink for the sergeant and one for himself. War thundered and whined around the dugout and battered at the door. There was a rending of wood and splinters flew through the room. "A bit of a near thing," said Captain Mitty carelessly. " The box barrage is closing in," said the sergeant. " We only live once, Sergeant," said Mitty, with his faint, fleeting smile. " Or do we ? " He poured another brandy and tossed it off. " I never see a man could hold his brandy like you, sir," said the sergeant. " Begging your pardon, sir." Captain Mitty stood up and strapped on his huge Webley-Vickers automatic. " It's forty kilometres through hell, sir," said the sergeant. Mitty finished one last brandy. "After all," he said softly, " what isn't ? " The pounding of the cannon increased ; there was the rat-tat-tatting of machine guns, and from somewhere came the menacing pocketa-pocketa-pocketa of the new flame-throwers. Walter Mitty walked to the door of the dugout humming 'Auprès de Ma Blonde.' He turned and waved to the sergeant. " Cheerio ! " he said . . .

Something struck his shoulder. " I've been looking all over this hotel for you," said Mrs. Mitty. " Why do you have to hide in this old chair ? How did you expect me to find you ? " " Things close in," said Walter Mitty vaguely. " What ? " Mrs. Mitty said. " Did you get the what's-its-name ? The puppy biscuit ? What's in that box ? " " Overshoes," said Mitty. " Couldn't you have put them on in the store ? " " I was thinking," said Walter Mitty. " Does it ever occur to you that I am sometimes thinking ? " She looked at him. " I'm going to take your temperature when I get you home," she said.

They went out through the revolving doors that made a faintly derisive whistling sound when you pushed them. It was two blocks to the parking lot. At the drugstore on the corner she said, " Wait here for me. I forgot something. I won't be a minute." She was more than a minute. Walter Mitty lighted a cigarette. It began to rain, rain with sleet in it. He stood up against the wall of the drugstore, smoking . . . He put his shoulders back and his heels together. " To hell with the handkerchief," said Walter Mitty scornfully. He took one last drag on his cigarette and snapped it away. Then, with that faint, fleeting smile playing about his lips, he faced the firing squad ; erect and motionless, proud and disdainful, Walter Mitty the Undefeated, inscrutable to the last.

— Vintage Thurber

Explorations

1.   Thurber described his stories as 'mainly humorous but with a few kind-of-sad ones mixed in'. Is there a similar blend of sadness and fun in the present story ? If so, point out examples of each.

2.   In Mitty's mind the world of reality is constantly colliding with the world of fancy. Study how Thurber makes the links between the two. One link is different from the others—see can you find it.

3.   What sort of wife has Mitty ? What sort of man is he ? If one of them were different would he dream so much ? Explain.

4.   Is Mitty a normal man or is he a little mad ? Explain.

5.   Do you find his dramatizations of the sea storm, the operating theatre, the courtroom and the dugout exciting ? If so, is it because they are very vivid ? because you have read such descriptions many times before ? because you have imagined such scenes with yourself as the hero ? Answer honestly.

Exercises

1.   Most normal people indulge in fantasies. Describe in detail three of your favourite ones. Try to explain why you have these particular day-dreams.

2.   As Mitty drives home he turns on his radio and hears news of a police hunt for a murderer on the New York roof-tops. Try to write his fantasy on the subject.

3.   Write a brief essay on the value of detective stories, television westerns and simple adventure tales to you and your friends. Do they fulfil some important need ?

BIOGRAPHICAL NOTES

DANIEL CORKERY

Daniel Corkery (1878–1964) was born in Cork and educated there by the Presentation Brothers. He trained as a primary teacher and taught for many years at St. Patrick's School in the city. From 1913 to 1916 he was an organiser for the Irish Volunteers, and took part in the War of Independence from 1918 to 1921. His first volume of short stories, *A Munster Twilight* (1916), established him as a writer of unusual talent. It was an important event in the genesis of the Irish short story : after the rather sardonic detachment of James Joyce and George Moore and the lyrical whimsy of James Stephens, Corkery's deep spiritual seriousness, his unquestioning acceptance of his people, his strong reverent feeling for tradition, were profoundly influential. His next volume of stories, *The Hounds of Banba* (1920), dealt with the Irish struggle for independence. Even here his sense of the serious prevailed : there is no delight in battle as one finds, for instance, in O'Flaherty. His mood is finely summed up by Benedict Kiely when he compares it to that of " a singing procession of fighting men silent for a moment as they march in the shadow of a convent wall."

His novel, *The Threshold of Quiet*, also a deeply contemplative work, still enjoys a high reputation. His subsequent collections of short stories were *The Stormy Hills* and *Earth Out of Earth*. Perhaps his most influential book was *The Hidden Ireland* (1925), a critical study of Irish poetry and culture as it survived through the period of the Penal Laws.

In 1930 Corkery was appointed Professor of English in University College, Cork, and in 1931 he brought out his last major work of criticism, *Synge and Anglo-Irish Literature*. He was one of the most influential writers of his generation : at different times Frank O'Connor, Sean O'Faolain and Francis MacManus have acknowledged their debt to him.

LIAM O'FLAHERTY

Liam O'Flaherty was born on Inishmore in 1897. He was educated at Rockwell and later at Blackrock College. After a short period at University College, Dublin, he joined the Irish Guards and served on the Western Front in the First World War. Invalided out of the army with severe shell-shock, he returned to Aran. Since then he has travelled widely and worked in a great variety of jobs. He travelled to Rio de Janeiro as a sailor and stayed to teach Greek at the Colegio Anglo Brazileiro there. He has worked in Liverpool, Cardiff and Smyrna. In America he has worked both as lecturer and labourer, and as an oyster fisherman off Long Island.

His writing career began in 1923 with the publication of his first novel, *Thy Neighbour's Wife*, and since then he has lived by his pen, dividing his time between Ireland and America. So far he has produced six collections of short stories, fourteen novels, three books of autobiography and a biography of Tim Healy. It is difficult to decide whether his reputation is to stand on his short stories or on his novels. He has written memorable novels on the Irish struggle for independence, such as *Insurrection* and his best known, *The Informer*, which, under the direction of John Ford, was made into a film classic. But his greatest novels were, perhaps, *Skerrit* and *Famine* which showed men struggling with the problem of survival against the implacable forces of nature. This primeval relationship between man and the elements is O'Flaherty's richest theme and it has also yielded him some of his greatest short stories. He sees life as an endless competition : the rockfish struggles for freedom ; the fisherman struggles to land him ; the reapers contend with each other while carrying out an endless struggle with the soil. The same conflicts operate in the animal world which the author seems to understand as vividly as the world of men and women : the fledged bird must face the terror of flight alone : the wren, the lamb, the goat, the conger eel, the cormorant and man himself, move through his stories in violent, primitive, vivid patterns. In his book on Joseph Conrad he wrote : " I was born on a stormswept rock and hate the soft growth of sunbaked lands where there is no frost in men's bones. Swift thought and the flight of ravenous birds, and the squeal of terror of hunted animals are to me reality."

FRANK O'CONNOR

Frank O'Connor is the pseudonym of Michael O'Donovan who was born in Cork in 1903 and educated there by the Christian Brothers. He took part in the struggle for independence and later in the Civil War. He was imprisoned during 1922–23 and the experiences of these troubled years influenced his subsequent life and work as well as giving him the material for his first collection of short stories, *Guests of the Nation* (1931). During these years also he came under the influence of Daniel Corkery who excited his enthusiasm for the Irish language and the Gaelic past. After his release from prison he went to work as a librarian, first in Wicklow, then in Cork, and finally in Dublin, where he was encouraged in his literary career by A. E. (George Russell) and W. B. Yeats. He was for a time a director of the Abbey Theatre. In 1939 he took up literature as a full-time career and in subsequent years he taught and lectured in many American universities. While he is, above all, a great short-story writer, he has worked in many *genres* : *The Saint and Mary Kate* and *Dutch Interior* were novels ; *Irish Miles* was a travel book ; *The Big Fellow*, a biography of Michael Collins, and his *Kings, Lords and Commons*, a volume of outstanding translations from the Gaelic poets. *The Mirror in the Roadway* was a study of the modern novel while *The Lonely Voice* examined the art of short-story writing. A moving and illuminating account of his Cork childhood is to be found in his autobiographical volume, *An Only Child*. But his most enduring work is in the short story where he has achieved a world reputation. He was a writer who reshaped and repolished his stories over and over again so that in many cases the final version differed substantially from its first published form. The bulk of his mature work in the *genre* is therefore to be found in *The Stories of Frank O'Connor* (1953) and *Collection Two* (1964). Frank O'Connor died in Dublin in 1966.

SEAN O'FAOLAIN

Sean O'Faolain was born in Dublin in 1900 but was reared and educated in Cork City. He went first to the Lancastrian National School and later to the Presentation Brothers' school there. He graduated from University College, Cork, and went on a travelling scholarship to Harvard University, where he spent three years, emerging in 1929 with an A.M. During his student years at University College, Cork, he made friends with Frank O'Connor and came under the influence of Daniel Corkery. He took part in the War of Independence and later in the Civil War. A vivid account of these experiences is to be found in his autobiography, *Vive Moi* (1965), which is also a useful account of his development as a writer. He is a writer of great breadth and versatility. His first collection of short stories, *Midsummer Night Madness* (1932), established his reputation in this *genre* and was followed by collections such as *A Purse of Coppers*, *Teresa*, *The Man Who Invented Sin*, *I Remember, I Remember* and *The Heat of the Sun*. His selection, *The Finest Stories of Sean O'Faolain* (1958), contains the two stories in our present anthology. (Unlike Frank O'Connor he refuses to revise stories after they have been published. When a story is written, he holds, " the experience, complete or incomplete, is fixed forever. You can rewrite while you are still the same man. To rewrite years after is a form of forgery "). He has also written three fine novels, *A Nest of Simple Folk*, *Bird Alone* and *Come Back to Erin*, also five full-length biographies including his study of Daniel O'Connell, *King of the*

Beggars and *The Great O'Neill* which deals with the great Irish leader, Hugh O'Neill. He has written three books of travel, one on the Irish temperament entitled *The Irish*, and two books of criticism, *The Short Story* and *The Vanishing Hero*, the latter an examination of the modern novel. In more recent years Mr. O'Faolain lives in Ireland but travels to America as a visiting lecturer.

MARY LAVIN

Mary Lavin was born in Boston, Massachusetts, in 1912 but was reared and educated in Ireland. She went to Loreto College, Stephen's Green, Dublin, and later to University College, Dublin, from which she graduated with distinction. Her first volume of short stories, entitled *Tales from Bective Bridge* (1942), took its name and setting from the farm on which she was reared and where she still lives. She has written two successful novels, *The House in Clewe Street* and *Mary O'Grady*, both of which deal with Irish family life, the theme which has always been her chief concern both in her stories and her novels. It is, however, by her stories that her reputation has been established. *The Long Ago*, perhaps her finest collection, appeared in 1944 and was followed by *The Becker Wives*, *A Single Lady*, *The Patriot Son*, and *The Great Wave* (1961). A collection of her best stories has appeared since in *The Stories of Mary Lavin* (1964). A new collection of stories, *In the Middle of the Fields*, was published in 1967. "Brother Boniface" is taken from her first collection and "The Widow's Son" from her 1944 collection, *The Long Ago*.

BRYAN MacMAHON

Bryan MacMahon was born in Listowel, Co. Kerry, in 1909. He was educated at St. Michael's College, Listowel, and at St. Patrick's Training College, Dublin. He is at present Principal of Scoil Réalta Na Maidine (2), Listowel. He is a versatile writer who has written plays for radio, television and the stage : the most distinguished of which are *The Bugle in the Blood*, *The Honey Spike* and *Song of the Anvil*. He has written one remarkable novel, *Children of the Rainbow*, which is a sort of lyrical elegy for a village and the traditional Irish values which it enshrined. He has said on television that his object as a writer is to " celebrate the pieties of his people," an ambition which puts him in the tradition of Daniel Corkery, Padraic Colum and Francis MacManus. His most enduring work is likely to be his short stories. He has produced two outstanding collections to date—*The Lion Tamer* (1948) from which " The Holy Kiss " is taken, and *The Red Petticoat* (1955) which includes " The Windows of Wonder."

BRIAN FRIEL

Brian Friel was born near Omagh, Co. Tyrone in 1929. He was educated at his father's national school at Culmore before going on to St. Columb's, Derry. He was at St. Patrick's College, Maynooth, for two years and later at St. Joseph's Training College, Belfast. For ten years he taught with the Christian Brothers and in Intermediate schools in Derry. As his life was taken up increasingly with his writing he decided, in 1960, to devote himself to his work in the drama and the short story. In the theatre his first success was *The Enemy Within*, a study of St. Columcille, which was produced at the Abbey Theatre. He followed up with *Three Blind Mice* and later *Philadelphia, Here I Come* which went on from the Dublin Theatre Festival to spectacular success on the Broadway stage. His first collection of short stories from which the present three are taken was *The Saucer of Larks* (1959). His second collection, *The Gold in the Sea*, was published in 1966.

JAMES PLUNKETT

James Plunkett was born in Sandymount, Dublin, in 1920 and was educated by the Christian Brothers, Synge Street. He attended the Dublin Municipal School of Music where he studied the violin and viola. He worked as a clerk in the Dublin Gas Company and was, for a period, secretary to the great Trades Union leader, Jim Larkin. He played with the Radio Eireann Symphony Orchestra and during the same period he wrote several plays for radio. His greatest dramatic achievement was his play, *Big Jim*—renamed *The Risen People*—which was based on the life of Jim Larkin and his fight against the Dublin employers in the Great Strike of 1913. He has since become a producer with Telefís Eireann for which he has written several features and plays. The present stories are taken from his 1955 collection, *The Trusting and the Maimed*, which is still regarded as one of the most important short-story volumes to come out of modern Ireland.

MICHAEL McLAVERTY

Michael McLaverty was born in Co. Monaghan in 1907 and was educated at St. Malachy's College, Belfast, and later at Queen's University, Belfast. He has lived most of his life in the northern capital and was headmaster of St. Thomas's Secondary School there. He began his writing career with a novel, *Call my Brother Back* (1939) and in it he introduced the theme that was to dominate most of his sub-sequent work - the alienation and suffering of simple, rural people amid the bigotry and squalor of the industrial city. His next two novels, *Lost Fields* and *In This Day*, explore the same theme. His short story collections, *The White Mare* and *The Game-cock*, won great critical acclaim and it is felt by many that it is on his work in the shorter form that his reputation most securely rests.

McLaverty is almost Wordsworthian in his devotion to the Irish landscape and the rural way of life. For his characters the countryside is the source of health, wisdom and innocence. As Benedict Kiely has written "even when his uprooted people find themselves in the streets of Belfast they bring with them, through poverty and pogrom, the innocence of children examining flowers or speculating on the myster-ious flight of birds."

BENEDICT KIELY

Benedict Kiely was born in Dromore, Co. Tyrone, in 1919 and was educated at the Christian Brothers' School, Omagh, and later at University College, Dublin. He took up journalism as a career, working successively for *The Standard*, *The Irish Independent* and finally as literary editor of *The Irish Press*. In recent years he has worked in many American universities as lecturer and writer in residence. He is best known for his novels, which include *The Cards of the Gambler*, *Honey Seems Bitter*, *There was an Ancient House* and *The Captain with the Whiskers*. He has written a critical study of the nineteenth-century Irish writer, William Carleton, entitled *Poor Scholar*, and his book, *Modern Irish Fiction* (1950) is an extremely valuable survey of Irish writing in the novel and the short story. "The Dogs in the Great Glen" is taken from his collection *A Journey to the Seven Streams* (1963).

BRENDAN BEHAN

Brendan Behan (1923-1964) was born on the north side of Dublin and received his early education from the French Sisters of Charity. He came from a strongly nationalist family, his uncle Peadar Kearney, being the author of the Irish national anthem, " The Soldier's Song." He became involved in I.R.A. activities during the years before the Second World War. He was arrested in possession of explosives in December 1939 in Liverpool and sentenced to three years Borstal

detention. This period furnished him with the material for his celebrated autobiography, *Borstal Boy*. The book, profane and ribald on
the surface, is a most sensitive study of youthful innocence confronting
a sordid and often cruel world. Back in Ireland, Behan was quickly
in prison again—first in the Curragh, then in Mountjoy—for renewed
I.R.A. activities. Released in 1946, he lived by writing and house-
painting until the production of his first play, *The Quare Fella* (1954)
which immediately established his reputation. In it he drew on his
prison experiences to compose what many still regard as the most
powerful indictment of capital punishment to be written in modern
times. His next great success was his spectacular adaptation of his
Irish play, *An Giall*—said to have been inspired by Frank O'Connor's
"Guests of the Nation"—which had been produced at Dublin's Damer
Hall in 1957. It was called *The Hostage* and had immense success
throughout the world. The present story is taken from his sketchbook,
Brendan Behan's Island (1962).

SAKI (H. H. MONRO)

Saki—the pen-name of Hector Hugh Monro—was born in Burma
in 1870 and spent his childhood in North Devon in the care of his
aunt and grandmother. He was further educated at Exmouth and
Bedford Grammar School. Upon his father's retirement from service
in British India he was taken on a tour through Europe. He served
for a time in the Burma Police and then returned to England where
he began his career in writing and journalism. In 1902 he was Balkan
correspondent for *The Morning Post* and later correspondent in Warsaw,
St. Petersburg and Paris. During the First World War he enlisted as
a private in the Royal Fusiliers, refused a commission several times,
and was killed at Beaumont-Hamel in one of the wasteful offensives
of 1916. His pseudonym is taken from the name of the cup-bearer
in *The Rubaiyat of Omar Khayyam*.

Among his best-known books were his novels and such collections
of short stories as *Reginald*, *The Chronicles of Clovis* and *Beasts and Super-
Beasts*. His most memorable stories concern children and their constant
battle for happiness in a world of menacing adults. It is believed
that his work in this field was influenced by the unhappiness of his
childhood when he was separated from his parents and left in the
guardianship of harsh and unsympathetic female relatives. Though
his work is often macabre, it is rarely without humour; and he is
one of the few writers who enjoyed almost perfect insight to the minds
of children. "The Lumber-room" is one of his most famous stories.

AMBROSE BIERCE

Ambrose Bierce was born on a farm in Ohio in 1842. He fought through the American Civil War (1861–1865) in an Indiana infantry regiment where he experienced the horrors of war at first hand. He was wounded and when he returned to civilian life he took up journalism in San Francisco, later travelling to London and Washington. Like some of his stories, his journalism was frequently angry and cynical. Books with titles like *Cobwebs from an Empty Skull* and *The Devil's Dictionary* earned him the title "Bitter Bierce". His *Tales of Soldiers and Civilians* (otherwise titled *In the Midst of Life*), from which the present story is taken, was rejected by American publishers because of its savage portrayal of war. It was eventually published by a friend of Bierce in 1891. His other famous collection, *Can Such Things Be*, containing stories of supernatural horror, was published in 1893. In 1913 Bierce went to Mexico to join the staff of Villa, the rebel general, and was never heard of again.

O. HENRY

O. Henry is the pen-name of William Sydney Porter who was born in North Carolina in 1862. As a youth of nineteen he went to Texas where he tried various occupations. In 1898 he was wrongfully convicted of embezzling funds from the bank of Austin and was sentenced to the federal prison at Columbus, Ohio. Three years in prison developed in him the talent which was to make him one of the most celebrated short-story writers of his time. On his release he travelled to New York where, as O. Henry, he began a writing career that was to yield two hundred and seventy short stories before his death in 1910.

Ingenuity is the most striking quality in O. Henry's technique. He makes great use of the ironical " whip-crack ending." He has the gift of keeping the story's secret till the precise moment when it can be most tellingly revealed. His technique is still imitated in the popular magazine story throughout the world. But his very skill seems to have acted against him and prevented his stories from reaching that degree of depth and human insight that the great short story must have.

WILLIAM SOMERSET MAUGHAM

William Somerset Maugham (1874-1965), spent much of his childhood in Paris. He received his education at King's School, Canterbury, and later at Heidelberg University. He trained as a doctor at St. Thomas's Hospital, London, and his first novel, *Liza of Lambeth* (1897), dealt with his medical experience in the London slums. The book's success encouraged him to give up medicine and devote his life to writing. His career proved to be one of the great success stories of modern times. At the time of his death eighty million copies of his books had been published. On one occasion three of his plays were running simultaneously in London's West End. His most celebrated novel was *Of Human Bondage* (1915) which has already been filmed three times. Other best-sellers have been *The Moon and Sixpence*, *The Painted Veil*, *Theatre*, *Cakes and Ale* and *The Razor's Edge*. His success in the short story has been similar and there are many critics who think that it is in the shorter form that his possible immortality lies. A useful insight to his work can be found in his *A Writer's Notebook* (1949) where he presents the hundreds of ideas, characters and incidents that he jotted down with a view to turning them into fiction. The method reflects his attitude to experience and to the writer's trade : he writes as an observer rather than as a participant in life. His attitude to his characters, while not without compassion, is detached and clear-eyed—while not always cynical, it is usually clinical. He is an ironist : he is fascinated by the frequent disparity between what people are and what they seem ; he is most at home when working within this double vision. He is not a writer with great richness of style and language but he has the important gifts of economy and clarity. Writing of his first novel he states, " I was forced to stick to the facts by the miserable poverty of my imagination. I had at that time a great admiration for Guy de Maupassant and it was after the model of his tales that I began to fashion my own. When I think of the bad examples a young writer may easily follow I am happy to think that I took that of one who had so great a gift for telling a story clearly, straight-forwardly and effectively." "Louise" is a very representative Maugham story.

WILLIAM GOLDING

William Golding was born in 1911 at St. Columb Minor, Cornwall, and educated at Marlborough Grammar School and Brasenose College, Oxford. He served in the Royal Navy from 1940 to the end of the war. He had a distinguished navy career and towards the end of the war he was in command of a rocket ship. In 1945 he went to teach at Bishop Wordsworth's School, Salisbury, and in 1962 he was appointed to an academic post in the U.S.A. His most celebrated book, *Lord of the Flies* (1954) established him as one of the outstanding novelists of modern times. It concerns the fate of a group of British school children marooned on a desert island in the course of a nuclear war. It demonstrated not only his remarkable insight to the minds of children—a feature of the present story—but his profound appreciation of the evil that is at work in human nature itself. The novel made a successful film in the hands of the director, Peter Brook, and it was followed by other distinguished novels such as *The Inheritors, Pincher Martin, Free Fall* and *The Spire*. The present autobiographical story is taken from his collection of occasional writings, *The Hot Gates* (1965).

V. S. PRITCHETT

Victor Sawdon Pritchett was born in 1900 at Ipswich, Suffolk, and educated at Alleyns School, Dulwich, England. He has had a distinguished career both as journalist and author. He worked for a period as special correspondent for the *Christian Science Monitor* travelling to Ireland, to Spain and other countries of the Mediterranean. He has written books of travel like *The Spanish Tempter*, novels such as *Mr. Beluncle* and such distinguished works of criticism as *The Living Novel*. He is a well-known broadcaster and lecturer and he has worked as a scriptwriter for films and television. "The Fly in the Ointment" is to be found in his *Collected Stories* of 1956.

H. G. WELLS

H. G. Wells (1866-1946)—the initials stand for Herbert George— was the son of a professional cricketer and was apprenticed to a draper at the age of thirteen. But through grants and scholarships he was able to attend the Royal College of Science, London, and obtained a B.Sc. degree in 1890. Stimulated by the teaching of T. H. Huxley, the great evolutionist, Wells taught science for a few years and then began to embody his scientific insights and speculations in articles, stories and novels. Novels such as *The Time Machine, The Invisible Man, The First Men on the Moon* and *The War of the Worlds* pioneered the new *genre* of science fiction in English literature. His realistic novels of contemporary life, often humorous and satirical, include *Love and Mr. Lewisham, Tono Bungay, The History of Mr. Polly* and *Kipps*. His *Outline of History* was a massive attempt to interpret the origin of the universe and the development of civilization in purely materialistic terms. Like that of his great contemporaries, Chesterton and Belloc, a great deal of his work is now forgotten but in his time he was one of the most energetic and original thinkers on the literary scene. It is in his less controversial work, perhaps, that his fame is most surely enshrined. Such a story is this strange tale of the "Diamond Maker".

G. K. CHESTERTON

Gilbert Keith Chesterton (1874-1936) was born in London and educated first at St. Paul's School and later at the Slade School of Art. But though he had definite talent as an artist—he illustrated some of Belloc's books as well as his own—he quickly discovered that his real bent was towards writing. He began as an art critic in *The Bookman* and as he put it himself—" I had discovered the easiest of all professions which I have pursued ever since." He seems to have been one of the very few men to whom writing came with genuine ease because in the following years he produced a prodigious amount of work in many forms. In fact had he written less, and more carefully, he might have achieved a more lasting literary reputation than his farflung energies gained for him. He wrote novels of fantasy such as *The Flying Inn, The Napoleon of Notting Hill,* and *The Man Who Was Thursday;* works of literary criticism such as *Chaucer* and *Dickens;* poems like *Lepanto* and *The Ballad of the White Horse ;* hagiography such as *St. Thomas Aquinas* and *St. Francis of Assisi ;* works of spirituality and apologetics such as *The Everlasting Man* and *Orthodoxy ;* autobiography, innumerable essays, and a history of England.

While a good deal of his religious writing is likely to endure, much of his strictly literary work may become dated because many of the issues on which he spent himself have become, with the passage of time, unimportant. But his Father Brown stories have already become classics of their *genre*. As well as being detective stories these are often shrewd moral explorations—his detective is not so much concerned with bringing the criminal to justice as with bringing him to repentance. Perhaps their greatest single appeal lies in the personality of their hero. Like Sherlock Holmes, Maigret, Albert Campion and Hercule Poirot, Father Brown is an unforgettable personality : short and dumpy, he blinks through his spectacles, has frequent fits of absent-mindedness and seems quite unable to manage his large, shabby umbrella. As a detective he combines a clear-eyed simplicity of insight with great logical ingenuity. His constant opponent is the great French criminal, Flambeau, who appears in the present story. In the very first of the Father Brown stories, *The Blue Cross,* when he captures Flambeau disguised as a priest, he sums up his strength as a criminologist in the following exchange ; "Has it never struck you that a man who does next to nothing but hear men's real sins is not likely to be wholly unaware of human evil ? But as a matter of fact, another part of my trade, too, made me sure you weren't a priest." " What ? " asked the thief, almost gaping. " You attacked reason," said Father Brown. " It's bad theology."

There has been a very successful film based on the Father Brown stories with Sir Alec Guinness in the title role.

KATHERINE MANSFIELD

Katherine Mansfield (1888-1923), whose real name was Katherine Mansfield Beauchamp, was born in Wellington, New Zealand, and spent her early years there. She came to England with a musical career in mind and completed her education at Queen's College, Harley Street, London. She married George Bowden in 1909 and soon began to write for such magazines as *The New Age* and *Rhythm* which was edited by John Middleton Murry. She married Murry in 1918 having divorced her first husband. Her first book, *In a German Pension*, was published in 1911 but her great talent was not fully recognised until the publication of her famous long story, *Prelude*, in 1916. Her next two collections of short stories, *Bliss* and *The Garden Party*, confirmed her status as one of the finest short-story writers of modern times. The last years of her life were dogged by ill-health and she died of tuberculosis at Fontainebleau on January 9, 1923.

JAMES THURBER

James Thurber was born in Columbus, Ohio, in 1904 and studied at Ohio State University. He worked for some time as a clerk in a department store before turning to journalism. In 1927 he joined the staff of *The New Yorker*. He quickly made his name as a writer of humorous sketches and stories and also for the remarkable sadly-comic drawings with which he illustrated them. Drawings such as those in *The Seal in the Bedroom, Men, Women and Dogs*, anecdotes such as *Fables for our Time* and stories like *The Night the Bed Fell in, The Macbeth Murder Mystery*, and *The Car We had to Push*, have already reached the immortality of folklore among people who read. "The Secret Life of Walter Mitty," for all its apparent slightness, has a good deal to say about the tragi-comic predicament of twentieth-century man, reduced to insignificance by urban civilization yet living in his imagination a life of heroic action. It was made into an out-standing film with Danny Kaye in the title role.